MAIDEN TO NONE

THE TERKIAN TRIPLETS

BOOK ONE

BY D.A. GATLIN

I dedicate this first book to Stephanie...
the strongest woman I know.

For Ellie and Mattie too.

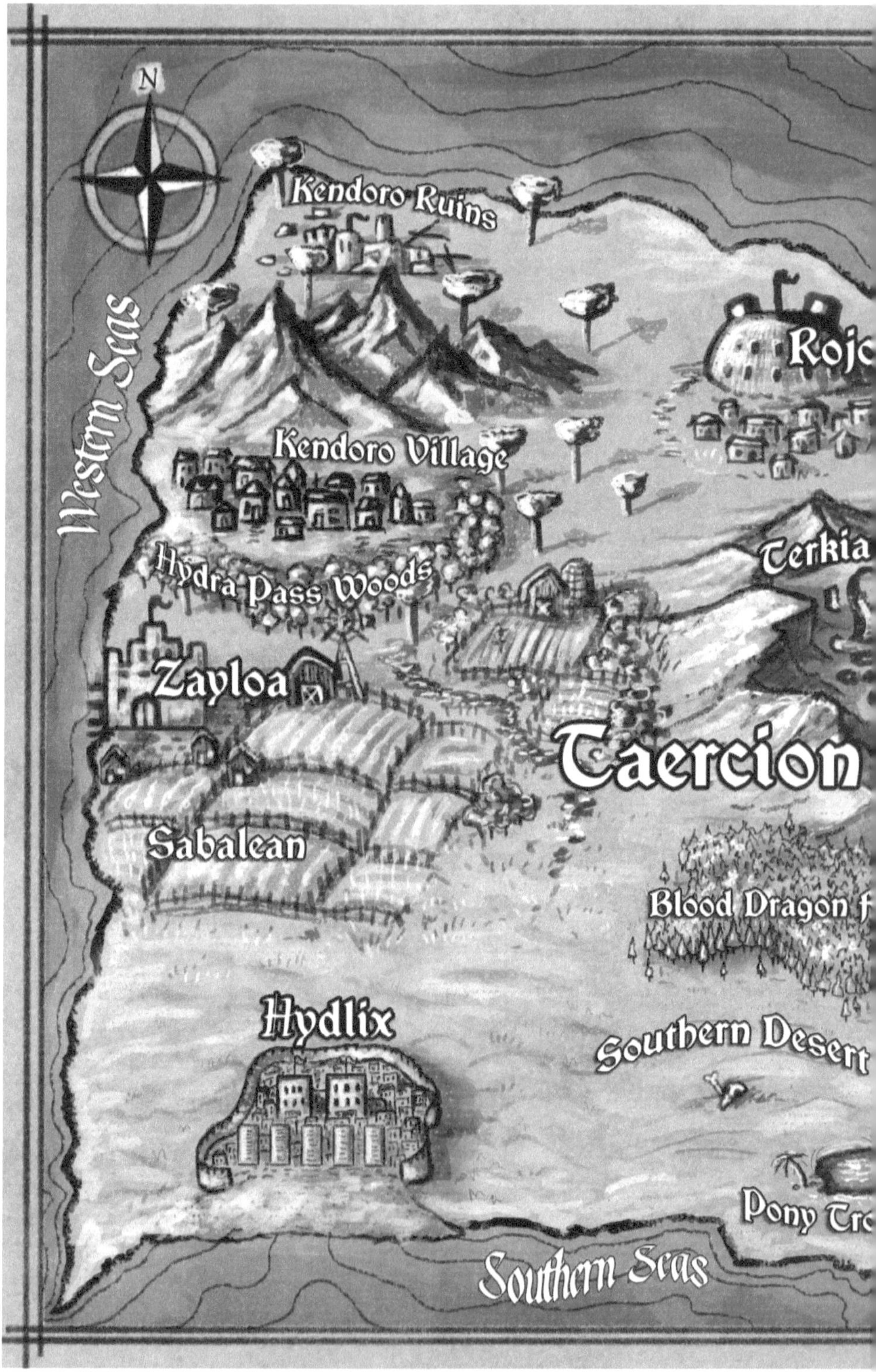

N
Western Seas
Kendoro Ruins
Rojo
Kendoro Village
Terkia
Hydra Pass Woods
Zayloa
Taercion
Sabalean
Blood Dragon f
Hydlix
Southern Desert
Pony Tro
Southern Seas

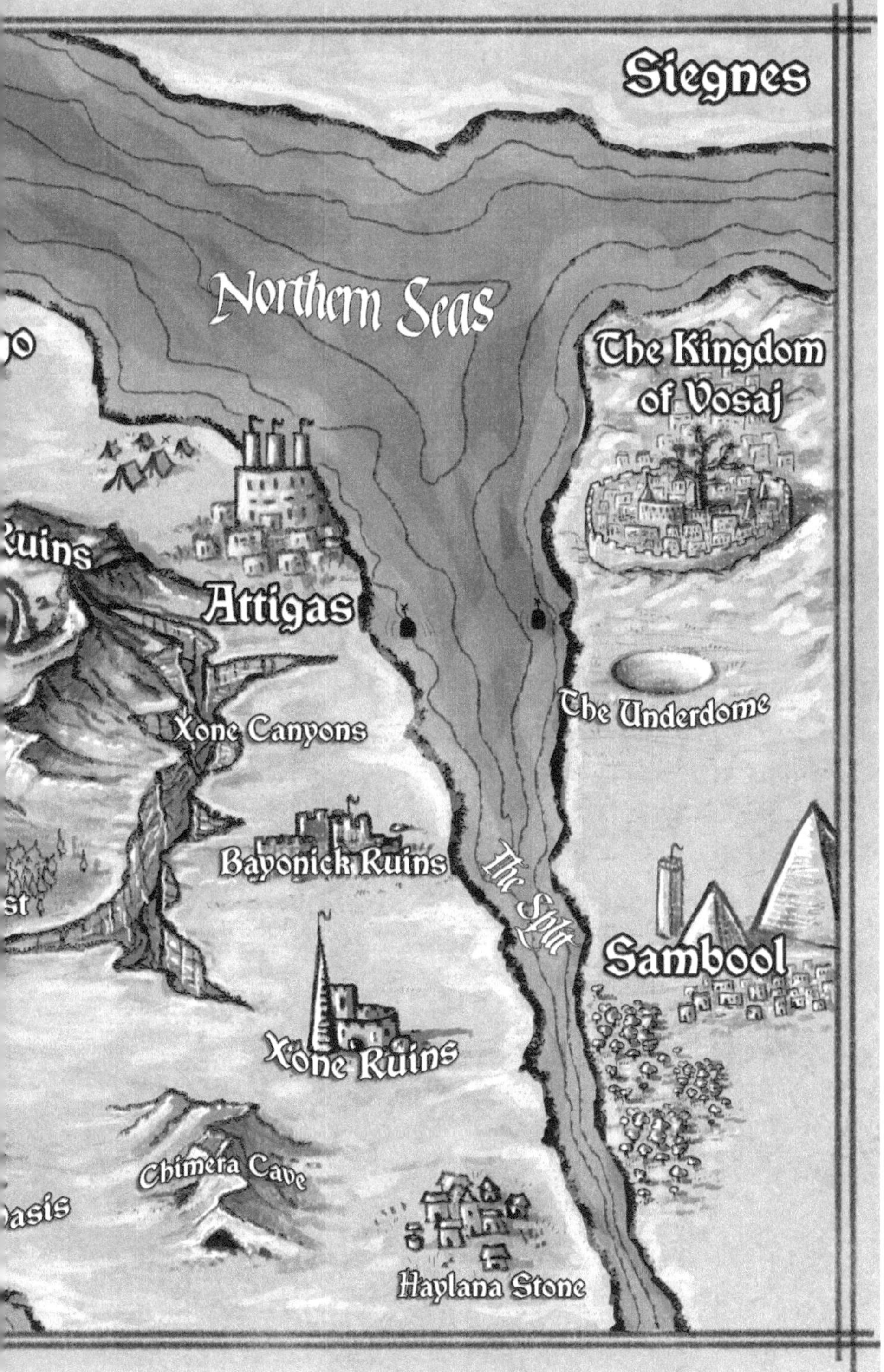

Siegnes
Northern Seas
The Kingdom of Vosaj
Ruins
Attigas
Xone Canyons
The Underdome
Bayonick Ruins
The Split
Sambool
Xone Ruins
Chimera Cave
Oasis
Haylana Stone

CONTENTS

PART ONE

MEMORIES

CHAPTER ONE

THE AQUA DUCK

"**A**m I boring you again, Lady Ikena?" Master Ihsotah's nasally voice teetered between anger and annoyance as he tapped at the spot on the page where Trinity's gaze should have been. He'd been going on about the hydra beasts discovered in the northern kingdom of Kendoro for what felt like forever and somehow, in the middle of it all, Trinity's mind had wandered back to the sweet roll she'd had for breakfast. A trace of drool was still warm on her lips.

"Oh, sorry. Right. Hydras scary. Got it." She straightened in her seat, yawned, and quickly pretended like she was interested in the place her teacher was pointing in the book. "Um, how many heads—wait, I see right here. Two. Well, that's not very scary, is it?"

Master Ihsotah let out a heavy sigh and muttered something about little princes being much easier to teach than eight-year-old princesses. Trinity hid a giggle.

"As I was saying—alternative routes had to be found, though hydras are elusive and are known to only come out every few years or so," he said, peering out one of the narrowed window slits in the room. "Do you know what alternate routes were considered for the trading caravans, Lady Ikena?"

Trinity furrowed her brow. "Alternate?"

Ihsotah put his hands on his hips. "Which way on the map should they go to avoid the big scary two-headed lizards?"

"Ohhhhh," Trinity said, as she began searching lazily for a map in her book. "I guess they could just go around."

"Oh, naturally." Ihsotah sounded frustrated. "Scale the blue mountains, why don't they? Be torn in pieces by timberwolves, obviously." He scoffed. "Sounds as if I've not lectured on Taercion topography enough, hmm? Perhaps some extra studies are in order."

Trinity rolled her eyes. Why did any of this matter anyway? She didn't know what topography meant any more than she knew what the world looked like beyond her kingdom's walls. Why did Ihsotah never lecture on any interesting subjects like wars, or sieges, or even beheadings? Once more she let her mind wander. Ihsotah had a name for her constant daydreams: "Letting your mind chase idle fancies."

Master Ihsotah continued to drone on as he searched through stacks of scattered scrolls along their study area. Trinity went back to ignoring him and turned her attentions elsewhere. It was then she spotted a boy who, unlike her, seemed to be enjoying the book that he was reading. He was strolling between the stacks of books on the shelves beneath her on the first floor of Hydlix's library. She gazed upon him through the iron grates. It seemed very strange how he managed to walk and read at the same time. Whenever he neared an end in his clearing, he simply turned without looking up and then continue on his way.

But even more peculiar perhaps was what he was reading. She couldn't make it out too clearly from her raised height, but it appeared that the book had a picture of a dragon. *Dragons?* Nobody ever read about interesting subjects like dragons in Hydlix. *Who is this boy?*

After Ihsotah's lessons had *finally* concluded for the day, Trinity raced downstairs. By the time she got there, however, the boy had already left. She asked the librarian about him, and the elderly woman directed her to the book registry tablets on a nearby table. There Trinity saw only one marked name for the day:

Schobe.

Schobe...I'll meet you yet.

It wasn't until a few weeks later that she saw him again reading a book beneath the concrete columns of the Hydlixian aqueduct. The other children around him were playing a game with a rounded ball made from dried animal skins, but Schobe seemed uninterested. His eyes examined the pages like a cook waiting for a pot to boil. Trinity would've jumped at the chance to play ball with the other children—though she had never done such a thing before. First, though, she would introduce herself to Schobe. Maybe he'd tell her all about the book he was reading. Maybe they could even be friends. She'd never had a friend before, but this seemed the best path towards making one.

Unfortunately, Trinity's aunt Evita had other plans for their morning.

"Come along, Trinity," Evita told her, as she took her by the hand and pulled her away from where Schobe sat. They scaled the cobbled steps leading towards the upper districts of the multi-layered kingdom of Hydlix, to a place where Trinity never saw any other children outside playing. Here it was mostly sour-faced, finely-dressed grown-ups who roamed the streets. They never played games, unless opening fattened purses again and again counted as a game. Trinity's feet always dragged along the cobble whenever her aunt would visit the upper districts' boutiques. She knew though that any complaints she made would result in receiving a lecture about the importance of always dressing one's best. In the end, Trinity usually found herself trying on heaps of dresses to the "aww's" and "precious darlings" of the store clerks. The clerks were very good at their job, Trinity believed, because they always made sure her aunt spent a lot of money.

Trinity instead decided to ask about the large, water-filled cement slopes that she had seen Schobe sitting beneath earlier. Though in truth, she was trying to take her mind off of the boy who was filling her every thought.

"*Aqueduct.* Not aqua duck," Evita told her. "The aqueduct has been here since the kingdom was built. Hydlix was the first of the great kingdoms that learned how to build structures using cement—very useful, as it can withstand water. And since we have naturally flowing water geysers here, it became the perfect place to transfer mail."

"It's for mail?" Trinity asked, disappointed.

"Yes. The aqueduct's water slopes run throughout the kingdom. When someone has a letter to send, they drop it off in a sealed bag and place it at one of the designated mailing spots. Tell you what, if you're a very good girl today, I shall let you come with me the next time I have a package or letter to send. I may even let you help me seal it in the water casing, though we must be careful." She flashed a rueful smile. "We wouldn't want to ruin our mail."

"Are you sure it isn't a slide, or something fun?" Trinity asked.

"I'm positive. What a silly notion."

Trinity wasn't convinced. From the high windows of the first boutique they visited, she looked down and saw the rushing gallons of water across the hard surfaces of the aqueduct. There were twists and turns along the paths, making it hard to see where the water might end up. Maybe, she guessed, her aunt didn't see a slide because she wasn't a kid anymore. All grown-ups ever seemed to care about was shopping and boring history lessons.

She felt a gentle tug on her tight, emerald-colored braid. "Hey Trin, come try on this dress," Evita said, cradling an elegant dress with big poofy sleeves.

"Not another one," Trinity whined.

"Last one today. I promise. Oh, this one would be so cute for this year's royal imprints. Father is planning for them soon."

"Don't we have enough pictures of me in dresses?"

"*Trinity*. A girl can never have too many pictures of themselves. Especially us princesses." She tapped her playfully on the nose.

Trinity sighed. "Well, I think they can, Aunt E."

"Just the two dresses today, your highness?" asked one of the seamstresses measuring the dress. "For you and your—" she hesitated.

"My niece, yes. Thank you, Gama," Evita said, fishing for money in her purse. She apparently hadn't noticed the woman's hesitation. Or maybe she was choosing to ignore it. Trinity, however, could never unhear people's sudden pauses when talking about her.

For years now Trinity had known that Evita wasn't really her aunt, the same as the king wasn't really her grandfather. Trinity's mother had been adopted at birth by the king and (once reigning) queen of Hydlix. She'd been from an eastern kingdom, said to be found in a wide canyon filled with green gorillas. Her father lived there too. And while everything about her birth-kingdom sounded fascinating, Trinity had no memory of Terkia. Or either of her parents for that matter. Both of them had died in Terkia on the night she was born, and Trinity was taken in by the only family she had in a distant palace by the southern seas. Her aunt Evita had been raising her as a royal ward of Hydlix ever since.

After putting on the stuffy dress with the poofy sleeves, Trinity had to stand atop a crate so that she could see herself in the boutique's mirror. She was short for eight, and she felt like a shrimp caught in a net as she looked at herself in the oversized dress.

"Why the scowl? I think it's very pretty. And such fine fabric," Evita assured her.

"I look puffy," Trinity said, hugging her body. The sleeves made a "whoosh" sound.

The door to the boutique opened and a large man wearing a suit of silvery armor stepped inside, lowering his head beneath the threshold as he did. He carried a brown package and he bore a very long sword fastened to his waist.

"Here's the rest of your shipment, Mother." He handed the boutique owner the package.

"Thank you, Doto," his mother said.

Doto's eyes drifted over to where Evita and Trinity were. He then quickly turned his gaze to the floor.

"Your highness," he said, before bowing and seeing himself back out of the door.

Trinity looked at her aunt's reflection in the mirror as Evita watched the knight leave. Evita's dark, flittering eyes remained fixed on the door long after the knight had gone.

By the time they'd left the boutique, Trinity was itching to yank off the dress, put on her breeches, and run around her grandfather's courtyard in a loose-fitting tunic, letting the trimmed grass cover her toes like a damp pillow. What's more she'd undo her uncomfortable braid and let her green curls loose upon her shoulders. Why did her aunt always go through such trouble buying dresses when you couldn't even play in them?

Good as her word though, Evita did indeed have something to send in the mail that day to one of the king's subjects, whom Evita had not yet paid for a job. Trinity followed her up several more flights of stairs until the whole of the kingdom was laid out before them beneath the orange sky. From this view, the Hydlixian kingdom seemed to hover over the shimmering southern sea. Trinity caught a whiff of the crashing waves far beneath her as she listened to the gulls playing overhead. The palace towers shone a ruby red under the setting sun, and the folks in the lower market square moved about like colorful insects. There amongst them was a procession of silver and white moving down the city streets; a long, rippling line, like a silver river flowing effortlessly through the crowds.

"So, it's true. The knights have returned," Evita said. "Father will be holding a banquet tonight."

"Do they get to eat special every night?"

"Hardly." Evita narrowed her eyes and checked over her shoulders. "I shouldn't be telling you this, but they've been investigating rumors of planned strikes in the desert lands, east of Bayonick. Entire towns burnt to rubble."

"Why would somebody burn a town?" Trinity began picking at her elbow. It was a nervous habit she could never seem to break.

"There isn't a good reason. But Father suspects it's Gazenga."

"Gah...zuh?" The word was harder to say than aqueduct.

"Gazenga. He's the ruler of Sambool. Nothing for you to worry about though. All I'm saying is our poor knights have had nothing to eat but whatever they could hunt in the desert for weeks now. When they weren't waiting to be attacked, I suppose."

Trinity's eyes grew wide with worry. "Do you think the bad men will come here, Aunt E? Burn Hydlix?"

"If they do, our knights will be ready for them," Evita said, sounding more confident than before. "This is what they have trained for. Hydlixian knights are the bravest warriors in all of Taercion. Though it's times like these I wish Commander Guren had never retired."

Guren. Trinity had heard his name many times before while seated at her grandfather's banquet table, despite never once seeing him. He was the famous commander who had successfully prevented war with the Reiwanian isles in the south. Everyone in Hydlix—even the king—respected Guren for his bravery. Many of the king's knights had trained under the gray lion of Hydlix, as Guren was sometimes called. Trinity wished that someday she could meet him. Maybe even ask him to train her. Oh, how she longed to be trained to be a knight.

Ordinarily, voicing her opinions on the subject of becoming a squire was met with laughter, usually by members of the king's court. Evita would frown or remind her that such foolish talk would only upset the king. Still, there was something about seeing the knights riding into the kingdom at that moment which ignited a fire within her belly.

"I could be brave like Guren. I bet—that I'd make a good knight too. I'm plenty strong!" she declared, loud enough for Evita and all the passing seagulls around them to hear.

Evita seemed taken aback by this sudden declaration. She cleared her throat, looking as if she was trying to reign in any more unexpected outbursts. "I know, little cub. You are very strong," she said, running her fingers through Trinity's hair. "But we must be careful with that *strength* of yours."

Trinity always hated the way her aunt said the word "strength" when speaking to her. Trinity had caused one too many accidents in their home to know what her aunt truly felt about her special abilities.

"Besides, we let the men serve as knights. This is how things have always been, and they will continue to be this way," she continued, adding a light laugh, "so long as you are my niece. Let the boys have their heavy armor. *We* have our beautiful dresses to wear and our handsome princes to marry."

Trinity pouted. "I'd rather have the armor."

Evita must have pretended not to hear again for she had already moved across the skyward corridor and approached a locked metal door on the opposite ruby-colored tower from where they had come. Trinity looked one final time upon the river of knights before scampering off after her aunt.

Evita used a special golden key to open the door. Inside the tower, Trinity saw a round stone room, with a high pointed ceiling. In the center of the tower was a gushing geyser, which held its place remarkably without leaking everywhere, and came up to the height of Trinity's shoulders. The excess of water flowed onto the starting point of one of the aqueduct's mail slopes. There were packages in this room too, and large bags with black paw prints imprinted upon them.

"This is the royal mail tower. We are the only ones besides Father with access to this room. When I put mail here, it is always sorted and delivered first by the postmen down at the sorting pool, near the kingdom's depths."

"No one else comes here?"

"No one."

Evita opened her purse and pulled out a few thin strips that looked like crispy golden flakes. She began to delicately count the flakes in her hand as Trinity played with the water rushing up to greet her outstretched hands.

"A few stekis short. I'm afraid I'll have to ask Father for more tonight," Evita said, biting on her lip. "He won't be thrilled."

"Well, maybe you could take back some of the dresses."

"But then *I* wouldn't be thrilled. Come, I've prepared the letter. Let's send it."

Trinity sealed the envelope with the steki flakes shifting about and closed them up in a damp green pouch. She placed the pouch onto the mouth of the aqueduct and sent the letter sliding down the soggy slope. She looked down as far as she was able until the swift letter was well out of sight. There were few words that could convince her that the aqueduct wouldn't make for a fun water slide.

The next time she ran across Schobe was nearly a week later when she broke her aunt's rule about appearances and ran down to the market square in the wee hours of the morning, wearing her dark-tanned breeches and gold-dyed tunic. Strictly speaking, she was never allowed in this part of the kingdom without wearing a dress, though she didn't understand why. Whether here or in the king's courtyards, today was too perfect a day to wear petticoats and hoop skirts. *This was breeches weather.*

Schobe was there in the market, sitting by a brick wall near the stables and, for the first time, Trinity got a good look at his face. It was narrow, with a pointed chin. His eyes appeared heavy, as if he needed a great sleep. His skin was dark like her aunt's and grandfather's skin, and quite unlike Trinity's own. His hair was cut short with remnants of curls still atop his scalp. Perhaps the thing she found most remarkable about him though was his eyes, racing across the pages of the book he was reading like rolling chocolate pebbles. Just the sight of them made her breaths grow still for a second or two.

She ducked past a few wooden stalls and slinked between a couple of the early-morning vendors who were preparing their wares for the day. Just before she could reach Schobe though, someone came and stood before him. It was an older boy wearing the silver armor of the knights. He leaned down towards Schobe and handed him a letter, then went on his way.

Trinity peered around a wooden stall and watched him for a while after he'd received the letter. She was unable to see what was written on the parchment Schobe had been given, but whatever it was made him shut the book he was reading.

Finally, she plucked up her courage and stepped forward to say something to him.

"H-hello!" she said. Actually, it was more of a shout.

Surprised, he stared up at her with those chocolatey pebbles of his, but only for a second before returning his attention to the letter.

"I'm Trinity," she said.

"I know that," he said, without losing his focus. "You're the princess."

She joined him by the wall and sat with her back to the bricks. "How do you know? Do I look like a princess?"

"Not really. But everyone says that you are one."

"Do you like princesses?"

"Not really."

"What's that letter?"

He hesitated. "It's from the king," he said, tapping the folded parchment on his book. "Says I'm to begin my squire duties soon. Before the week is out."

"You mean—to be a knight someday?"

"I guess. It says Gazenga's threat upon the other great kingdoms is real. King Eslon says he needs all boys seven or older to report for training. And since I'm already nine—"

"Oh Schobey, you're so lucky," she said, practically squealing. "Think of it, you'll get to wear armor, and use swords. Ride a horse even."

Schobe scoffed. "I don't care about any of that. Wars are nothing to be excited over. And my name isn't Schobey, it's Schobe."

"S-Schobe?" It sounded wrong to her somehow. Like an old person's word.

"Sure. You know, like robe. Or, earlobe," he said, flicking at his own ear. "And wait a minute. How—how do you even know my name? That's weird."

"Um," became the first word she could muster. Her face crinkled up as she tried to remember the spelling of the name in the registry. "Someone—I heard it somewhere," she choked out, hoping he bought the lie. "And it is too Schobey. You have an "E" at the end of your name." She specifically remembered the odd letter placement.

"It's silent. You don't say it, and you don't add letters either."

"Silent? How can an "E" be silent?"

"It—" he started to say, but then his cheeks rose, and his lips curled. Soon, he was laughing.

"Hey! I'm being serious," she objected.

"I believe you are," he said, still grinning. "I wish I had a good answer for you. Sometimes E's are just silent."

"Well, they shouldn't be." She placed her hands behind her head and leaned further back on the wall. "It's very confusing."

"Do you like to read? You find many examples of silent letters in books."

"I don't," she said, assuredly. "But I have to, sometimes. In my lessons. There aren't even any good pictures in my books. They're very boring. Except for this one book I have on swords. Oh, but I'm not supposed to talk about that one."

Schobe studied her words. "You know, not all books are boring. This one here is about dragons."

"That's right! Yes, I wanted to ask you about it the other day."

"Other day?"

"When you were at the library. I was watching you."

Schobe's eyes grew wide. "*Right.* Well, anyway it's a story about a knight who—" but he stopped himself short, and then slowly placed the letter inside of the book's cover. "Ah, it doesn't matter. I won't have much time for reading anymore."

She could sense his bitterness now. They'd taken the one thing he loved. She couldn't imagine having lost something so important to her. She reached forward and took his hand. Her determined jade eyes locked onto his unwavering pebbles. His smile disappeared.

"Maybe you can still read. While you're a squire, I mean."

"*Yeah*," he said, in a tone she knew wasn't serious, "and maybe *you* could be a knight."

A few days later, Trinity was there waiting for Schobe to return at the same spot where they'd met. When he arrived, she begged him to tell her all about his day as a squire. She wanted every grimy detail, right down to the number of piss pots he'd scrubbed. Though Schobe was tired, he stayed and shared the details of his day with her all the same, much to Trinity's delight.

It wasn't long at all before Trinity found herself being invited to Schobe's home for supper with his family. Evita didn't usually allow Trinity to play in the lower parts of the kingdom, especially near suppertime. Trinity managed to convince Evita though that she was staying in bed because she was feeling too sick to dine in the banquet hall that night. Trinity snuck out shortly after her aunt had left for the evening.

The two-window, one-room home where Schobe lived was fixed below three other dwellings, all carved alike in the faces of the city's concrete walls. Along the wall were several other homes which looked similar to Schobe's. The people who lived here prepared their meals outside on shared spits in the center of their neighborhood. They sang songs and drank dark ale while the children ran and screamed through the streets, playing games still despite the late hour. Trinity never knew a place like this was still inside of the Hydlix she had always known.

Inside Schobe's home, lion-paw banners, and cloth tails were strung about the drafty room. The king's banquet hall had similar banner designs, though on much larger, hand-embroidered tapestries. Trinity preferred the hanging cloth tails; she thought they were cute. Schobe's younger siblings bounced about the small living quarters. The brother and sister team quickly convinced Trinity to play a game of chase with them. She had no siblings of her own and had never done such a thing before. She thought it was splendid fun. By the end of the evening, Trinity was learning braiding lessons from Schobe's four-year-old sister, while Schobe's three-year-old brother curled atop Trinity's back like a frog ready to spring into a pond.

At first, Schobe's mother had been shocked to see the princess of Hydlix enter into her home, but she welcomed Trinity all the same and fed her a warm bowl of trockan stew. The purple goop appeared unappetizing at first, but Trinity soon found she was asking for seconds. And then thirds. She thought Schobe's mother was a charming woman who was so easy to talk to about anything. Trinity loved watching Schobe fidget in his chair as his mother told stories of his early childhood. When Trinity finally left later that night, she kissed Schobe's siblings each on their foreheads. His mother caught her on the way out and gave her a long hug.

"You're all he ever speaks of," she whispered into Trinity's ear. "After his father's passing, Schobe he's—" but she broke off, "...thank you, little Princess. For letting him be your friend."

She met the woman's deep, brown-colored eyes, and for the first time felt shy around this family. "Yes mam," was all she could manage to say. She had always felt the opposite about Schobe. *She* was grateful to be his friend. And for the first time in her life, she had known what it felt like to be surrounded by a normal, non-royal family. She couldn't help but be a little jealous.

As Schobe walked her back up to the royal district, near the courtyards where she lived, Trinity stared up at the star-filled sky. She wondered if Schobe too liked to stare at the stars sometimes.

"Your family, they're very sweet," she said, as they ascended the last flight of stairs. "I'd give anything for a brother. Or even a sister."

"They wouldn't be so bad if we didn't all have to share the same bed," he assured her.

A week later Trinity gathered her courage and asked her aunt if she could invite Schobe and his family for supper in the king's banquet hall. Evita ignored her question for the better part of the day, but that night as she was tucking Trinity into bed, she gave her answer.

"We can't."

"I don't understand. There's lots of places at the table. To feed twenty families even."

"I said no. Now let that be the end of it."

Trinity wouldn't accept this. Not even the next day when Schobe tried to explain the situation after he'd returned from his squire's duties.

"It can't be done. Peasants don't eat in the grand hall. Don't blame your aunt. She doesn't make the rules."

"You're not peasants. Peasants are poor, and don't have any money. You're going to be a knight. You have a family coat of arms."

"There's very little difference now that my father has died."

"No, that's not fair. It's a stupid rule," she whined, as she sat atop their favorite brick wall. "If I were Queen, I'd let anyone eat in there."

He chuckled as he helped her back to the ground. "You'd run out of food. Lots of hungry people in Hydlix. Especially now, when all the best stock and crops are taken by the king's army."

Or the king, she thought angrily. Schobe's answer did nothing to change her mind. She knew there'd be no way to sneak his family into the banquet hall without them being spotted. There had to be a way for her to give him something the way he'd done for her. It wasn't until he'd walked her halfway back to her and her aunt's home that an idea suddenly came to her.

"The slide!"

"Slide?"

"Yes, the aqua duck."

"*Oh*," he said, sounding amused again, "you mean aqueduct."

"Yes. I know where the slide begins," she boasted triumphantly, realizing then that this was the only royal perk she could offer him. "It's the best spot in the kingdom. Even better than your home even. I've always wanted to slide down the aqua duck. You can go with me."

"Down the...*aqueduct?*"

"Yes."

"You're joking. It's for mail, Trin. We could be hurt. Fall to our deaths. And that's only if they didn't catch us. Which they would."

"Who?"

"The knights. The postmen. Take your pick."

Trinity snickered. "They aren't very scary to me. Come on, it'll be fun," she said, taking his hand. "We'll feel the water splash in our face. We can see the whole kingdom from there. And I want you to go because, well, because I have nothing else to give you. Oh, and I know where my aunt keeps her key."

"Wait. What?" he asked, loosening his hand from her grip. "Who says you have to give me anything?"

"Fine," she said, rolling her eyes. "If you don't want to play with me, then go and read a book or something. But I'm going down that slide."

"Trin, you're crazy. What will your aunt say? Won't you get in trouble?"

"Only if we get caught. Which we won't."

"And what if we do? You, you'll probably get a talking to. Me? They'll throw me in the dungeons for endangering the life of the princess."

"Well, if you're going to protect me, then you'll have to go too, won't you?" she asked, testing him with her raised eyebrows.

"I won't," he declared, folding his arms and rooting himself to the spot.

Only he did go. He followed her all the way to her room and waited in the main hall as she changed her clothes and went to grab Evita's key.

Trinity found the golden key hanging on a hook inside Evita's empty room. She knew Evita wouldn't be home for a few hours, and that she'd be able to replace the key before her return. Strictly speaking, Trinity was supposed to be studying with Master Ihsotah this morning while Evita was attending a tea with some of the court members. But this was Trinity's one chance to share something with her one and only friend. She wasn't about to give that up now, especially when she'd already come so far. Hesitantly, she unhooked the key. She had never stolen before, and something didn't feel right about this action. She left her aunt's room and closed the bedroom door quietly, despite no one being home. It was then her head started hurting her. It felt like a dull, but annoying pinprick in the center of her forehead. *Why is this so difficult?* She placed the key around her neck, letting her regret pass for the moment. Still, the pain remained.

Trinity led Schobe to the royal mailing tower. Along the way, she scratched at her forehead wondering if maybe she'd been stung by a bee. It was beginning to feel as if a great weight had been placed atop her brow. She wondered if she was becoming sick. Turning back, she saw that Schobe was grabbing hold of a wall to steady his balance. He was trembling with every step.

"It's just here," she said, holding onto her head as she approached the door. "Hurry up."

Inside the dank mailroom, Trinity removed the key from her neck and placed it on a small hook by the door. She leapt up and steadied herself on the aqueduct's edge, right where the water was spilling over before pouring down the slope.

"So, are you *going* with me?" she asked, as Schobe slunk his way through the threshold and examined the sight of the apparent slide for himself.

"H-how do you know we won't die?"

"I don't," she admitted. "But I'll never know unless I try." She focused on the slope dropping down before her. She leaned forward slightly, but the pain in her head was growing stronger. Now it felt like someone was punching the top of her head with two fists. She winced, then looked back at Schobe. "Hey, you don't have to go, Schobey. I'll be alright."

She hoped so anyway. The sight below seemed much more intense than before, now being here on the edge of it. Her fingers creased the slippery sides she was holding onto. But just before she pushed herself forward, she could feel Schobe climbing up behind her. He seated himself down with a bit of a wobble and grabbed onto her shoulders. Trinity's face felt hot; she kept her eyes looking dead ahead.

"Thank you, Schobey."

"Don't call me Schobey."

"Are you ready?"

"No."

"Go?"

"I said *no!*"

She had heard him clearly but pretended not to over the sounds of the slapping water being blocked up by their bodies. "Then let's gooooooo!" she screamed. She scooted them forward with a mighty—and maybe too strong—pull along the aqueduct's smooth inner sides. Half a second later the two of them were rushing down the slippery slope in a full whoosh.

Trinity's whipping hair danced from the swiftness of her descent, covering Schobe's face as he let out shrill-sounding screams from behind. Downward they shot, spiraling and skidding past the first sharp turns of the plummeting aqueduct. Trinity's fear from earlier had gone; she couldn't hide her fits of glee any longer. The view from here was as spectacular as she knew it would be. She took in the sights and wondrous beauties her kingdom had to offer. The seven high towers glistened under the setting sun. The crowds below appeared from this height like a ripple in a rainbow-dyed pool.

"This is *amazing*," she squealed.

"If *you* say so!" Schobe shouted, hiding behind his soggy shield of fingers.

As the water grew thin up ahead where they neared a jut on their path, her headache suddenly intensified again. Trinity was then swept with a dark, unshakeable feeling. Her heart was growing still inside her chest, before suddenly pumping vigorously to correct itself. Her eyes welled with tears, which she at first mistook for the water splashing in her face, but the dropping pit feeling in her stomach left little doubt. There was an intense *pain* inside of her. Uncontrollable pain. Her lips started to quiver, and her jaw tensed as she cried out, overrun with emotions.

"Trin?" Schobe called to her, "Trin, are you alright?"

But she wasn't. The pain was only growing. The stabbing prick in her head worsened. She felt as if she could see the hands hitting her now. Only…they weren't connected to anybody. She gasped as two lifeless hands covered in blood both appeared in her mind's eye. They felt so real she could almost reach out and touch them. And for a second, she wanted to. Instead, she turned in disgust as tears began flooding from her eyes. Her screams turned into earsplitting screeches. *Something* was happening. She felt so angry, so sad, and so helpless all at the same time. The line between reality and what her mind was seeing started to blur. She started lashing out with her fists, knocking off a few of the rapidly passing edges of cement along the aqueduct's path.

"You're breaking the wall, Trinity!" Schobe yelled.

She couldn't hear him, or maybe she just couldn't respond. Her body demanded that she make the pain stop, but she didn't know how to do this. The convulsing heartache felt unreal. It was as if someone was reaching inside of her and squeezing her life out. *Whose hands are these?!*

"Trinity! Trinity, what's wrong?"

She snapped out of her apparent vision, but the pain couldn't be stopped by Schobe's words alone. The two of them hit the jut in the aqueduct at top speed and soared over the spot where they should've landed. Trinity threw her fists forward to protect herself from falling flat on her face and broke through the solid duct altogether. She and Schobe were sent plummeting to the ground some fifty feet below. Despite her growing terror at the looming death before her, the merciless pain refused to cease. *Something, or someone,* was making her feel as if her entire world had been destroyed, and that her happiness was gone forever. She turned in mid-air and clutched onto Schobe for protection. He did the same to her. Then, all she knew was darkness.

THE GRAY LION OF HYDLIX

Six years later...

No one could see Trinity's lively smile under the loose iron helmet. Her brambly hair bent and tugged beneath the headpiece. She'd never smelled the inside of a knight's helmet before and there was a crunch to the odor, like sniffing dried fur. The T-shaped slit on the front visor was thinner than she'd expected, making her breath hot and her eyes scrunched. Still, she had never been happier.

"Hope the helmet fits you better than the armor," Schobe said, though Trinity couldn't see where he was talking from. He then added, "You look like you're in a metal bubble."

"Will I pass on a horse though?"

He hesitated. "Eh, you might pass on a horse. In the middle of the night."

"*Schobey.*"

"Don't start that," he muttered, checking the straps on her silver cuirass. "I can't believe you talked me into this Trinity. If the king finds out—"

"You didn't *have* to help me. All I did was ask if I could borrow your armor."

"And my horse. And a lance. You want me to stand in front of you out there? Use me as a shield?"

"Listen. Thank you. Really."

"Yeah, yeah," he said, as he finished with the straps and moved on to fastening his gauntlets over her arms. "This isn't the first time I've risked my neck for you."

"Besides," she said, taking his chin in her gloved hand, "who says he's going to find out?"

She could see her worried accomplice now; his eyes were checking for unseen listeners around the room like a rabbit awaiting the hawk's talons. And though Schobe was only a year older than her, he too didn't quite fit into the pearly armor he'd lent her. She used to tease him for this, but now as she wobbled about in the borrowed knight wear, she began to feel just as clumsy as Schobe usually looked. Even with the extra grass padding in her sabatons to help make her a few inches taller, she could barely keep her loose helmet pointed straight. *They definitely don't make armor for girls*, she thought.

"Your aunt will spot you. I've no doubt," he said, waggling his finger in front of her visor. At least she thought it was his finger. He could've been waving his foot in her face for all she could see.

"She's shopping today—she hates going to jousts. Which means we have a good half day without a royal interruption."

"And what about Guren? If there's one person in that audience who'll know, it's him."

Trinity smirked an unseen smirk at the mention of Guren's name. "Let him." More than anyone else who might've spotted her at the joust, Guren's opinion mattered to her the least.

* * *

Trinity's first encounter with Guren had happened late one night when Trinity was eight. Her aunt had been scolding her for eating sugar cookies in bed again; the regal silks lining Evita's oversized mattress had become encrusted with dried jam fillings and crumb flakes. Who was her aunt trying to impress anyway? Even at a young age, Trinity knew there wasn't an answer to this question. The marble-floored, ivory-columned room had never known a man's presence other than Evita's own father, and he hardly ever visited.

"Why are you always eating in my bed, Trin?" Evita asked. "My linens are ruined."

"Your room has the best view," Trinity said, jumping off the high bed and running to the drafty stone window. Beyond the curtains and under the moon was her favorite sight in the whole of the Remsphere. The southern sea. The waves crashed against the seaweed laden rocks far below her aunt's window. The smell of the ocean was intoxicating. It was like a candle you never wished to see extinguished. She could feel the mist upon her cheeks. *The ocean's kiss*, she sometimes called it.

Evita sat on the now unmade bed and beckoned Trinity to join her. Trinity crept towards her side. Evita's onyx eyes were staring out the window, unfocused as Trinity came and sat beside her. In the light of the moon, which danced through the curtains, Evita's ebony skin seemed to glow. Her dreadlocks adorned the shoulders of her pale nightgown. Trinity had always been jealous of her aunt's beauty. There was a refined elegance in the way the older Hydlixian sat with such a perfect posture. Even when upset, the older princess never looked anything less than royal. Always so poised and so righteous.

Trinity on the other hand had always felt like her aunt had adopted a peasant. Her pasty skin was lined with freckles. She wore a nearly toothless smile—all through natural causes—yet it was often a topic of conversation at the airless suppers she was forced to attend in her grandfather's banquet hall. There her hair and eye color were also frequently mentioned. Questions of hers and Evita's relationship were usually brought up by dining members of the court, even though many of them had once known Trinity's mother—the first adopted princess and Evita's older sister. It was said that Trinity's mother had long golden hair, while Trinity's hair looked more like crinkled seaweed. Maybe this was the reason people doubted Evita whenever she'd tell them Trinity was her niece. Trinity didn't know why her skin was not dark or why her hair and eyes were green, or why it mattered. She would just sit there at the banquet table and rely on Evita's repeated explanation to silence the murmurs. Still, there was never a day in Hydlix where Trinity didn't feel like a white weed in a bed of dusk tulips waiting to be plucked.

Trinity slouched beside her aunt who was now sitting on the crumb-covered bed. "Sorry about the cookies."

Evita smiled as she corrected the girl's posture into one more like her own. "Yes. Well, you could at least clean up after yourself. Just like your mother. You know she was always a messy eater too."

"Really?"

"Oh, it was dreadful. And the floor was so sticky you'd have to wear shoes to bed."

"Sounds like my floor."

Evita scrunched her nose. "You two would've made a pair, that's for sure."

Trinity laid back in the bed and let her feet kick in a dangle. She sometimes wondered if her mother would've enjoyed some of the same things she did: sweets, watching the knights train, sunsets atop the eastern towers. Her mother surely would've approved of these non-princess activities.

"She loved the view in my room also," Evita explained. "So much so that she used that *strength* of hers to punch a hole in her wall just so she could catch a sight of the ocean. Father was so angry with her, but he never mended the wall."

Trinity's eyes lit up. "She made a window? How— why did I never think of that? A room with a view." She bounded to her feet. "I'll get started right away."

"Not so fast," Evita said, catching her by the wrist. "There's still the matter of these linens."

"Oh," Trinity said in a deflated voice. "I was hoping you'd forgotten."

"Hardly. You'll take these to the laundry. And *you* will be washing them tomorrow."

"Don't we have handmaidens for that?"

"Yes, we do. But you'll not have them cleaning up your mess. Am I quite understood?"

"Got it. Clean bedsheets. No more night sweets. Any other demands, your majesty?" Trinity asked. She then performed an over-embellished curtsy which had her plopping onto the floor.

"*Yes,*" Evita said, with a tense look that Trinity recognized at once. She loved seeing her aunt lose that *proper poise* of hers, if only for a second. "If I hear of any unplanned redecorating going on around here, you'll be confined to that room without a view. For a month."

"Two days. Tops," Trinity muttered under her breath.

She snatched up the linens, nudged open the front doors in the main hall, and scooted past the knight on guard duty outside of their home, who snickered at the sight of her. She ignored him, instead bounding up the stony steps into the courtyard. Admittedly, it was embarrassing to be strolling the gardens at this hour with a pile of laundry looming over her. Where was Schobe when she needed him? He would've jumped at the opportunity to help the princess. It was a title she detested, but nevertheless found useful at times.

The trimmed hedges within the kingdom's mile-long rose garden were shaped to resemble the royal emblem: a lion's black paw print on a yellow sun. This made walking across the yard difficult. Trinity felt like she was navigating a labyrinth of sweet-smelling bushes. She even bumped into the white lion hedge at the center, shaped with white roses and standing ten feet tall. She wondered for a second if she had dropped anything when a soothing, but brusque voice broke her thoughts.

"Do you need help, little one?"

The sound startled her enough that she dropped the linens onto the ground. A fortress of a man was leaning against the lion hedge, smoking from a long pipe made of tan wood. Green rings of dense smoke illuminated his figure. His narrow eyes cast a red shine from his lit tobacco and his well-trimmed beard of razor-thin black hair seemed to melt over his face. Even while leaning, he towered over her, looking almost as tall as the lion hedge, or so she believed in the moment. He rubbed one big hand along his high cheeks until his fingers grazed his chin.

"N-no thanks, I think I can manage," she said, picking up the soiled bedding. *I'm going to be washing all day now,* she thought, grimacing.

"My apologies, little Princess."

Who was this man? If he was someone important, she would've seen him at her grandfather's suppers. He wore on his neck a golden chain with a medallion bearing the lion stamp mark. *A knight?* She knew most of the knights in the kingdom. She'd been sneaking down to their barracks to watch them train for years now. He was like no knight she had ever seen before.

"Are you...a knight, sir?" she asked.

He nodded very slowly, and then took another puff on his pipe. "I was indeed. Though happily retired. Name's Guren."

"Guren?" She could feel her stomach drop to her feet. "*The* Guren? Former knight commander? Leader of the Battle for Reiwania?"

"I'm sure there are plenty other useless titles too. Call me Guren."

"Sir, it's an honor!" She dropped the bed linens again as she stepped forward and shook the man's hand vigorously. His face winced, and she loosened her grip. "Sorry. I'm just—I've always wanted to meet you. I didn't know you still lived in the kingdom."

"Came back a few weeks ago. Nice to see Hydlix standing in one piece." He cupped her hand into his rough palm. "That was some grip. You're Zepolia's girl alright."

"H—how do you know my mother?"

"When someone has yellow hair in this kingdom, everyone knows them." He released her hand and began tapping out some of the ashes in his pipe. "Though yours is a, forgive me, calming shade of green. No doubt inherited from your father. Yes. I am almost certain of it."

"You knew my father?" She practically shouted the question at him. No one had ever spoken about her father before. Not even Evita.

Guren gave a short sigh. "Not personally, no. I'd only been told stories, hear. Of the green-haired king with the strength of a hundred men. I mean, besides your mother, it wasn't every day we were blessed with a *Terkian's* presence in Hydlix."

She knew this word, but not well. She'd heard people call her that before. Often court members, but sometimes by those she saw in the marketplace. No one ever had an answer when she asked them what it meant. Trinity had considered the word a dirty swear of sorts, what with how it was usually said when referring to her. But Guren used the word another way. There was a glimmer of respect in his voice. His eyes lit up. And the slightest of smiles creased his lips.

"That word. What *is* a Terkian, sir?"

"You do not know of your own people? Your original kingdom?" he asked, now rubbing his chin again. The rugged Hydlixian accent was strong in his voice, like stones plunking into puddles making words short-sounding, but powerful. "Didn't you ever wonder about that strength of yours?"

"My strength?" She closed her fist tight. Her *strength* had always caused accidents. It was a curse she kept hidden. No one had ever spoken of her strength like a gift, especially after the aqueduct incident.

"Your kind possess the strength to change the very tides in the ocean. I once spoke to your mother of those abilities. Requested she join my ranks. But your grandfather wouldn't have it."

"You asked my mother to be a knight?"

"Course I did. I know talent when I see it."

She wondered if he saw any in her. But then what did it matter anyway? She knew the king's law. If her grandfather wouldn't allow his own adoptive daughter to become a knight, what chance did she have? *The pasty princess.*

Guren cast her a knowing grin. "I've heard stories about you too. Some of the men call you a thief. Said you stole some weapons."

Her eyes grew big. She knew what he was referring to. One late night she had taken some weapons from the training dome after it had been cleared. It was just an old rusty sword and a bow with a small crack in the wood. She never thought anyone would miss them, and had been so careful to hide them and only train delicately with them. Most of the time she was afraid they were going to break if she held them too tight.

Is that why he was waiting for her out here? Was he going to take back the weapons? Turn her in for her crime? She watched as the old knight took one final drag on his pipe and let the last of the green smoke fill his insides. He stood in the same manner her aunt often appeared. He had a straight, narrowed stance. *A poised gentleman.* She didn't think any existed in her kingdom. Not even Schobe stood like that.

He gazed down at her and seeped out the pleasant-smelling fumes from his nose. "I'd feel like a damn fool if I did not ask this," he said, "but perhaps you'd like to learn how to use those weapons. Properly."

* * *

Guren's lessons had meant everything to her. They were proof of the value of her ambitions. She knew she wouldn't be sitting in this saddle holding a lance today if it weren't for Guren's guidance.

How she missed those days. His kind words, rare as they were, had filled her with hope. If he was still her teacher, she was certain of the words he'd have for her before her first joust. The words echoed in her head and warmed her heart as her chestnut mare galloped at top speed down the track. *Don't lose your opponent. Not even for a second.*

Her joust was over as quickly as it had begun. She scored a direct hit on her opponent's shield; her lance exploding onto his chest. The opposing knight was lifted from his horse and thrown across the track, falling onto his back as Trinity's weapon crumbled to the ground. She had won. The roar from the stands ricocheted in her helmet like a swarm of gathering bees. She clutched the reins of her horse and turned on the spot.

Schobe was running to meet her now. He was sweating, struck with a look of what appeared to be mixed joy. Trinity stumbled off her horse and clanged over to greet him.

"I won! I won!" she squealed, grabbing his arms and leaping giddily.

"Easy," he said. "Knights don't squeal when winning a joust."

She could see her adoring crowds now. The cheap seats were lined with men and women, most of whom were wearing stitched, handmade lion manes. Many had painted faces with three red lines across their left eyes, trying to look like Sachrezzar, the lion of legend. Some of the women wore long, white tails made of sewn linen fabric, which could be purchased inexpensively by vendors walking the stands. Trinity had several of these tails at home. She used to wear them all the time until her aunt forbade her. Evita said they weren't proper for royalty. Her aunt never much approved of any fan gear.

The crowds were chanting something in Hydlixian, which was a language Trinity hardly ever used. Even at home or at royal events with the king, she and Evita spoke in the TCL: Taercion Common Language. It was the most well-known tongue on the continent, and most traveling merchants even spoke it. But whatever it was the crowds were chanting, she believed they were saying it about her.

"What does *kilik ma stebana* mean?" she asked Schobe, wondering about her own pronunciation.

Schobe almost laughed. "Lance-crusher. It's a well-earned title. Hard to come by."

Trinity gazed back into the stands. The children were frantically waving their paw print banners in her direction. The men drank ale from tin goblets and feasted on charred sagme fat. They belted out choruses of "Pardon Our Claws" completely out of tune. Trinity soaked it all in with sheer happiness as the pride within her welled to new heights. Here in the lists, beside the wooden posts separating the horses, she was privy to a view of her people unlike any she'd ever seen before. No one was staring at her in disgust. No one was whispering behind her back. She was no longer the little white princess with dirty green hair. Here—in her borrowed armor and damp helmet—she was accepted. *So, this is how it feels to be poised.*

"Your aunt is here," Schobe whispered. "And I've just seen Guren."

Trinity turned to where the king's box was located. Her own plush, cushioned chair sat empty, but her aunt now sat there beside the unfilled spot. Evita was wearing some spiked, silver animal's fur atop her snowy dress, staring directly at Trinity through a pair of tiny binoculars. Without thinking, Trinity dashed behind her friend.

"She can still see you," Schobe said.

"She must've finished shopping early. That scarf is hideous."

"Focus Trin. What are you going to do?"

Trinity looked just above her aunt's seat and saw her grandfather biting into the charred fat on a stick. King Eslon of Hydlix looked like he hadn't even noticed her victory. The round-faced, beady-eyed man had gravy running down his black chins and pouring onto his diamond-studded robes. There was no pause between stuffing his gullet and raising his chalice of ale. The froth smeared across his lips like a breaking wave. Trinity thought to herself that the only feature separating him from the drunken, gorging peasants—besides his rich garments and raised vantage point—was his elegant crown. It was shaped to resemble a lion's head with strands of pure gold nestled together, and two perfect, round-cut rubies attached to where the eyes would be.

It's a wonder he hasn't started nibbling on it, she thought.

"Where's Guren?" she asked.

"He—"

Schobe's words froze in his mouth. The opposing knight was approaching them both. He bore a great dent from where Trinity's lance had broken off at the center of his chest. The knight removed his helmet. Trinity knew this stone-faced man with livid eyes. Schobe made a clumsy four-fingered salute to the man. *Hardly a proper lion's paw salute.* Trinity hesitated to follow his lead as her own hands shook by her sides. Of all the knights she thought that she would be facing here in the lists, she didn't think her first opponent would be the knight commander himself. *Why didn't I pay attention to his armor?* Unlike the other soldiers, his dented breastplate bore gilded lines. He had also fastened on his long pearl commander's cape—most likely to hide the dent and dirty armor—yet Trinity suspected another reason. *He probably wants to look official before coming down on us.*

"C-Commander K-Kuza," Schobe sputtered out. He sounded like a kicked dog begging for another stomp.

"Attend to me squire! Who in MAI's name is this soldier? Who let him ride the track?"

"Sir, I—"

"*You?*" Kuza screeched at him.

"No," Trinity declared, taking a small step forward. "I chose to ride. All on my own. I bested you in the joust."

"Who—was that a girl's voice?" He pushed past Schobe and yanked Trinity's helmet from her shoulders.

The crowds grew silent. The king was watching now. He nearly choked on his food. An outraged Evita covered her mouth with both hands. And there standing behind Evita was none other than Guren. He was the one person in the stands who didn't look surprised. Trinity hoped against hope that he might say something, or even acknowledge her knightly accomplishment with the slightest of expressions. Instead, she watched helplessly as the former knight commander turned his back on her and walked down the flight of wooden stairs into the throngs of speechless cheap seaters. He disappeared without a word, just as Trinity feared he would.

CHAPTER THREE

DAUGHTERS
OF THE REALM

Trinity's toes felt trapped within the pair of heels that she'd been forced to strap on almost an hour ago. This, of course, had happened before her half-mile march to the gilded throne room with Evita walking close behind her, breathing like a dragon down her neck. They walked so fast that Evita was breaking a sweat. She wasn't even stopping to check her make-up, which was something she normally did about a dozen times before having an audience with the king. Trinity half-believed that her aunt might keel over before arriving to the throne room. But then she remembered that Evita was far too stubborn to die before giving her a proper earful.

The steel-tipped boots from the joust had been discarded—along with all of Schobe's armor—beside the brick wall where they used to play as children. Trinity hadn't planned on walking back to her chambers in only her breeches and undershirt, but Evita had only given her five minutes to ditch the armor set and meet her back in their chambers. These clothes were hardly proper attire for the late Fall chill thick in the afternoon air.

Trinity had never undone armor on herself before and may have broken a strap or two as she slipped out of the heavy gear. Schobe was unable to assist her this time. Last she saw of him he was being chewed out by Commander Kuza. *Poor Schobe*. She'd never meant for her friend to be involved in her defiant act. It had been her own reckless desire to compete in the king's jousting tournament, not his. Yet, the most admirable trait about her best friend was his ability to forgive even when he ought not to. She knew she had chosen a proper friend all those years ago. She hoped his punishment wouldn't be too severe.

After an embarrassing and frigid trip back to her chambers, Trinity discovered that her aunt had already instructed the handmaidens to draw a bath. Evita had also laid out an emerald-studded dress that Trinity loathed wearing. She always thought that it made her look like a walking piece of broccoli. And the dress was so tight that she was certain a couple of deep breaths would surely split the gown down the sides. Still, she thought it best not to question her aunt's wardrobe choices for her at the moment.

Trinity was bathed and dressed in minutes. Her post-bath, sopping curls clung like spider webs across her face. The oldest of her aunt's handmaidens took her in hand and brushed all the tangles out, despite Trinity's whines and protests. She had concluded long ago that her hair must be naturally tangled and no amount of brushing would change that. She also believed that this particular handmaiden got some sort of twisted joy out of watching her suffer for the sake of a too-tightly-taut braid. *Braids... like a dungeon for your hair.*

Once she was changed and ready, she and Evita set off for their meeting with the king. Trinity tried her best to stay far ahead of her aunt during their trek. Her own experience with walking in heels was nothing compared to Evita's though, and her aunt was able to match her hurried pace with ease.

Trinity wanted to avoid the lecture she had coming to her for as long as she could. She'd been so rushed since leaving the lists that she and Evita had hardly spoken, which was fine with Trinity. If she'd known Evita was attending the king's tournament, she might've reconsidered competing. It wasn't her fault the king had proclaimed such a rare and tempting opportunity for her to show off her skills. It was a real chance to prove herself and show her grandfather the capability of her strength. But she hadn't known Kuza would be her opponent. That man had always hated her. She wasn't sure if he was jealous of her inherited abilities or something else entirely. But then, this was not the first time she had embarrassed him in combat. He never should've made her so angry on her ninth birthday.

* * *

Trinity's ninth birthday had begun early in the morning, as she snuck into the training dome to watch Schobe attend to his squire duties. Most knights in the dome barracks had seen her there before, and felt as if she was an unwelcome presence. She'd had to hide herself behind straw dummies and archery posts, and was, for the most part, ignored save for the passing comments:

"—why is that brat down here again—"

"—don't the princess keep this one on a tight leash—"

"—watch it little mouse or I'll step on ya—"

Trinity had felt particularly brave that day, seating herself on one of the wooden benches lining the dirt-covered floors of the dome. There was no place in all the kingdom that gave Trinity more excitement than watching the men train, wishing and hoping that one day she could join them. She'd made a plan of it. At her birthday supper tonight, she would ask her grandfather's permission to become a squire. He would have to listen then, or he'd look especially mean in front of the visiting royalty that would also be dining tonight. They were coming all the way from the kingdom of Zayloa. Her plan had to work in front of them. At least, she thought it sounded good when she'd told Guren about it yesterday.

As she sat on the bench watching the knights continue with their morning drills, she noticed that Schobe was having difficulties of his own. Each morning he was tasked with filling the water barrels near the well by the armory racks, and then maneuvering them back to where the men trained, but he looked to be struggling and he was drenched with sweat. She didn't think going to help him would cause any harm, so she did.

This, however, was the first time Commander Kuza had seen her in the dome. From the second she saw the commander riding up to them and their water barrels, she knew she'd done something wrong.

"You girl!" Kuza called to her, as he sat atop his white horse. He was bare-chested, and the sweat from his dark ponytail soaked onto the towel atop his shoulders. "What knight do you squire for, Princess?" he asked. His rigid face and close-set eyes made him appear as if he'd just told an unfunny joke.

Trinity had been busy balancing a filled water barrel atop her head, as Schobe dragged his barrel slowly behind. When she heard Kuza's barking request, she turned to him quickly and sloshed some of the water onto her boots. She dropped the barrel with ease to her waist, and then lowered it to the ground. She saluted Kuza with the salute she'd seen done hundreds of times before by the men. It was four outstretched fingers and a tucked thumb: the lion's paw salute.

"Sir!" she exclaimed, matching his heavy tone. "Just helping my friend, sir!"

"Can't handle your task on your own, squire?" The commander was addressing Schobe now. He drove his horse closer to the shrinking squire. "Needed a visit from your...*royal* friend? The white mouse princess."

"Leave now, Trinity," Schobe whispered to her. "Go now and he'll forget all of this."

She ignored her friend's request. Kuza had riled something within her. "Sir, I'm not a mouse, sir! And I am going to be a knight someday...*sir*!" She added this final "sir" with an extra air of snark.

"Leave!" Schobe told her again. There was hurt in his eyes, and Trinity knew she was the cause.

She dropped her salute. "I'm sorry Schobey. Let me finish helping you and then I'll go."

She knelt and stretched her arms around the barrel. But just then there was a sharp tug at her shoulder. She turned to see that Kuza had already dismounted and was beside her. She tried to pull away from him, but the man clenched his hand onto her violet tunic and lifted her off her feet.

"Princess or not, do you know what I do to little mice who don't know their place?" he asked. She could feel his hot breath in her eyes. It smelled of burnt coffee and raw meat.

"Please Commander," Schobe begged, "she's leaving now. I'll attend to my duties alone. Please!"

"Let go!" Trinity shrieked. Don't you dare rip my tunic! Guren made it for me for my birthday."

Kuza abruptly dropped her and Trinity fell to the dirt floor with a thud. "Oh, my greatest apologies, Princess," he said, chuckling. "Didn't realize Guren had taken up knitting after he retired."

She checked her tunic for any rips. She could feel her face growing warm with embarrassment. "You *almost* ripped my tunic," she muttered through grit teeth.

"Right. About that," he said, bringing his hand down and dusting off her back with sharp whaps. "A girl should know better. Princesses, women, they have no place on my training grounds. They should be shopping. Or better, learning to knit. You should ask Guren to teach you."

There were snickers from a few of the watching knights. Trinity knew her face was beet red by this point. Her fists curled at her sides.

Kuza continued, "I don't much care who your mother was or why everyone in the kingdom is supposed to call you Princess." He placed a heavy hand upon her shoulder, tightening his grip. "You do well to stay away from my knights, girl, or next time I may not be so...*nice*."

She turned to face him. She grabbed his wrist with both her hands and dug her nails into his skin. Kuza's pinched face wretched in pain, but Trinity didn't loosen her grip.

"Me neither," she replied. Trinity yanked Kuza's arm forward and launched him over her body, sending him flying well over his horse and then down onto a set of unsuspecting knights nearly forty feet from where he had once been standing.

Kuza's body smashed onto the ground and crumpled. The other men in the room stopped their exercises. Some began to guffaw at the sight they'd just witnessed, while others ran to examine the commander. Kuza was coughing out the dust wedged in his nose from the point of impact.

Trinity turned with a smile towards Schobe. He wasn't smiling back though. Instead, he was giving her a pure look of fear. His eyes trembled in his head, and his bottom lip was quavering. Schobe steadied himself, and spoke aloud his one single thought:

"Freak."

* * *

She never forgot the look Schobe had given her on that day. It was the same look her aunt was giving her now as they stood before the castle-sized doors of the throne room. Though Trinity had long ago forgiven her best friend for his misspoken word, the hurt from years ago still remained. She wondered if this was how Evita felt about her as well. Warm tears began to form, but she forced them back. *Don't*, she told herself. *I won't cry before the king.*

Evita stood facing the door and then heaved a deep sigh. "...Listen," she finally began, "when we get in there you let me do the talking. Interrupting a kingdom-sponsored joust is a serious offense."

"I wasn't interrupting it. I was winning."

Evita narrowed her eyes. "You—yes, you rode beautifully."

Did she just—Was Evita pleased with her? This wasn't the same woman who was nipping at her heels on the stairway seconds earlier. There was pride in her voice. She even had a spark in her eyes. What in MAI's name was going on?

"Aunt E?"

"Zepolia…she would've been proud."

Trinity said nothing. Just hearing her mother's name was enough to break her. Instead, she did something she'd not done since she was a small child. She took Evita's hand into her own and gave a soft squeeze as her emotions won the fight. *Damn these tears.*

"I'm sorry Aunt E. I only rode—"

"I know why you rode. You're very skilled Trinity. You didn't have to prove that to me, or to them." She embraced her then, letting Trinity sob onto her new scarf. "None of that matters to Father though. And you knew that."

"I won't accept his plan for me," Trinity said, her voice cracking. "I-I'd rather die."

"Trinity, it is our duty as daughters of the realm. I've accepted my role, just as you should yours. You can't change it. Any more than you could—" Her eyes wandered for a thought.

"Change the tides?" Even now, Trinity found comfort in her former teacher's words, though it had been over a year since the last time he had spoken to her.

Evita nodded. "Precisely."

After ascending the marble stairs within the royal ruby tower, Trinity and Evita entered the throne room. Kuza was already there, standing guard beside the king on his cushioned throne. He was wearing a long-sleeved shirt with wooden toggles now. The dented chest piece he'd worn at the joust laid beside his feet.

Trinity didn't make eye contact with him or the king. Despite waiting outside the doors for a few extra minutes to stop her crying, she couldn't hide the puffiness around her eyes. She knew she was showing these men before her a weakness, and she was certain the knight commander would find some way to use this against her and gobble her up. She wondered then how the king would feel if she challenged Kuza to a rematch. *I'll make him snort dirt again for sure.*

She and Evita walked down the center of the amber-lit room, where the setting sun pierced the glass walls. There would be no white carpet treatment today. She hardly felt like a guest though. The clacks of her heels reverberated off the stone floors of the rustic throne room. This was one of the oldest rooms in the kingdom. Her—or Evita's, she supposed—great-great-grandfather had built the room to overlook the ocean. When the towers of the palace were finally erected after his death, the room was raised with them. Because of this, she always had a shaky feeling when walking these floors. Her knees felt like they were swaying. She was convinced that if her grandfather got any fatter, the tower would collapse.

Evita took Trinity's hand once more and the two of them curtsied before the king. *How does Evita manage it in those heels?* Suddenly, and without much effort, Trinity's pinky toe punctured a hole through the right shoe's top end. She was impressed with her own toe's strength since it was a muscle she had never once trained. She tried the same with her left shoe and found equal success. She wiggled her pinky toes freely now under the safety of her dress, feeling relief at last.

"Princess Trinity," grumbled King Eslon, as he attempted to set himself upright. "You stand accused of entering my jousting tournament, even though it is forbidden for women to do so. Do you deny it?"

"No, your Grace, she doesn't," Evita said.

"I want to hear it from her," Eslon grumbled, wiping at the sweat falling over his puffed-out cheeks and squishy brow.

"No, your Grace," Trinity said, feeling a bit foolish for having to address her grandfather by his royal title. "I entered the tournament." *And I would've been champion too*, she thought, though not aloud.

"Grave offense," Eslon told her, leaning back on his throne and scratching at the fold between his chins. "The joust is a very lucrative tournament for the kingdom. I can't have some *girl* bankrupting my crown because she wanted to play knight and horsey."

The present members of his court chuckled. Trinity was familiar with this chorus of rehearsed laughs from along the lines of robed steki-squeezers, as she liked to call them. They only cared about money—*the king's money*—and as such never had any problems telling her grandfather how to spend his stekis. Trinity always thought that the court members sounded like dying bullfrogs when laughing together.

"I'm very sorry, your Grace," Trinity said, convinced her words sounded genuine.

"Yes well, any other child who attempted such a thing would be thrown in the stocks and have the key tossed away. What am I to do with you, girl?"

She wasn't sure if this question was meant to have an answer. Evita seemed to share in her perplexity and spoke once more on her behalf.

"I assure you, Father, your Grace, that I will have a *long* discussion with her. And she will be participating in no further knightly events."

"She could've been hurt, Princess Evita," Commander Kuza said, stepping forward now. "The lists are no place for a girl, least of all a princess."

"Weren't you the one knocked to the flat of your back?" Trinity asked, sharply.

Evita gave her a stern, "Hush. Not another word."

The knight commander continued his advance. "This can't be easy on you, Princess. Having to take care of such a disobedient child. And at your tender age, too. Knowing what *she* is."

Evita glared at him. "Stop right there. I knew taking on my sister's baby when I was fourteen would have its challenges. But I have never once regretted the decision to do so, sir."

"Gorilla people, you know," he said, now addressing the court. "That beast blood of hers is what makes her so dangerous. No telling what wild thing she'll do next. Do you not remember what she did to our aqueduct years ago? All that ruined mail. And the streets flooded."

"You are bringing up ancient history," Evita said, with callousness in her voice. "Furthermore, if it weren't for that *blood* of hers, she and the squire would've died."

There was no denying this. Trinity still couldn't understand what it was that made her so upset that day six years ago. Fortunately, her body had broken Schobe's fall and he was able to walk away from the scene she'd caused relatively unharmed. Even her own wounds had only amounted to a bump on the head. When she regained consciousness, her intense pain and dark visions from before had ceased, almost as if they had never been. There was a crater in the stone road beneath her. At first, she didn't know that she was the one who had caused this great big hole in the ground. She stood guiltily beside Schobe and felt as if all the eyes in the kingdom were upon her. Wooden stands in the market had been swept away by the rushing waters spilling from the broken aqueduct. Everyone in the market place was drenched from head to foot. The "Aqueduct Project," as it came to be known, took weeks to repair.

She had also never seen her aunt so angry before. Evita's scolding stretched long into the night, harping on about her disappointment over the stolen key until Trinity had nodded off atop their feather-stuffed bench in the main hall of their home. The next day Trinity was forced to go out and help clean up the mess that she had made, though she was only there for a day.

She supposed she'd gotten off easy. Schobe had revealed to her sometime later that when his mother found out about all the trouble that they'd caused, she took her broomstick to the back of his legs. Trinity knew Evita would never do something so harsh, no matter how mad she was. Besides, if the aqueduct incident had taught her one thing, it was that she had tough skin. Even still, Trinity had never stolen anything from her aunt again.

Commander Kuza was circling Evita and Trinity now, as he continued his attack on Trinity's character, "Please understand your Grace, present members of the court, that we knights will not be able to stop her if she one day decides to use that *strength* against us. Against our kingdom." All around him were whispers and several nods coming from the court members. "I assure you Princess Evita, that if she were my responsibility, I'd have tamed those animal instincts the way I would any wild beast: with a long whip and a small cage."

"Then let us be thankful you were not responsible," Evita said, as she stepped in front of Trinity and met the man's gaze head on. "You might have brought the whole kingdom crashing on its head. She is my responsibility, and mine alone. And you are forgetting your *place,* sir!"

Trinity looked past her aunt's dress towards the source of further whisperings filling the room. The faces of her grandfather's court were laced with dread. Was she so horrible? Even her own aunt had just voiced her worries of the girl's destructive abilities. *I hate my strength. I hate my strength.* She'd not chanted that inside her head for some years, before ever meeting Guren. Once she had begun his strict training regimen, her only fear had been being not strong enough. But perhaps this was why Guren had stopped talking to her, stopped training her. Maybe he too had been afraid of what her strength could do.

"Enough of this," King Eslon growled. "Kuza, my daughter has stated her piece. And my granddaughter has spoken her apology. That will be the end of it."

Kuza stepped back and bowed his head slightly before the king. "Yes, your Grace. And my apologies, Princess Evita. I was only concerned. For the safety of the kingdom, which I dutifully serve."

"Save it," Evita told him. "What have you done with the squire who helped her?"

Schobe? Why was she mentioning Schobe?

"The squire? H-he's been given additional tasks," Kuza began, though shakily. "Latrine digging, just outside the kingdom. As well as a month's watch patrolling the dungeons."

"Very well," Evita said. "He shall have a partner."

"He—what?" Kuza bellowed.

"My niece committed her crime looking like a knight. It is only fitting that she faces the same fate as a knight."

Trinity was taken aback, but her aunt gave her a quick smile then. Kuza was looking absolutely outraged as he curled his hands to fists.

"There you have it," the king said. "You'll start tomorrow, young lady. Best you wear appropriate attire."

"Thank y—I mean, yes, your Grace," Trinity said, holding back a smile of her own. "I understand. I accept your justice."

"Very well. Court's adjourned. You may leave us, Kuza. I need to speak to my family. You're all dismissed."

The knight commander hesitated to follow this order as the court members filed out of the room. Trinity had never been met with a glare more intimidating than his was in that moment. But she wasn't afraid. Instead, she struggled not to laugh as Kuza stomped out of the throne room like a pouting child, carrying his dented armor and muttering Hydlixian swear words.

"Trinity," King Eslon called, summoning her attention once more.

"Your Grace?" She turned to him, feeling confused. What else could the king possibly have to say to her?

"Is something wrong, Father?" Evita asked.

"Not at all," Eslon said. "I received a letter recently. From a *Zayloan* messenger."

Trinity's heart sank. Her feet felt so heavy upon hearing this that she feared she might shatter through the floor and bring the tower down around them.

"W-what did it say?" Evita asked, stepping by Trinity's side and clutching onto her arm.

"It seems they want to hold the wedding in spring. We'd best start preparing," he said, with a hearty chuckle. "Four months. Hayden, of course, sends his love, Trinity."

She should've known better. Just when her life seemed to take a positive turn by giving her a chance to work side by side with Schobe and feel like a real knight, she was reminded of perhaps her greatest fear. The image of a snaggle-toothed demon entered her thoughts. She could hear the whistle in his voice again, see those vexing eyes. He, too, had called her a Terkian with *disgust* in his voice. How could she ever forget Hayden? His face haunted her every dream. Now, his presence would soon be inevitable. The man—*the monster*—they intended her to marry would be here in half a year's time.

ANOTHER DAY EARNED

The next day, after being so unnecessarily reminded of Hayden's impending arrival, Trinity rose early and went to the royal mailing tower alone. The sun hadn't yet risen. By now, the cooks in the kitchens would be heating the leftover oils and beginning to fry up the sagme strips that would be served for breakfast in the banquet hall. Trinity's favorite cook, a jolly woman named Phes, always left her the darkest pieces of meat alongside a fresh-squeezed glass of grapefruit juice and a poached egg. Trinity usually thanked her with fresh cut roses from her grandfather's garden. Today, however, she'd be skipping breakfast.

Schobe would be outside the palace walls soon. Trinity would soon meet him beneath the eastern bridge so they could begin their day's tasks. In the three weeks she'd been digging the outdoor latrines with him, they'd managed to carve a shaft through the mud and all the way down the craggy cliffs to where the tides came in late at night. They now had to reinforce the dug latrine with cut wood which they collected from the carpenter. At first, Trinity was bringing the long boards—each six feet in length—down the cliff, seven to ten at a time, stacked atop her fully-gloved arms. It wasn't long though before she noticed that Schobe was having difficulty keeping up with her.

He never asked her to ease off, but Trinity changed tactics midway through the job and began carrying only two pieces of wood at a time. She also slowed her pace considerably. This gave her a chance to walk directly beside her friend as they found their footing down the damp rocks. And, fortunately for her, Schobe had so much to say as of late.

His youngest brother, Dary, had just become a squire. The boy was lightning fast in his tasks and Schobe boasted that he was already a finer piss-pot polisher than he ever was. Schobe's sister, Ellacryse, had also been busy. She'd taken to selling wares in her own corner of the market, handmade jewelry made of colored twine and smooth beads. Upon hearing this, Trinity made a special trip to the market and purchased a dozen necklaces from her. Ellacryse was beaming as Trinity paid her two handfuls worth of stekis. Trinity began making a habit of wearing a different piece every day. But today, she'd forgotten to wear one entirely.

Her Aunt Evita never stirred at this time of day. She was always asleep when Trinity was readying herself in the morning. Trinity would sometimes voice a hushed farewell before leaving, or sneak into her aunt's room and give her a light kiss on the cheek. She always had to stifle a giggle when hearing Evita snoring. *Snoring definitely isn't poised.*

Sometimes for fun, Trinity would take the opportunity to move pieces around on hers and her aunt's never-ending game of King's Circle, played on a fine oak set on the rounded table in their study. She'd found it was hard to get away with moves like reviving some of her fallen pieces such as the handmaiden or king's piece, but Evita never seemed to call her out on moving her newborn prince piece closer to the center of the board. Trinity would never take advantage of the extra move, putting her piece back before their game resumed. She just wanted to see if Evita ever noticed.

There were usually leftover dessert plates on their game table from the night before, which Trinity would stack and set aside for the handmaidens. A new bakery had just opened near Evita's favorite hat shop. For the past several nights Evita had brought home various cakes for the two of them to try. Trinity learned that she couldn't stomach carrot cake, but raspberry-lined frosting was perhaps the most exquisite taste in all the kingdom. Last night she reminded her aunt that she wanted this type of cake again on her birthday next summer. Evita then bit her lip and sighed.

"...Maybe for your wedding," she finally said later on, before the two of them had gone to bed that night.

Today, Trinity didn't stack the plates. And, she told herself, she didn't much feel like playing games or eating cake. *Not today.*

The harsh reality of Evita's words stung like an arrow through the chest. Even now, as Trinity stared across her kingdom after jumping up to the top of the royal mailing tower, she felt a heavy ball of emotions welling in her throat. She knew her destiny had been decided for her long ago, but thinking of Hayden again sent a ghostly shiver through her bones. Soon there would be no more birthdays in Hydlix, no cakes and games with her aunt, no time for her friends and favorite people in the kingdom. Soon, all of these things she loved about her Hydlix would be only memories.

But then she reminded herself—as she had done every day since the first day she'd met Hayden—that today was not his day yet. No, she wouldn't let him steal her joy as he had done for so many nights as of late. The snaggle-toothed prince wasn't expected until spring. The winter season had not even begun to fall upon Hydlix yet, though the days grew shorter and the air had a biting chill. *I still have time.*

And that was why today, Trinity believed, was a good day to train. Though her path had been set forth by others long ago, she still held on to her one guiding hope. *Maybe, I could still be a knight someday.*

She undid the bolts and loosened the slats on the tower window she was standing beside. Trinity had discovered that she didn't need her aunt's golden key to gain access into the royal mailing tower. She gripped onto the window's ledge and lowered herself inside. The fall below was some thirty feet. The softest—though less preferred—landing came with falling onto where the gushing waters rose and spilled out onto the aqueduct. But this led to wet clothes, and sometimes questions from Evita.

Trinity instead had taught herself how to gracefully land onto the toes of her boots. There was never any sting after doing so, which often made her wonder just how high a fall she could survive.

She loosened a stone from the floor inside the tower, revealing a stack of wet papers. She'd gotten the idea of hiding her papers beneath stone from watching others in the kingdom send their mail and packages out by lifting the marked paw-print stones found throughout the kingdom. If a person—who wasn't royalty—wanted to send something by mail in the kingdom rather than hand deliver it, they'd lift the marked stones on street corners and drop their mail down to the watery caverns below. Once or twice a year the kingdom's postmen would have to fish out packages clogging up some of the tunnels. Trinity once heard during her teacher Ihsotah's lessons that the kingdom was filled with numerous tunnels below ground, and not every one of them ended up filtering back into the aqueduct. The thought of it was enough to make Trinity squeamish. She couldn't imagine going down there and running into a swarm of rats or something.

Trinity pulled up her stack of papers. The ink was smeared on many of them, and some had torn due to age and the moistness of the room. Trinity set about hanging these tattered pages around the tower on bolted hooks in the stones that she nailed in herself. Some of the bolts required her to jump across the room. She kicked off the walls and clasped onto the outstretched hooks until every one of them held a paper.

Next, she pulled from the loosened spot on the floor two iron swords, which were dull and rusting. The original blade she had stolen when she was eight had broken long ago. These swords had been a secret gift from Guren. She held the iron swords together and studied one of the hung papers. On the hanging page was the drawn figure of a man wielding two blades identical to her own. He was thrusting forward with one while his elbow jutted out and appeared to be swinging in from an alternate direction with the other. Trinity followed the paper's directions obediently. When she was satisfied with this exercise, she moved on to the next hung page.

This was how she had come to train herself every morning for the last year, ever since Guren had suddenly stopped training her without an explanation. She had come now to rely upon these handwritten lessons and drawn pictures, which were a poor substitute, she knew, compared to having a real teacher. Despite this, she'd come to master some of these techniques through continued exposure and refinement. And though she was lacking a training partner, she had come up with a solution to this problem as well.

Behind one of the cabinets holding letterheads and mailing bags was a straw dummy, whose body was wrapped tight with sacking, which she'd acquired from the waste piles beside the training dome. The dummy had two outstretched arms as long as Trinity's body. When she discovered him, he was torn and headless, but she'd fixed him up as best as she could, even painting a face on him: two crossed blue eyes, a button nose, and a pair of frowning lips with a sketched snaggletooth between them.

Her steel thudded and rang against the post he was tied to as she hacked at the straw fixture mercilessly.

The dummy's innards fell from his shirt as her sword cleaved across his lumpy chest. One of her favorite techniques with her stuffed training partner was to swoop down low with a twist and slice the dummy's head off its shoulders. The stuffed head bounced against the stone walls and rolled by her foot. She kicked the head up high and then smacked it back onto the post with the blunted edge of her sword. *No!* The head had landed on the body backwards. She never could get the head on just right.

Trinity looked up and noticed the sky was beginning to brighten. She hurried to loosen the dummy and stash him away again. Quickly, she collected all of her training papers around the room and stashed them, along with the swords, back into the hole on the ground. Next, she pulled out a wooden bow and a leather quiver stuffed with steel-tipped arrows. Carefully, she tied a bowstring down across the ends of the bending wood. She'd already broken three other bows this year. Stealing another one would be difficult. Inside the quiver was another stack of rolled papers—targets this time. There were twenty in total: red circular marks with tattered holes throughout. She set about hanging each one in the same manner she'd done with the sword-training papers.

Trinity steadied herself at the center of the room and nocked an arrow. She looked to the ceiling, then crouched down and leapt hastily upwards towards the window she'd come in from. Her body slipped through the opening and for a few brief seconds Trinity was suspended high above her tower. Her curled hair flailed over her eyes. She was met with the most remarkable sight. A golden sliver had just risen on the southern horizon. The light rushed across the calm waters. *MAI has made another promise.* She remembered these words that her aunt used to say when the two of them would sometimes wake early enough to catch the view together. *We have earned another of his days.*

She flipped her body over as she descended back through her window. Lifting her bow swiftly, she nocked an arrow and held it beside her cheek. She loosened the zipping steel tip into one of the targets within the tower, before firing off another three and coming back to the ground. Each one found their targets as well. Once more she kicked off the ground towards a wall. She fired another, and another, and another, until there was but one left. Her favorite target caught her eye. She'd posted this one high above the others, near the tower's ceiling. Quickly, she pulled from her breeches a folded piece of dark cloth, which she then tied around her eyes. *I'll get it this time*. Taking a deep breath, she readied her feet by feeling around until her right foot was near the hole in the floor. She prepared her final arrow and then leapt up once more, counting silently to three before nocking the arrow fully.

"Plunk," she whispered, mimicking the sound of the bow's string shooting the arrow.

There was a tearing sound. Was it the paper? She peeked out beneath her blindfold and saw that the outermost ring of the high target held her arrow. *Damn!* She had been so sure of a center hit. *Why did I miss?* The shock of her failure didn't remain for long. Before she could stop herself, her head smashed hard onto the stone ceiling above. Her body toppled down as she let fly several Hydlixian curse words that she was grateful her aunt couldn't hear. She pulled the blindfold off and held onto her pulsing head as she landed back to the ground harder than she'd intended. Bits of rubble fell from above. They were followed by a large dented stone which missed hitting her head again as it smashed onto the floor.

Slowly she collected her arrows and targets from around the room. When she had placed them back safely under her concealing floor stone, she picked up the fallen piece from the ceiling.

"Stupid stone," she muttered, rubbing at the back of her head, though the pain from her misfire still hurt worse. It was, perhaps, a good thing that Guren *hadn't* been here to see her latest training blunder.

Nevertheless, she'd managed to train some. And she supposed that would have to be good enough for the time being. Now, it was time to see what this newly earned day would bring her.

CHAPTER FIVE

SNOWFLAKES

Schobe was waiting for Trinity outside the palace walls. He stood on the black sand cliffside overlooking the foamy waves. He didn't seem to notice her carrying the fractured piece of the tower's ceiling until she was nearly at his side. With a low-sounding grunt, Trinity chucked the stone as far as she could. The two of them watched as the stone soared into the horizon and made a splash far off into the distance.

"Hit your head again, did you?" he asked, fighting off a smile.

"Be quiet, Schobe." The bump on her head felt like it was starting to swell. "It actually hurt this time."

"I'm sure it did. Anyone else would've caved their head in. You keep bumping into the roof like that and you're going to collapse the tower. Just you watch."

She peered at him as fiercely as she could manage before breaking down and laughing right along with him.

"Hey, did you skip breakfast again?" he asked.

She nodded. "Mhmm. I was worried I was going to be late."

"Thought you might. Here, I brought you something."

"Oh, Schobey dear, you didn't." She peeked over his shoulder as he reached down and undid his leather knapsack. "Now I almost feel bad for telling you to be quiet."

"If you call me Schobey again, I'll eat it all for myself."

He pulled out a folded white cloth which was warm to the touch. He unwrapped it and held the concealed treat up to Trinity. Her eyes lit up as a savory aroma filled her nostrils. There in his hand was a large, freshly baked donut, in the shape of a turtle with a jelly-filled shell. She knew this treat well.

"Your mom baked me a turtle this morning?" she asked, squealing with delight.

"She *baked* them for Mrs. Malakena's stand. And you should count yourself lucky. It's not as if she just gives these things away. Especially with jelly getting to be more expensive. Those donuts are at least four steki apiece in the market, but I snaked you one before I came down. I was thinking we could share."

"I get the shell!" she exclaimed, ripping the pastry from his hand and sinking her teeth into the crunchy, sweet shell as if she were a wild animal devoid of a meal for days. "You can have a foot or something," she told him, between ravenous bites.

"Oh MAI, doesn't your aunt feed you?" he asked, tearing off one of the turtle's feet.

"Of course, she does. Or Phes does anyway. But no one cooks like your mom."

"I'll tell her you said so."

"Can she come to Zayloa with me? Be my personal cook? I'll make sure she's paid well." Though she meant the words as a jest, they somehow lightened her mood. She turned to Schobe expecting some sort of quick-witted response, but the boy's face was patient. He was watching her as she ate.

"What?" she asked, feeling embarrassed. "Do I have jelly on my chin?"

"Do you—do you really mean that?" he asked, stumbling over his question.

Trinity waited on her next bite. "*Yes.* Naturally. I wish they could all come. Ella and Dary. Your mom. I'm going to miss them terribly."

"Just them? Not...anyone else?"

"Like who?" she asked with a knowing scoff. "Oh, do you mean you? Well, I suppose we need someone to build latrines in Zayloa." She watched as a handsome smile creased his lips. There was a dangerous look in his eyes now. *Success!*

He rubbed his hands together. "How many days will I get in the dungeons for throwing you into the ocean?"

"Schobeyyyy," she warned, holding onto the false vowel. "Don't you even think it."

"Better yet. How many days for a mud-pie to the face?" he asked, stooping over and gathering a clump of mud resting beside the latrine.

"You wouldn't dare," she said, with a growing grin.

She reached down to gather some mud also. Schobe was quicker. He chucked a gob of the wet earth towards her face, though most of it got in her hair. Trinity hurled her gathered pile also, but Schobe expertly knew when to duck. He swiftly scooped up another handful and launched it. The mud exploded over her face.

"You're dead," she declared.

The battle of the flying mudpies lasted for several minutes. By the end, their faces and clothing were both drenched and filthy. Trinity also felt like she was going to die from laughing.

Neither of them heard the approaching knight on horseback. He was an older boy with a narrow brooding face, stubble on his chin, but he still wasn't quite at an age where he would be considered a man. He had coiffed ebony hair, raised with care, and a polished gloss to his breastplate. He wore a thick, broadsword at his waist, and towered over Trinity and Schobe—even when not on the horse—at over six feet tall. His eyes, Trinity thought, were the bluest blue she'd ever seen, like the ocean's water on the hottest of summer days.

"Hey, it's the turd-tunnelers," he called to them. "Getting a little caught up in our work, are we?"

Schobe stopped the muddy duel with Trinity and saluted the approaching knight. Trinity, however, hadn't finished her fun yet, and delivered a kick—as soft as she could manage—to Schobe's backside. He yelped out as he was lifted two feet into the air.

"Ugh, what do you want Qua*tas*," Trinity asked him, saying the tail end of his name as if she'd just chewed on a rotten lemon.

"Oh, me?" Quatas asked. "Now let's see. What do I want? I could always use a new horse. Flick here looks to be on his last trot," he said, patting the sickly gray horse beneath him. "A date with that gorgeous aunt of yours, that'd be something."

"Princess Evita would never date you," Schobe said, rubbing at the spot where he'd been kicked.

"Don't say that," Trinity said, "she hasn't been on a date in years. I'll bet she'd jump at the chance to date again. Even with Quatas."

"Is that a glowing recommendation?" Quatas asked, raising his trimmed eyebrows tauntingly.

"Not really. Only that you're not entirely hopeless." She smiled fiendishly up at him.

Quatas grinned good-humoredly. "In that case, I've always wanted a barrel full of good ale. One I wouldn't have to share with others."

"You aren't even old enough to drink yet," Schobe reminded him.

"Oh, is that a fact? Do you hear this little gnat, Princess?" Quatas asked, stepping down from his horse. "I'm plenty old enough to kick your ass as well."

The older knight darted forward and locked Schobe in a headlock. Schobe tried to struggle away but he was no match for Quatas' strength.

"Be nice to him," Trinity said, giving Quatas a stern look. "I need his help finishing the latrine."

"Ah. That's why I'm here," Quatas said. He released Schobe, but not before adding a sharp elbow to the younger knight's side which left Schobe gasping for air. "I've just been given orders. Commander Kuza says today's the last day he can spare Schobe. The latrine is finished as far as he's concerned."

"Last day?" Trinity asked, looking as if she'd had the wind knocked out of her too. She knew there was much more work still left to do. *It can't be the last day.*

Quatas looked up at the sky. The light from the morning was beginning to fade behind heavy clouds, which were a dark and somber gray. "Agh, it's getting too cold for this type of outside work anyway kids. Yup. I expect the first real snow of winter to be here soon."

"It won't!" Trinity snapped.

"Oh? Can you predict the weather, then?" he asked.

"No. But—it isn't even that cold. Winter isn't here yet."

"Right. Whatever you say, Princess."

Schobe was readjusting his tunic now after Quatas had finished roughing him up. "Do I still have my dungeon watch this evening?" he asked, glancing quickly over at Trinity as he did.

Quatas smirked. "Of course. Who else is going to do it at this late notice?"

"I will," Trinity said. "It's part of my punishment too."

Quatas snickered in a nasally sort of way. "Princess, Princess, Princess. You know nobody's going to let a royal highness down into the dungeons. When you got assigned the same tasks as Schobe, Kuza had no intention of letting you go down there yourself."

"But it's only fair," she complained. "I entered the joust. The king said—"

"Then take it up with him," Quatas interrupted. "Because the rule is that no girl goes down to the dungeons. Unless she's a prisoner that is."

I've been to the dungeons plenty of times, she thought. She didn't bother to mention this to either of them though, or fight Quatas on the subject anymore. Who would believe her anyway? No one else knew about her secret trips to the dungeon, which she'd kept well-hidden ever since she started doing them at age nine. For it was there, in the darkest depths of the kingdom, where Trinity had a *special friend* who had spent the last five years locked away. He was someone whom she could share anything with. He never judged her, nor did he ever question her decisions. *Tonight.* Tonight, she would be sure to go and see him, regardless of what anyone said about her going to the dungeons.

"Trinity! Just look at you. You're a positive mess!" Evita shrieked, while grimacing at the mud Trinity had just dragged in from outside onto the white rug in their home. "What were you doing down at the latrine? Taking a mud bath?"

"I'm fine, Aunt E. Besides, job's all finished now. No more mud, I promise."

"Oh, thank MAI. The smell from your room is horrendous. Are you certain you're taking your clothes to the laundry every day?"

"I am certain...that you asked me to take my clothes to the laundry. Every day."

With a curt nod from the older princess, Evita's handmaidens prepared a non-mud bath immediately. Before Trinity could protest, she found herself in the water, shivering. *It is getting colder.*

"Am I to assume you will *not* be joining us for supper this evening?" Evita asked. Her tone made her sound like she was biting rather than inviting. "It's three times this week you've been too tired to attend."

"I'm not hungry in the evenings," Trinity confessed, as she began blowing bubbles atop the dirty water's surface. "And I had a big lunch."

"Sweets again, was it?"

"...I'll join you tomorrow."

Evita stood beside the edge of the large, in-floor tub. Her gown was long enough that her skirt became soaked in the muddy water along the marbled tiles. Trinity wondered if she even noticed.

"You know, it's not just me you disappoint. Father misses you too. He hasn't seen you in over a week."

If he's so disappointed, then why is he sending me away?

"I'm sorry, Aunt E," she said, keeping her thought to herself. "I just...I haven't been myself lately."

"Is that—is that a bump on your head?"

Trinity touched the swollen spot atop her matted hair. "Bump?"

"How did you get that?"

"I probably, um, fell. Out of bed?" She was aware how unconvincing she sounded. "Stone floors, you know."

Evita cast her a knowing scowl. Her eyes always looked like a lion's right before a pounce.

"You *will* join us tomorrow, Trinity. And you *will* dress nicely."

"If not, I'm sure someone will anyway," Trinity muttered into the water.

"What was that?"

"I said—supper sounds good. Best be on your way."

Evita looked as if she had more to say, but with a flustered sigh she turned and walked away. Before leaving though, she paused at the door and delivered one more chilling reminder about the weather. "Should you change your mind, be sure to bundle up. I expect it will be freezing tonight. Father will probably schedule the Snow Day Ball soon."

Ugh. Why was everyone so focused on the weather today? There were still plenty of pre-winter days to enjoy. Rainy nights to run home in. And warm, baked treats to sample. Her favorite part of Fall was the roasting fires which still made you sweat. This wasn't the time to be discussing formal dances and snow. Besides, she didn't even know where to begin searching for her winter attire. Fortunately, she was relieved to see that one of the handmaidens had laid out a freshly pressed, lilac tunic and rose-colored breeches. *A fine Fall outfit.*

When she was certain that the handmaidens had retired early for the evening, Trinity went to the wall in her room and began feeling around for loose openings. One by one she pulled out several stones from her wall until there was a wide gap. Evita had once forbidden her from adding a window to her room, but she'd never caught on to Trinity's method of removing and replacing the stones in her wall every time she needed a majestic view. Or in this case…a quick exit.

Trinity scaled down the outer wall from where her removable window formed, and stepped along the damp, black stones leading towards the ocean waves like an ebony trail. Her bare toes on the wet rocks felt like they were stepping on frozen needles. She pushed on until at last she reached a small cove near the end of the reef. It was here she would perform her second bout of training for the day, the same as she had done two other times this week.

Under the safety of the cove, Trinity set about preparing herself for the training. The tide would be high soon, enough to cover the reef entirely. There wasn't a second to waste. She began by digging up clothes from underneath a marked spot beneath a rock. She pulled out from the sand a rough spun shirt and a pair of short, gray pants. Both were wet to the touch and stank of mold and seawater. Under the cove's coverings, she quickly changed out of her current clothes into the moldy ones, and then folded her fresh outfit onto a nearby rock.

Next, she unearthed a fat, broadsword, nearly the length of her body. The unpolished steel was rusted along the metal and would've made a poor weapon choice had she used it for combat. Trinity, however, did not intend to use this blade on an opponent. Near the place where she'd uncovered the large sword, Trinity rolled out two rounded stones with some weight to them. A rope wrapped each, with about six feet leftover in slack between the pair. Trinity fastened the two rope ends around her ankles and took deep, heavy breaths.

"It's not that cold. It's not that cold," she told herself, pepping up for the plunge. She hoped her body would believe these words.

Trinity stood near the edge of the cove. There was a drop off into the water about five feet out from where she stood. Trinity stuck the broadsword into the sand beside her, and lifted up the two great stones.

It's not that cold. It's not that cold.

She hurled the rocks forward. As they both plopped down into the ocean water with loud splashes, she snatched the blade up just as her body was pulled forward by her feet as the stones did their job of helping her sink. Trinity's body was rushed down towards the depths of the ocean, becoming submerged in the ice-cold waters. The pain in her body felt like a thousand piercing arrows hitting her all at once. She refused to scream out. She knew better than to lose her air so quickly, having trained long ago to hold it for as long as her strong lungs could manage.

* * *

"Come on, you're faster than this," Guren growled at her, while Trinity pulled him along atop the slapping waves of the ocean.

She was still eight then. Guren had only been training her for a few months. A short rope was tied to her foot, connected to the man's longboat. There were no oars to assist them today; she set the course on this grueling training session. Her arms cut the water rhythmically at her sides as her scrawny legs kicked and jutted along the edge of the water's surface.

"I thought you wanted to be a brave warrior," he called. "Stop slapping the water like it's offended you somehow. *You* control the tides."

I control the tides? The thought offered her no comfort as her lungs felt ready to burst.

Later on the beach, as she laid on the wet sand wheezing for the lost air she'd spent, she asked him, "H-how do I...how do I go faster?"

Guren was sitting on the beach beside her, resting on one of the stones under the arch of the cove. He was whittling the figure of a lion on a dry woodblock with his ruby-hilted dagger. He glanced up at her. "Oh, it's very easy. You stop swimming like a girl."

"That's bad advice," she spat, punching at the wet sand. "I am a girl."

"Then that is all you will ever be."

Trinity gaped. "There's *nothing* wrong with being a girl."

"There is," he replied, "in this kingdom. And every kingdom. I don't have to tell you what our world thinks of girls, because you know already, don't you? Girls are arm ornaments at fancy balls. And quiet seat-fillers at banquet tables. Baby-makers, who serve their husbands until his death, and then weep bitterly because they cannot live without him. That is all a girl is. Unless—"

Her breathing stilled. "Unless what?"

"You change their minds," he said, with one of those rarely seen smiles of his. "Of what a girl is. And what she can do."

* * *

She didn't understand his meaning then. Even now, at fourteen, his words puzzled her. How could she change people's ideas about what she could do? She was born a princess, just like her mother so many years before her. And though she'd imagined so many times her mother being strong like her, Zepolia had accepted her role and married the Terkian king. She liked to think her mother was free enough to make the choice willingly, but Trinity knew better. Her parent's union strengthened the bond between the Terkian and Hydlixian kingdoms, the same as her own marriage to Hayden would strengthen the bond with the kingdom of Zayloa and her kingdom of Hydlix. Her mother must've been a victim to this same fate. They must've seen her as *just* another girl.

Trinity swung the huge sword with all her might as she stood tall again, far beneath the ocean's waters. A line of ripping water lashed out from her swing, and jettisoned far along the still, dark abyss. She swung again. Each stroke slashed through the ocean like a fired arrow. *How many more before I can change the tides?* Tonight, her body could only produce seven cuts before the chills of the water constricted upon her lungs.

She knelt down the way she'd done earlier that morning in her tower, and launched herself as high as she could. The rocks pulled with her. Each one felt so heavy beneath the weight of the water. She kicked and tugged with every last ounce of strength she still possessed, clutching onto the sword with one hand and paddling upwards with the other. The air inside her felt so thin. *I should've ascended sooner.* She knew she wouldn't make it. She tried clumsily cutting at the rope, but the sword wasn't sharp enough. Regrettably, her hand—making the difficult decision her heart couldn't—dropped the sword. She pushed towards the surface with the help of both arms now. The fallen blade fell down to the place where she'd trained. At last, she breached the surface.

Trinity laid out by the cove, panting and feeling her muscles tingling beneath her wet clothes. All she could do was watch the gray sky overhead darken. Then, as if they had waited for her to return to the surface, a blanket of snowflakes began to tumble down. They drifted and danced to the world below. Some fell to the ocean's waves, melting instantly. Others flailed along with the cold winds and landed all around her. With this downfall came the gushing outpour of emotions which Trinity could no longer hold back. It was here in the presence of such beauty that she felt only an empty sadness. Winter had once been her favorite time of the year, but now that the long-awaited season had finally arrived, all she felt was pain. She knew that Spring would be here soon. And with it, the man she'd be forced to marry.

After night had fallen and she'd crept back through her window—now dressed in her much warmer clothes— she saw that her aunt had still not returned from supper. She restored the stone wall to what it once was and put on thick boots and the first coat she could rummage from her aunt's closet. Her nose was red and swollen and her eyes felt puffy. She knew she'd taken a risk with the underwater training, but she hoped she wasn't getting sick.

She visited the kitchens. Phes wasn't working this evening. Luckily, Trinity managed to find two cooked flank steaks and take them without much fuss from the current staff. She walked the long route down to the underbelly of the kingdom, so that she could avoid making contact with Evita or anyone else who expected her to be home on a night like this.

At the lowest point of the kingdom, beyond the poorest homes and the broken-cobbled roads, lay the dungeons. There were two knights posted at the silver doors on the crumbling stone tower, but they were more fascinated by the falling snow than their post. She didn't expect anyone would want to be working on a night as beautiful as this. She waited until their curiosity got the better of them and they started making snowballs. She stayed to the shadows, and to her own surprise was able to sneak in the front entrance without raising suspicion. *And here I thought I was going to have to bribe them.* Still, she thought it safer to use an alternate—though much less preferred—exit on the way out of the tower. The prisoners were just a little too close for comfort along *that* entryway.

She followed a line of lit torches down a leaky corridor. The cells were too poorly illuminated to see who was there, but she did know some of the men from previous visits here. Some were kind enough to ignore her. Others made lewd comments and blew whistles and jeered as she walked by. Trinity, however, was not deterred from her current route.

"W-what are you doing here, Trin?" Schobe asked, barely above a whisper, as she finally approached him in the center hall where the lines of cells ran up along the length of the tower into a dark chasm.

"I told you I was joining you this evening," Trinity said. "Sorry I'm late. I couldn't find a coat."

He held a torch up to her face. His own appearance beside the flame was timid looking as usual. He ran his eyes across her face. "Trin you're—well, you look miserable."

"*Thanks,*" she replied unhappily.

"I mean it. Are you feeling alright? You look sick. Look, please don't argue. For just one night, listen. Head home. Get some sleep."

"What? And let you have all the fun?"

"Honestly? Fine. Suit yourself. If Kuza catches you—"

"He *won't* catch me. Besides, I won't be here long. Aunt E will be home soon. Here, I brought you something."

She handed him one of the flank steaks. Schobe's face brightened at the touch of the lukewarm meat. "Thank you," he told her, sounding surprised. "That's funny."

"What is?"

"I brought you breakfast and here you are bringing me supper."

"Well, I had just thought you might be hungry." Her eyes fled from Schobe's perceptive gaze.

"I was. Mom was still roasting the trockan when I had to report. Thank you," he said, biting into the steak. "You're very sweet."

She could feel her cheeks growing even warmer. "...You're welcome. Do I still get baked turtles now that you're done digging latrines?"

"Do you ever not get baked turtles is the real question? Say, who's the other steak for?"

"This? Um, it's for my...*other* friend," she said, after a second's hesitation.

"You have friends? Here?"

"Only one." She took the torch from his hand and walked closer to the center of the tower.

"Wait—no!" He turned his head nervously. His eyes darted across the darkness of the center hall. "You're not talking about him. Are you?" he asked, his words filling with dread.

Trinity raised the torch and placed the stick onto a sconce near an iron cage. She tapped on the bars and waited.

A rustle came from within the dark cage. She and Schobe watched as a menacing-looking beast on four legs approached the edge of the bars, licking its huge, spotted lips. It hobbled like a heavy bear but stepped as silently as an alley cat. The monstrous creature purred at the sight of Trinity, his huge green eyes, like thick summer treetops, locked onto her as she reached her hand inside the bars.

"What are you doing?!" Schobe exclaimed.

A low growl resonated from the creature. Schobe stepped back, grabbing Trinity's arm as he did.

"Wait," she whispered, handing Schobe the other steak. "Just watch."

Trinity reached her hand inside. The giant beast within mashed his face up to the palm of her hand and closed his eyes in acknowledgement of her presence. His purring intensified. Trinity reached her other hand in and began to scratch behind one of his ears.

"Trinity? You know the white lion of Hydlix?" Schobe asked in disbelief.

"Yes."

She'd known him for years, ever since the two of them first locked eyes so very long ago. As it so happened, they had met on the day she first learned that she would be marrying Hayden.

"You know it took like a hundred soldiers to get him down here, right?"

"I was there," she said.

"You were? Where was I?" he asked, scratching at his head.

"Missing out apparently. It was quite the show."

She took the second steak back from Schobe and presented it to the lion, tossing it into his cage. The white lion ran along the bars and snatched up the piece of meat, devouring it in a single gulp. He then turned and sprinted back to the far side of the cage, baring his fangs. He appeared desperate for another snack.

"I've known him for a long time. He's one of my very best friends." She flashed a bright smile at Schobe, and even relished in his doubt. "I've even named him."

"You named him? The kingdom's lion? W-what do you call him?"

"Snowflake," she replied.

CHAPTER SIX

SCARS

As suspected, Trinity woke the next morning feeling sicker than ever. The king's doctor was quickly dispatched. After the check-up, Evita decided to keep her at home until she was feeling better. Trinity was so sick that she couldn't even complain about her aunt's decision. The whole Remsphere felt like a hot brick crashing onto her congested head. *Stupid bricks!*

At first, Trinity hated being stuck at home. Missing her morning training sessions in the tower felt almost unbearable. And not seeing Schobe was so unfair. She didn't know how much more time she'd have to see him or her beloved kingdom before her exile ceremony to the Zayloan castle, or as everyone else called it: the wedding.

Much to Trinity's surprise though, Evita had been nothing less than terrific the whole time that she was sick. She was being a fun aunt rather than the stern one Trinity had always known. The two of them had taken to playing several games of King's Circle during the day, and pigging out on handmaiden-delivered food straight from the king's banquet table. By the end of the week, Trinity believed she'd eaten her weight in cakes and turtle-shaped donuts.

When they weren't playing games or eating themselves into sugary stupors, Evita would read to Trinity. Her aunt didn't read very exciting stories as Trinity would've hoped. They were mostly historical texts about the kingdom, or tedious tales about princesses with giddy desires to marry princes and make babies. The women in these stories always wore such lavish sounding dresses, and Evita would read these pages about courtly gowns with a reserved gusto.

Sometimes during these stories, Trinity would prop her head upon her aunt's lap as the two of them relaxed on the cushioned bench in the main hall. The goose-feather stuffing beneath her always made Trinity sleepy by story's end. Before she'd fall asleep though, Evita would sing softly to her as she caressed Trinity's clump of unbrushed green curls. Trinity never minded the singing. It reminded her of when she was a little girl, and Evita would sing to her when tucking her in for the night. Evita's voice was always a beautiful, golden thing that could both warm ears and calm troubled minds.

One night, Trinity struggled so much to rouse herself from the cushion after recovering from dessert and Evita's hypnotizing melodies that she believed she was going to die right there on the bench. *It won't be so bad. At least I won't have to get married.* To her surprise though, Evita scooped her up in a single, unbecoming motion.

"Whoa. You're still able to pick me up?" Trinity asked, yawning. "At your age?"

"I wanted to see if I was still able to. You planning on having a growth spurt soon, little cub?"

In the sconce light, Trinity caught a glimpse of Evita's smirk. Oh, how she hated being so much shorter than everyone else in the kingdom. Though she was halfway to fifteen, Trinity was still only a fraction of Evita's size. She wondered if she would ever grow taller. Or were Terkians just short?

"Aunt E, be careful," Trinity said. "I don't want you to break your brittle old back on my account."

Evita's eyes grew wide with a reserved fury. "I am *only* twenty-eight."

"I'm not so sure. I think I heard your bones creak when you lifted me."

"Such nerve," Evita spouted. "If you keep talking about me like I'm some old hen, I won't play King's Circle with you anymore."

"Perish the thought," Trinity said, grinning. "*Whoever* will I beat now?"

"If you weren't so sick, I'd drop you."

Trinity laughed lazily. Her aunt's empty threats always had a way of making her feel better. "I'd make another hole in your floor again. Like the time I jumped off my bed."

"*Yes*. How is it someone so small can create such large holes?"

Trinity didn't have an answer. During fittings, the ladies in the boutiques would sometimes compare her to the porcelain dolls displayed at the window fronts. Even her muscles—after hundreds of hours of training— weren't particularly big. It was hard to know exactly how her Terkian strength functioned, but she knew for certain though that if she stepped hard enough without thinking, she could fracture the ground beneath her. Cobbled streets or marbled floors, her feet had at one time shattered them all.

"What do you want for your birthday this year?" Trinity asked, now laying beneath her covers.

"To spend some money of course," Evita said, standing at her bedside as she compared Trinity's forehead to her own.

"Don't you have enough dresses?"

"Never."

It was no coincidence that the Snow Day Ball coincided with her aunt's birthday. The whole court turned up for the yearly celebration, as well as several of the more revered knights. She wondered if Guren would attend this year. *He's probably found an excuse*, she thought bitterly.

"Are you going to go with me to the Snow Day Ball again this year?" Evita asked.

"Aren't I always your date?"

"Yes...but I thought you might want to bring someone else this year. Schobe perhaps."

Schobe? Why was her aunt being so kind lately when it came to Schobe? First there was the outside kingdom work after her failed joust. And now this. Schobe had never been able to attend any of the king's functions before. *Would he even want to go?* Trinity tried to picture Schobe wearing dress robes. Even in her fantasy, he looked miserable wearing them.

"I haven't asked him. I didn't know I could."

"It's typically up to the boy to ask on you. I just figured—what with it being your last winter ball here— maybe he could—"

"Oh," Trinity said, as her aunt's words began to make sense.

"Sorry. I shouldn't have said anything." Evita sat beside her now, looking flustered. "Of course, I would love it if you attended with me. I could go shopping for our dresses soon. When you're better, you can go with me and try them on. That would be a fine gift, really."

"…Alright."

The two of them said nothing more. Evita kissed Trinity on the forehead and blew out the candles in the room.

The next morning Trinity woke convinced her bed was shaking. Was she still with fever? No, the fever had broken. She laid there for several moments trying to recall what she'd been dreaming of. Whatever it was, the visions had been horrible and the sleep unsettling. She'd heard some people call this shaky feeling a visit from the midnight fairies, who had come to collect bad dreams to feast upon. *The fairies are in luck*, she thought. *I've plenty of rotten dreams to spare.*

But for the first time in a week her headache had disappeared, and her nose was no longer cherry red and swollen. Trinity rose and went to tell Evita the good news, but when she came to her aunt's room, she found only an empty bed instead.

The handmaidens who were there in the main hall tidying up their home had no answer for where Evita had gone. Trinity decided to go and find her, but first had to do a great deal of fibbing to convince them that Evita was allowing her to finally leave. Her least favorite of these servants—a harsh, narrow-eyed woman named Birtess—wouldn't allow Trinity to go anywhere until she'd eaten and had her hair properly brushed. Trinity eventually relented to woofing down some lix bread made by one of the local bakers and a hunk of dried cheese. The bread was considered a delicacy though it was hard and gray and would've chipped a tooth—*probably*—if her teeth weren't Terkian also. Next came the hair brushing, which Trinity was dreading. Her knots had grown twice as gnarly over the last week.

"Keep still!" Birtess snapped. "I'll have them out in a minute yet."

"Can't I brush them out myself later?" Trinity whined.

"No better than me, Princess," she said, shaking the brush at Trinity within her chubby-fingered grip. "Besides, if you'd done this once a day while you were sick, your hair wouldn't be in this wicked mess."

"Ouch! If you brushed a little softer, it wouldn't hurt as much."

Birtess glowered at her, before suddenly howling with laughter. "Oh MAI, girl. You Terkians are such a confusing bunch." She puffed her rounded cheeks out in a frustrated sigh and glanced over her shoulder at one of the handmaidens watching. "Tonok, eh? Pelas ke eke Tonok."

She laughed again as the thin, frightened-looking handmaiden behind her quietly joined in. Birtess was laughing so hard that her chins were shaking beneath the silk wrap on her neck.

"Alright, what's the joke?" Trinity asked, crassly. "I may as well know what you're calling me."

"Oh, don't get your curls any more twisted up. I was saying you reminded me of Tonok, one of the lions of old. You know the story, don't you?"

Trinity shook her head.

"Doesn't the Princess ever tell you stories?"

"Not stories about lions. She usually tells me stories about royal weddings," Trinity said, her voice fragile.

There was a flicker of understanding in Birtess' creased smile. "Well, then I shall tell you. Tonok, see, was one of the strongest lions our Hydlix ever had living in the dungeons. Don't know which king it was, maybe the first, that decided our kingdom always had to have one of the sacred white lions living up in the dungeon, but Tonok was as tough as they came. Big mangy sort of cat. Lots of tufts in his hair, the same as you," she said, giving one of Trinity's curls a soft yank.

"It's not—he's not the lion down there now?"

"No, no. This was years ago. Back when I was just a cub myself. They say Tonok was so strong that the knights couldn't even pull him out of his cage for cleaning. They'd strike him with whips and tug on him with chains. It wasn't enough for old Tonok. That lion was the fiercest cat you ever saw. And there was never much of a scratch or scarring on him, truly. It's as if his skin were as strong as he was."

Trinity's eyes grew big. She rubbed at her left forearm. "No scars? You mean to say he never felt any pain?"

"That's what we all believed. But then one day a wasp got into his cage. A little one, no bigger than your finger. They say it landed right on the top of Tonok's mane and stung. MAI, you'd never seen a lion more agitated then. He rattled his cage so terrible that they thought the dungeon tower would come falling down on his head. They had to settle him with some fresh goat. Poor dear. He never reacted like that again, but we all knew then that he could feel pain the same as us."

Trinity hesitated with a response. "...Are you saying Terkians don't feel pain?"

"Of course, you do," Birtess said. "These tangles are proof enough of that, dear. It's just you're strong enough, usually, to not feel the pain that most of us would. Just like that lion. I remember when you were a wee lass and we were teaching you to sew. The needles would bend against your fingertips instead of giving you a prick." She grinned. "It's funny, we all thought you was made of stone or something. I just never thought a tangle would be something that could hurt you."

Trinity considered this as she stared down at the place on her arm where she'd been rubbing. A visible line of a dark gray scar was there, nearly the length of her hand. She folded her arms, feeling embarrassed suddenly. She knew that Birtess had seen the mark before, just like so many others who saw Trinity regularly. She'd gotten the scar over a year ago. It too was proof enough that she, like the lion, was capable of being hurt.

When she was finally allowed outdoors again after having her "mane" fully brushed, Trinity basked in the freshness of the outdoor air, although it was much chillier than she remembered. Bundled up beneath a thick fur coat, she made her way first across the white courtyards with their frosted plants and dying flowers. Even the white lion hedge looked somehow paler and drearier as the effects of the season took their toll.

She was met by several onlookers as she passed beneath the palace alcoves. They commented on her brightened expression. Trinity realized then that word of her sickness must've spread. If Evita had been the one to tell them, then she couldn't have gotten far.

She went down to the market square. Trinity thought it unlikely her aunt would come here, but wanted to check nonetheless. The square was often filled with children playing around the vendor stands, but now they were building snow people and having snowball fights. Some of the shopkeepers had covered their stalls with tarps, and many of them had convened around lit fires in the square's center. Ellacryse was huddled around a fire, rubbing her bare arms together.

"Where's your coat, Ella dear?" Trinity asked as she joined Schobe's sister by the fire.

"Outgrew it. But it's not that cold yet," Ellacryse said, her teeth chattering. "Mom says I'll have a new one before long."

"Hey, I may have some old ones that will fit you until then."

"Really, Princess? Real royal coats?"

"Several. Each one fluffier than the last. Come on, let's get you one."

Rather than retrace her steps, Trinity thought it best if they took a shortcut back to her home. She usually avoided this route, but maybe Evita would be found along the way. The two of them dashed up to the goldenrod balconies that oversaw the square. Up here in the alcoves there were wandering priests in white robes, with jangling golden chains and dangling rubies carved like lion heads attached to thick ropes adorning their shoulders. Trinity recognized one of these priests from behind by the way he waddled. He was a portly man named Palthar. Of all the priests, Palthar was the last person she wanted to spot her.

"Why are you covering your face?" Ellacryse asked, as Trinity moved behind her.

"That priest over there. He hates me."

"The Great Father? He can't hate anyone."

"I wouldn't be so sure about that."

She took Ellacryse's hand and hurried down the corridor. Luckily, Palthar was caught up in conversation with members of his congregation. Trinity and Ellacryse turned the corner without him spotting them. Then Trinity saw the sight she'd most wanted to avoid. Her stomach did a flip.

"I know that door," Ellacryse said, referring to a ragged, wooden door along one of the stone walls, covered with nails and posted pieces of paper. "What's with all the papers?"

"Oh—I'm not sure," Trinity said, averting her eyes to the chiseled lion faces in the balcony beside her. One of the papers from the door had ripped off and now lay in the wet snow beneath one of the faces. She hesitated, but crouched down and picked up the parchment. Smeared on the paper was the figure of a man holding a sword, performing a horizontal slice. Her hand trembled as she turned the paper around. A fading message was written:

Sorry. Still sick.

"Wait a minute," Ellacryse began, "this is Guren's door, isn't it? Schobe told me all about it. He posts a different paper every day. Most of them blow off and end up in the square."

"Do they?" Trinity asked, already knowing the answer for herself.

"Yes. Why do you think he does it? Who are the notes for?"

Trinity remained frozen where she stood, glaring at the door. She could tell some of these papers had been here for weeks. They were torn and weathered, flapping in the breezy corridor where they were posted. She'd not been here in some time.

"I don't know," she said, sighing as she glanced down once more at the place where the scar on her arm was, now covered by her coat sleeve. "Ella, let's hurry and grab the coats."

* * *

The first paper posted on his door came just one day after an incident she'd had with her bow. It was last year just before summer had ended, shortly after her thirteenth birthday. They were up bright and early, the pair of them, running, fighting, and training along the beach.

"Again," Guren commanded. "Hit me as if each strike is your last."

Trinity swung her rusted short sword at the man's abdomen. He deflected the blow with his own steel, redirecting the attack such that her sword stuck into the sand. She was ready for this. She squeezed the pommel of her sword and twisted her body into the air. Her foot met the man's chin, though the blow was soft like she'd intended. Guren snatched at her ankle and threw her body from him. Trinity fell forward, her face smushing into the wet sand. Guren picked up her blade from where it had been stuck. He now wielded two swords.

"You throw like an old woman," she spat at him. She hopped to her feet and wiped the caked sand off of her cheek.

"Calm yourself. I've taken your sword."

The challenge was hers to accept. She dug her feet into the sand and with a short sprint she bounded and leapt over her teacher. She landed on her knees on the opposite side of him, quickly becoming buried, then she shot up and dashed towards the other weapons laid along the beachside. She picked up her bow and pulled two arrows from her quiver. Guren gave no chase.

"Foolish. Always take the shield first."

"Tough *skin*," came her earnest, yet mocking reply.

"That may be. But tough skin didn't save your people from being put to the sword."

He readied his two swords into an attack stance and placed one foot behind the other. She knew this stance.

He was going for a full-offensive strike. If he could cut her bow, she'd be finished. *Should've grabbed more arrows.*

Guren began his attack. The old knight moved with such a fierce stride that Trinity began to doubt the limp she sometimes saw him walking with. His feet carved through the sand with pinpoint accuracy. He never stumbled nor showed any sign of fatigue. His gray cloak fanned out behind him as the fading, woolen sweater he wore beneath bulged, making his arms appear three times their size. He gave no warning of how he would strike first.

Trinity readied her bow and fired the first arrow. The shot was too swift. Guren didn't even need to swing at it. He shifted his weight to one foot and the arrow missed him by inches. Trinity nocked her second arrow. Guren was so close now. There'd be no way he could dodge another shot, or so she told herself. She loosened the arrow and watched the flying wood hiss towards Guren's rock-steady face. Still, he was a charging mountain. With a single cut, he broke the arrow in two, dodging the steel tip as it swirled overhead.

Guren whipped his sword down in an attempt to slice her bow, but Trinity stepped back just in time, able to roll out of the way, though she felt the slice of his blade nick the end of her weapon. She sprinted to the quiver and slung the bag around her shoulders. Relentlessly, Guren was still on the move. Trinity readied another shot. Taking a single solid breath before releasing, she let off another arrow in his direction. This one mustered a reaction from the old man. He ducked to the side, only just quick enough as the arrow barely missed grazing his shoulder. *Now's my chance.* Her fourth arrow would find its mark. *I've got him.*

Or so she would've, had the mysterious pain not found her again. All at once her body bent double and she bared her teeth so hard that she thought they would break. She seized up with a spine-tingling ache. Her arms twisted back as she choked on her scream. Two heavy streams of tears were running down her face now, but she hadn't the strength to wipe at them. *My strength?* Her body felt completely devoid of any power that her Terkian blood might have given her. She was helpless now, experiencing a private torment that could only be compared to the first time she'd felt pain like this—during her aqueduct misadventure.

Suddenly, the string on her bow snapped. The bow's rough wood exploded with pressure. She'd pulled too hard, unaware that she'd still been prepping an arrow to fire against her teacher. A wooden shard slashed across her skin, slicing her left forearm open with a deep cut.

"Trinity?" Guren was beside her now, his swords laying at his feet. He helped her to the sand as she continued convulsing in her lonely agony. "Hold on, Trin. Try to steady your breathing. You'll get through this." He took her arm in his hands and carefully removed the wooden shard from her cut. Trinity screamed out.

Then she could see them before her. There were... bodies. *How?* It had only been her and Guren on the beach that morning. But there they lay before her, several men bleeding out from grotesque wounds as if they'd just lost some horrible battle. They had been cut open, dismembered, and strewn across a vast blur that seemed to separate reality from the nightmare world she'd landed herself in. Guren, the beach, her Hydlix had all faded from view. All she could see now was death and darkness.

She attempted to step forward, but immediately regretted it. There beside her boot was a bloody head, cleaved clean from its shoulders. She wanted to gag, but found that she couldn't. The inside of her mouth tasted like burning fire. *Am I drinking fire?*

Seconds later, the pain in her body ceased and the vision dissipated, just like it had before, as though it had never been. Unable to stop herself then, she threw up onto the wet sand. Guren pulled her hair back and wiped at her mouth with his cloak.

"Such a bizarre wonder. For a moment, why, you had lost all consciousness, though you were still standing. It seemed you wish to respond, only—"

"I couldn't," she said, in a raspy voice.

"My dear child. How do you feel?"

"...Dizzy. Really dizzy."

When she was able to regain her composure, the two of them sat upon the damp morning sand and Trinity told Guren everything then, including the feeling from last time when her heart felt like it was being ripped out of her chest. This time was different though. This time her heart felt fine, but her stomach was still churning. And unlike last time, her strength had definitely left her for a moment, only now feeling as if it were returning. *Is that why I was cut?* She kept this thought to herself as she examined her arm carefully. The blood had stopped leaking out but the slash still remained. Just the sight of the blood was enough to make her shudder as visions of the bodies came creeping back to her mind. She didn't know people bled so much when they died.

Guren listened closely to her words, but asked no questions. He cut a piece of his cloak off and wrapped her cut, promising that he'd treat it properly when they returned home. She was disappointed by his quiet reaction, hoping he'd have at least something to say about the two visions. There had to be some sort of connection—other than the pain and spilt blood—between the hands from her first vision and the dead bodies now. She wanted to press him further and try to squeeze a guess out of him, but Guren remained tightlipped as he concluded their training for the day. Afterwards, the two of them walked home in a strained silence. *Why is he being so distant?*

Later that night, at supper, Trinity's grandfather became the first person to notice her cut. She thought it unlikely at first, since she and Evita were sitting opposite him along the stretched pine bench in the banquet hall. The king's jowls quivered as he studied her arm.

"MAI's sake, girl, what's that mark on your skin?"

Trinity had been afraid of this inevitable question. She even tried to hide her arm under a napkin until she accidentally forgot about the wound when reaching for a roll. The cut was as Guren had said before: something bizarre. The place where the wood had slashed her hadn't fully healed yet. While the gash itself didn't feel too painful, the long, dark-gray stripe across her left forearm remained. She wondered again if this had something to do with the pain she'd experienced earlier when she snapped her bow. After all, she'd been completely fine after falling on her head from the aqueduct. So why then had this pain left her with a scar?

"I must've scratched myself," she said, covering the cut with her napkin again.

"Scratched yourself?" Evita asked, as she and her father exchanged worried glances from across the table. "That's no scratch. You really expect us to believe that?"

"...I do."

Supper ended soon after these words. Evita stood, thanked her father for bringing the cut to her attention, and then ordered Trinity to accompany her home. The king waved a half-hearted goodbye as he continued with his meal alone. Neither Evita or Trinity returned the gesture.

Back at home, Evita rushed Trinity inside and had her sit down on her bed. She paced Trinity's bedroom for a moment, searching for words that would start the conversation again. She didn't give any motherly glares or shouted threats as Trinity first suspected she might. Instead, Evita's face remained stone cold until she finally quit pacing and sat beside Trinity on the bed, studying the cut for herself. She took a calming breath, then asked, "Alright, what is this all about?" Trinity had never heard her aunt ask a question so softly before.

"What do you mean?" she asked. "What's got you and grandfather so upset?"

Evita took Trinity's arm and rubbed her fingers along the cut. "I—we worry for you. I've never seen a cut on your skin before. Seems strange, doesn't it? Given your heritage."

"Well, not so strange."

Now came the infamous glare Trinity had been dreading. Their locked eyes squared off in a pathetic waltz, waiting for either one to look away first. Trinity was the first to tilt her head and instead focus on her fingers nervously scraping at her elbow.

Evita sighed. "I'm not even too sure how I'm supposed to ask this. So, I'm just going to come right out and say it." She released Trinity's arm. "...Did you do this? Did you cut your own arm?"

"No. Not on purpose. It was an accident." She stared at her cut incredulously for a second before looking at Evita. "Why would I cut my own arm?"

Evita made no reply. She was watching Trinity with a jutted chin and a pang of suspicion in her eyes.

Trinity drew back on the bed. *Why is she acting this way?* A thought occurred to her then. If Evita had found out about the secret training or the accident with the bow, she would've mentioned these things right away. No, something else must've been bothering her about the cut. The older princess was even beginning to slouch. Besides buying expensive dresses and eating pastries, good posture was what her aunt did best. "I don't understand. What's wrong, Aunt E?"

"Nothing. Forget it."

Trinity's jaw dropped. "Do you think I was trying to hurt myself?"

Evita's eyes glassed over with fresh tears. "Trin—no. I would hope you'd be smarter than that. After all, I didn't take you to church every week just so you could...but if this is because of Prince Hayden—taking your life into your own hands like that seems so...reckless."

"Hayden?" Trinity fired back. "You think I'd kill myself because of Hayden?"

Honestly, the thought of causing herself bodily harm had never occurred to Trinity until then. Why would anyone ever want to cut themselves, or worse, take their own life? It was beyond her understanding. And Hayden of all people was not worth it.

"I'm not trying to kill myself," she said, sharply.

Evita mopped at her falling tears. "I know. I know you wouldn't do that. Please, excuse me." She stood up and went to the kitchen, leaving Trinity to ponder her aunt's next move. When she returned moments later, Evita had with her a chalice full of wine and a stack of sugar cookies.

"Trinity, I've never told you the story of my mother before, have I?" she asked, sitting back down and taking a long sip from her chalice. She offered Trinity one of the cookies.

"Queen Ada?" Trinity asked.

She had heard the stories alright, but none of them came from Evita. It was a well-known fact throughout the kingdom that the former Queen—Ada of the Attigas kingdom—had returned home to her father despite the protests of Eslon. Her grandfather and the former queen had nullified their marriage years ago, and Ada was sent home on a wagon with an escort of hand-picked knights.

Guren was among these men and he'd told Trinity what he saw on the trip. The queen rode not as a prisoner, but as a broken and defeated woman. She'd not said one word the whole ride to Attigas, nor did she eat or even sleep. When she was returned to her father, Ada was not welcomed with open arms. It was said she retired to her chambers and had never been spoken of by King Eslon since.

"They called her mad," Evita began, though her chalice was nearly empty now. "Said she was a fool woman to divorce Father. He'd given her everything. Including a child of her own, after she thought that she'd be barren forever."

"What's barren?"

"It means she was unable to have children of her own. Her grief was known by many, even early in their marriage. But then your mother came along."

Trinity decided upon a sugar cookie after all. She also tried to help herself to what was left of the wine in Evita's chalice. Evita smirked at her, but let Trinity have the last sip. The taste was bitter on Trinity's tongue, like a nasty, dying flame in her mouth. She remembered how dry her throat had felt on the beach earlier. *Is that what I was tasting?*

After Evita had gone to pour herself another chalice, she continued her story. "They say a baby was found crying just outside of mother and father's chambers, though none of the men assigned on patrol that evening had seen anyone enter. But they found your mother there, wrapped in a blood-stained blanket. And when one of the knights handed her to my mother, they say that Queen Ada never looked happier. Father too. There was never any question that Zepolia was their daughter then. Father would always say, because of Zepolia's golden hair, that she was his *little sunflower*."

Trinity tried to take another sip from her aunt's second chalice, but Evita shooed her hand away.

"Did they ever find her?" Trinity asked, settling for another cookie instead. "The woman who gave birth to my mother?"

Evita nodded. "They did. Outside the knight barracks. She was lying against a brick wall. A pale woman with green hair. A Terkian. The first to have ever entered our kingdom."

Trinity took a long curl of her own hair into her hand. She knew the wall her aunt was describing well. It was the same one she'd first met Schobe at years ago. A wanting smile grew upon her lips. *My grandmother...she had green hair too.*

"Five years later, I came along. Needless to say, Mother and Father weren't expecting me. Zepolia would sing at my crib. She'd call me *My Evita*. She used to tell me that mother was so happy during those days."

"What changed then?"

Evita's face turned hard again. She held the chalice firmly on her knee. "I wish I could tell you. She and Father never got along while we were growing up. But I never believed it to be so bad until—" her voice trailed off.

Trinity gasped. She covered the cut on her arm with her hand. "...She tried to kill herself?"

"Many times. Eventually, Father had enough. Told her it would be better if she returned to Attigas. *Without us*. He didn't want us to see what she had become, or so Zepolia would tell me. I was...quite young when this happened. So much was left unsaid to me." Her narrowed eyes gazed upon the freshly emptied chalice. The tears on her cheeks had dried, having stopped when Evita spoke about her mother.

Trinity was left with much to ponder that night after she helped tuck her tipsy aunt into bed. She wondered about Queen Ada, and what had made her so miserable here that she wished to end her life if she wasn't brought back to Attigas. Trinity didn't expect anyone would return her back home, no matter how much she hated Zayloa. Or Prince Hayden.

She thought about her other grandmother as well— the Terkian one—and why she had chosen the kingdom of Hydlix to deliver her baby in. Maybe her grandmother had been on the run. Or maybe, she'd had no other choice.

And before falling to sleep herself that night, Trinity thought of her aunt Evita. She could see now why her aunt so rarely opened up about her past. It was a scar that Evita carried, and one that couldn't be seen. But most of all, it was a scar that pained her to reopen.

The next morning after her incident with the bow, Trinity had gone to Guren's room to seek him out for their day's lessons. There was a note posted at his door. The message upon the note was written clearly:

Sorry to do this Trinity, but I'm feeling sick. Follow the lesson on the back. Maybe tomorrow?

Until then, he had never missed a single day of training with her. Thoughts about the broken bow, the uncomfortable dinner, and barging into his room right then and there flooded her thoughts. But obediently, she chose to listen to her teacher. If she had known this would be the first of his many excuses in note form, she'd have never taken the paper from his door.

* * *

Ellacryse was sent back to the market square with three new coats folded atop her arms, and a fourth covering her chilled, bony little frame. Trinity watched as Ellacryse scooted away, practically leaping with excitement. Trinity folded her arms, slid up her sleeve, and let her fingers traipse over the vertical gray scar once more. She would never forget the day that her bow had cut her, for it was also the last day she'd ever trained with Guren in person.

Finding Evita would have to wait. Quietly, she returned to Guren's door and collected the posted papers. Each one bore similar messages about the man's supposed illness, and each one contained a new lesson for her to try. Every time she came to this spot in the kingdom, she considered knocking on his door—though breaking it down still seemed the easier answer—but she knew neither action would do much good. Guren had made his choice and, for over a year, Trinity had lived with her choice of blindly following his written words. As if by not doing so he'd somehow turn his back on her more than he'd already done.

She went to her tower alone. Once inside, she removed the stone which held the rest of the papers and placed the new stack upon them. *Maybe tomorrow?*

There had once been a time when she believed those words.

CHAPTER SEVEN

PLAYING AT KNIGHT

Early that morning, a great number of foreign ships passed the archipelago, docking in the Hydlixian harbor. They were huge vessels with high white masts and timber-cut hulls that cast shadows across the blue waters. Trinity counted seven of them from her vantage point, atop the royal mail tower where she sat with her knees tucked under her chin. The ships bore no flags, and didn't appear to be invaders. *No war drums.*

Guren had told her stories of the beating war drums and the pawprint flags when he and the knights under his command had set sail for the islands of Reiwania many years ago. It had been one of the bloodiest battles in Hydlixian history according to him. In the end Guren and his soldiers had settled the land dispute on the island colony, leading to the establishment of good trade routes. Trinity knew the ships entering into the harbor weren't from the Reiwanian isles. Reiwanian ships, which were black as night, carried cargo like fruits and fauna, and had tropical flowers sewn onto their flags. They usually had a handful of tan-skinned sailors that mostly stayed on the boat after making deliveries. But the tall ships she saw in the harbor now carried no goods or sailors that she could see. Instead, they carried hundreds—if not thousands—of cloak covered, sand-caked, face-wrapped peoples.

"Who are they?" she asked Schobe later that day after he had finished his tasks and was sitting down for lunch. The two of them watched from the goldenrod balconies near the glass chapel. From here they could better see the people unloading from the ships. Many traveled in large family groups. They wore meager coverings—mostly heavy, rough spun wraps—and carried with them bundled possessions.

"I think they're from all over Taercion," Schobe told her, while biting into a juicy, green apple. "Refugees, some of the other knights were telling me. Kuza's been assigning posts dedicated to watching over all new arrivals. Keep these people from entering the cities gates."

"But they're allowed on the beach?" she asked, her head tilting slightly.

Schobe snickered. "Not even Kuza can just go and tell a thousand people to leave. I think the last thing he wants is to upset all of them. The king has been made aware, but nothing else has been reported to us. They started making camps under the cliffs."

Trinity watched some of the younger refugee children clinging to their parents. Some of them looked as if they'd not eaten for days.

"I still don't understand why we can't just let them into the kingdom. There's no food on the beach," she said, squaring her shoulders and clenching her fists. "That doesn't seem fair."

"They're strangers, Trin. They could be dangerous."

They didn't look dangerous as far as she could see, only tired and hungry. She saw crying children, panicked mothers, and tunicked, beardless men huddled in groups around built fires on the beach. There were elderly among them too. An old woman crossed the freezing beach sands barefoot, accompanied by a young girl wearing a fading yellow dress under thick, ash-colored robes which wrapped all the way up to her umber-colored face. The girl peered up through the narrow, oval slot her robes made at her face level. Trinity could swear she was watching them watch her.

"I wonder why they came here," she thought aloud. *And why they left wherever they came from.*

"Bet it's a lot safer than wherever they're from," Schobe said, wiping the apple from his lips. "Could be Bayonick, but they don't look like swamp people. I heard that lot does their traveling in muddy canoes. Most likely they're from the far deserts, like those in Sambool. That's a dangerous kingdom, Trin. Gazenga's realm."

She knew the name of Gazenga all too well. The scary warnings of the eastern warlord and his malicious tyranny across the land of Taercion had been recited to her by just about everyone she knew. It was he, the man in ivory armor wielding a bloodstained battle axe, who had destroyed Terkia on the night of her birth, along with his ruthless Samboolian army. They laid siege to her parent's kingdom and killed everyone within a matter of hours. She was the sole fortunate who had been able to escape, along with her aunt. It had always seemed strange, Trinity thought, that a kingdom full of strong people like herself would fall so easily at the hands of a foreign invader. But whenever she tried to ask Evita about the fateful night, the older princess would grow silent and angry. Sometimes Evita would even begin to weep. After all, her sister Zepolia had died the same night. What a dreadful monster this Gazenga must've been. To kill a woman after she had given birth...the horrid thought was enough to make Trinity shudder and scoot closer to Schobe.

Still, it was a piece of her past Trinity was burning to know more about. She always swore she'd get a straight answer from Evita someday before having to marry Hayden, but her time until that end was drawing painfully closer by the second. She knew she'd need to find out the truth soon, before it was too late.

"Schobe...do you think we're safe? From Gazenga's army?" she asked.

"Well, I don't think we'll ever *really* know until we're attacked. But I think he'd be nothing short of a mad dog to fight us here, in our kingdom. We have the advantage. Our ships patrol the harbor. And the height of our kingdom gives us some extra security. And, there's also the alliance."

"*Right*. The alliance."

The cursed alliance. She didn't think anyone besides herself minded the wedding, so long as the two great kingdoms became allies. *Hydlix and Zayloa.* She wondered when the vendors would begin selling flags with stitched mustangs and lions standing side by side in unison.

"Want to hear something really scary?" Schobe asked, leaning in close. "I heard it from Quatas, who says it was a rumor he overheard from the commander himself. Gazenga isn't alone. He has a helper."

"A helper?" *Were there two tyrants now?* Another shiver shot up her spine.

Schobe nodded. "I hear he's real strong. Like, shatter mountains strong."

Trinity gaped. She stared bewilderedly out over the ocean. "Shatter mountains?" She didn't know if she was even capable of such a feat.

"He uses an axe, just like Gazenga."

"Does he—what's his name?"

Schobe's face scrunched up. "Quatas didn't mention a name. But he sounds like a Terkian to me though. What do you think?"

She had thought precisely the same thing. But a soft "maybe" was all she could muster.

After Schobe returned to his newly appointed post, which was standing watch within the market square, scanning for pickpockets and settling squabbles over the prices of fabrics, Trinity continued her search for Evita alone. Though she knew her aunt wouldn't be in the lower ends of the kingdom, Trinity decided upon checking the dungeon tower all the same. It had been a week since she'd last gone to see her lion friend. She hoped he wouldn't be cross with her for not visiting. Sadly, she had no steaks with her today, only a handful of cookies that she'd managed to shove in her coat pocket before Birtess could catch her in the act. Snowflake would probably eat them all the same though, she knew.

The lion had always been a gentle ear to bend whenever her mind was heavy with worry. He would purr and listen to her problems with a hungry, but certainly understanding, expression. Or so she liked to tell herself. But what was she worried about? *Another Terkian?* To think there was someone else like her who was still alive and had a strength far beyond the average person. Maybe his powers were always getting him into trouble too when he was growing up. Perhaps he was younger than her. Whatever the case was, she knew one thing for sure. People probably feared him the same as they quietly did her.

"Ah, the Mouse Princess approaches," Quatas said, scoffing as Trinity neared the dungeon tower. He was standing guard outside the entryway while another posted knight was dozing beside him in a chair. "Don't tell me. You've come to relieve me for a piss?"

"What? Definitely not. Don't be so disgusting," Trinity replied. "I'm here to—to see someone."

Quatas scratched his brow with the dull edge of the long halberd he was holding. "Someone? You mean...me?"

"N-no, definitely not." She cast her gaze down at his shiny boots. She'd not expected to see him on dungeon assignment today. For a flickering second, she had hoped he might let her in rather than having to sneak in once more. But now she was not so sure. He showed no signs of stepping aside for her, instead settling himself wider against the doors. Even his weapon was still held firmly. "Quatas, I'm just visiting someone. *Inside*. Now let me past. I don't want to stand outside here all day. I have better things to do. Besides napping or hearing terrible jokes." It was then she looked up and noticed the top of his forehead was beaded with sweat. The water trickling down from his hairline looked sticky and darker than any type of sweat Trinity had seen before. "What's that on your head?"

Quatas' eyes grew big. He stooped down and picked up the steel helmet laying by his feet and put it on. "Ignore that. I woke up late. I don't think I got all the soap out of my hair after my bath this morning."

"But if you were running late, why did you take a bath?"

Quatas laughed. "Some of us like our hair to look good all day long. Unlike that Schobe of yours, eh? I swear, he just falls out of bed and shows up for his posted assignment. Well, not me."

"He takes care of his hair," she protested. "But I'm not here to talk about hair. If you'll excuse me."

She walked forward but as she feared Quatas thrust the handle of his halberd out beside him, blocking her path. Trinity's breath was stunted by her sudden stop.

"Step aside Quatas," she told him, looking jolted. "Why are you stopping me?"

"Now, Princess," he began in a lecturing tone. "It's my knightly duty to watch over this tower. Keep out all the intruders. Even the cute ones."

"Intruder? Me?" It was hard to know whether she should smile at the missed joke here or call him out for his rudeness. "Stop this little game of yours. You know I'm not an intruder."

"Oh, someone needs to be stopped. That's for sure," he said. He then grabbed her forcefully by the arm, twisting her clumsily on the spot.

Trinity jerked away from his grasp, pulling back angrily. "Quatas! What's your problem?"

"You're the one with the problem. Sneaking around here looking for trouble." He stopped himself from reaching out for her again, instead settling on a crooked smile. "I wonder what Princess Evita would think of you being here. Heard she went to the chapel this morning. Shall we go and have a word with her?"

Trinity could feel her face turning red. She sensed a tightness in her throat. "Y-you're being a jerk. You've never been this serious about guard duty before. What?

Are you hiding something in there I'm not supposed to see?" She tried to look past the girth of his armor but Quatas once more clutched onto her, gripping at her shoulder with his gauntlet. Trinity glared at him, now realizing for herself that this was no joke. "Careful," she warned. "The last knight who grabbed my shoulder like that got tossed across the barracks."

"Ooh, you got me trembling in my armor, Princess," he said, though his grip did loosen. "I ain't scared of some nosy Terkian brat who keeps forgetting her place."

"Place?"

"Sure. Up in your grandfather's district. With the rest of them courtly fools who wear furry coats and eat themselves sick."

Quatas' eyes shifted back suddenly to the guard behind him who was beginning to stir. Trinity used this distraction to once more try and go around the defending knight but Quatas beat her to the door and stood in front of it, barring the way.

"Come on, Trinity. You need to listen and understand for once. While you're off trying to play knight, some of us are doing the real thing."

"Oh, I can see that clearly," she said, gesturing at the waking knight.

"Enough! This is my job. Don't do anything stupid or you're going to get us both into trouble."

Trinity was still scowling at him and resisting the urge to reach up and punch the tall knight on the jaw, even if she had to hop. This was strange behavior, even for Quatas. Even if she wasn't allowed in the dungeons, Quatas had never been one for enforcing rules. True, she wasn't as close with him as she was with Schobe, but he had never acted so terribly to her before. He was always telling jokes and encouraging her and Schobe to get into mischief. Today, however, he was acting nervous, and even violent.

She stepped forward once more, defiantly, but the slightest change in his normally calm-looking face made her pause. He looked at her—for only a second—like a viper ready to sting. His blue eyes narrowed, looking like trembling sapphires. Out of fear or anger, she couldn't say for sure. Reluctantly, she stepped back.

"Fine. Just-fine," she stammered. "I'll visit later. And maybe the next posted knight will remember who I am. And *who* my family is."

"I'll be sure to remind Kuza we need extra guards posted here then," he said, leaning back on the door. He looked relieved, and even smiled at her again as Trinity walked away from him backwards.

"I can't believe *you'd* treat me this way," she shot back at him, wondering if he even cared. "I'd expect this sort of treatment from Kuza. Even other knights. But never you. And you know what? You can just forget about dating my aunt. I was even going to suggest it to her for the winter ball. But not anymore."

"Ah, now don't be like that, Princess. I'm only keeping you safe. Honest. Dungeons are no place for kids," he jeered, laughing this time as he did. "Now, I think I hear your aunt calling. Best behave and get on home, Little Mouse. Before someone steps on you."

Trinity was prepared to scream at him every possible Hydlixian swear she could think of then. And she would've too, if the knight beside Quatas hadn't woken fully and hopped to his feet quickly, looking as if he were the one who had given her some offense. Quatas threw his arm around the startled knight's shoulders and whispered some private joke. With both fists clenched, Trinity twisted and stomped back down the road she had entered from.

At least she knew where her aunt was now, though this provided little comfort. Quatas had embarrassed her, this much was true. But by turning tail and walking away...it shamed her more than she'd ever felt before. Quatas' words stung worse than any cut. Perhaps she was nothing more than a mousy little rich girl who played at being a knight.

TALES AND SECRETS

When Trinity returned to the sanctuary, she'd found that the priests had gone. It was midday and they had probably stepped out for lunch down in the market. This meant she could avoid seeing Great Father Palthar but still search for her aunt within the chapel.

She didn't know why Palthar seemed to detest her so, but she had some notions. Usually during his early morning sermons—which seemed to last until well past noon—she would nap on Evita's shoulder, or sometimes even the pew itself. It wasn't entirely her fault, she believed. The chapel's plush pews were irresistibly comfortable. If it weren't for the glaring sun bleeding in through the blue-stained glass walls, Trinity would've slept the whole of her sabbath mornings away.

And then there was the time when she was ten and had made the foolish decision to pee in one of the sacred ale barrels. Again, she was convinced that she didn't deserve *all* of the blame for this. There was a well-known tale passed amongst the children of Hydlix which said there was once a Great Father from the past who had prayed to MAI for a barrel that could turn water into ale. Schobe told her that he knew which of the barrels in the chapel's pantry it was, and he had even seen Palthar sampling some of this "magical ale" when the church was not in service. Quatas was the one who tricked her though, telling her that *any* liquids which went into the barrel would instantly become ale. Trinity's curiosity prevailed, and having nothing other than her own liquids that fateful morning, she relieved herself upon the open container. She remembered her stomach doing flips the next time she went to church with her aunt. Palthar's round face grew rigid and his half-closed eyes shot daggers at her. Even though he never made an accusation against her, she was sure he knew of her misdeed.

She thought it a shame that the Great Father didn't like her. Rumor had it that beneath the glass chapel lay a long tunnel which stretched all the way to the dungeons. She didn't know what possible use Palthar could have for easy access to the prisoners, but had she been more welcome in the church, she would've used the rumored tunnel to go and visit Snowflake whenever she chose. After what happened this morning with Quatas, she knew that sneaking into the dungeon tower would be her only option from here on out.

Don't even start thinking about that jerk. Besides, she wasn't trying to see Snowflake right now. Or the Great Father. Muddled with worries, Trinity stood hesitantly beside the chapel's closed doors and listened carefully. There was a resonating music coming from within, like quiet humming. The sweet melody seemed to grace the cracks in the door and fill her ear. *Is someone playing the piano?*

She opened the door a crack and snuck in. Staying low, she crawled on all fours along the long train of white carpet stretching through the church as the sounds of the piano grew louder, amplified within the tiny chapel. The pews lining the walkway had golden lionheads etched into them with eyes made of jade stones. The eleventh one had a chipped fang on the right and she paused there as a familiar voice started to sing.

> *"I wouldn't slay the dragon*
> *Whose name I didn't know*
> *He flew me to the mountain*
> *Where men could never grow"*

Trinity peeked beneath the remaining pews towards the front of the chapel. She could see a pair of dark heels clicking onto the piano's pedals, the mystery player's legs were covered by a blue, silky dress. The airy tones of the piano continued their resonances, and the singer began the second verse, quieter than before:

> *"I kissed him with a blade*
> *And watched his green blood flow*
> *But the dragon freely gave*
> *He shared his ember glow"*
> *"I've flown with the dragons*
> *We've conquered every foe*
> *His sins are now my sins*
> *We both know where we'll go"*

"Have you ever walked the sky?
There my face was singed.
Did you say I should have burned?
I never even turned.
I killed him, though I was singed."

Trinity couldn't help herself. She jumped up from where she was hiding and clapped aloud. As she suspected, Evita was the one letting the last note ring out on the big instrument before becoming startled at the sight of the unexpected listener.

"H-how long have you been here?" she asked.

"Long enough to hear your song. It was so pretty Aunt E. I really loved it."

Trinity joined her at the pearl-colored piano, taking her place on the long gray bench beside Evita. Evita looked displeased that she'd had a hidden audience member.

"You know, you really shouldn't sneak up on people like that. And shouldn't you be at home, young lady? Last I saw you your head was so heavy you could barely lift it. Even Terkians need to take it easy every so often."

"But I'm feeling loads better now. Won't you teach me how to play a song like that?"

Evita winced. "I'd love to, but I was just leaving. Besides, you remember what happened the last time you tried to play the piano."

"I'll play it softer this time. I promise."

"Not now Zepolia—Trinity." Her eyes crinkled with embarrassment. "Sorry. What a silly thing to say."

Trinity was used to this mistake by now. Her aunt had accidentally called her by her mother's name several times over the years. Why did this slip-up embarrass Evita so?

"Did my mom ever play the piano?" Trinity asked, trying to stay on the subject.

"No," Evita said, snickering. "She broke more keys than you, believe it or not. But she always liked to sing along. Especially to the song I was just playing."

"What song was it?"

Evita hesitated. "Well, it's not really a song meant for church, which is probably why you've never heard it. It's called *The Turtle and the Dragon*. One of my favorites."

Evita turned to the previous page in her song book that was sitting on top of the piano's keys. Along the aged, yellow pages were drawn sketches of silver dragons breathing fire and several violet turtles who were swimming across the musical notes and stanzas.

"Did you color on this?" Trinity asked, giggling.

"Your mother and I."

Trinity reached forward and caressed one of the crinkled turtle shells. "Someone actually wrote a song about turtles and dragons?"

"They weren't just any turtles and dragons. They were the sacred ones. You know, *MAI's* animals?"

Trinity rolled her eyes. She knew these animals, of course. The sacred beasts were as rudimentary to her private instructor Ihsotah's lessons as the alphabet of the TCL: Taercion Common Language. There were eight animals in all: the white lion of Hydlix, the black elephant of Sambool, the orange giraffe of Attigas, the blue wolf of Kendoro, and the red mustang of Zayloa, where Hayden was from. There were also two kingdoms which were long ago destroyed. The swamp kingdom of Bayonick, which had their golden dolphins. And then there were the winged hydras of the sky kingdom, Xone. She remembered seeing the pictures of these flying behemoths in her books. They were truly terrifying monsters, but she yearned to see them up close. Finally, there was the green gorilla from her fallen kingdom of

Terkia. Again, she'd only seen pictures of gorillas in her study books. She wondered sometimes if gorillas still roamed the Terkian canyons after the kingdom had been destroyed. Still, despite the importance of these sacred animals, pictures in books were hardly enough to hold her interest for long.

"*Yes*, I know the sacred animals," she said, sounding annoyed with the assumed lack of her knowledge. "But wait, I don't remember any turtles and dragons in the stories."

"*No*. They usually aren't mentioned in the tomes or holy books," her aunt confessed. "But they are told in the stories. Don't you listen to Palthar's sermons?"

"I...must've forgotten."

"Hmm," she said, sounding unconvinced. "Let's see. The stories tell of ten animals in all. And each was assigned a special place by MAI. To govern the whole of Remsphere and watch over his creation. They helped man establish laws and kingdoms. The violet turtle was assigned to the depths of the deepest oceans, where no human dwelled. The other animals freely coexisted with humans. I'm sure you remember when the knights brought a white lion here to live in our dungeons."

Trinity shifted her attention to the ivory piano keys. "Oh yeah...I sort of remember that."

"Why, even dolphin could frolic among the top shores, working with fishermen. But not turtle. He had to live his life scrounging the ocean floors with a heavy shell on his back. He wished to soar the skies, like the silver dragon."

"I think I'd take my chances in the sea."

"Ah. You *are* a Hydlixian at heart, my child," Evita said, smiling. "Now, turtle was the most deceptive of the ten animals. One day he encountered dragon and tricked him into giving him a ride on his back. Turtle claimed he wanted to see the sphere as dragon did. Dragon allowed him to ride with him as he flew across the blue horizon."

"Must've been a sight."

"Quite, I'm sure. But then, at the highest point of the heavens, turtle betrayed dragon. He attacked him in his one weak spot." Evita reached behind Trinity's shoulders and touched the soft part behind her mess of curls, on the other side of where her heart lay. "Dragon was killed here, see, as was the legacy he surely would've left behind."

"*So...*turtle just killed dragon mid-flight? How did he survive the fall?"

"He wasn't just an ordinary sea turtle after all. And don't forget. He had his shell to protect him. It would seem his burden must've been his saving grace."

Trinity narrowed her eyes, unsatisfied with Evita's answer. "Uh, how does a turtle even stab a dragon?"

Evita shrugged. "The song mentions a blade."

"A blade?" she asked, her eyebrows raising.

"I wasn't there, Trinity. I don't know what he used," Evita said, sounding flustered.

Trinity leaned back and folded her arms. She was still unsure how the beautiful song her aunt had just sung was somehow related to sword-wielding turtles. Still, she wanted to know how the story ended. "Alright, turtle kills dragon. Dragon's legacy suffers. What about MAI? Was he fine with all of this? I don't think he would just sit back while seeing his animals kill one another."

Evita studied Trinity's face for a second, as if surprised by the cleverness of what she had just said. "You are very right. Dragon's death meant sin was introduced to the Remsphere, our world. Naturally, MAI had to intervene. He banished turtle for his crime. Back to a lonely life beneath the sea. But by then it was too late. Man had followed turtle's example. Surely you know that murder is one of the most atrocious sins. But—" Evita's face hardened, "it's considered even more vile to kill one of MAI's chosen animals. Even the descendants. The very act is unforgivable."

Trinity said nothing, though her thoughts fell upon Snowflake. *Guess it's not a sin to keep them locked up though, is it?* She started scratching at her elbow, frowning as she did.

Evita continued on, seemingly unaware of Trinity's mood change. "Amazing when you think about it. The thought of a turtle being able to slay a dragon. It all happened because the turtle took the one piece of power the dragon freely gave."

"...What piece of power?"

Evita caressed a strand of Trinity's hair in her hand. "His trust."

Trinity's mood improved soon after they stepped out of the airless chapel into the crisp, afternoon air. She even successfully convinced her aunt to eat at one of the food-stands in the market square for lunch. Evita made it no secret that this was a huge gamble for her.

"Everything here is going to stick inside my stomach," she said, grimacing.

The two of them settled upon a stand selling steamed cabbage plates with roasted fire- carrots. Trinity loved the spicy, red carrots, one of the few vegetables she didn't detest. They helped themselves to one of the wooden benches scattered around the market and several of the children Trinity knew came and greeted her. This included Ellacryse, who gifted Trinity with a new red and orange bracelet.

"Your favorite color and mine. I've just made it," Ellacryse said, still looking puny in her oversized coat.

"Thank you, Ella dear. I'll wear it every day," Trinity said, admiring the handiwork of the bracelet.

Ellacryse turned and gave a small bow before Evita. "If you ever need handmade jewelry, Princess, I'll gladly make you one. Any color you like."

Evita gave a slight nod and Ellacryse scooted off. Trinity could see Evita watching after her for some time.

"Seems you've made many friends here," Evita said, examining the handmade jewelry on Trinity's wrist. "Especially that little bracelet seller."

"Ella's great. She's like a sister," Trinity admitted.

Evita drew back some, but she wore a convincing grin. "I must say, that coat of hers was remarkable. She really has fine taste."

Trinity couldn't help but smile at this.

Evita elaborated for some time during their meal about the recently opened bakery in the upper district. They were serving a new type of drink that she wanted Trinity to try, a cup of heated milk with sprinklings of chocolate mixed within.

"Why would anyone heat milk?" Trinity asked.

"You had no problem with heated milk when you were a baby."

"Well, that's just it. I was a baby. I couldn't complain yet."

"Oh," Evita said with a practiced sigh, "you complained about plenty."

When they finally headed home, the two of them walked arm in arm. Trinity insisted they take the longer path, avoiding the chapel entirely, and Guren's door, though she kept this afterthought to herself. The sun was covered by heavy clouds, but Trinity sensed it must've been late in the afternoon by now. It wasn't as chilly anymore. Even the onlookers who greeted them as they slowly ascended back up to their home in the upper districts had seemed to shed some of the heavier layers from earlier. Trinity was certain her grandfather would have a great fire built in the hearth of the banquet hall. For once in her life, she was grateful to dine there. She couldn't help licking her lips as she wondered what Phes and the rest of the kitchen staff had prepared for them. *Anything but cabbages.*

It wasn't until they were nearing the courtyards that Trinity finally asked her aunt the one question which had been eating at her ever since she'd woken up.

"Why did you leave me this morning, Aunt E?"

"S-Sorry," Evita sputtered, as if the question had come unexpectedly. "I was—troubled this morning. I had to clear my head a little."

Troubled? Why would she be troubled? Trinity couldn't help but remember the refugees arriving on the beach earlier. Their troubled and hungry faces still pressed at her mind. What could Evita, who had never known hunger or the wants of the poor, possibly have to be troubled about?

"I don't understand. What's wrong?" Trinity asked, in a callous tone.

Evita stared straight ahead, but she had stopped walking now. Trinity stayed by her side.

"Everything…it's all happening so quickly," she began, "just like before. With Zepolia. Her wedding day. That was today. I went to the chapel this morning. To pray for you mostly. Funny how so many of my trips to church have ended with me playing the piano." She bit at her bottom lip. "No matter how many ways I think it, there's no question. I feel horrible. Just horrible. As if I'm losing you the same way I lost her."

"Oh."

"Don't misunderstand me. It's a brave thing you're doing, Trin. I want you to know that."

"If you really feel so horrible," Trinity said, as she loosened herself from Evita's arm, "then why let the wedding happen at all?"

"Why—I'm afraid we don't have a choice, dear."

"I don't believe that. Grandfather, he might listen to you. He could call off the whole thing."

"No, it's not that simple."

"It is!" Trinity snapped, gritting her teeth.

Evita shook her head. "Trinity. You've no doubt seen the arriving boats in the harbor," she said, still biting at her lip nervously. "The Samboolian threat is real. Unless we form an alliance with another kingdom, Father fears there will be war."

"You don't know that. None of you know that." Her heart raced within her chest. The words she'd kept pent up for so long were coming to her at last. "Marrying Hayden fixes nothing. It just ruins my life."

"Oh, here we go again. You're being dramatic."

"Am I? I'm only *fourteen*. I have to leave everything and everyone I have ever known. You have no idea the sacrifices I'm making."

Evita's eyes were trembling within her head. Trinity sensed an advantage in the moment. Now was her chance to strike.

"What about my mother? Did she accept her arranged marriage? Did she even love my father?"

"Don't!" Evita warned, scowling, as the fear from before seemed to vanish behind her furrowing brow and pursed lips. "I've told you before. We do not discuss that man."

"My father? Why not? I'm not the one who decided to stop talking about him."

"*Trinity!*" Evita said the name as if she were casting a curse. "Enough."

"I have a right to know. You've never told me anything about him. Only that he left her when she was delivering. But there was a battle going on outside. And maybe," she had said the words so many times in her head that they'd felt like a recitation, "maybe he had his reasons. Maybe he thought he was being brave."

Evita scoffed. "There's *nothing* brave about leaving a woman who loves you. Especially when she needed him most."

Trinity couldn't stop herself then. The words came out like an unpreventable sneeze.   "You did."

Evita reached back and slapped Trinity across the face. Trinity felt more surprised by the blow than pained, as she sensed a slight tingle on the right side of her face. She could see Evita's hand start to swell. Evita appeared equally startled.

"Trinity—Trinity I'm so sorry."

"...Save it."

Trinity sprinted down the steps they'd come up from, as Evita tried in vain to call out for her. But Trinity had no intention of turning back to face her aunt again. She had meant every word she said. And it was true. Evita had left her mother's bedside, the same as her father. Why should his neglect matter more than hers?

Trinity had grown weary of all the secrets. After being told off by Quatas today, she was starting to wonder if anyone was being truthful with her anymore. Guren had long ago stopped confiding in her—or speaking to her altogether. And Evita had been keeping secrets from her since she was born. Even now, as Trinity was about to start a new life in a new kingdom with a new horrid husband, Evita wouldn't reveal her own past to her. *If she won't tell me*, Trinity thought, *I'll find the answers myself.*

* * *

"Lady Ikena, are you—possibly here of your own accord, Trinity dear?" asked her teacher Ihsotah, who sounded as shaken as if he'd just seen some terror of the night rather than a girl in the library reading a book.

She had been eleven when her and Evita had their last argument about Zepolia's failed husband. They'd been discussing gorillas of all things that morning at breakfast. But when the topic shifted to Terkia and its former king, Evita shut her down by banging on the table with both fists. Trinity knew better than to push the questions further. Her curiosity, however, got the better of her, and she retreated later in the day to the library. She hoped this would be a quieter place to find some answers to her questions.

"Lady Ikena, you are aware we don't have any lessons today?" Ihsotah asked.

"I'm aware," Trinity said, her eyes never leaving the dusty tome open before her.

Ihsotah sat to join her. Trinity turned her head slightly to meet his heavy gaze. A proud looking smile was on his face.

"What?" she asked.

"You've come to better your understanding of something, haven't you? All on your own. This warms my heart, child. I feel I should capture an imprint of the occasion. Can you wait here until I retrieve a picture box?"

"*Ihsotah*," she grumbled. "I'm trying to study. Only, I just, I don't really know where to begin."

"Here, let me help you."

Ihsotah showed her the Hydlixian word for the animal she'd been searching for in the text and retreated to gather several more books. Trinity read the passage, written just below an illustration of a hairy beast with vicious eyes and bared fangs.

Illiag — in TCL: Gorilla. N. The largest ape creature in all the Remsphere. Located in the center of Taercion, with smaller subspecies located in Siegnes. In the MAIjos religion Gorillas are believed to be part of the eight (originally ten) different animals appointed by MAI to serve as guardians to Remsphere. The larger green species inhabit the northern central mountains of Taercion, known as the "Terkian Push", now inhabited by the kingdom of Terkia. (See Terkia). Gorillas have become rare sights in modern times with many believing they are nearing extinction. Gorillas are aggressive, difficult animals, and should be approached with extreme caution. Gorillas are herbivores but have also been known to display carnivorous signs.

"Trinity, dear, why do you wish to know of gorillas? If you don't mind my asking," Ihsotah said, placing three encyclopedias and a thick, leather-bound religious text on the seat beside her.

"They're the sacred animals of Terkia. I guess I was just curious. I wondered if I might ever see one," she said, deflating into her chair. *I didn't know they were all gone.*

Ihsotah shook his head. "Oh, I don't think so, Princess. Most of them died out before your father's reign. Hunted to near extinction."

Her eyes grew big. "My father, did you know him, sir? I can't find anything about him."

"I'm afraid not," Ihsotah admitted. "My work keeps me here mostly. The siege on Terkia during your father's reign is still fairly recent history. I doubt we have any materials on the subject."

"I don't even know his name." She closed the book in front of her.

"That is perplexing," he said, scratching at the curly wisp of gray hair on his chin. "I would expect a Terkian to know plenty about her own people."

"No. My family tells me nothing."

"Hmm." He cleared his throat. "To deny knowledge of one's origins is truly cruel."

"Origins?"

"Indeed. They are what you seek, right? Kulumnus et vasotah esh kishibiti van nuuse."

She laughed guiltily. "I've not been studying Hydlixian lately."

"It means knowledge found is greater than the already known. You have to find the knowledge you seek, not just rely on what you know."

"*So*—I should try asking my aunt in a different way?"

"Perhaps." Ihsotah pondered her words for a few seconds. "Maybe the answers you are searching for won't be found by asking the same questions of someone who doesn't want to answer them. Discover your own answers, Princess."

* * *

It had taken her years to heed his advice, but now she knew exactly what she must do if she ever hoped to learn more about her past. She waited to return home until just before dusk. There was a good chance Evita was out there looking for her, and the handmaidens usually had gone home by this hour, meaning her home would be empty. Still, Trinity was somewhat surprised that the knights and handmaidens hadn't formed a search party yet. She knew she and Evita would be having a conversation again soon. Probably after supper. She hoped there would be less yelling and hitting this time.

Trinity snuck through Evita's window. As she guessed, there was no one home. She set to work searching the polished, well-organized room. A guilty feeling—much like the one she'd had when she first stole the key to the mailing tower—swept over her, but she ignored it as she peeked under Evita's finely-made bed with fresh-pressed linens. *Nothing.*

She tried the dresser, the chifforobe, the spacious closet. She found nothing at every corner of the room. What was it she was searching for? She didn't know the answer herself. But she knew that some part of her past must dwell here. Some answer that must lay hidden. At last, she found a small wooden chest tucked away on the top shelf of the closet. There was a small, metal lock on the lid. She considered breaking it, knowing full well that she'd reveal her crime by doing so, but she spotted a small brass key tied to one of the iron legs of the chest. She unraveled the key and opened the chest.

There were various trinkets within: jewelry, hair ribbons, and a crumpled letter with some weight to it. She picked up the letter, which had the shape of a heart written on the seal. Inside the heart was the letter "Z".

"Zepolia," she whispered to herself. *Mother.*

She placed the letter beside her and continued rummaging through the chest. There were a couple of imprints at the bottom. She had a few imprints of her own hanging in her room. The process for these pictures was a lengthy one. It involved dying glimmer bugs and oily papers, or something like that. She hated having to pose for an imprint every year. The stuffy dresses and forced smiles were enough to make her gag.

She picked up one. There were two girls in the picture who she recognized immediately. Evita looked so young here, and short, standing beside the fair-skinned girl holding her in an embrace. The older girl had long, golden hair, and eyes as blue as any sapphire pendant Trinity had seen in a shop. *Her eyes*, she thought. *They aren't green like mine.*

"Mother...she's so beautiful," she said quietly to herself.

She looked so happy. They both did. Trinity couldn't remember a time her aunt had ever looked so pleasantly at peace.

Trinity picked up the other imprint from the bottom of the chest. As her eyes focused on the new picture she held, her stomach dropped and her heart must've skipped several beats, for she suddenly felt short of breath. *What in MAI's name?*

Her mother was on this imprint as well, but a great many things had changed. She was a woman now, but her face was sad and more wretched than before. It was as if any semblance of joy had never existed within her. She was sitting on a bed, and there in her arms was not one, but two babies.

Two babies?

She tried to examined the imprint more closely, but just then an earsplitting sound from a barrage of horns and trumpets filled the air around her. *Could it be?* She knew this sound, though only from her time spent hiding in the barracks. It was a call for the knights to take up arms. *Are we being attacked?*

She didn't know what to think anymore. She tucked her mother's letter and the imprint with the two babies into her tunic, then closed the chest up once more. The answers she sought would have to wait a little longer.

THE BANDITS OF BAYONICK

Trinity ran to her room and quickly changed out of her dress and coat, pulling on a fresh, long-sleeved tunic and pair of thick breeches. If there was really an attack happening on her kingdom, the last thing she wanted to be wearing was something that prevented her from being battle-ready. After refastening her boots, she stepped out of her empty home slowly, unsure of what to expect.

Several knights were already clanging past her doorway like a wagon load of metal. Their lanterns cast long pillars of light as early evening settled upon Hydlix.

"Wait! What's going on?" she called out to the knights. "Why are the trumpets being blown?"

Not a single knight acknowledged her. They didn't even seem to care that she was a princess without an escort, or they were pretending not to notice her. She couldn't be sure. Instead, she followed their path. It wasn't long before she could see others out on this strange night as well. There were Hydlixians—unarmored—dashing frantically across the courtyards scurrying for places to hide. Trinity was confused by their reactions. Had a great army suddenly risen up out of the depths of the kingdom? The knights were surely ready for any and all attacks. Or was that a lie too? *What is going on?*

"Princess?" called one of the shimmering soldiers charging past her.

"Quatas?" She knew those blue eyes of his anywhere. Even beneath his open-faced helmet, both eyes shone in the darkness like sapphires. She met him on the snowy grass, hesitant to hear him out. She'd not forgotten the way he treated her earlier. "Quatas...do you know what's happening here?"

"We need to get you to safety, Trinity. We're under attack."

"None of this makes any sense. Who would attack us?"

"Bandits. Whole mess of them just popped up in the market square. There's fifty, no. Maybe a hundred."

"You're joking."

Again, she was having trouble reading his expression. Once more he wasn't acting like the same friend from her childhood. There was the same brashness in his voice from earlier, as if he selfishly enjoyed telling her what to do. He was also standing so close she could smell the burnt meat he'd eaten for dinner. She tried to step back, but he leaned in closer.

"Quatas, bandits wouldn't attack here. Not with such low numbers."

"Only they have!" he shot back, as his eyes narrowed in on hers. "They've even killed some people. We're on strict orders. Any members of the royal family or high court are to be immediately taken to the glass chapel." He yanked aggressively at her arm, trying to pull her along as if she were a captured bandit, and not someone he was trying to escort safely.

She could've fought him, and for a second, she almost did. It would have given her some small satisfaction to give him such a punch after the way he'd been treating her. But there again in the intensity of his eyes was a look which reeked of fear. Was he really so afraid of her? Or was he afraid of what would happen if they stayed there much longer? Perhaps the situation was worse than she had guessed.

"Quatas...are you taking me to where my aunt is?" she asked, warily.

"Yes Princess. I told you already. She and the king are being held in the chapel for safety."

Trinity stopped walking. Quatas couldn't budge her. "I don't understand," she said. "Why would they be taken to the chapel? Seems the safer place would be the throne room."

"Look!" Quatas snapped, looking more flustered than she'd ever seen him before. "I have urgent orders to follow. You are in danger. Now are you going to come with me or do I need to carry you there?"

She tapped a finger harshly on his breastplate. "You're not carrying me anywhere. I'll go. Not because you're telling me to, but because I'm trusting you, knight. Now, lead the way. And don't you dare screw this up."

He looked taken aback by her words. He choked out a quick, "R-right this way then, Princess." His hold on her arm softened some.

Trinity continued following him, though her suspicions had grown. The throne room was the safest place in the kingdom, and far away from the market square. The glass chapel was too close to where the fighting was taking place. It also seemed strange that none of the other knights were as eager to escort her to the chapel. Could Quatas have been given orders that they'd not been given? *But who gave him those orders?*

Quatas led her down the cobbled steps past the courtyards and into the openness of the kingdom's lower district. The market square was indeed under siege. Fires had been set on several wooden stands. The vendors were scrambling, some clutching onto what they could salvage from their wares to keep them from burning. Trinity watched in disbelief. How could all of this have happened so quickly? Whoever was attacking her home had certainly wasted no time.

Then she saw them—hooded figures slinking quickly across the alleys directly beneath them. Beyond that, in the market square, she could see several of the attackers more closely. They were masked, with cobalt smocks each wielding a strange blade that resembled a large fishing hook. The bandits were fighting with some of the knights who had arrived on the scene. They moved with fierceness, repelling the knights' attacks by hooking their blades and throwing them off their strides.

One of the masked men, a lumbering figure with blood dripping from his hooked blade, turned and spotted her and Quatas on the steps. He rushed towards them, and Quatas forced Trinity back with his hand, drawing his blade to meet the scoundrel head-on.

Trinity wanted to protect herself until realizing that she didn't have a sword. She didn't expect any of the knights would let her borrow one, and she had no idea how to use one of the enemies' hook blades if they fell. Instead, she watched to see if Quatas needed any help. He was having no trouble pinning the hooded man's hook onto the ground, elbowing him in the face as he did. Trinity was admittedly impressed.

She focused her attention away from their fighting, peering out into the burning market. It was difficult to see in the middle of the moonlit battle if there were any Hydlixian subjects roaming amongst the chaos. She wondered if everyone had sought shelter or known to run. All around the once-bustling square were shrieks of men being pierced with swords and halberds. The knights had already begun lining the golden balconies above; their longbows were nocked and were taking aim.

They'll make short work of it, she thought, feeling some contentment. But it was then she saw an unmoving armored figured lying near a broken vendor's stand. The armor was far too big for the one wearing it, and the breastplate was rusted. She knew at once who it belonged to. Her heart skipped a beat. *Schobe!*

She moved past Quatas and raced down the steps, leaping from the bottom one as if this would get her to Schobe's body faster. She landed in the paved streets of the square below with her fists outstretched before her to break the fall. Her fists smashed through the cobble like glass, sending a fierce rumble rippling through the ground and knocking the battlers around her askew. She found her feet and kept running, despite the startled shouts swelling all around her.

"—the princess—"

"—she has to leave; this is no place for a girl—"

"—such strength from a child—"

"—she's no knight—"

At last, she reached the place where her fallen friend lay. His sword lay unsheathed and bloodied at his side. "Schobe! Schobe!" she screeched, rolling him over to his back so she could find some life in those deep brown eyes of his.

He moaned, and his face tightened. "I'm alright," he managed to say. "One of the bandits cut me. Used that weapon of theirs to hook my sword down. He took a dagger to my stomach, but he didn't cut too deep. I got him...I think."

"You killed someone?" Her gaze steadied upon his face. Schobe's eyes began to twitch, as the realization of his actions seemed to set in. He didn't cry, though his bottom lip shivered some. Despite his unease, he still maintained a rigid expression. It reminded her of the one he wore when she had first introduced herself to him by the brick wall—back before either of them had ever held a sword.

"...I did," Schobe said, sounding unsure himself until then.

Trinity could feel her own emotions welling up. "Schobe, you—what were you thinking?!" she shouted, as she pounded onto his breastplate with her fist, denting it slightly. "You scared me to death. You barely fit into your armor. And don't even get me started on your sword handling. Why are you down here where all the fighting is? You never have a post in the market."

"Ouch. Hey, I'm hurt here. You could at least pretend to be nice," he said, through shallow breaths. "I came here to look for Ellacryse. She hadn't come home yet. When we heard the trumpet's call—"

"Ella?" The image of the expensive coat she'd given Schobe's sister that morning flashed into her mind. "Where is she?"

"I don't know. I thought maybe she might be looking for you. We were all out searching after your aunt told the commander that you'd run off. I need to find her, Trin."

Quatas had finally caught up with them, having apparently won his scrape. A line of blood—not his own—smeared across his shoulder plate. A scrap of fabric, which looked to be a remnant of the bandit's smock, dangled from Quatas' sword. Quatas reached forward for Trinity's arm again like a nipping pup. "Come along, Princess. We've no time to waste."

"No! I have to find Ella," she said, twisting her body away from him.

"Damn it, Trin. You're getting on my last nerve," he said.

"Schobe's hurt here, can't you see? He needs help, not me. Fetch my grandfather's doctor. His name is Mokin. Hurry."

"I have my orders!"

Trinity ignored his bark. She stayed knelt, resting her hand behind Schobe's head now. "You sure she never went home, Schobe?"

"Positive."

"She's here then. I'll find her," she said, peering towards the flaming stalls. Just hang on."

"...Hey Trinity," Schobe started, weakly, "if I don't make it..."

"Shh. Don't you dare die on me Schobey. Or I'll be sure they write the extra "y" on your gravestone."

Schobe laughed, clutching at his side as he tried to sit up. "Listen, if you find her, please, keep her safe."

She smiled at him. "You know I will."

She stood, glancing at the flustered Quatas. "Protect him with your life, sir knight."

Quatas bumbled to make a reply, but Trinity didn't wait for it, running further into the streets of the still flaming market. She thought it best to begin her search by checking beside each of the empty stalls. The king's archers had already dealt with most of the bandits, it seemed, and the area had grown eerily quiet since her fist-led entrance. Her breathing grew rushed as her eyes darted across the still ground laden with firelit corpses. What if one of these rogues had noticed the value of the coat she'd given her friend? *Oh, why didn't I tell her to be more careful? Don't you die on me either, Ella.*

It was on her second fast-footed sweep across the cracked cobbles when she suddenly saw it—the heavy fur coat she once owned. The coat was bundled in on itself in the center of one of the streets. Traces of clumped snow lay atop of the wet fur.

"E—Ellacryse," she cried out in a broken whisper.

A pair of hands slowly emerged from beneath a nearby tarp. Fortunately, they were attached to Schobe's sister. Her teeth were chattering, and she was too frightened to stand.

"T-T-Trinity."

"Ella!"

Trinity pulled Ellacryse to her feet and held onto the trembling girl as tightly as she could, uncaring of whether or not it was too much hug for a Terkian to give. Ellacryse clasped ahold of her waist just as tightly and began to sob.

"I thought they had you princess," she said, weeping onto Trinity's tunic.

"Ella, dear. That was so clever of you to hide like that."

"Trinity, I-I heard them," she stammered, "the bad people. They said they were going to steal the crown."

Trinity's eyes grew big. "Did they?" There'd be no way bandits could seize the crown. Surely the kingdom's prized piece—along with her aunt and the king—were under heavy protection from Commander Kuza's finest knights. Not that this comforted her any. If Kuza had been the one who ordered Quatas to bring her to the glass chapel, then his judgement was seriously off. But even he wouldn't be so foolish as to attempt to move the crown, or leave it unguarded. The Hydlixians had a rule about the crown. *Heavier protection than the king.* Her grandfather's orders, and those of the kings that came before him. *The crown must still be in the throne room.*

She took Ellacryse by the chilled hand, considering whether or not she should hide her back at her home. Off in the distance, she could see Schobe. He had risen to his feet and was standing alone, still clutching his left side. All the fighting around him seemed to have ended, though the fires were still burning. She decided it best to lead Ellacryse back to her brother. *They both need to get out of here.*

"Thank you, Trinity," Schobe said, softly, while embracing his sister. There was an unmistakable shame in his voice. Trinity wasn't sure why though. She hadn't done anything so remarkable. Ellacryse had managed to save herself. Still, Schobe was wringing his hands together now and refusing to meet her eyes. "Thank you," he repeated.

"Schobe, get yourself patched up. And take Ella home." She looked around. "Where's Quatas?"

Schobe snickered. "I—I told him to piss off. I don't know. He just kept going on and on about dragging you up to the chapel. I didn't like the way he was ordering you around. You're the princess, after all."

Her heart felt as if it were kicking her in the throat. "You stood up to Quatas? For me?"

He nodded. "Let the others flee to safety. We need you here, helping us defend the kingdom. That's obvious."

She couldn't stop herself after hearing this. She kissed him then. Oh, it was nothing more than a light brush of her lips upon his cheek. *A peck.* But a sudden warmth pressed upon her as she did so, a kind of peace, which almost made her feel like she was floating. Only Ella's giggles and Schobe's surprised look could bring her back to the ground. They stared at one another for a few seconds, she and him, neither really knowing what to say. If Ella hadn't been there, she may have kissed him again. But she knew now was not the time to think about such things.

"See you soon," she told him, assuredly.

"Don't do anything reckless," he told her, smiling.

"...No promises."

She tore herself away from Schobe's gaze and sprinted back up the stairs, towards the upper districts again. Quatas had taken her far from home, and the glass chapel was still close by. Maybe he had misheard his orders. *But he seemed so sure.* Nevertheless, she wouldn't be going to the church. Not yet. She slowed her pace and pondered her next move.

Ellacryse had mentioned the crown was what the bandits were there for. Trinity knew from her lessons with Ihsotah that the lion-mane crown was forged by the first fires back when the kingdom was formed over seven generations ago. It was said that Sachrezzar, the original white lion, had taken his pride to the southern coast and rid the land of wolves—not blue ones—and giants, on MAI's sacred orders. Sachrezzar himself protected the first men who started construction on the ruby kingdom, as it came to be called by merchants and passersby who awed at the beachside fortress. It was even rumored that traces of Sachrezzar's mane were sewn within the ancient, royal headwear. Surely a bandit—regardless of birthplace—would know the priceless value of her kingdom's ancient crown. Though Trinity had no personal love for her grandfather's hairy old headwear, she knew she must protect it. *This* was a knight's first duty after all.

Along the way to the throne room, Trinity saw other hooded bandits who had fallen in battle. Their hook blades were piled in the streets and their bodies were being prepped for burning by the battle-weary knights. She could see the bandits better now under the light of the bonfire the knights had drawn. They had bronze skin, and black tattoos twisting up their arms. One man she passed had needles lining his ears like jewelry, and another had some speckled paint on his cheeks. Beneath their gray cloaks were leather cuirasses and long daggers fastened to their belts. Perhaps the strangest thing about them though was their boots. They were such a curious sight that Trinity had to stoop down and feel a discarded pair for herself. They felt like rubber, but the material was tougher and more durable. Each pair was colored golden, but Trinity couldn't be sure if the boots were made of gold or just dyed. *They can't be real gold.* Even Evita, she believed, would never pay for something as extravagant as golden boots.

The fighting seemed to be over now, but the soldiers around the bonfire were still tense. In a huddle under one of the arches of the aqueduct, Trinity saw a group of gold-booted prisoners being escorted somewhere. The captured bandits walked with their hands bound as they marched slowly between their knight escorts to the western part of the plaza, towards the dungeon tower. She wondered if the bandits would be locked up, or if they were to be hung immediately. *It's been a while*, she recalled to herself, *since we've had a hanging.* She wondered if Guren would be there to see her grandfather's justice enacted upon these men. Guren never did much care for hangings.

* * *

The last execution she could remember was shortly after her ninth birthday. It was a particularly dark period in her life. She had only just found out that she was to be betrothed to Prince Hayden. She'd also been at odds with Schobe, after the boy had called her a "freak." *I hate my strength. I hate my strength.* She'd been repeating those words all day as she sat on a half-log bench in the lower slums near his home, waiting for him to return from his squire's duties.

It was dusk, and the slums were aglow with activity. Dary and Ellacryse were running between the legs of adults who were either cooking, drinking, shouting, or laughing in the dusty streets. Trinity was watching the mischievous pair for Schobe's mother while she prepared supper over one of the open fire pits near their home. But she was really there for Schobe. She had to see him again and apologize in person for embarrassing him the way she did in front of Commander Kuza and the rest of the knights. Word had it the knight commander was still recovering from her infamous throw. And ever since, the squires—mostly Schobe—had been extra busy taking orders from the current knights in command. She'd been to visit with his family twice already, but both times it grew too late and she had to retreat back home before her aunt asked any questions. She was beginning to wonder if Schobe was purposely avoiding her.

Suddenly, she heard a great commotion coming from the center of the plaza. A woman in a torn green dress was screaming and running towards where the children were playing.

Trinity stood atop the bench so she could get a better view of what was happening. Two men chased her—big, loping, men who stumbled and laughed as they gave pursuit. The woman however did not appear to be in a joking mood, and Trinity saw one of the men remove a knife from his belt as the other grabbed onto the woman's arm and began tossing her around.

"Stop it!" Trinity yelled, but only one person overheard her above the growing crowd's excitement.

"You stay there, Princess," Schobe's mother told her, stepping before her and blocking her view. "None of that concerns you, my little lady. Those men are too dangerous."

"But they're going to hurt her," she said, trying to look past her.

"And you, if you try to interfere. They're drunk. Run home my sweet, and ask your grandfather to send us a knight here. Hurry."

When Trinity hadn't done as she was bid, Schobe's mother tried to lead her away with a surprising show of strength, but Trinity was stronger still. Trinity whipped out of reach of the woman's hand and ran closer to the commotion.

No one else tried to stop her as she approached the two men. Everyone either huddled up or had begun returning home quickly. *Cowards.* Why were they allowing this to happen? And why were these men trying to hurt this poor woman anyway? *I don't need a knight.* The only thing she did need was this cursed strength of hers.

"Stop it!" she repeated to the men, louder this time. They turned, finally noticing her.

The two of them stared at her with cold, glazed expressions for so long that she began to feel uncomfortable. One man had the shrieking woman pinned down on the road. The other man was holding the knife, which he now pointed at Trinity.

"Shut up girl," he spat at her. "Get out of here. This isn't your place."

"Leave her alone!" Trinity shouted, stepping closer. She was beginning to regret this bold move of hers, unarmed as she was.

"Didn't you hear me, you little brat? I'm going to carve you up unless you leave." The man stepped forward, knife thrust out before him.

Fear set in. It didn't matter to these men that she was a princess or a child. They would hurt her all the same. She wanted to run, despite the way her legs wobbled beneath her. But stubbornly, she stayed her ground and raised her trembling fists.

"I told you to...leave her—"

"Stop!" came a gruff bark from nearby. As quickly as day met night, another man had appeared in front of her. His heavy, puffed-out sweater smelled of fish and ocean salt. He nudged her back with his giant, callused hands and steadied himself in a weaponless, defensive stance.

"Guren," Trinity said, breathing easy again. She wanted to hug him, to hold his hand, *something*. Nothing felt right in the moment though.

"Stand back," he ordered.

"But Guren, you don't have a weapon. I can help you. I can—"

"Stand *back*," he repeated, sternly.

She did as she was told. She backed off and joined the edge of the watching crowds. The knife-wielding man slowed his drunken approach as he looked Guren over from head to foot. She knew he was sizing him up and looking for signs of a weapon.

"Piss off, Guren! This don't concern you, old fool."

"Guren?" the other drunken man asked, sounding shocked. He backed away from the pinned woman and struggled to his feet. "I didn't know Guren was going to be here. You didn't say nothing about Guren, Kury. I-I'm getting out of here."

"Shut your mouth," the first man, Kury, told him. "Stay here and help me fight off this old bother."

"N-no. Guren, I'm sorry, I didn't do nothing to her."

The woman in the ripped dress had already gotten to her feet and run off. Trinity was still focused on the man with the knife. He looked to be the more disturbed of the two, and she was afraid for her teacher. He must've just returned from a fishing trip. This, she imagined, was the reason he had come here so quickly, and without his weapons. Guren didn't appear phased by this disadvantage though. He stood confidently, hands steady, ready to strike, yet there was a calmness to him as well.

"I don't suppose the two of you will accompany me quietly to the dungeons," Guren said. "I've already sent word ahead. A garrison of knights will be here shortly."

The more scared of the two men began cowering. Kury, however, stepped forward again. "I ain't afraid of no has-been knight. Come on, and show me why they call you the gray lion," he mocked, before spitting at the ground near Guren's feet.

Kury charged forward and Guren spread out his feet, rooting himself to brace for the attack. Trinity gasped, stepping protectively towards her teacher before forcing herself to stop. *Don't distract him. He's got this.* Kury lunged the knife forward, but Guren smacked the man's wrist away with apparent ease. Clutching onto the drunk's throat, Guren threw his left foot behind the man's feet, sending him down onto his back hard. Guren reached down and plucked the knife from him, tucking it into his boot.

The other man had already begun to flee. Guren, still kneeling, looked up as if he was about to pursue, when Kury pulled from behind his back another knife. A short one, tucked back on his belt. He tried to jab it into Guren's ribs but the skilled knight blocked him with a quick hand. It was a false move, however, and Kury used the distraction to clasp onto Guren's boot and take possession of his first knife again.

Trinity's eyes grew wide with terror. There'd be no way Guren could stop an attack from so close. Kury spun the first knife skillfully in his hand, readying himself to stab through his opponent's leg, but Guren moved quicker. He broke Kury's grip on his second weapon and then fast as a blink scooped it up and slashed the knife across Kury's throat. Kury dropped the knife he was holding as blood spilled from his wound. Trinity heard a sound like air escaping a crevice. She shuddered.

True to Guren's word, the garrison arrived moments later. The knights took chase and were able to apprehend the other man who had been responsible for the attack. He was sent to be hung immediately, thanks to the testimony of many onlookers.

Guren left them to dispose of the other body. He came over and stood beside Trinity, his sweater and hands still covered in Kury's blood. What's more, he was shaking. He dropped to his knees and embraced her. As he held her in his arms, she could hear him begin to weep. He, who had led armies and killed countless warriors wept for this drunk named Kury. Up until now she had never heard a man cry. To be honest, she didn't even know that they could. She realized then that Guren must have hated killing more than anything.

* * *

Trinity reached the throne room tower with little difficulty, save for a few baffled stares by subjects still wondering if the attack was going on. A large squadron of knights were stationed around the area in front of the tower. They appeared to be standing watch only; no battle had fallen here. Strangely, there were so many knights here. She realized then that her grandfather and aunt must be inside.

"Princess?" Commander Kuza asked with a startled grunt upon seeing her run up to meet him. "There you are. We worried for you."

Trinity resisted the urge to roll her eyes. Even if her marriage to Hayden meant a great deal to the future of Hydlix, keeping her alive seemed like the least of Kuza's concerns. "Is my aunt in there?" she asked, noticing now that the big knight was wearing the breastplate she'd dented. *Don't giggle.*

Kuza's eyebrows raised. "*Yes.* They've been here the whole time during the Bayonick invasion. Where else would they be? The throne room is safest."

Bayonick invasion? So that's who was responsible. Her mind flashed to images of the refugees down at the beach earlier that morning. Was it possible that some of them had mounted this attack? They hadn't looked capable of using force. And Schobe had doubted the refugees were even from Bayonick. She didn't see weapons unloaded from their ships, but they may have been concealed. One thing was certain—whoever had started this whole thing must've been planning it for some time. How else could they have launched such an attack from within the kingdom?

"Many people died tonight," she said.

"Many of theirs. We lost few, Princess."

She narrowed her eyes at him. "Were there...orders—any orders, to take the royal family to the glass chapel?"

He peered at her, once more looking surprised by her question. "Chapel? Why would we take you to the chapel?"

"A knight tried to take me there. Said he was following urgent orders."

"Which knight said this to you?"

"...I never caught his name."

Why would Quatas have possibly tried to take her to the wrong place? She didn't need any convincing about which place was safer. But Quatas had seemed so sure. Something wasn't adding up. It was either Quatas or Kuza who was lying to her. And she didn't like either of her choices at the moment.

Just then she saw a gleam in the darkness, high overhead. It was right where the royal tower's battlement lay. There was something up there. *A weapon?* No, a figure, cloaked in the darkness of the night. The mysterious person only gazed down upon them, looking still as a statue.

"Who is that?" she asked.

Some of the knights turned their attention towards the skies. Kuza was still glaring at her, until some murmuring from his soldiers caused him to look at the figure overhead.

"What the—that's not one of ours. Men, look sharp!" he called out, as he readied his halberd in hand and refastened his silver helmet back on," I need four knights on the battlements immediately! Princess, we need to get you inside."

Trinity had no intention of going inside. Not when a possible answer was right there above her. She didn't know for sure if this mystery person was behind the attack, but they'd managed to scale the most secure building in Hydlix. *They have to know something.* Trinity leapt back several dozen feet and planned her jump. She was going to have to do this at a bit of a run.

"Don't you even think of it!" Kuza shouted. "You'll never make it. It's too dangerous."

"If you think you can stop me, why don't you go ahead?"

She dashed forward before the knight commander could respond. She slid to a crouched position and used her legs to push herself up high off the ground. She would have been lying to herself if she thought this jump would've worked the first try. Never before had she attempted such a feat with her strength. *Her strength.* Why couldn't they see her strength as something useful in a battle?

She knew for herself then. There was no question in her heart. As she sailed high through the night sky and watched the gawking men—and one outraged commander—below, she couldn't help but laugh aloud as the cool wind filled her lungs. *I would make an awesome knight.*

She hadn't expected to go sailing over the lone figure— who seemed to be watching her with a look of equal astonishment. Trinity's body eventually came rolling down hard onto the stone battlement. She could feel her knees scrape against the rough stone surface but she was able to stop herself from rolling off the tower, though just barely.

"What a *jump* that was," the watching one said, with a bizarre but lovely-sounding accent that Trinity had never heard before. Their voice sounded the way she would imagine a songbird's voice would sound if birds could converse. What's more, it was a woman's voice.

The cloaked bandit undid her hood. Her skin was bronze like the other bandits, and her hair came down in a fishtail-type braid beside her pointed chin. She looked several years older than Evita, maybe forty, and much stronger and scarier looking. Trinity could now see what was making the glimmer from before. A short, metal rod poked through the woman's long nose and rested on each of her painted cheeks. Both cheeks were painted with an array of colors. Gold, silver, red, blue, green, and yellow triangles seemed to shape her expression as if they were natural. But it was her gray and white eyes which shone brightest of all. Like two stars come together for all the world to see.

"I…" Trinity tried to say.

"You. Yes. Most splendid. I almost believed for a single second that you were a knight. Silly, no?"

Trinity had no trouble finding her words then. "How do you know I'm not a knight? Here to stop you and your army of bandits."

"Army?" The woman laughed. "No army. I only bring thirty-five men. Poor men. Stupid men. Untrained. Men to test your knights. And I must say little Princess, I am… *unimpressed.*"

"How—I'm not a princess. I'm a warrior, and I'm here to stop you." Though she realized what a foolish lie this was. Just like all those years ago with the two drunks, she had no weapons with her to back up these bold claims.

The bandit sucked on her teeth and walked in a wide, half-circle around Trinity, just out of range for an attack. "You do not look to be a knight. What do I see? Hmm. I see a rich girl's tunic. Bought in a shop, no? A boutique perhaps. Oh, and such pretty green hair. You washed yesterday. Lavender soap, yes?"

How did she know any of this? She wasn't sure the woman could smell anything with that metal rod fixed through her nose.

"And those boots. Very expensive, I'm sure. If I had more time to spare with you, little Princess, I'd take those boots right off your feet," she claimed with a snap.

Trinity peered down at the woman's boots. They were the same golden-type boots as the other bandits.

"Your boots are more valuable. Why would you want mine?"

"These old things? Hah! Do not be mistaken. They are nothing more than dolphin skins."

Dolphin skins? So, they really were from Bayonick. And apparently, these people had no trouble killing sacred animals.

"You would do well little Princess to jump right back to the safety of your men. Do you, perhaps, need a little push from me?"

"You try it and you'll be making a big mistake. Or maybe you forgot that I just jumped up here. From down there," Trinity said, jerking her head behind her. She didn't like how close to the ledge she was standing.

The woman's wry smile from before faded. "I might be scared of a strong princess. But you don't have weapons. And I do." She unfastened her cloak and unhooked a coiled instrument from her belt.

Trinity had never seen such a weapon before. It looked like a rope, but it had a thickness to its weight like leather and, as the bandit unfurled it, the end of the weapon dropped with a heavy thud onto the battlement's floor. She knew she should be scared, standing here, unable to defend herself. But her curiosity was growing.

"What sort of weapon is that?"

"Oh? You have never seen a whip? How fortunate. I assure you little one, they are worse than any blade." She reached up and lowered the collar of her cuirass. Three long, poorly-healed scars wrapped down the side of her neck. "A sword cuts through the skin. But a whip tears it from the body."

Trinity gulped. She was beginning to doubt the strength of her own skin. But just as the bandit began to draw closer, the sounds of footsteps could be heard close by, coming from the other side of the wooden canopy door on the stone ground. *The knights are here*, Trinity thought. She'd been able to stall the bandit long enough, or so she hoped.

The wooden door opened. Trinity's stomach sank as she watched Guren step up before them, alone, holding his drawn steel in hand. She hesitated to call out to him. The bandit woman stepped back towards the opposite edge of the tower.

"Ah, I see. What is a princess without her faithful knight, eh? I should've known a man would fight your battles."

"I *don't* need him," Trinity shot back. She stepped forward with a renewed confidence.

"Stand down," Guren growled at her, before he rushed towards the bandit with his blade tucked behind him.

But it was too late for either of them to make a difference. The bandit woman leapt back and fell from the opposite end of the tower. Trinity gasped. *Why would she throw herself from the tower?* She turned slowly to Guren, unsure what to say. His focus was elsewhere, studying the place where the bandit had jumped. His sword was still at the ready.

As she opened her mouth to speak a gust of wind quickly flooded the top of the battlement where they stood, drowning her out. Something below was causing a great wind to flare up between their legs. Trinity moved towards the source of the wind rising from the backside of the tower, but Guren raised a hand motioning her to stop. Before she could protest, a massive bird shot up from where the bandit had fallen. It was a brunet feathered, dome headed bird with pointed ears and snapping yellow talons. Huge white spots ran up the center of his pelt. And riding there on his neck was the burgundy-haired bandit woman clutching onto the bird's ruffled feathers, smiling smugly as if she'd planned this escape all along.

"Such a lovely kingdom this Hydlix," the bandit called to them. "Next time I come here I'll be sure to spend a day on your beaches, yes. I do so miss the water."

"How did you—" Trinity asked, unable to finish her thought.

The bandit scratched at one of the bird's pointed ears. "Hesper is very good at perching in the dark. And your knights are not very observant."

She'd aimed these words at Guren, but he said nothing.

"Why did you come?" Trinity asked. "Were you really here for the crown?"

"You ask a lot of questions, my little warrior princess. Be sure to fight your own battles next time, Trinity. How else will you ever learn?"

"Y—you know my name?"

"I know much about you. When next we meet, I hope you bring with you a sword. Cause I'll show you then, yes, why the whip is more...*dangerous.*"

She kicked the bird in the sides the way a rider would with their horse and the two of them flew off towards the black horizon. Trinity ran to the edge of the battlement and watched with her hands rooted atop one of the stone ledges. There was so much she wanted to know. So much she needed to know. But for now, all she could do was watch with the same look of fierce curiosity from before. *When next we meet?* What did she mean by that?

"A giant owl," Guren said, as he came and stood beside her and watched the same sight she was seeing. "I thought they were only stories. I've never seen one before."

She was surprised to hear him talking so casually to her. True, she always imagined his voice when reading the notes he left her, but this was different. She'd missed hearing him speak. For a second it felt like old times again, before she'd gotten her scar, and before he'd stopped teaching her face to face. This man hadn't said so much as a "good morning" to her in over a year.

She looked up at him. "…Guren?"

He scowled down at her. "That was quite stupid of you. Coming up here without a weapon. What were you thinking?"

Her fists clenched at her sides. "I could've handled myself. I didn't need you."

"No? You would've died believing that."

"Stop. I don't need a lecture. Especially not from you."

"You—don't you ever do something so foolish again. Do you understand me?"

"Or you'll do what? You don't get to tell me what to do, Guren. You're not my father!"

She could feel her face turning red. Seconds ago Guren's voice had comforted her. Now she was in a fury. Guren's face, however, had softened some. He dropped his scowl, looking as if he wanted to say something. Instead, he turned and left her standing there in the cold, waiting for his reply.

Evita was waiting for her down where the knights were gathered. Trinity believed there were apologies of all sorts that were being strained through her aunt's quivering lips, but she wasn't in the mood for listening. Not now. Today had been *such* a long day. She accepted Evita's weepy embrace and said nothing more for the rest of the night.

As the two of them walked back to their home, Trinity could see down into the lower plaza where folks had begun to gather around the gallows. Three men were hanging there from spindly ropes; their bodies were swaying in the cool night's wind.

"Best you don't look, dear," Evita said, cupping Trinity's face with a gentle hand. "Father's justice has found those awful men."

Yet Trinity still managed to glance back and see the dead men swinging. She wondered—though just for a second—if Guren had gone to attend the hanging. But then she remembered. Guren never did like hangings.

CHAPTER TEN

TOGETHER

There were several more drawn-out apologies from Evita over the next two weeks. Some were filled with tears, and others with presents. Trinity couldn't recall a time her aunt had ever put up so much of a fuss after an argument. Trinity was beginning to think Evita had accidentally stabbed her with how her aunt seemed to make a sobbing mess of herself over every meal as of late. It wasn't as if the strike she'd received had caused Trinity any real pain. More shock than anything. Evita was the one who had to wear a cloth bandage over her hand for three days after their shouting match near the courtyard. When people asked, Evita would tell them, "I hurt my hand hitting a brick wall."

The biggest problem came with how clingy Evita had become. Trinity was being checked upon in her room multiple times a day. Whenever she would try to go out, Evita always found some excuse to tag along. They ate every meal together. If Trinity tried to go and train early in the morning, Evita would be fully dressed and ready to accompany her, despite not knowing where she was going. She was beginning to think they'd somehow been sewn together.

Because of this, Trinity spent much of her free time in her room. She'd not even been to see Schobe in a week. The last time she checked in on him he was still recovering at home; his mother was doting on his every need. He'd never seemed happier. The word around the barracks was that Schobe had fought off a man twice his size. Some said he even ripped out the person's heart and bathed in the blood. Or maybe she had started that rumor. She couldn't be too sure anymore. There were lots of over-boasted stories lately about the night of the invasion.

Recently though, her time among the knights was always short. Evita would unfailingly find her with some pointless errand or shopping trip that Trinity was forced to endure. About the only time she could get away from her persistent aunt was when she was at home, lying in bed. It had gotten so bad that she'd taken to reading books, something she considered incredibly boring.

She'd also read her mother's letter about forty times since stealing it. She practically knew the words by heart:

My Evita,

We've been having a wonderful time of it here in the kingdom. Remember when we joked as children that we wouldn't marry a man unless he knew how to build a house with a slide? Well, I know you won't believe me, but there is the most wonderful slide here in Terkia. It goes all the way down into the quarry. I'm sure I've bothered most of the women fetching water in the river by now. To them I'm probably just that crazy Hydlixian woman who doesn't even know her own strength. I may as well not even be Terkian to them.

Oh, there is the most wonderful child here. Her name is Tricia. Ro and I are of course discussing children, but wouldn't it be wonderful to adopt? On several occasions, she has asked me if I could be her mother. Isn't that darling? Her green hair is absolutely gorgeous. You simply must meet her.

And that is why I write you. I know father is still angry about so much. I don't need to hear further lectures to know his feelings on the matter. But it's you I miss my love, my Evita. Mother's leaving still pains me greatly. And although I love it, being amongst my people...sometimes I've never felt so alone. I never knew I could miss someone so greatly. Evita, you remind me so much of her. I am jealous of you, because I will never have mother's beautiful hair. If you ever die- completely forbidden by the way-you must let me have your hair. Will it, and I will find you a husband. Although thirteen is too young. But you should see some of the men here. Don't tell RoRo I said that. He'd get so jealous, poor dear.

I write you to say this: You simply must come and visit! Be warned, if you do, I will never let you leave.

Ro asks about you often. I think you amused him with your report about gorillas that we found in our old studies box last time we were all in Hydlix. Remember? They are his favorite animal too.

He simply is wonderful Evita. I am so very lucky to have him.

I love you dearly, little one. Father never says it anymore, but I will never stop. Please come visit!

I await your reply. EAGERLY!!!
-Z

She sometimes couldn't read the last part of the letter without growing misty eyed. Her mother was so similar to herself—a fact she found strange yet comforting. She loved that Zepolia had an appreciation for slides, the same as her. The name Tricia reminded her of her own name. Oh, how she'd love to meet someone else with green hair. She also had no idea that her aunt Evita liked gorillas. Apparently, her father liked them too. *RoRo?* It sounded more like a nickname than a real one. To think her mother was so accepting of this man she'd been forced to marry. And how quickly Evita seemed to forget that Zepolia also had opinions about being too young to marry. Trinity wanted to remind her aunt of this, but knew there'd be no way to do so without revealing that she'd stolen the letter. She contemplated whether or not she should even return the letter, or the contents within the envelope.

The weighty object she'd felt inside the envelope before turned out to be a medallion, and it was a very strange one at that. For there on the palm-sized oval, plated in gold, was the chiseled etching of what looked to be a horn of some sort. Possibly a goat or cow, though it was longer than any she had ever seen on those animals before. The horn was held up by a single hand amidst a background of dark mountains, a full moon, and a gray river. At the tip of the horn there was blood. Green blood. Yet perhaps the oddest thing about this medallion was the name chiseled into the back. Near the bottom edge, one word: Trinity.

It belongs to me, she thought when first studying the medallion. But she knew she'd never be able to wear it without Evita catching her for sure. Even if she couldn't wear it though, there was something so calming about holding the medallion. The smooth plate on the back reminded her of water. She'd gotten into the habit of running her fingers along the etched shapes. *I wonder if Evita ever planned on giving it to me.*

Then there was the imprint. There was no doubt in her mind that it was her mother in the picture. But why was she holding two babies? It was impossible to tell the gender of the children by just looking; they both looked to be barely born. Both babes were swaddled in green blankets. She supposed the one on the right did sort of remind her of herself. Similar nose. She hated not having any imprints from when she was that age to compare. Who was the baby on the left? Another girl...or a boy?

She had heard of twins. A woman in the lower districts had given birth to a pair of boys only two years earlier. She wondered though if having a girl and a boy was a possibility with twins. It seemed unbelievable. She thought twins were supposed to look the same after all. Trinity would scrutinize over the imprint every night before tucking it under her pillow and falling asleep. She wouldn't be satisfied with guessing anymore. *Discover your own answers. Discover your own answers.*

"Where are you going?" Evita asked her, early one morning. She was already sitting on the pillowed bench in their main hall, dressed and ready for her day.

"...I have to go see a person in town. Alone...Mam."

Evita's eyebrows cocked. "Alone? What*ever* for?"

"They have something. A gift I wanted to get you. For your birthday. I was going to give it to you at grandfather's ball, but if you'd prefer that I tell you now—"

"No, no. I—suppose you do need to do that on your own. Straight back though. I've a busy day ahead of us. We still haven't picked out your gown for the ball."

Had her aunt actually bought into the lie she told? Why didn't she think of this sooner?

"Yes Mam," Trinity said, sounding more chipper than she'd intended. "I'll hurry back at once."

"Smart girl. You may as well get some of those jelly turtles for us. The ones you're always going on about. Here, I'll give you some stekis."

Privacy *and* breakfast? This was too good to be true.

After devouring three of the jelly-filled treats for herself later that morning, she was satisfied with bringing her aunt back one and a half turtles. *Half?* Her aunt would never eat the half. She could give it to someone. *Oh, it's still warm to the touch.* It would have been a shame after all to let such a treat go cold. There was no telling how long she would be out.

Trinity knocked on the door of a home belonging to a Mrs. Imelda Nask. She straightened her dress and brushed off the sugary flakes on her lips from the fourth turtle she'd just inhaled. She had never met Mrs. Nask and didn't want to start off with a bad impression. She was wondering if there was still jelly on her face when a robust, baggy-eyed woman filled the threshold, looking as if she hadn't slept in days.

"H...hi," Trinity said, feeling suddenly speechless.

"Hi yourself. What do you—oh, you're the princess aren't you?" The woman's face softened, but she broke into a very long yawn. "You're Princess Evita's cousin, or something like that?"

"Her niece, actually. Mrs. Nask, I was just wondering if I might ask you some questions."

Mrs. Nask looked taken aback. "Questions? The king is sending the princess to ask me some questions now, is that right? *Well,* I should feel right honored to have royalty enter my home, and on such short notice no less." Her tone sounded anything but honored in that moment.

Trinity shook her head. "No, Mam. The king didn't ask me to come here. I came because I had questions."

Mrs. Nask stood at the entryway for a few seconds sizing Trinity up. "…Are you selling something?"

"No." She scrunched her face. "Is that something people do?"

Mrs. Nask broke into a boisterous laugh. "Oh, MAI's sakes, dearie. You are as precious as they come, aren't you?" She cleared a path. "Well, step in. May as well. It's rude to refuse a princess, after all. Oh, and do mind the clutter, dearie. Had I known I were to be visited by royalty today, I'd have started cleaning last week."

Trinity entered the home. Mrs. Nask was not joking about needing a week to tidy up. There was a "positive mess," as her aunt would say, within the dim little house. Wooden toys were scattered all across the floor. Bits of food—both solid and splattered—were strewn across the walls and furniture. Linens were being folded in the center of the kitchen table, but there was still a mountain of clothing left to be tended to. Mrs. Nask pulled up two wooden chairs for the two of them to sit upon.

Mrs. Nask sat down and matted out the wrinkles in her dress. "Now then, what can I do for you, Princess? I'd curtsy, but my poor left knee would never forgive me."

"Yes," Trinity said, taking the offered seat. "Sorry for showing up unexpectedly. I just—I didn't know who else to ask."

"The questions, right. For me?"

"It's about your boys. The twins."

"Oh?" Mrs. Nask's face livened. "The king is interested in my boys? But he's recruiting sort of young, isn't he?"

"No," she said, stifling a laugh. "I'm not here to recruit them. I'm here to ask about them. Twins. Do they, I guess what I want to say is…how are they different from having only one baby?"

"Well, there's two of them, isn't there? Twice the mess."

"No, that's not what I mean." She didn't know how exactly to phrase the question in her head. She was beginning to wonder why she had even come here.

Mrs. Nask licked at her lips. "Can I get you a drink, dearie?"

"No, thank you."

"Nonsense! If I'm to entertain royalty, I'd best do so with style."

Mrs. Nask heaved herself off of the chair and walked through the clutter to her kitchen. She came back only a moment later with two large, wooden goblets; each were filled with a sloshing liquid.

"I usually have my evening wine in these. After the little'uns have gone to bed. We're in luck this morning, they've chosen to sleep in. Maybe I can get started on a little housework."

She handed Trinity the goblet. Trinity didn't even want to think about how clean the cup was. She took a small sip. *Water?* At least, she hoped it was water. Whatever it was, she began to feel calmer. She took another small sip, and then placed the goblet on her lap.

"Your twins, Mrs. Nask. Are they very close?"

"I should think so. Spend every moment together. Eat together. Make trouble together. Practically the same person. But then again, they are still very young."

Trinity took a deep breath. She touched at the scar on her arm as her eyes grew wide; the memories of her mysterious bouts of pain were coming back to her. "Do they ever feel things…together?"

Mrs. Nask looked to ponder her words. "Are you asking me if they can read one another's minds or something?

How would I know? They've only been two since last month."

"Oh. Yes, that makes sense." She sunk into her chair. *I knew this was foolish to ask.*

Mrs. Nask stretched back and scratched at her chin. "Now that you mention it though, there is something sort of weird that happened the other day." She leaned in close. Trinity could smell mint leaves on her breath. "Last week, my Keist, well he's the oldest by a minute, ran right into my table. Just smacked his head like that," she said, clapping her hands together. "Jost was in the other room, playing toys with his father. I swear to you, on the white lion himself, Jost started crying as if it were he who'd smacked himself on the table."

"Really?"

"Yes. His father came running in not knowing what he'd done wrong. I had to go and comfort all three of them. Guess they've always sort of been that way though, the boys. Whenever one is upset, then so is the other. And they both get so worked up on the giggles too. Practically the same," she repeated.

"Giggles," Trinity said, speaking aloud her thoughts. If giggles had been her only trouble, then she wouldn't be sitting here having this conversation.

There was a sound coming from the next room like a soft parade of rapid drum beats ringing through the floor. Trinity looked to see the two boys standing at the open door of their bedroom. They really were a pair to behold. They were the same height, same little bellies hanging out from their shirts, and both had the most adorable smiles Trinity had ever seen. They scampered over to Mrs. Nask together and she scooped them up in her arms and kissed each one on the cheeks.

"There's my boys," she said, sounding proud. "The Princess here has been asking all about you. You'll be good brave knights for her someday, won't you?"

"Knight," said one.

"Knigh," the other mimicked incorrectly.

The two dark-eyed boys stared at Trinity. They couldn't take their eyes off of her hair. She stood up and knelt beside them. One of the twins reached forward and grabbed onto one of her green curls. The other quickly followed the example.

"Careful dearie, they're getting to be plenty strong."

"I'll be fine, Mam," Trinity said, smiling back at the children. "They're so cute. And you're right. They do look so alike."

"Cute? Did you hear that boys? You've just been given a royal compliment. Best you mind your manners. Say thank you."

"Danku."

"Danku."

"Just like I told you dearie, one in the same. They're very lucky. To have one another. Share in each other's joys and pains. Together."

"...Together," Trinity repeated, as her smile left her.

* * *

Her fascination with twins had started about ten days earlier, just a few days after the bandit strike on her kingdom.

All of Hydlix had grown tense after the attack. People were staying indoors; shops were closing early. Even her grandfather would spend their family suppers griping to Commander Kuza about reinforcing security. Food would usually be flying from his mouth as he did. The knight commander would just stand there, taking the king's spit-filled orders, and then make a brief salute or bow before offering his own quiet suggestions. Most of the time he discussed strategy, or knight postings for the evening. Trinity couldn't help feeling a little impressed by some of Kuza's strategies. She still had her suspicions about the man, and still snickered a little every time she saw his dented armor, but his forces had managed to shut down the bandit strike quickly.

Still, there was something more sinister going on here. Everything about the bandit strike had been too random and unexpected. There had been no strange people in the streets that day, and no reports of anyone suspicious on the roads leading to Hydlix prior to the attack. But there had to be someone who knew about the strike before it happened. *Someone.*

"I already told you," Quatas said, sitting back on the barrel he was resting half of his rump on, "I heard a false report. One of the older knights had told me to go and fetch you. I thought it a little strange too that I was supposed to take you to the chapel. It's made of glass mostly and hangs over a cliffside. Too dangerous."

Trinity looked down and studied the King's Circle game board set out in front of her. Her handmaiden piece was already in possession of the newborn prince piece and she was close enough to the center space to smell victory. She peered up at Quatas, still somewhat surprised that he agreed to play the game with her. She had managed to sneak down to the barracks tonight—without her tagalong aunt—by refusing dessert after supper. To her even greater surprise, Evita had agreed to let her leave the banquet hall without her. Though Trinity hated missing out on the chocolate cake they were to have, she had far more pressing matters down in the barracks with Quatas. Simply put, they were matters she could no longer ignore.

"And you don't remember who gave you these orders?" she asked him, conversationally. She was trying her best to hide any tone of an accusation.

"Our helmets were on. And it was nighttime. Sorry, but like I told you before, I don't remember."

"You sure were trying to get me there in a hurry," she said.

"I had to. We were under attack. I wasn't about to go and disobey orders when I saw you there running around, confused."

Besides his harsh words when he had been on guard duty at the dungeon, Trinity had never had any reason to doubt Quatas before. Next to Schobe, he was one of the few knights in the kingdom who never seemed to mind her presence. Even now, as they sat on the barrels playing their game on one of the wooden overlooks in the barracks—which rested above the dusty training grounds—she could hear agitated whispers coming from the knights below.

"What's their problem?" she asked, focusing on the game board.

"Don't mind them. I think they're all still a little jealous of the jump you made up here. Did you really make it to the top of the battlement in one leap?"

Trinity couldn't keep herself from grinning. "I could've jumped higher."

Quatas returned the grin. "Now, there's no reason to go getting so full of yourself."

"Just thought you should know," she said, sounding pleased.

"Oh MAI. Strong and pretty." He leaned in, tilting his head. "You're quite the handful, aren't you Trin?"

She fidgeted atop the barrel. "...What do you mean?"

"A guy could get into real *trouble* on account of you."

She could feel her cheeks growing hot. Still, she was unsure if he was putting her down again or trying to flirt with her. There was something so wrong about the way he had said the word *trouble*. And it was just as jarring as the time he called her cute by the dungeons. *Why is he talking to me that way?* Quatas was practically a man's age. And even though she loathed the idea of having to marry Prince Hayden, Quatas knew of her engagement the same as everyone else. Yet, here he was talking to her as if she wasn't three years younger than him but someone who he was actually interested in. As if she wasn't just... *somebody else's maiden.*

"You shouldn't say things like that," she told him, looking away. "If my aunt, or the king heard you say—"

"They would get angry at me for giving the princess a compliment? Really?"

She hesitated. "No. I guess not."

She tried again to ignore everything but the circular game board. It was then she noticed the unfortunate move Quatas had made on his last turn. He brought one of his single remaining knight pieces down three squares. But there was no way he would catch her prince piece before the game ended.

"I see you messed up there. Is that truly the best you could do?" she asked, pointing at the little carved figure of the horse.

Quatas smirked. "Tell me. Why do I play this stupid game with you again? Ain't uh, your boyfriend Schobe much better at losing to you?"

"Don't talk badly about Schobe. And he's not my boyfriend. He's—only my friend," she said, feeling slight relief at the change of subject.

"*Right.* Cause I heard a little rumor that he was asking you to the king's ball."

"You did?"

"Ah, I thought that might perk you up." He shrugged his shoulders. "Only a rumor really. Course, I've been meaning to go and have some words with him. Don't much care for the way he spoke to me during the invasion. Especially because I was only—"

"Following orders?"

"…Precisely."

Trinity glared at him. "If you hurt him Quatas, I'll stomp your face in." She was only half joking.

"Temper, temper Princess." He sat back further on his barrel and folded his arms. "I only said have words. No one is going to hurt your precious boyfriend."

Trinity made no reply.

"Say, ain't it past your bedtime anyway? I don't want your aunt poking her nose in here again asking for you."

She rolled her eyes. "I was just leaving. But I have to beat you first."

"Get on with it."

"Hey, don't be angry just because I'm a better King's Circle player," she said, taking hold of her piece.

Quatas sighed, grimacing at the board. "You're a better jumper. That's all."

"Speaking of jumps—"

She held the prince piece dramatically up above her head. She was just about to place it in the center and win the game when the familiar sensation of pain struck her unexpectedly again. She dropped the piece and clutched onto her knees as her face began to scrunch up. Tears— those same mysterious tears from before—began to flow. Quatas jumped up and ran over to her.

"Trinity? Trinity?"

She started to scream. The pain this time was happening again in her chest. Only it felt harsher than the time before with the busted bow. More constricting. She was having difficulty breathing.

"Trinity?!" His shout sounded muffled.

He tried to help her to her feet, but her body wrenched away from him. She heard a snap. She realized that she had broken through one of the wooden railings on the overlook. Her body plummeted some twenty feet below before hitting the dirt floor of the barracks. But she didn't feel any pain from this. The real pain was still happening within. The tears were endless. She felt as if her heart were beating so strongly that she could hold it within her hands as it pounded through her chest. And then everything started to go dark.

She was seeing someone then, in the dark plains of her mind's eye. They were fuzzy at first, but grew clearer. It was a woman. At least, she believed it to be a woman. They were wearing a dress, tattered and aqua, but their hair was cut so short that it rose above her ears. And their hair was blue. *A blue-haired woman?* She was laying in the ground in some giant dug hole. Her face was covered in blood, as was the rest of her. But it wasn't red blood like she'd sometimes seen the knights produce after intense training bouts. This blood was a dark gray with shades of green and red flowing throughout. It was blood like Trinity's own. *Terkian blood?* The woman lay still as tears of tri-colored blood dripped down her cheeks. Her eyes seemed to be staring vacantly at Trinity. They were haunting, yet very distant.

Trinity writhed in the dirt for what felt like an eternity. But as her emotions began to settle—and the tears stopped running—her focus returned to her. The girl from her vision had gone. Now she could hear a commotion coming from the blurry knights who had gathered around her. Even Quatas had climbed down from the tower and joined them. The knights started moving aside. Quatas turned and saluted at whoever just showed up. Trinity squinted to see who he was addressing. She didn't have to wonder for long though. The dust had already begun clasping onto the skirt of her aunt's long, pearl dress.

"Trinity!" Evita shrieked.

* * *

The aqueduct. The bow. The King's Circle game. She knew without a doubt that all of these incidents were related. These emotions and pains she felt were very real, even if they weren't entirely her own. She had left Mrs. Nask's home later that morning and gone to the beachside alone. As she sat at the snow-covered cove watching the calm waves embrace the jagged stones along the sands, all she could think about was the imprint. Of her blue-eyed mother. Of herself as an infant. And...the other baby. *The other baby. Twins.* Was it possible? Was she sharing emotions with her twin? Was the other baby the reason why her aunt never spoke of the night she was born? Why had her aunt only saved her? Yet, there was one question that surpassed all others. If the other baby had died, then why was she still having these intense emotions? *Are they still alive?*

She watched as a fishing boat sailed out along the horizon. It was heading back to shore. When she was younger, Trinity would ride in these boats with Guren and help him pull up the nets. There was no greater sound in all of the Remsphere, she believed, than the sound of a full net of fish flopping out onto a boat's bottom. The fish would whack their scaly tales against the wooden deck, composing a rhythmic beat that made her smile every time she heard it, despite the smell.

Someone stepped out from the hull below and onto the deck. She couldn't see them well at first until she shielded her eyes from the sun. Then, they became as clear as the ocean. *Guren?* The old knight had emerged and was resting his hands on the boat's railings as he stared out across the harbor. He didn't see her, or he was choosing not to look at her. This seemed the more likely option. *Guren.* She had called him so many horrible names in her head in the past two weeks since their encounter atop the battlement. Yet here, sitting frozen on her snowy rock, she yearned for him to look at her. Speak with her. *Guren.* He would know the answers. He would know about the other baby. *I have to ask him!* She knew he'd been avoiding her for some time, making excuses, but this was the chance she'd been waiting for. *An answer.* Maybe he'd even know something about the bloody, blue-haired woman she saw that night. She was sure of it. She crunched the snow beneath her icy fingers and pushed herself to her feet. She was really going to do it. She was really going to brave the deadly cold waters. Until…

An unknown woman stepped out from the hull and stood beside Guren. She was beautiful, and walked as if she were gliding. Her dress was long and flowing and her skin dark and shiny against the reflection of the wintry sea. She wrapped her arms around the big knight's waist, and rested her head on his shoulder. He turned and embraced her.

None of this makes any sense, Trinity thought. But as she watched them standing there, holding one another, the realization became impossible to ignore. This woman was the reason behind all of Guren's secrets. The lies. The absence in her life. *Why wouldn't he tell me that he had a wife?* She wouldn't have cared. She might have even been happy for him. Seeing them together though—in secret like this—gave her a sick feeling in the pit of her stomach. It was proof that Guren no longer wanted anything to do with training the annoying little Terkian girl. All of these years she'd looked up to him, respected him, and regretfully even loved him like a father. But Guren, it would seem, didn't care about her at all. He'd successfully pushed her away and didn't even have enough honor to be truthful with her. Hot tears pressed at her eyes. She stood hesitantly, her boots crunching down further into the snow.

She had to get away. Be somewhere else. Anywhere. *Home?* No, she couldn't return home. She was certain Evita was already irritated with her after having been out for as long as she had been that morning. *Schobe?* Not Schobe. Not when she felt this way. And what way was she feeling? She didn't entirely know.

A man like Guren was at perfect liberty to be with someone, though the woman did look rather young compared to him. And Guren was more than allowed to be out on his boat, though fishing seemed to be the last thing on his mind. And why should she—the girl who trained for years to be a knight until her tough skin started to ache, until her tears became one with her sweat, until she shot every last bloody target in her tower with her eyes closed...*except one*—why should she care about any of this? About him? Up until now, this man had been nothing but a miserable remnant of her past which refused to go away. A gnawing memory of—she supposed—a happier time. It had been a time when she could run outside of her home with her hair in a mess. A time of breeches and ocean swimming and falling to sleep beside warm, comfortable fires. They were the moments when she sought more than anything for Guren's gentle, approving nod, or the four words he so rarely spoke to her: "Well done, my girl." She hated thinking of those times, but not as much as she hated thinking about the man connected to them all.

And it would seem Guren had already forgotten about those times. He'd already moved on to a new life. A life without her.

Trinity stomped swiftly back through the streets; the snow was still wet on her dress. She ignored the passing comments and greetings. Even Ellacryse's high-pitched "Hello!" was dismissed. Trinity kept moving forward, not really knowing where she was going. Not wanting to be anywhere, but here least of all. She found herself at the mailing tower. *Should I train?* Of all the doubts swirling inside of her, training seemed to be the most comforting notion.

She bounded up to the roof. It had been weeks since she'd come here. The snow was heavy up here. Every step she took produced a loud, crackling thud. The window was frozen shut. *No!*

There'd be no way in unless she broke the latch. But then they'd know. Everyone would know. About the training. About Guren. *Guren.* In her teary-eyed frustration, she stomped down on the snowy roof. Her boot caught a slippery step. It was a weather-torn tile. She upended and went sliding off of the roof. She screamed for all the world to hear as she hurtled down hundreds of feet below while the *weight* of her own world was still heavy upon her.

CHAPTER ELEVEN

THE GIFT

The next thing Trinity knew she'd become enveloped in a world of unfamiliar darkness. The tower, the people, and all of Hydlix had disappeared. She'd stopped falling now, but she had not risen. It was difficult to know whether she was asleep or awake. There was a coldness to this world, like winter, yet her body felt weightless as if she were still plummeting. But when she tried to stand, both of her feet took on the weight of a million pounds each, or so she believed. Even with her strength, they were impossible to move. All she could do was sit up, now realizing that she was stuck in a field of crusted grass and windless breezes beneath pitch-black skies.

She tried scooping her legs up with the help of her arms. "Move!" she ordered her disobedient legs. "Get up!"

There was something strange about her words though. It was if they weren't there, like they were still trapped behind her closed mouth. "Why am I not strong enough to move?" Again, the words had never left her mouth even though she was convinced of saying them. *Why am I not strong enough?* She was *very* strong. She was a Terkian after all. *Terkian?* Isn't that what Hayden called her? *A stupid, filthy Terkian.*

There in the darkness someone rose against the dry fields. They were difficult to see at first, but as they strutted closer to her, Trinity recognized them immediately. Her heart felt frozen in her chest. *Prince Hayden?!* The arrogant prince was exactly as Trinity remembered him. He walked with a noxious air of nobility, looking down upon her as if he were king of all Taercion. His ugly waves of pinkish-red hair bounced against his round, unnerving face. His smile—*that disgusting smile*—made Trinity's hair stand on end. His lone snaggletooth remained, causing his breath to whistle with every laugh. Oh, how he was laughing. He had been laughing ever since the first time he saw her with those vexing eyes of his. Those twisted, powerful eyes. *Red. Like a demon?* No. She was imagining red. No one has red eyes. They were blue, and such a blue. Those eyes were like ice. Perhaps it was only fitting that every time he stared at her she felt like she was frozen by his eyes.

Blue eyes. Mother had blue eyes.

Mother had twins. Evita knew the whole time. *Why?* Why wouldn't her aunt say anything about the other baby? Evita came then and stood shoulder to shoulder with Hayden. At least she thought it was Evita. She had the same stunning, dark skin that Trinity was envious of. And she had those flowing dreadlocks which made Trinity resent her tangled curls. Yet, Evita's face had changed.

The unpoised smile remained but her eyes were missing. They were replaced with money. They'd become two thin flakes of golden stekis, hardly enough to buy a new dress. But then when had that ever stopped Evita from asking for more money? Trinity's aunt didn't need a new dress though. The one Evita was wearing was glowing like a white ruby in the field of nothing. Nothing would, or could, shine brighter. Or so Trinity told herself. Before something—*someone*—started shining brighter. *There. Behind Evita.* Another woman stepped forward. Her face was glowing a fiercer white than the dress.

The glowing woman cackled. It was an unsettling, high-pitched cackle. She carried with her a net. *Fishing nets?* Was she only there to help Guren? *Was she only a friend?*

Guren was there now beside the woman, shaking his head, as if he'd heard Trinity's inner question. He held onto the glowing woman's shoulders and began kissing her on the neck, then her cheek, and soon he was kissing her on the lips. Both of their faces were glowing now. *Guren!* Why wasn't her voice working? *Guren!*

All she could muster were thoughts...very loud thoughts. Those watching her could apparently hear them too. They must've, for they all began to step closer. In each of their hands were more nets. The glowing woman's net had extended out to where everyone had a grasp now. They circled Trinity. She still couldn't force herself to move. *Please don't!* she thought. Heavy tears began to fall from her eyes. She could feel her face sinking in, and her cheeks being crushed, as if she were submerged in her sadness. *Why are these tears so heavy?*

Then, they were upon her. The net bound her. *Please!* She was scooped up and brought to the place directly behind her. A wooden set of gallows had been constructed with only one rope. She knew who the rope was for even before they began to hoist her up the stairs. *Stop it. Stop it!* She was brought to her feet. They still wouldn't move for her. *Move! Run!*

Guren himself was the one who placed the rope around her neck as Evita tucked Trinity's hair back. *Why are you doing this?* Her aunt only smiled, as if she understood the weakened thought. *Please Aunt E! Please don't let them kill me.* Evita and Guren stepped aside. Everyone else had departed also. They weren't even going to watch.

Trinity looked down desperately from the gallows, searching for help. Instead, she saw a lone woman standing there now, watching her, and crying. Trinity had only seen this person once before, in a vision. *When did she get here?* It was the blue-haired woman, her clothes still ragged and stained with blood. Her body seemed to be filled with broken bones, and her neck looked to be snapped. Had she been hung too? *Who are you? Can you hear me?*

A sound of clanging armor and heavy bootsteps rose from the side of the gallows. Trinity turned her head as best as she could until she could see who was stepping up to spring the lever. A man dressed in Hydlixian armor stood there. There was a dent on his breastplate.

Kuza? Commander Kuza, please don't!

His breathing grew heavy as his eyes pierced through her like arrows. She watched him grip the lever. The rope felt like it was burning around her neck.

"I sentence you to die, Princess," he said, with a triumphant air in his voice.

She could feel the floor release from below her. She started plummeting again. A feeling of weightlessness filled her for what seemed like minutes. When would it end? When would she feel the snap of death? She couldn't scream or struggle. All she could do was watch as the ground and empty field disappeared before her. In its place was more darkness. And there in the darkness came a figure of a familiar white lion charging towards her with hunger in its eyes. *Snowflake?* Her secret lion friend approached, baring his fangs. They grew to the size of her body. This was no friend. She could feel herself being devoured whole. She tried once more to scream out.

Her breath came to her all at once as she sat up in her bed. It felt like the same long breath she'd taken that time before when she almost didn't resurface from the ocean. The rope was gone. Her lion was too. She was back. Back from whatever cruel hell she'd dreamt of.

"Trinity!"

"Trin!"

Evita was sitting beside her, but she threw herself upon Trinity as she struggled awake. There was a heavy, sticky warmth between them, like there was something coating her skin. She leaned back and saw her body covered in blood. Her linens were stained too. The blood was not red. It was the same color as the crying woman in her dream—dark gray with traces of green and red—and she recognized it at once. *Terkian blood? Why am I bleeding?* She didn't feel any pain in her body, or tightness around her neck anymore, but she did lift her blanket to check her legs, fearing the worst. Both legs wiggled comfortably beneath her blankets. She took a deep sigh of relief.

She looked around her room. Schobe was there, standing just over her aunt's shoulder. His armor was stained with gray blood as well. His eyes were swollen and puffy as if he'd been crying. He looked too nervous to step forward.

"You had quite a fall, young lady," came another man's booming voice in the room. Trinity turned to see a thin-haired man in a brown, blood-spattered cloak. "We were beginning to wonder if you were ever going to wake up," he said, tipping his glasses to her.

"Doctor Mokin," Evita said, as she released her grip on Trinity and turned to face him, "is she going to be alright? Should I bring her in for a further examination?"

"Now, I don't much see the good in that. The fact that she can sit up on her own after falling from that height is astounding. That's twice this blood of yours has saved you from a fall, or so I've heard."

"...Yes," Trinity said, dryly.

"Any pain?" he asked.

She shook her head slowly, not wanting to speak again. In truth though, her head did feel a little tender after the fall. Evita handed her a cup of water. Trinity drank. She could feel the dried blood in her mouth also.

"Even still, I'd recommend keeping her in bed for a while. Away from any battlements or rooftops," he said, laughing. "Bring her in soon for a follow-up."

"I *assure* you," Evita said, in a scary tone, "she won't be anywhere near a roof in the future."

"If you say so." Mokin turned to leave. "Oh, and be sure to thank the knight here. If he hadn't turned the princess over when he found her, she'd have probably drowned on her own blood." He slapped Schobe on his metal arm and then grabbed his hat and left the room.

"You found me, Schobe?" Trinity asked, ignoring the death glare her aunt was giving her.

"You fell right outside our home. Crashed right down onto the street. You left a big hole again. N-nobody thought you were going to survive. Ella and Dary will be happy to hear you're alright. Mom too. Though I'm sure she's going to be plenty mad at you for giving us all a scare."

"That makes two of us," Evita said.

"I'm so sorry, Aunt E," Trinity said. "I didn't mean to worry you."

"What in MAI's name were you thinking, child? Why did you climb up that dangerous tower?"

"I just...I had to check something."

"Check *something*?"

Trinity nodded. "Yes. It was stupid. I know I shouldn't have gone up there. I wasn't in my right mind." Her eyes scanned the room. She smiled halfheartedly at her aunt. "Guess I lost your baked turtle too."

Evita's eyes grew even more livid. "Trinity—I don't care about some baked good!" she exclaimed. "You *lied* to me. You endangered your own life. They said you fell right on your head. All the way from the top of the mail tower. And for what? Hmm? I just can't believe you would do something so—"

Trinity scrunched her eyes closed. "So damn foolish?"

"Watch it," Evita warned. "You are in enough trouble as is."

"I know," she said, slumping her shoulders. "Look, I said I was sorry. And I am. But it's like I told you. I had to check something."

Evita said nothing more, though she still looked plenty angry. She balled her fists and stood up. She began pacing in short huffing strides across the room, not walking a clear path. Her aunt appeared to want to say a great many things to her, but Evita amazingly kept herself calm and silent. Trinity didn't know if she should cower or feel grateful that Evita wasn't on the rampage that she'd expected her to have. Trinity pulled the bloody blankets up to her chin. Evita grimaced and then resignedly walked over to where Schobe stood and gave him a light thwack on his breastplate.

"And you," she began firmly, "I suppose I do owe you my thanks, Schobe. Sir Schobe, I ought to be saying. For saving my hard-headed niece's life. Though why she ever had to be saved in the first place—I'll never understand."

"A-anytime," Schobe sputtered.

"I'll be sure to tell Father and Commander Kuza about your quick actions." She turned back, peering at Trinity out of the corner of her eye. "Will you—" she took a deep, calming breath. "Will you be alright if I leave for a little while? I'll have the handmaidens check in on you, but there's something I urgently need to take care of."

Trinity gulped. "I—yes." She weighed her aunt's words, trying to decide if waiting was a good thing or bad thing.

Evita's scowl lessened. "You need to rest. Get some more sleep. I don't imagine I'll be long. But don't you set a *single* toe out of this room until I return. Am I understood?"

"Yes Mam." Trinity couldn't argue with this demand. Something in Evita's all too calm demeanor suggested that the woman wasn't above chopping off feet as a form of punishment.

"Then I'll be back." Evita placed her hand on Schobe's shoulder. "Don't you go staying too long either. She does need her rest."

"I-I'll only stay a minute," Schobe said.

Evita leaned into his ear and whispered something which Trinity couldn't hear. Schobe's eyes widened and his mouth gaped. Evita pulled away from him.

"I mean it. Only a minute," she said.

"Yes Mam, uh, Princess. Very short. Time, that is. That I, uh, will be here."

Evita left them, though Trinity could hear from the other room that she was giving her handmaidens an earful. Trinity still couldn't decide if this was actually happening, or if she was still dreaming. She was alive. She had survived her fall with no injury again, save for the blood.

She had once woken in her own blood before, much to her shock and horror. Evita had been the voice of comfort on that day though. She explained to Trinity about why her blood was a similar color to Zepolia's. She also went on—for several, lengthy hours—about how Trinity was growing into a woman and would soon be able to make little princes and princesses for Hayden. The sick feeling in Trinity's stomach that morning only intensified upon hearing this. *I don't want to have his anything.*

Schobe—who had still been standing patiently in her doorway—stepped forward with caution. Trinity motioned for him to join her where Evita had been sitting, but Schobe remained standing.

"...Hi," he said.

"Hi," she said.

"Are you feeling alright?

"My head sort of hurts."

"Yes, I can imagine."

"What happened exactly?"

Schobe folded his arms. His eyes weren't on her, but instead on the bloody sheets. "Well, I think everyone knew it was you who fell. We didn't see you on the tower, but we could all hear you screaming. I saw you while I was stopping in to see Mom for lunch. Trinity—I thought you were dead. You weren't breathing. When you started breathing you were coughing up blood. Lots of blood. I had to keep your face down. I'm sorry, but you ruined your dress."

Trinity snorted in appreciation. Smiling, she reached out and grabbed his gauntleted hands into her own. "I don't care about some stupid dress. You saved my life, Schobe. Thank you."

"You saved mine last time. Remember the aqueduct?"

"Not so well, honestly. Only bits."

"Hmm. Well, if I had tough skin like you, I wouldn't even wear armor. It's too heavy."

Trinity showed him the scar on her arm. "It's not that tough. I don't know how I keep surviving."

Schobe traced her scar with his fingertips. "Hard to believe anything could hurt you. I really didn't want to believe that all of that blood was yours." He bowed his head. "On my honor as a knight, I swear I won't let any harm come to you again, Princess."

"*Schobey*. You know I hate formalities."

"Alright, fine. On my honor as...your friend. Happy?"

"Very."

Schobe heaved a great sigh and took a knee by her bedside. "Please don't ever do something so reckless again." He tucked a piece of her blood-crusted hair behind one of her ears. "I know you like to train there. The tower. But it's too dangerous with all the snow."

"I'll have to use the door next time, won't I?"

He rolled his eyes. "May I ask you something? Something I've always wondered about, ever since we first met." He met her gaze. There was an earnestness to his expression, and a softness that made her feel so comfortable around him. "Trinity, why do you want to be a knight?"

She was surprised by his question and didn't have an answer immediately prepared, but she wouldn't dare let him know it. Instead, she snickered, puffed herself up, and gave Schobe the biggest grin. "Guess I'm just really great at protecting people," she said in a tough sounding voice, tapping a finger on Schobe's armor.

"*Right*," he said, skeptically. "No doubts you are good. And I'm certain you'd make a better knight than most. But how about you tell me the *real* reason?"

She bit her lip. "Well, uh…I've been told I'm pretty strong."

Schobe narrowed his eyes. "You're pretty on a lot of things. Like being stubborn."

"Am not."

"Honestly, if I could be half as stubborn as you, I'd have my pick of positions. Maybe a guard who protects the royal library or something."

Now it was Trinity's turn to roll her eyes. "You have the most boring dreams of anyone I know."

"Maybe," he said. "But they're my dreams. The same as you have your dreams."

"My dreams?" Her dreams were now nightmares. She felt bound still—even here—by the heavy, enclosing net. "My dreams don't matter."

"Now that I don't believe. You remember the time you stuck up for me against the commander?" His grin grew. "The way you chucked him across the barracks. I was so mad at you, remember? But look at you now. You get to enter the barracks whenever you wish. No complaints from the commander." There was a glimmer in his eyes as he spoke. The same one he always seemed to have whenever the two of them would get into an argument. It was as if he secretly enjoyed them. "Knowing you, you'll find a way of making your dreams a reality."

Trinity said nothing. If there was some way to do what he said—to stop the wedding and have everyone accept her choices in life—she certainly hadn't found the answer.

Schobe waved his hand in front of her face, breaking her from her thoughts. "You know, you still didn't answer my question, Princess. Why do you want to be a knight?"

She sighed, resting the side of her face onto her hand as she let her mind wander towards the truth. "…I suppose it's for the same reason I find you reading sometimes on your post. I can't change what I love doing."

Schobe's eyes grew wide. "You shouldn't have to," he told her.

There was only one other answer she could think of then. The same one she had been thinking of since the first time she saw the silver stream of knights entering her grandfather's kingdom.

"And...I don't like being told that I can't do something. Just because I'm a girl."

"Whoever tells you that—they don't know the real you."

Trinity looked at him sincerely. As she did, her face drew slowly closer to his.

Schobe leaned towards her but quickly stopped himself. He sprang up and scratched at the back of his head as if he had an itch that wouldn't go away. "Hey, um, I got you something," he said, frantically avoiding her eyes. "I was, well you know, I was going to give it to you later, but now just—it seems right to give it you now. Here. In your room—or, just you know, now. It doesn't have to be in your room. It could be outside. Let's go outside. Oh wait, your aunt said not to. Well then here. Now."

Trinity sat deflated, leaning back in her bed. She knew all the answers of why they couldn't kiss just now. But none of them helped make any of this any easier. She attempted to show mild interest in what he'd just said. "...You got me something?" she asked.

He nodded quickly. "A gift. One that might cheer you up."

She tried to brighten up as she turned to get out of bed, but Schobe put his hands on her shoulders and kept her from rising.

"You know, you could probably have this gift sitting. Would it hurt you to be still and wait for once in your life? Build up the anticipation? Show patience?"

She narrowed her eyes at him. "Where's the fun in that?"

"Here," he said, fishing on his belt. He pulled from one of his tied leather pouches a small white box.

Trinity slowly took the box from his hand. She raised her eyebrows. "Am I allowed to open it now? Or do I have to remain still? Be patient?"

He snickered at her. "Open the stupid box, Trinity."

She did, smiling contently in the knowledge that she had irked him slightly.

Within the box was a single golden necklace. It was simple but elegant, or so her aunt probably would've said if she'd seen it in a shop. When she lifted the necklace to her face though, she could see the attached pendant. And she knew then without a doubt that Schobe had put a great deal of thought and hard-earned stekis into this gift. For the glistening pendant twirling before her eyes was nothing less than the most beautiful golden snowflake she'd ever seen.

* * *

Trinity remembered so well the first and only other time Schobe had ever come to visit her at her home. It started with a sharp knock on the door, which Evita went to answer. The two of them had just sat down for lunch; Trinity had been crying her eyes out again. Still, Evita wouldn't let her skip another meal.

Her aunt opened the door. There standing outside was none other than Schobe. At the time, Schobe's arm was being roughly handled by one of the knights regularly posted near Trinity's home.

"This one says he has business with our Princess Trinity," said the knight. "Should I toss him on his ear, Princess Evita?"

"What business have you with my Trinity, boy?" Evita asked, sternly.

"Please Mam. Uh, Princess. I'm—well, she's—if I could just speak with her a moment."

Evita turned back to Trinity, who was still at the table. "Do you know him, Trinity?"

Yes, she knew him. He had been her very best friend for nearly a year before she'd embarrassed him down at the barracks a month ago. *Freak.* That's what he had called her. That's what she still felt she was. Nothing more than an overpowered freak.

"I know him, Aunt E. This is Schobe. The squire boy. My...friend."

"*Oh*? So, you're the one she's been crying over for the last few weeks," Evita told him. Schobe looked frightened by her words. "You must've said something dreadful young man, because I've never seen her this upset."

"I'm sorry," Schobe said, looking past Evita and speaking directly to Trinity. "That's why I came here. I wanted to say that to you. I am sorry for what I called you."

"Should I have him flogged in the streets?" suggested the knight.

"*Perhaps*. Trinity, what do you think?" Evita asked, sharing a smile with the knight.

Trinity shook her head and went to where Schobe was being held. "Please don't hurt him. He came all the way here. To see me."

The knight released Schobe's arm and Evita eventually gave her approval for the two of them to talk alone, though Trinity was certain her aunt would be listening in since she didn't close the door all the way. Standing outside near the courtyard, Schobe said what he came to say. Trinity listened, first to his apologies, then his explanations, and then his eager requests on whether or not she could join him and Quatas for a game of ball down in the market square. They were words she'd imagined hearing all month—words that somehow didn't feel necessary anymore. Just his presence was somehow enough.

"I'm sorry too, Schobey. I shouldn't have been there in the barracks. I know I'm not wanted there."

"I want you there," he said, unable to meet her gaze.

"Then I'll be there."

"Are we still friends?"

"Yes." *My best friend,* she thought to herself. *The one I want to keep forever.*

* * *

Schobe hadn't appeared in her dream. He hadn't tried to cause her harm or pain. And he respected her decisions, always, the same as she tried to respect his. There was so much of him, even now, that reminded her of that nervous little boy who'd shown up on her doorstep years ago. Yet he had also grown. He was becoming more a man every day, more handsome and knightlier even. She sometimes wondered if he still saw her as the annoying girl who kept pestering him while he tried to read. But the snowflake necklace suggested something different. *Something wonderful.*

He undid the clasp and put the chain around her neck. She shuddered, like she'd done with the rope in her dream. But she wasn't scared. Not now. Not with Schobe beside her.

"What did my aunt whisper to you before she left?" she asked.

Schobe's eyes grew wide. "She said...I'm not allowed to leave until I ask you to the winter ball. I was always going to. Only, I didn't know if you'd say yes."

Yes! Yes! A million times yes, she thought to herself. "I would be delighted," she said, aloud.

Schobe leaned down and embraced her. She couldn't stop herself then from crying on his breastplate. He leaned back and wiped her tears away.

"Why are you crying? Are you hurting?"

"No." She wiped clumsily at her face.

"What's wrong?"

"Nothing. I'm just remembering this moment." And she was. For it was the moment she was going to miss most of all when she had to leave this place. *Forever.*

CHAPTER TWELVE

MISJUDGED

E vita knocked upon the note-covered door. There was no answer. She knocked again, harder this time. After a moment, the door opened. Guren stood in the threshold, looking as if he'd just woken up—despite it being the middle of the day.

"Oh," he said, blinking the sleep out of his eyes. "It's you."

Evita's nostrils flared. "Is that any way to address royalty?"

He bowed his head slightly. "Princess Evita, what can I do for you?"

"You could quit blocking the doorway and let me in."

He appeared to ponder her words for a second, as if searching for some reason to leave her out in the cold. "...I suppose I could let you in."

He moved aside, allowing Evita into his home. The man kept a pristine dwelling. Not a single thing was out of the place. The dishes, few as they were, were all stacked with care. Two wood chairs were tucked in neatly at his table; the only other furniture in the main room was an old rocking chair, set before a dying fire in the polished hearth.

Evita stood, staring into his kitchen, hands folded against her dress. "Are you going to offer me tea? As I recall, you make a delicious cup," she asked, sounding more polite than when she'd entered.

"If that is what you wish, Princess." He snorted beneath his breath. "Feel free to liven up the fire while I fetch the kettle."

Evita stepped over to the dying flame and picked up a piece of kindling—delicately with her fingertips, so as not to catch a splinter—right off of the stack by the hearth. She tossed the wood onto the fire and stoked the flame with an iron rod. She then looked behind her at the rocking chair.

"Take the chair," Guren told her. "Best seat in the house."

"You never did have much furniture," she said, scooting the rocking chair closer to the fire and seating herself upon it.

Guren returned to the living room with two iron mugs and a black kettle which he set onto the spit before grabbing one of the two chairs from his kitchen and setting himself before the fire. He pulled from beneath his gray sweater his long yew pipe and began stuffing it with green tobacco he'd taken from his pocket.

"Want to smoke?" he asked.

"No, thank you." She straightened in the chair. "Haven't smoked since I was young."

"That's right," Guren said, lighting his pipe with a thin piece of kindling that he'd placed in the fire. "You and your sister both smoked for a time. Was it your mother or father who caught you? All I remember is we were on orders to hide all the tobacco in the kingdom for over a week. I had to start hoarding."

Evita cracked a smile. "Father's order. He was so cross." She swelled her stomach out. "Smoking is bad for you. It isn't proper for princesses," she said, in a mocking tone matching her father's. "Wasn't until we were told our teeth would fall out that we finally quit."

"*Smoking* does that indeed," he said, taking a drag on his pipe.

Her face stiffened again. "I suppose you're wondering why I'm here?"

Guren's eyes were still on the fire. "No. I have my suspicions though." He scratched at his beard, taking another slow puff. "How is she? I trust that since you're here instead of home she survived her great fall."

"You knew of the fall?"

"Everyone knows of the fall."

Evita grew silent. She stared at the base of the reddening kettle. A loud, steamy whistle began to pour from the spout. Guren poured her some tea. She let the mug warm her hands, and then she took a small sip. Guren, meanwhile, stared gravely down at his own mug. Neither one of them said anything for a few moments more. Outside of Guren's thin door came the muffled sounds of Great Fathers walking and shouting holy recitations, and passerby conversing in the echoing corridors.

"You must think I'm a terrible parent," Evita finally whispered.

"...No. You were never really her parent to begin with. If you were, you'd have a strength equal to hers."

Evita shot him a hostile glare. "Oh, so I guess *nothing* I've done in the last fourteen years matters. All the feeding, and clothes buying. Drying her tears and doing my best to keep her from trouble. All for what? Myself?"

His face remained as unfeeling as a block of wood. "Maybe."

Her jaw clenched. "Damn you Guren." She rose from her seat. "I know. I know you've been training her still. That's why she was going to the tower, isn't it? You told me—you told father even—that you were going to quit training her after the scar that she got training with you the last time. You lied!"

"*Evita*," he growled in his gruff voice, "you know nothing of what that girl does every day. If you had, you'd have realized she's been training herself for over a year. Long after I stopped teaching her."

Her watery eyes widened. "S-she has?"

"Don't you remember the joust? You think she did that on some child's whim? I am certain with the way she rode, the way she performed, that she practiced for months before besting Kuza." His face softened some, as the glow of the fire danced in his eyes. "I had heard a rumor about a certain squire-turned-knight recently who was fetching horses from the stables in the sunless hours, and bringing them to the lists. Probably the same knight who let her borrow his armor for the event."

Evita's mouth gaped open. She slunk down into her seat, holding the sloshing beverage loosely on her lap. "I had suspicions. The early mornings. The bits of straw I'd sometimes see on her clothes. I always assumed she was going to the marketplace. Maybe the beach. But somewhere, not training. Though I guess...I guess I always knew the truth. I really am a failure of a parent. Or whatever I am."

Guren adjusted his seat to face her. He took the hot teacup from her and set it down on the ground. Evita placed her face into her hands. Guren took a drag on his pipe to stoke the fire within and then handed her the smoking wood. She looked up, hesitating, but finally took the yew pipe from him and smoked a little of the green tobacco for herself. It didn't take much before she began coughing.

"Goodness, I forgot about the coughing," she said, pounding on her chest and handing him back the pipe.

"You did beautifully," he said, chuckling. "Smoked like a true knight."

She settled a little upon hearing this, but still wore her frown like makeup. "At least I've not failed at one thing."

"We all failed her, Evita," Guren said, and his voice had become unusually weak. "Marrying her off at this age. Not using that strength of hers to better the kingdom. I failed her—the same as you."

Evita crinkled her skirt beneath her palms. "Is that why you trained her? To help the kingdom?"

Guren placed a fist against his mouth. He stared at the fire with a brooding expression.

"You've heard the rumors. Of the Terkian living in Sambool?" he asked.

Evita grew still, making no reply.

"Gazenga has acquired a Terkian of his own," Guren said. "A deadly young man who they say single-handedly killed a thousand refugees trying to flee here."

Evita swallowed. "Do...do they know he is Terkian for certain?"

Guren turned and studied her face closely. "Yes. Seems another survived. A boy. From what I hear, he's about the same age as her."

"...I see." Her hands were trembling in her lap.

Guren leaned back, sighing heavily, and then checked the inside of his pipe. "With Trinity properly trained, we stood a chance of defending ourselves from these enemies. Now, she is Zayloa's weapon to use."

Again, Evita maintained her silence.

"Shame," he said. "She could've learned a lot more. And not just from me."

"What do you mean?"

He looked sharply at her. "I'm not the only one who knows how to defend our kingdom properly."

She scoffed. "Me? I haven't trained with a blade for years."

Guren nodded. "True. But you and your sister were good. Especially you and those twin sai blades of yours. Your suitors had the cuts to prove it."

She stared down at her mug on the floor, holding back a grin. "I must've had a good teacher."

He scratched sheepishly at his beard. "One of the best."

"So, is that the only reason you trained her then? Nothing to do with the promise you made me?"

"Ah—the promise." Guren tapped out the remaining ashes from his pipe. "To be her MAIda. Her protector and keeper of the faith. Hmmph. I've made a pretty poor one, admittedly."

She reached forward and touched his hand. "No. Don't say that. I know you've always watched out for her. For us both." She turned fully to him now, her eyes boring into his withheld expression. Her own manner had changed also. She grew calmer, looking into his eyes. "I remember yours was the first horse I could see on the horizon when we fled Terkia. She rode in the crook of your arm the whole ride back to Hydlix and never made a sound. She's always thought very highly of you."

Guren snickered to himself. "I'm not so sure anymore. The king didn't just forbid me from training her. He said if I were to spend any further time with her, even so much as talk to her, he would—"

"I know," Evita said, curtly. "Father told me. I suppose I should be thanking you, after all. He's made good on his promise to not send her away until the Zayloans come calling. Fourteen years still wasn't enough time though." She withdrew her hand. "They'll be here soon. A month. Maybe a few weeks."

"Winters never did last long in the ruby kingdom."

Evita saw herself out shortly after she'd finished a second cup of tea. Before she left, Guren gave her a birthday gift: a ruby-colored shawl, made from raskworm silk, which gave the fabric a creamy, transparent texture.

"I probably won't be attending your birthday celebration. I don't want to upset Trinity any further," he said, while standing beside his door.

"You can come out for one evening. Whether you speak to her now or...when she leaves, it makes little difference. Come on, bring this lady friend of yours everyone keeps talking about."

"Heh," he grunted. "You always were too nosy for your own good. You and Zepolia both."

She smiled, turning to leave. "I suppose I got it from her then."

Guren reached for her arm, stopping her. "Earlier— what I said—I'm sorry. I'm sorry I misjudged you. You may not be her mother, but you are her parent. I can't imagine how hard this is on you."

Evita acknowledged his words with a respectful nod. "Seems I misjudged you too, Guren. I thank you."

Guren said nothing. He only watched as she walked away. But just as she neared the glass chapel, she turned to face him once more as a final thought came to her.

"It's too bad really that she wasn't born a boy. I'm certain you would've made her into the finest knight we've ever had. Instead…well, she's a girl. Her path was decided the moment she was born a princess."

"No," Guren said, grinning in his gentle, reserved way. "Even without her strength—she is so much more."

When Evita opened the door to her home, the handmaidens were busy at work, polishing the silver and scrubbing the stone floors. Trinity stood over the threshold to her bedroom, dressed in a robe, having changed out of her stained clothing. She had taken a bath also, since there were only a few traces of blood still clinging to her wet hair. Evita breathed a sigh of relief upon seeing her.

"Are you still angry with me, Aunt E?" she asked, in a timid tone, unbecoming of her.

Evita shook her head slowly and walked a dry path where her handmaidens hadn't scrubbed yet. "No dear. I'm not angry with you." She pulled her niece into a tight hug.

"I'm sorry. I am. I'll never do something so foolish again," Trinity said, sounding sincere.

"Good to hear." Evita looked down and examined the golden necklace around Trinity's neck. "This is lovely." She admired the jewelry with her hands.

"Schobe gave it to me." Her cheeks became rosy, and her eyes filled with starry-eyed hope. "He's asked me to the ball. Am I really allowed to go with him? What I mean is, do I have your permission?"

Evita gave her a solemn grin. "Yes. I think that will be fine."

Trinity looked relieved. "The only thing is…do you think maybe we could help him purchase dress clothes? He didn't want me to ask, but I don't think he has any of his own."

Evita nodded. "I'd be delighted to, little cub."

Trinity beamed. "Thank you! Thank you so much. I can't believe this is happening. This is going to be the best. I'm going to the ball. I'm going to the ball with Schobe. I...I love you Aunt E. Really, thank you."

Evita closed her eyes, soaking in the moment of her niece's acceptance. "I love you too."

Trinity was practically bouncing with glee now. "I can't believe he asked. I was hoping he was going to ask. I didn't really know if he would. I hoped he would. But then when he did—oh, it was like diving into the ocean. I felt so happy. And I—" her voice tightened. "Well, he left shortly after asking. Just like you instructed." She suddenly frowned. "Oh no. I feel so horrible. Your gift. I never got around to getting you your gift."

Evita shrugged it off. "No matter. Having you here with me for one more birthday is *gift* enough. Tomorrow we'll go get you a dress for the ball, and help Schobe with his clothes. Maybe after the ball the three of us could have cake and you and I could play a round of King's Circle. Since it's my birthday tomorrow, you could let me win."

Trinity smirked at this. "I guess. Though don't be mad if I forget and win again."

Evita poked her playfully in the side. "You better not. It's my birthday after all. I'd like to win too every now and again."

"We'll see," Trinity said, giggling. She then began snooping around, looking for some clue to Evita's latest activities. "Hey, you didn't buy any gifts for yourself, did you? You were gone so long, Aunt E. Where did you go?" She gasped. "You didn't get any donuts without me, did you?"

It was Evita's turn to laugh. She paused her niece's nosiness and cupped Trinity's warm cheek softly with her hand. A recognition dawned on her then, as she remembered previously striking Trinity upon this same cheek only days before. Her bottom lip quivered, but she held back her approaching tears. "No dear. I would never do something so mean as eating donuts without you."

Trinity's eyes grew suspiciously wide. "Oh. Good. Me neither."

"Hmm," Evita said, sounding unconvinced. "If you say so."

Trinity tilted her head. "So where did you go then?"

Evita sucked in a breath. "It's as you said. I was shopping dear. Only shopping."

"No bags?"

"Not this time. Plenty of orders to pick up though."

Trinity rolled her eyes. "I knew it. You're always shopping."

"Yes," Evita said, as her smile faded. "...I'm always shopping."

Later that night after seeing her niece off to bed, Evita retreated to the emptiness of her spacious room. She lingered at the mirror for a few seconds, looking deeply into the two dark eyes in her reflection. Silently, she went to her closet and slid the door open. There at her feet was a locked chest. Evita knelt beside the chest but did not open it. Instead, she moved the rattling contents within until she could grasp the stone tiles on the floor of her closet. It took some doing, but she was able to dislodge the stone and lift it from the ground.

There within the hole lay the items that she sought. Two steel sais, each the length of her arms, glinted beneath the peeking moonlight from her window.

Evita pulled out the weapons and held the long, skinny, dagger-like blades to her forearms. She stood before her mirror once more, examining the weapons and checking for signs of rust. They were in need of a good polish, but they maintained their sharp edges well. It was always the sign of good craftsmanship, or so she had been told by her teacher. And Guren was just as good a smith as he was a teacher.

CHAPTER THIRTEEN

SECRET WEAPONS

Trinity had considered it quite good fortune that her evening with Evita had ended with dried cake and another victory at King's Circle. Still, in spite of herself, early the next morning Trinity snuck out once more by using her room's hidden window. It had been far too long since she had gone to see her lion friend. She hoped to make a quick return before her aunt woke. She also hoped that she'd be able to sneak past the guards once more at the dungeon tower. *Please let it be anyone but Quatas posted today.*

The whole kingdom was in a bustle today preparing for the ball. Though only families from the upper districts were usually invited to attend, as well as the knights, everyone else in the kingdom seemed to be making preparations also. The gardeners were doing final touches in the garden, removing clumps of snow from the hedges. Members of the kitchen staff were zipping through the halls carrying large pots and pans, as well as the finest ingredients they'd purchased from the lower districts. The servants were polishing stone and the florists were spreading out new arrangements along the golden alcoves. Even the nearby stables were looking cleaner than normal.

Down in the market, the vendors were busy as well. People from the upper districts always ventured to this part of the kingdom during big events, searching for new garments and other wares that the upper district couldn't supply. The finest silks were on display. There were even dresses and suits hanging from the stalls of a few vendors. The food stands had all been freshly stocked also, making the square smell like a blend of fish, cheese, and donuts. Trinity would've stopped to help herself to a freshly baked turtle donut, but she knew time was limited.

Before turning towards the road leading to the dungeons however, a strange new sight caught her eye. There on the outer parts of the market, clumped in a corner, was a poorly laid out tarp containing a wide array of flowers, so beautifully arranged. And there in the center of the tarp was a bouquet of orange flowers with sharp green thistles that Trinity had never seen before. Standing beside the bouquet was another curious sight. It was a young girl wearing ash-colored robes wrapped up to her head. Only her cobalt eyes were visible, as well as the yellow dress she was wearing beneath. Trinity had never met her before, though she'd seen her on the day the refugees first started arriving on the beaches.

"Care for flowers, milady?" the flower girl asked, sounding even younger than Trinity first suspected. Her accent was thick and treacle-like, making her words sound like they were slathered in butter. She also sounded very different to the Bayonick woman on the rooftop.

"They're lovely," Trinity said. "Are you allowed to sell in the kingdom now?"

The flower girl nodded proudly. "Oh yes, milady. But only for today. The king has allowed us to sell in the kingdom, and make deals with some of your local florists. We brought many flowers from home, but only a few survived the trip. Even fewer thrived on your beach sands. These here are my finest wares." She waved her hand over the tarp. "So, won't you hurry fast and buy one?"

Trinity pressed a finger to her lips. "Hmm. So hard to choose. I did like this one."

She took one of the orange flowers from the bouquet and brought it to her face to sniff; the flower gave off a striking aroma that she couldn't quite say that she liked. Her eyes suddenly stung and filled with water. She wiped at them, feeling as if she'd just finished smelling fresh, hot peppers. An uneasy, tricking feeling jolted between her shoulders, causing them to seize up with pain. She put the flower back into the bouquet, adjusting her neck as the unsettling feeling eventually ceased.

The flower girl knelt and rearranged the bouquet. "No one ever buys these but they are most good for treating cuts. My old mam sometimes drinks them crushed in her tea. Says they are a great Samboolian cure-all."

Trinity gasped. "You're from Sambool?"

The girl's eyes grew big. She started to tremble as she began clumsily rolling up her flowers into the tarp, crushing some as she did.

"N-no more business today, milady," she said, her voice quivering.

Trinity was taken aback. "I've said something wrong? I didn't mean to. I just wanted to know where you were from."

"I'm sorry," the girl said, avoiding eye contact. "I must—"

"Please don't go."

"I must. I should not say these things."

"Wait!" Trinity placed her hands on the tarp and kept the girl from rolling any further. "I'm not going to tell anyone where you're from. I understand."

The flower girl paused and slowly glanced at Trinity. Her eyes appeared to be studying Trinity's words, as if they were hanging in the air. "How...how could you understand?" Her tone had changed. She no longer sounded like a foreign child peddling her wares. Her voice had become cold and defensive. "You don't know anything about us."

"I know," Trinity said, softly. "Only what I've heard."

"I am sure that whatever you have heard about Samboolians is wrong. We trueborn are not killers and thieves."

Trinity shook her head. "I don't judge you for being from Sambool."

The girl was clutching at her tarp still. "Why not? There are many here who do. Many believe we were responsible for the attack on your kingdom. I suspect this is why none buy from me. Or the other Samboolian merchants. But we did not attack your kingdom."

"I believe you," Trinity said, remembering the look of the bandits clearly. "The ones who attacked us carried hooked weapons and had tattoos on their arms and faces."

The flower girl huffed. "If your people know this, then why do they still treat us so poorly?"

Trinity bit at her lip. "It's just...ever since I was girl, there's been terrible rumors going around about Sambool. About Gazenga. His sieges on small villages. How he's destroyed some of the great kingdoms. And now, I hear he has a strong young man who works for him."

The flower girl looked squarely at her, with an intensity that made Trinity have the urge to look away.

"We...my people...we are not them. We are not the king and his strobanth."

"Strobanth?"

"Yes. The strong boy you speak of. He protects the king. Like a shield protects a warrior. He is supposed to be a symbol of Sambool power. But he is not Samboolian. He is not trueborn."

Trinity felt her whole body tense up at these words. "Is he—he's a Terkian! Isn't he?"

The flower girl looked terrified, and her mouth snapped shut. She stood, lifting the remnants of her flowers into the crumpled tarp.

"Please," Trinity begged. "If there's anything you can tell me. Anything at all. Do you know his name?"

The flower girl turned to walk away, but hesitated. Though she wasn't facing Trinity anymore, she slowly nodded. "Yes, milady. I know his name," she said, sounding pained by her own answer. "It is Duke. His name is Duke."

Duke? His name is Duke. Trinity could've asked about a hundred other questions after getting the first real answer towards this mystery Terkian from far away. *How old was he? What color was his hair? His eyes? Who were his parents?* She, however, didn't have a chance to ask. The flower girl left, racing back to the beach where the other refugees were camping. Trinity thought about chasing her. Maybe she'd even have a knight accompany her down to the shores. But what good would it really do? The flower girl was terrified to say any more, and Trinity didn't wish to frighten her any further. Besides, the flower girl had already given her more answers than anyone in Hydlix had ever given her. It was a start to be sure. Instead she chose to share her barrage of questions with the only other "someone" in the kingdom who might listen to her at this hour…Snowflake.

She was spotted by the four posted knights at the front entrance of the dungeon; she'd have to find another way in. She considered going and pleading with Great Father Palthar to let her use his tunnel beneath the glass chapel—though she was still uncertain of how real this tunnel actually was—but she just couldn't summon the courage to speak to the holy man. Besides, Palthar would've snitched her out to Evita for sure, and she knew there'd be no way to explain to her aunt why she was in the dungeons that morning.

Trinity realized she'd have to resort to breaking the promise she had made the day before. She made her way to the far side of the tower and jumped up to the nearest open window she could spot. She crouched and looked below her on both sides, hoping nobody had seen her. Her aunt would be furious if she was discovered climbing a tower again, but there was no other way. Trinity was worried that Snowflake may have forgotten about her by now; this was the longest she had ever gone without visiting him.

She made her way through the dank tower and down to the lumbering lion's cage. He whimpered upon seeing her, but when she approached his cage, he bounded up and nuzzled the iron bars, looking forgiving for her absence. She scratched the soft fur above his nose for several minutes, before tossing him in the steak she'd brought him. Snowflake devoured the meat in a single gulp then continued purring and looking at her longingly. She was happy to see him again, though her mind was still troubled over thoughts of the name she'd just heard about. *Duke.*

"Do you think he's my brother, Snowflake?" she finally asked, after explaining her situation to him. She looked into the lion's vacant stare. "I know it seems stupid. Impossible, really. But I always thought all the other Terkians were dead. If this boy really is out there somewhere—maybe that's the cause of all this pain I've been having. Like with those twin boys…maybe we can feel each other's pain. Maybe we share more than just a mother." She sighed. "I mean, it can't all be for nothing, can it?"

Snowflake yawned. He appeared to have grown bored of her further lack of poached steaks to offer. He rested himself along the bars while his long tail swayed back and forth across his stone floor.

"You're no help," she said, scratching behind his fluffy, unbathed ears.

She was relieved to see her lion friend so docile after not visiting him for a few weeks. It comforted her to know they were still content with each other's company. After all, it was Snowflake's jaws closing around her in the nightmare which had given Trinity the greatest scare yesterday. She knew he was capable—even with her inherited strength—of killing her with a single swipe of his giant paw. Perhaps that strength was what comforted her most, though. Snowflake had a calming power, like a warrior with a sheathed sword. He was a mighty beast who yearned for the same freedom she wished for herself.

She guessed it a cruel coincidence that their first encounter came on the day she learned she was to marry Hayden.

*　*　*

It was her ninth birthday but she didn't have reason to celebrate. Her best friend in all the Remsphere had just called her a terrible thing. Trinity sat against hers and Schobe's brick wall, weeping and hoping no one would notice her. For the first time in her life, she wanted to be completely alone.

"Stand clear!" shouted a man stepping past the wall, a heavy clang in his step. "The prisoner approaches!"

Kuza? No. He was still inside being attended to by his men after Trinity had managed to toss him an hour earlier. Besides, this knight wasn't walking towards the barracks. He was walking a slow, yet determined, pace towards the lower plaza where the dungeon tower lay. A chorus of tinny steps followed close behind the knight; a dozen other soldiers were marching after him as best they could, though it was clear their movement was hampered by someone between them. Whoever it was had enough force to pull against the chains that the knights were using to restrain them.

A crowd of spectators lurked nearby. Trinity couldn't see beyond the gathering Hydlixians. Who was giving the knights such a struggle? *A single prisoner?* Maybe he was strong, like her. *Another freak?* She had to know who it was. She swerved through the crowds like a slippery fish, drawing ever closer but still unable to see the mystery prisoner.

A fierce roar rose from the center of the commotion, causing most of the onlookers to shriek and cower away. Trinity stayed her ground. She spotted two knights that had fallen to the ground, while the rest were still struggling with the chains. She stepped forward, wondering if she should help them. *Help them with what?* Why were they even chaining up this prisoner in the first place? It was then she caught a glimpse of the one who had roared.

The massive white lion surrounded by knights broke loose from his captors and yanked several more knights to the ground. He bounded over their bodies and hissed as several more soldiers came running over from the barracks. They approached with their swords drawn, their shields covering them. The lion paused, apparently assessing his surroundings. He was drooling over his large fangs and his big green eyes narrowed. The fur around his mane stiffened; his long claws were drawn and ready to strike. He looked ready to strike—maybe even kill—but there was something else in his panicked demeanor that Trinity recognized. *He's scared.* With no one left to stop her, she stepped forward until she was able to meet the lion's fearsome gaze with her own softer, undiscouraged expression.

"Don't hurt him!" she commanded of the knights. "Please, don't hurt him! Can't you see he's terrified?"

The lion stared at her. The four green eyes between them locked for what felt like minutes. He looked as if he were trying to parse her words. Impossible, she knew. Lions didn't understand the common language. And they most certainly couldn't speak. But something calming had passed between them. Maybe he was tired. Or maybe, her words had somehow made sense. Either way, his intensity lessened. His hair softened and he closed his jaw. He continued to watch her closely as a swarm of knights closed in around his body and bound him in chains once more.

"There you are!" her aunt Evita said, clawing through the crowds and taking her by the hand. "What are you thinking? White lions are dangerous. You could've been killed."

"Why are they taking him?" Trinity asked, looking back as the lion was dragged away once more.

"Who?" Evita asked, sounding winded.

"The lion," Trinity cried. Her voice had grown thin.

Evita gave her a stern glance, but then recognition dawned on her face. "Ah. I see. You didn't know, did you? The kingdom has always kept a white lion, Trin. When one dies, another is captured," Evita said, sounding casual as she did.

"But why?"

Evita squeezed her hand. "He is our symbol, Trinity. A proud one we Hydlixians respect. With him here our enemies will see us as strong and powerful. Our allies too. Did you forget? The Zayloan king banquets here tonight. And his son, the prince. They must know of our strength if we are to reach a fair treaty."

Respect? There was nothing respectful about the way the knights had treated the lion. Unsatisfied with her aunt's answer, Trinity couldn't help herself from asking another question.

"Why keep him locked up? He wasn't going to hurt anyone. He was just scared."

"Wait," Evita said, "you'll see. One day, you'll understand why we do the things we do."

* * *

She never did understand. Not really. Snowflake was a fearsome lion, but there was a gentleness in his eyes too. And though he was unchained within his cage, she knew those tender, heavy eyes of his were still longing for the freedom he always craved. Perhaps this was why the two of them had always gotten along so well, she thought. They were so alike. And she supposed—maybe naively, or maybe just hopefully—that Duke was like her lion friend as well. Snowflake and Duke were symbols of strength for their kingdoms. Secret weapons. In a way, it was what she imagined herself to be for Zayloa soon. *But maybe*, she thought, *just maybe...Duke was a prisoner too.*

CHAPTER FOURTEEN

THE ONE WHO WAITS

Most prisoners were barely awake at this hour, but the ones who were came ready with the familiar whistles and catcalls when Trinity hurried past their cells. *I'm only a child*, she thought, sidling back out the window she'd snuck in from after leaving her lion friend to nap. *Why would they say such things?* Trinity disregarded them as best she could, though the rattling from their bars and unflattering words stayed in her head long after she'd gone.

Once outside again, she tiptoed across the snow-covered roof and checked to make sure no one saw her.

She jumped back down to the cobbled road and headed home. On her way, she made sure to stop in and apologize to Ellacryse, who was found once more selling jewelry near her usual place in the market.

"You gave us all a scare," Ellacryse said, unpeeling herself from Trinity's waist. "I knew something was wrong; I just knew it. Is that why you ignored me?"

Trinity nodded. "Again, I'm sorry Ella dear. I didn't have the right head yesterday."

"Do you have the right one today?"

She laughed. "I think so."

Ellacryse closed her eyes, smiling. "You and Schobe are so lucky. I wish I could go to the winter ball."

"Be my date next year."

Ellacryse's face scrunched up. "I would. But you won't be here next year, Princess."

Trinity made a face. "*Right*. Keep forgetting that."

Ellacryse giggled and took Trinity's hand; she gave her a woven green bracelet from her wares. "Take this one tonight."

"Oh, thank you. I was planning on wearing the one you made for me the other day."

"Yes, but green is Schobe's favorite color. He says it reminds him of your eyes. And—" she reached up and yanked one of Trinity's curls. "Can I tell you a secret? Only, you can't tell Schobe or he'll be very angry."

"But it's such fun to make your brother angry."

"Please."

"Oh, go on then. I won't say a word."

Ellacryse sucked in a deep breath. "He likes you," she blurted out. "I think he's sad because you're going to marry someone else."

Trinity's face froze, though her cheeks felt flushed. "Is that—are you certain?"

"I am."

"I see." Her hand clutched at her snowflake necklace. "Guess that makes me sad too then, Ella dear." She looked down into Ellacryse's big brown eyes. They were the same as Schobe's. "Do you want to know my secret?"

Ellacryse nodded.

Trinity knelt down and whispered into the younger girl's ear.

"Really?" asked Ellacryse, looking pleased. "I thought as much. Well, I won't tell anyone. I promise."

"Good," Trinity said. "A secret is only as good as its keepers."

Trinity left Ellacryse to her business and visited one other shop before continuing on home. She already had the perfect plan in place for the inevitable question she was sure to receive upon returning.

"And *where,* though I'm afraid to guess, have you been?" Evita asked, both hands were balled into fists on her hips. "I never even saw you leave."

"Uh—you see, the truth is—I just felt so horrid," Trinity began, "about yesterday. With your baked turtles that I ruined." *Turtle,* she remembered. *There had only been one left.* "I've brought you some."

Evita's face lost some of its rigidness. "Turtles? You went and got me baked turtles?"

"Of course, Aunt E. I wanted to do something special. It is your birthday, after all."

"*Really*? No tower walking? No armored trips to the list?"

Trinity shook her head fiercely. "None worth mentioning."

"I'm not going to hear a single report when I enter town today of a mad child breaking through the aqueduct or smashing up city streets?"

Trinity shrugged. "Probably not today."

"Hmm." Evita's eyes narrowed in on the white pastry bag at Trinity's side. "Alright. Let us have this breakfast."

"Thought you'd never ask," she said, giggling. "Happy birthday, Aunt E."

Not long after their jelly-filled feasting there came a knock on their door. Trinity ran to greet the expected visitor.

"Hi!" she said.

"Hi," Schobe said, holding back a smirk. "You, um, have some jelly on your chin. A lot, actually."

Trinity's face grew stiff. "I was saving it. For later. And you could've had some donuts too, had you gotten here earlier."

Schobe snickered. "I somehow doubt that."

Evita came and stood beside Trinity, throwing her arm around the girl's shoulders. "Ah, the knight is here. Lovely. Shall we?"

Schobe looked thunderstruck. "I—yes. I wanted to thank you, Mam, Princess! For, um, helping me *purchase* dress clothes. Happy birthday, by the way. I'll pay you back, as soon as I have the money."

"Handsome, and thoughtful," Evita teased. "You're too kind, sir knight. And I should be thanking you. For saving my hardheaded niece's life." Evita lassoed Trinity in with her arm and rubbed a knuckle on the top of her scalp.

Trinity tried to pull away but she was too busy refraining from laughter. "Hey. My head is still tender up there. Schobe. Schobe! Tell my aunt to stop being such a bully."

"I—uh, well, I'm not..."

"Have you always been this well-versed in the presence of ladies, Schobe?" Evita asked.

"Be nice to him," Trinity told her, slipping from Evita's grasp. "Don't mind my aunt, Schobey. She's just excited. She doesn't get a chance to shop for men often. Ever really."

"Why you little—oh, and just look at your face. How dreadful. You're a positive mess. I swear, this one eats more donuts than half the kingdom," Evita proclaimed. Just then she pulled out a kerchief from her purse, licked the end, and began dabbing the cloth onto Trinity's chin.

Trinity's face turned a blinding shade of pink. "Aunt E! This is so embarrassing. And gross."

"No more embarrassing than having you walk around with your face looking like a broken jam jar. And if you think that's gross, perhaps I should regale our Schobe here with the infamous tale of the wool diaper on your head."

Trinity's eyes grew huge. "No, no, no, no, no."

"You...put a diaper on your head?" Schobe asked.

"I—well it wasn't—*yes*." She slumped. "I was just using it for a hat."

"Tell him what you told me when I caught you," Evita taunted, tugging on Trinity's arm playfully.

"Grow up. I was only two, you know."

"Go on. I just love what she said. So precious."

"Yes, I'm quite curious now," Schobe admitted.

"You're as bad as she is," she said, rolling her eyes. "Fine. I told her...my...my head smells funny," Trinity muttered.

Evita and Schobe burst into fits of laughter. Trinity knew she was beet red by this point. She finished wiping the jelly from her chin and was eventually able to nudge the cackling pair outside. As embarrassing as the tale of her misused diaper was, she was pleased to see Schobe and Evita in good spirits again.

"What do you think?" Evita asked later, once they'd returned home and dressed in their purchases for the evening. She was wearing a stunning pearl gown with golden trims. Her new heels matched her gown as well. Her dreads were yanked back into a single braid and she wore a colorful head wrap; her face made up with some of the expensive powders they'd purchased. She smelled of a pungent perfume which Trinity wrinkled her nose at. Her aunt, however, insisted it was an acquired smell one learned to love.

"Wow," Trinity said, genuinely. "The knights will be drooling."

"Oh stop," Evita snarled, her eyes glinting at the compliment. "Come here and let me button you."

Trinity twirled over to her aunt and stood before the body-sized, brass mirror in their entrance hall. Evita stood behind her and struggled with the large buttons on the back of Trinity's new dress. From the moment Trinity had seen the dress she'd known it was the one she wanted: an orange evening gown with a beautiful embroidery sewn throughout. She also bought a black belt, some painful heels her aunt purchased before she could protest, and a white shawl that Schobe insisted on. Trinity had no idea that Schobe had a taste for fashion, especially with such patriotic colors.

The pair had had their fun during the shopping venture. Evita made them try on so many outfits—despite Trinity's constant complaints about already finding the perfect dress—that they started making a game of their appearances. Each time one would spring from the dressing room they'd do a little jig, or break down in mock tears as they declared this was the most spectacular outfit they'd ever worn, much to the annoyance of Evita and the boutique owner. Trinity's ribs had begun to hurt from all the laughter.

"Do you want your hair back?" Evita asked, after finishing up with Trinity's dress.

"No. Schobe likes it this way."

"I see. Does he like matching green bracelets too?"

Trinity touched the bracelet she was wearing. "This is a gift from his sister."

"I wasn't going to say anything at the boutique. But they clash you know? Green and orange."

"I don't think so. I think they were made for each other."

Evita laughed. "If you say so."

Trinity held her fingertips beneath her chin and stared into the mirror. Her pasty skin somehow appeared brighter with these colors. Her hair swooped over her shoulders with a natural bounce. She may have cursed once or twice as the handmaidens removed all of her tangles, but they had done a fine job. Trinity looked into the face her reflection made. She looked more scared than anything.

"Do you think Schobe likes freckles?"

"He'd be daft not to. They're very cute."

"I don't want to be cute. I...never mind."

Evita gave her an understanding look through her own shared reflection. "Trinity? Would you like to wear some of my make-up?"

"...Really?"

"Come on," Evita said, leading her by the wrist.

Trinity had never been concerned with her appearance before. She was usually more concerned with earning scrapes and bruises, rare as they were for her tough skin. Yet something inside of her found the idea of make-up pleasing in the moment. *Did Schobe even like make-up?*

"There," Evita said when she was finished lathering on Trinity's make-up. "I think your freckles accent your face. I made sure not to cover them."

Trinity looked once more into the mirror. She felt like a painted jester. But she looked…beautiful. *Me? Beautiful?* She wondered then—if only for a fleeting second—what Guren would've thought. But this notion left her as quickly as it had come. *Who cares?*

"Thank you, Aunt E."

"Ohhhhhh," Evita cooed. "I can't even—just." She started fanning her eyes. "If I cry my make-up will smear and—"

Trinity wanted to change subjects fast. "So, do *you* have your eye on anyone at the ball tonight?"

This broke Evita from her weepy fit. "Absolutely not," she declared, in a stark tone.

"Why not? There's plenty of good knights attending. I could set you up a dance."

"You had better not. I'm perfectly content with greeting guests and drinking refreshments. I don't need some armored buffoon on my arm."

"They don't wear their armor at balls."

"You know what I mean. It's not dignified for princesses."

"But it is for me?"

"You're different. You have an intended. Schobe is only accompanying you as a friend."

Trinity's stomach felt like it fell to her feet. "…Oh…I see." Her mouth fell open as she cast her eyes down to the bracelet.

Evita sighed. "You must understand. The royal court can be very—petty sometimes. If I am seen dancing with anyone who isn't a prince, they will begin rumors. Nasty, awful rumors."

"You can't have friends?"

Evita shook her head, though there was a familiar sadness clouding her features. "Not male ones. Especially if they aren't born from royalty. And since Taercion is short on princes these days—at least, ones that don't have a claim to their own throne...I must wait."

Wait, Trinity thought, remembering. She'd heard her aunt say something similar before, on the night Trinity first met Hayden.

* * *

Both she and Evita were wearing the kingdom's colors on that night over five years ago. Pearl dresses and black belts. Trinity supposed the dress wasn't completely terrible. Evita had picked them up last week at the boutique and commented that they could both be matching for the event.

"It's hot," Trinity grumbled, tugging at the collar as she examined herself in the brass mirror. Though her height was barely half the mirror's length at the time.

"Simply adorable!" Evita squealed. "When you get a little bit older, I'm going to have to start summoning the knights to protect you. All the boys will be wanting to court you."

"I don't want to court boys."

"I know," came Evita's dry reply, "You don't want to wear dresses. Or go to banquets. Or court boys. You want to be a knight. Right?"

"I will be a knight," she declared with a stamp. "I'll even protect you when you're the queen."

"Well, that's not going to happen for either of us," Evita said, folding her arms and staring into the mirror they were both standing next to. "You are to live as a princess. And I...I will wait."

"For what?"

"For—well, a husband of course. Then, and only then, can I become a queen. You know that, darling."

Trinity scrunched up her face and folded her arms. "I thought you got to become queen when grandfather dies."

"It...would be my title," Evita said, hesitantly, "but the royal court would never recognize me as a ruling figure until I married. And I'd need their backing, both financially and politically, if the kingdom were to survive."

"Finanshulee?" Trinity asked, butchering Evita's word.

Evita laughed and patted her on the head. "Nothing you need to worry about, little cub. I just have to wait for the right husband to come along."

Trinity grinned mischievously. "If all you need is a husband to become queen, then I can help with that. I'll find someone for you tonight."

"It's not that easy. There are rituals. And courtships. And talks with fathers."

"That all sounds boring. I think you should just marry a knight. A strong one. I can help you find one. And all I ask is that you do your royal duty and make me a knight too." She smiled at her aunt's rising brows. "I mean also, your grace. Queen Evita." She curtsied clumsily before her aunt.

"Oh, that will be the day," Evita said, scoffing. "Your beautiful hair crushed beneath a helmet. Which reminds me—" she grabbed a hairbrush off of her dresser. "If you think I'm going to let you go out looking like that—"

"Aunt E, no!"

But it was too late. Evita had declared war on Trinity's tangles. Trinity knew she was on the losing side.

"Ow! I'll bet you were never this mean when you brushed my mom's hair."

Evita stopped brushing. "...Well, actually Trinity, it was the other way around. She taught me how to style mine. Oh, your mother wove some of the best braids.

She even helped me dread my first set of locks," she said, running her fingers along her own hair. "She always used to say how jealous she was of my hair."

Trinity studied her aunt's expression closely. "Aunt E... do you know how my mother died?" This was the fourth time in her life Trinity had asked this question. She knew her aunt had never once given her a straight answer, and instead always changed the subject, or hid behind the mystery. The only thing Trinity knew for sure was that her mother died on the day she was born.

Evita sighed. "Maybe it is time I told you."

"You...you're going to tell me?" Trinity squeezed both of Evita's hands.

"Not so hard Trinity," she said, wincing.

"Sorry." She loosened her grip. "How?"

Evita chewed on her bottom lip; her jaw clenched. "Childbirth," she whispered.

Trinity gasped, as her eyes filled with tears. She stepped back, feeling her knees grow weak. *Could it be? Was she responsible for her own mother's death?* "How can that be? Babies are born every day. Wasn't she strong like me?"

Evita cleared her throat. Her own eyes were misty now too. Trinity could sense her aunt was struggling to find the words. "Yes honey, she was very strong. The strongest person I have ever known." She balled her trembling hands and furrowed her brow. "...It was his fault. He's the reason she couldn't hang on. She kept calling for him, but he was never there. Her blood is on his hands."

Trinity wiped at her eyes. "Do you mean...my father?"

Evita glared at the ground as she nodded. "*Everyone* in the Terkian kingdom died the night you were born Trinity. Everyone. There was a fierce battle going on just outside the hospital. The Terkian forces were unprepared, but they still believed they could win. That their strength would keep them alive. Your foolish father thought he was better off helping them than staying by your mother's side. The coward ran out—Zepolia called for him! Instead, he just ran to join a lost cause. His lost cause." Tears streamed down her face. She looked angrier than Trinity had ever seen before, like a pot ready to boil over. "That monster left you both to die. But in the end... you and I are the only ones who managed to escape. His kingdom fell. And Zepolia..." She couldn't finish, letting the word catch in her throat as she wiped at her face with her handkerchief.

Trinity was thunderstruck. The man she'd imagined to be her father all this time was suddenly slipping away, replaced with a selfish king more interested in his walls than his family. She didn't want that man to be her father. He couldn't be. If only there was some way that she could see him. Ask him for herself.

A thought seized Trinity then. One she feared to ask, but asked all the same. "If he never came back...then do you think my father's still alive?"

Evita took a deep breath. "I seriously doubt it. But I'd be lying if I didn't say that a part of me has always hoped that he is." Her tone was cold and vicious. "If he is still alive—still out there somewhere allowed to breathe," she looked into Trinity's eyes and her anger weakened, "...I... never mind. We should go."

"Aunt E?"

"Come on." She checked her reflection in the mirror one last time. "We must not be late."

Not long after their conversation, Trinity and her aunt attended the banquet that the king was holding for the visiting Zayloan royalty. The king's table was teeming with a wide selection of Hydlix's finest delicacies: roasted lamb, caramel chocolate pie, broiled sagme carcasses (a northern dish) and everything was topped with shaved mushrooms and Hydlix's own silver cheese. Hydlixian cheese was one of the most valuable exports on the market, and even in its own motherland was considered too expensive for most. Trinity thought the smell of it was enough to make one vomit.

She sat at the long pine table next to her aunt, along with several distinguished members of the king's court. At the center of the table sat King Eslon himself. He was busy biting into his roast lamb and drinking wine with his invited guests.

Several performers flooded the banquet hall offering a variety of acts. Trinity never held much interest for the kingdom's fire-breathers or illusion performers, though she had heard rumors that the white lion was supposed to make an appearance. She thought this very unlikely after witnessing the difficulty the knights had with him that morning. *I wish I could see him once more.* She wondered if this were possible. *Maybe I could bring him something to eat.*

Other concerns were still weighing on her mind. Her thoughts dwelled on her father. She couldn't imagine a man so cruel as to leave his own family when they needed him most. She wanted to meet him, if he were still alive that is. *If he is still alive, why has he never tried to meet me?* Just the thought of his absence being intentional made her want to punch him in the face. But in a strange way, she also wanted to get to know him better. He was her father after all. *Would he even know that I was his daughter?*

Evita tapped Trinity on her shoulder. "Did you hear what Father asked you?"

"Asked me?" Trinity hadn't realized there was a conversation still happening around her.

"Now, now, Evita. I'll ask her again," Eslon mumbled as he downed the last of his wine. A wine servant was there with a freshly filled goblet at once. "I said what did you want for your birthday this year, girl?"

Trinity immediately noticed the many eyes around the table gawking at her just then. Most were familiar court members. There were other people at the table though, seated at the king's right side. Trinity had never seen them before. *The Zayloans*, she guessed.

One was an older man wearing an emerald robe. He was long in the face and his hair was trimmed and pink beneath his crown of stringed diamonds, which reflected his hair with all the intensity of a sunrise. His crown resembled a cherry mane. She remembered then that Zayloa's sacred animal was the red mustang. The older man gazed at her with half-lidded eyes as if the anticipation of finding out a nine-year-old's birthday gift was quite enough to put him to sleep. *Definitely the king.* Though until today she didn't know kings could have pink hair.

Sitting beside the king was a sour-faced boy who looked several years older than Trinity. His hair looked absolutely ridiculous. It was pinkish-red like the king's hair, but long and poofy. Parted down the middle, his hair stretched down on two opposite ends and looked like brightly-colored waves crashing just above his shoulders. She found it difficult to look away from such a bizarre style. That was, of course, until her eyes connected with his from across the table. Those eyes of his were so cold looking that Trinity shuddered at the sight of them. He tapped his fingers impatiently against the tablecloth. Trinity realized then that both the boy and the king had light-colored skin, the same as her. *Oh MAI, please don't let us be related somehow.*

The boy continued to stare at her as Trinity tried once more to ponder her grandfather's question. For some reason, she couldn't take her eyes off of him. He opened his mouth to yawn and she saw a set of misshapen teeth behind his plump lips. Trinity had to force herself to look away to keep herself from laughing. She glanced back at her grandfather; his chins trembled under his exasperated breathing.

"Well?" he asked, sounding irritated. "We are waiting. I haven't got all day."

Trinity took a deep breath. She hadn't forgotten the question she'd been preparing for months to ask him, ever since she first started training in secret with Guren.

"Grandfather...I wish to be a knight. May I become a squire? Please?" She seemed to recall her aunt telling her one day that if she ever needed anything from the king at all, she had to add the word please at the very end.

Evita sighed, but rubbed Trinity's back in support all the same. Several at the table chuckled politely—everyone except the boy, who sniggered behind his snaggleteeth. Trinity was beginning to think he looked stupider and uglier by the second.

Her grandfather belched and then started to laugh. He was looking as if he were more amused with his own disgusting feat than the question that she had asked him. "Now, see here, my girl—my knights are all men and I don't intend on changing that. Dangerous playing with swords. You could—I don't know, break a nail." He let out another boastful laugh, and several others at the table joined in.

Trinity ignored the tears she could sense coming. "I handled myself against Commander Kuza today. Ask the knights. Ask Schobey, even." Oh, why did she have to think of Schobe right then? Wasn't losing him as a best friend a bad enough way to spend a birthday? She knew there was no stopping the tears now.

The king puffed up his cheeks and blinked rapidly. "The captain of my knights? Beaten by you? What an outrageous lie." He squeezed the life out of the silverware in his fists. "I will not indulge these stories of yours, girl. Now you'll mind your tongue, or I'll have you sent to your room."

"But it's not a story, Grandfather!" she cried out, wiping at her warm tears. "I'm stronger than him. I'd be a great knight. Let me prove myself."

"Enough of this," Eslon growled, raising his hand in front of him. His posted knights on both sides of him raised their weapons but Eslon shook his head, looking uncomfortable, and the knights settled. His voice softened some, "Now, Evita tells me you've had your eyes on one of my palominos. I shall give you any one of them that you choose, and that will be the end of this discussion." He sipped from his goblet of wine, and others followed his example.

"I don't want a horse," Trinity said, although she could no longer be heard above the clinking of metal and loud, drunken laughs. "I want to be a knight."

Evita leaned over to Trinity and whispered into her ear, "You knew he would say this. I'm sorry Trinity, but this is the way it must be. Thank your grandfather for the gift."

"I won't," she piped out.

Evita moved away with practiced poise and managed to slurp a spoonful of soup without making a sound. Trinity knew Evita was just trying to hide her humiliation. She didn't care about who she embarrassed anymore, or the trouble that she was now in. As she looked around the table and watched the men and women laugh and drink with the king, she could feel her dreams shattering around her. This wasn't the life she wanted. She had no business sitting at these fancy suppers, smiling only when everyone else was, and talking in a sweet voice to the king even when she didn't feel like saying sweet things. Her strength—which bested the knight commander earlier—was of no aid now. For the first time in her life, she felt weak. Trinity stopped fighting off her tears and trembling lip. She looked at her food and hoped no one would take any further notice of her.

"Right," Eslon said, clearing his throat as he rose with difficulty from his chair. "We do have another reason to celebrate this evening. If I could have your attention!" Upon raising his voice, the knights in the room stomped their halberds or spear handles onto the ground. The room fell silent. "Visiting with us today are some very special guests. It is so fortunate that on this day they have also become close, personal friends of mine." The king gestured his hand to the bearded man in the emerald robe and the wavy-haired boy. "Please welcome, visiting all the way from the great kingdom of Zayloa, his Majesty, King Saito Barshim. And his son, Prince Hayden!"

A resounding, well-rehearsed applause filled the room as King Saito and Hayden waved. Eslon continued his speech, "I have been in contact with King Saito for several weeks now, and I believe I have come up with a treaty that unites two of the great kingdoms. Such a feat, of course, hasn't been done since before the fall of Terkia." His eyes fell to his empty plate. "Back when my...dear Zepolia—"

"Excuse me, your Majesty, but I believe *I* helped form this treaty," King Saito piped in, interrupting Eslon. A few of the braver guests in the room began whispering amongst themselves.

"Right, right. Formalities, Saito." He stifled an irritated chuckle. "Never take credit from a Zayloan, they say."

Trinity listened to some of the rising murmurs coming from some of the other tables in the hall. Some of the lords were questioning why the king would allow this foreigner to interrupt him. Others were lightly laughing, claiming that they knew this truth about Zayloans also. Despite the unrest Saito's interruption had caused, everyone was still seated stiffly, including Evita, and they all had their eyes glued to the two kings. About the only person besides Trinity who seemed uninterested in all this royal talk was Prince Hayden, who was busying himself by swirling his goblet on the tabletop and sloshing out his drink everywhere. An unnerving grin formed on his lips as the napkin beside his goblet became stained.

King Saito rose. When he spoke loudly, he sounded like someone who inhaled when they should've exhaled. "Thank you, one and all, for welcoming my son and I into your lovely kingdom. Rumors of the kingdom sieges have hit our shores, as well as yours, and we must band together in these trying and grim times if we are to ever bring peace back to Taercion."

Eslon grunted in approval and wrapped his arm around Saito's back as if he were an old drinking acquaintance reunited in a tavern. The two kings raised their glasses as did everyone else in the room. All except for Trinity and Hayden. He was now watching her with a fixed gaze.

"A toast!" Eslon exclaimed.

"Yes, a toast!" Saito proclaimed. "To our treaty. And to the future marriage between our children."

The drowning noise of clapping and cheers masked the sudden outbursts that followed Evita's spitting of soup at the word "marriage." Trinity looked over to see her aunt rise to her feet and pound the table in front of her. Trinity was also gravely shocked by her grandfather's words. Was her aunt really going to marry that ugly looking boy? Eslon looked back at his daughter and then leaned over to the wide-grinning Saito. Trinity leaned in but could still barely hear what they were saying.

"I told you to wait until I had a chance to tell her."

"High society demands promises, Eslon. Whether we are ready to present them or not."

"Father!" Evita shouted. "W-what is the meaning of this?"

The applause waned. All eyes became drawn again to the king. "Take your seat, Evita," he demanded in a loud whisper.

"Are you joking? You said you'd formed a treaty. You never said anything about me marrying some—some boy."

Eslon blinked quickly and chuckled as he attempted to save face in front of his subjects. "You? I'm not marrying you off. You're the next in line to our throne." He pointed his chubby finger towards Hayden. "Prince Hayden will wear the Zayloan crown someday. He'll be needing a princess to marry. And besides, you're far too old for him."

"Then..." the word fell from Evita's lips like a plate about to be smashed.

"Her," he said, now pointing at Trinity. "Hayden and Trinity are to be wed."

Trinity felt a violent shiver race up her spine. Evita grit her teeth and curled her fists onto the table. Trinity expected her to say something—*anything*—that would change her grandfather's decision. Instead, Evita slowly fell back into her seat, looking as if she'd just been bested in a duel. She didn't raise up another protest or make any further scenes; she just sat there like a crumpled handkerchief and started weeping into her hands. Trinity couldn't believe what was happening. Her heart began racing, and she could feel her blood boiling within as her hands gripped at her knees ever so tightly. Even her insides felt like they were being tossed and drowned in an ocean of her unspoken emotions. *Why would she—why are they—why is this happening to me?!*

As the applause around her waned, Hayden stood up from his seat and joined at the two king's sides.

"Thank you, Father," he said. "I for one am most honored to be marrying for the enactment of the treaty amongst our kingdoms." His words whistled and accented themselves through his gate of crooked teeth, causing some people still listening to hide their laughter behind hands and napkins. Trinity didn't think his voice was funny at all, only annoying.

There was some scattered applause for Hayden, but the guests in the room resumed their noisy feasting again after a few polite seconds had passed. Evita was sopping up the remainder of her tears and the makeup around her eyes was now smeared onto her hands. Eslon was busy snapping at the servants for another goblet of wine as Saito scratched at his thin mustache in a very unkingly sort of way. It would seem that nobody cared about what Trinity thought of all this. She scowled into her intended's eyes and studied his expression the way she would watch an arrow about to be shot at her head.

Hayden continued smiling at the banquet goers as he walked over to her and leaned down to where she was sitting. He spoke only loud enough for her to hear him now. "I guess I'm supposed to be pleased as I look upon a face such as yours, Triny. Yet all I see…is a disgusting, toothless child."

Trinity clumsily covered her mouth with her hand. Her three missing teeth had all been baby teeth. But she didn't feel any comfort about this. Only unexpected shame.

"They tell me you are a *Terkian*." He said the word as if he were going to hurl his dinner up right back onto the table. "I hear your kind were monkey people. That you used to breed with them. Probably explains your ridiculous hair color."

Trinity said nothing.

"Not talking, eh? Make no mistake, Terkian girl, when I'm king you'll fall in line and respect me the same as everyone else. Can your stupid monkey brain comprehend that?"

Trinity balled her fists. She was so angry she was shaking.

"I can only hope that our children will not have green hair too. Or these disgusting freckles of yours. An ugly, spotted little ape girl. That's what you are. A stupid, *filthy* Terkian."

Prince Hayden bowed before her before smiling back at the crowd, who had mostly lost interest by now, though he waited by her chair as if he were expecting some sort of last-minute cheer. He placed a clammy hand on her bare shoulder, causing Trinity to flinch. "Let us kiss then!" he shouted, loud enough for the two kings to hear him. "To seal our engagement."

Trinity rose to her feet. The two kings settled the crowd. Everyone—including Evita—was watching now. Trinity realized she had an audience, and smiled. She proudly showed off her missing teeth. "My name is Trinity, not Triny. And I'd rather have no teeth than teeth like yours."

After saying this, she caught the prince on his jaw with a rapid swing. Prince Hayden was whirled into the crowd of astonished partygoers. As his face smashed into one of the tables, several of his own teeth popped out and scattered themselves amongst the remaining food items.

*   *   *

Trinity stepped away from the mirror where she'd been admiring her made-up face—with hints of her freckles still remaining—her styled green curls, and orange dress; she took a seat on the cushioned bench beside her. Everything was coming back to her: the mistrust, the anger, the hurt. Hayden would be here in a few weeks. Evita and Schobe could do nothing to stop this. *No one can. Even my strength won't be enough to...*

"Trinity?"

She looked towards the entrance door. There stood her date for the evening. He was dressed in pale orange dress robes, with similar embroidery to her own. It was as if the two outfits were meant to be worn together. *Together.*

"You look radiant, sir," Evita told him, as she welcomed him inside.

"Thank you, Princess. You—look nice also." He stepped inside, and sort of shuffled over in his pointed shoes to where Trinity was sitting. He stood there, confused about what to do or where to stand. "Trinity...you are..."

"Disgusting?"

Schobe laughed aloud. "No. Not at all. I was going to say beautiful. Only I didn't think that word would be enough to describe you."

Trinity's lips curled into a small grin. Regardless of what she was feeling, Schobe could always make her smile. She reminded herself then of a comforting thought. *Hayden isn't here yet.*

Schobe sat beside her on the bench and put his hand cautiously beside her leg. "I read once—in a book of poems—of a word that sounded so much better than the word beautiful that I had to look it up in one of the libraries dictionaries to be sure of its meaning."

"And what word is that?" she asked, resting her hand atop of his.

He leaned close and whispered his reply into her ear. "Dazzling. You look *very* dazzling tonight, Trinity."

Dazzling. She'd never heard the word before. But she wouldn't soon forget it.

FIFTEEN

With Evita's help, Trinity pinned the orange rose corsage they'd purchased yesterday onto Schobe's jacket and took Schobe's arm. Being the gentlemen that Trinity knew he was, he lent his other arm to her aunt without any of them having to say a word. Evita smiled at his gesture, though she seemed hesitant to take it. After a reassuring glance from Trinity, Evita accepted the knight's offering. Together, the three of them walked to the banquet hall.

The night was clear, smelling of warm mead and roasted chestnuts. Phes and the rest of the kitchen staff had surely been kept busy accommodating the large number of guests. Seven hundred court members and invited knights were expected to show. The king had extra security posted along the corridors leading up to where the event was taking place. Even the lower districts were sealed off by garrisons of knights.

The three of them walked through the courtyard. Trinity's feet shivered as her heels crunched through the snow. Her skirt was so long she had to take it up into her hands to avoid getting it wet. The white lion hedge in the center of the courtyard was still caked with snow, and little lanterns adorned its every crevice, including the place where two eyes would've been if the hedge were real. They glowed with an amber radiance.

It was hard not to think of Guren when seeing the lion. After all, this was the first place they had ever met. She wondered—try as she might not to—if he would be there tonight. *He's probably still sick,* she thought resentfully. If she were to see him, she convinced herself that ignoring him would be the best plan of attack.

"I don't know all the steps to the Hydlixian waltz," Schobe confessed, interrupting her thoughts as they stomped through the snow. "I've been practicing, but my mother kept stepping on my toes."

"It's the easiest dance to screw up," Trinity said. "Aunt E still won't dance that one with me after I sent her home one year with a broken toe."

"I remember that," Evita said. "I hope you wore steel boots Schobe. Or you're in for a painful night."

"I walk a lot softer now, *thank you,*" Trinity remarked.

"Our floors back home would say otherwise."

"Schobey, ask my aunt how much fudge she ate last year."

"Well, I—" Schobe murmured, not looking entirely comfortable with proceeding further into the conversation.

"The nerve!" Evita spat. "There are some conversations a lady should never discuss. And it was—is my birthday. I'm at perfect liberty to eat whatever I like."

"Alright. By the way, do you want me to help you fill your purse again? The chocolate did leave a stain last year, remember?"

Evita glared daggers at her. Trinity fought off the giggles and ducked behind her date. Schobe shook his head in disbelief.

"You two fight like sisters," he said.

Evita's glare lessened. "Hmm, that figures. You know she is often mistaken by many to be my adopted little sister. Must be my *youthful* appearance which keeps people guessing."

"That or I look like I'm fifty," Trinity muttered beside Schobe's ear.

"What was that?" Evita asked, suspiciously.

"I said...these new dresses are...*spiffy*. Thank you, oh, gracious Aunt."

The inside of the ballroom was more lavish than Trinity had ever seen it made up before. Constructed only a stone's throw from the king's tower, the ballroom was the largest building in Hydlix; the illuminated, blue-glass tiled floors stretched on for what felt like a mile. Trinity didn't think she'd ever seen the whole of the building from the inside, since it was usually filled with party-goers. She wondered how long it took for the servants to light all the candles beneath the clear floor to give off that luminous effect. Upon entering, they were treated to loud music flooding the grand hall; Trinity spotted bladder pipes, lyres, and lutes. *What a terrible sound they all make.* She wanted to hear music like the kind her aunt played on the piano. There was certainly enough room here for a piano. *Why do we always get stuck with bladder pipes each year?*

An open-shirted minstrel with a hairy chest was crooning at the top of his lungs from the amplified, wooden stage in the center of the hall. He sang some song about kings of the past who had ridden on the backs of white lions. The crystal chandeliers overhead twirled and flashed their sparkling reflections onto his body, making him glow like a screeching angel. Trinity, however, was convinced that MAI himself would be offended by the singer's offkey voice.

She recognized a few faces among the attendees. There was Sir Paul and his wife Lady Karin, a charming older couple, and members of her grandfather's court. They'd given Trinity a box of expensive chocolates one birthday, though she couldn't remember which. They pledged their loyalties from the West Reach, a beautiful place to visit in the Fall (or so she had always been told) because of the changing colors of the giant parasol trees. The trees were said to bloom into blinding shades of pink and orange right before the winter frost settled in. Trinity had longed to see them, sit beneath them, or even climb up to their canopies. But even on clear days when looking beyond the kingdom's walls, she couldn't see the West Reach. Her imagination had to fill in the gaps.

"Princess," hummed Sir Paul. "Ah, both princesses, yes." He bowed and his wife Karin followed suit with a well-practiced curtsey. It was the kind that made Trinity wonder about the strength of the woman's ankles hidden beneath her dress. "You grow more beautiful every time I gaze upon you, Princess Evita. And you as well, Princess Trinity."

"My, she has grown too. So pretty," Karin said. Her accent was thick, but Trinity didn't know where she was originally from. Her hair was a dark shade of burgundy, but her brown eyes were glassed over. *Too much to drink, perhaps.* "Ah, such a handsome man you bring," Karin continued, reaching out and caressing the side of Schobe's face with her fingers. His face grew stiff, and he glanced rigidly over at Trinity for some sort of assistance. "He looks too young to be a dashing knight," Karin continued. "Perhaps he is a boy knight, no?"

"No. Schobe is a full knight," Trinity corrected her. She lifted Schobe's lion print medallion that dangled from his neck and held it to Karin's eyes. "One of the youngest to ever complete his squire services, actually."

Karin glanced for only a second at the medallion before moving her sights towards Trinity. She strung her fingers through Trinity's hair, which made Trinity reel back. Karin clicked her lips, and sounded as if she were cooing.

"You certainly are a real Terkian, my dear. Oh, I have read the stories of their shimmering green curls riding down their back like a jade army. And eyes so purple you believed you were staring at a painting. But, forgive me, your eyes are...*green*," she said, sounding disappointed. She was standing uncomfortably close now. The wine breath was strong on her. "Did you know you have green eyes? Not purple ones?"

"I—yes?" She wasn't sure how to answer the almost insulting question. She winced, looking to Schobe now for protection. He had a vacant stare. *No help there.*

Sir Paul must've sensed her apprehension. He took his wife by the arm and gave them all a quick grin. "Now Karin, that is no way to address a princess. Come, let us get you more wine."

"Lovely seeing you," Karin said with a fleeting wave.

"Eh—you too," Trinity said.

"Hmm, it seems the drinks are already being served," Evita said, scanning the rest of the room with watchful eyes. "You really must forgive them. Birthdays are, of course, a chance for everyone else to get drunk. But then Father only holds one royal spectacle a year lately."

"Are we allowed to drink tonight?" Trinity asked, sounding more excited than she'd intended.

"Absolutely not. No alcohol of any kind. For either of you. I think I saw a cider table in the corner. You children have at it."

"Blech, cider," Trinity complained.

Evita ignored her and turned her attention towards Schobe. "Keep your eyes on her, will you?"

"I—well," he sputtered.

"I've just seen Father," Evita said before he could answer, adjusting her wrist corsage. "Probably already spending the Zayloan dowry. Better help myself to some wine before he finishes it off. So, I'll leave you to it." She took Trinity's hand into both of hers and gave a gentle squeeze. "Have some fun. But behave yourself. Remember your royal duty."

"You *never* let me forget," Trinity said, taking her hand back and folding her arms.

"And I won't. Not so long as you are still my little cub to protect." She frowned slightly. "Ah, here I go, nagging again. Go. Enjoy yourself. For my sake. It is a party after all. One of us should anyways." Evita put on a convincing smile and embraced her tightly, then sauntered away towards her father.

Honestly, she still treats me as if I were a little kid sometimes. After all, she was soon to be a married woman. What was the big deal about consuming a little alcohol? Wasn't she considered a grown-up now too? Besides, she didn't need any further reminding of her royal duty. Hayden was already a looming enough presence in her life. Tonight, was hers and Schobe's night together. She turned to him, feeling slightly embarrassed for the way they'd both been talked down to so far. And the night was still very young; plenty of other remarks from members of the high society were certain to occur. Schobe was still looking jumpy as ever; he stood there like an upright orange fish gasping for air.

"Um, so," he began, scratching at his head, "shall we... have some cider?"

"Or some ale."

"W-what?" he sputtered.

Trinity rolled her eyes and sighed, leading her date by the arm towards the cider table. "Come on, Rule-keeper. Let's go behave like good children."

* * *

"The treaty stands!" barked Eslon, who could be heard shouting from the other room. Trinity couldn't see the argument unfolding. She was sitting in her bedroom where she was confined until further notice. Not that she cared. She didn't want to see any of the people in her home right now anyway. *Maybe ever again.*

"She's *just* a girl," Evita cried, though Trinity had had just about enough of that for the evening as well. No amounts of tears from either of them was going to save her from marrying that awful prince that she'd just punched. She remembered the sounds of his teeth bouncing onto empty plates. A selfish, mean-spirited joy rose within her. She would've punched him again if she hadn't been escorted away from the banquet hall so quickly. A slew of curses and cheers erupted in the hall and rang through her ears as she left the supper during a feast that was supposed to be celebrating her ninth birthday, not honoring *rude princes!* She was sure of one thing tonight: *Worst birthday ever.*

"She will not be marrying my precious Hayden," King Saito spat spitefully. "Not until she is older. And more obedient. I want to see that she is *wholly* mature, and better trained. If she is to be our queen someday, we can't have her flexing that—that *strength* of hers against our kingdom. Against my son."

"I was o-only...I was only telling her how beautiful she was," Hayden howled, through sniveling, gap-toothed shrieks that Trinity believed sounded more akin to the whimpers of dogs than those of spoiled princes. "I was just thinking how happy I am. And how happy our kingdom will be—" He sniffled loudly. "—To look on one so fair. I am only thinking of the promise we've made tonight. The promise for her and I to be together forever. If I've caused any offense sirs, I desperately am sorry."

A ruckus of kingly voices reassuring Hayden of his innocence followed. Of how the cruel Terkian girl was only having a tantrum. Of how she would be punished, and forced to make an apology. Trinity took it all—including Evita's silence—with a growing tension in her chest until she'd had just about enough to last a lifetime. She rose from her bed and undid the stones from her window. They wouldn't have her. Not tonight. *Not ever*, she told herself.

She leapt from her window into the cold, and crashing ocean far below. Her body carved the waters like a spoon lapping milk. She started to swim, despite the pain in her body. Now, she knew of a worse pain, cutting deeper than any blade. Where would she swim to? She couldn't say. For how long? *Forever*, if she must. Because as long as she was swimming, she controlled the direction her life was going to take. *I control the tides.*

* * *

"Trinity?" Schobe asked, breaking her chain of endless thoughts once more tonight. "Your cider."

"Oh." She took the warm cup from his nudging hand and sipped. "Sorry. I was just thinking about—"

"Well, well, well," shouted an approaching Quatas, cutting her off. He was wearing unremarkable dress robes, dark and plain, the same as so many others there in attendance. Even his hair looked dull tonight, and a lighter shade than Trinity had ever seen before. She wondered if perhaps it had something to do with the lighting in here. Still, his blue eyes shone bright beneath the lit chandeliers. Trinity couldn't help herself from staring into them upon his stumbling approach. "I didn't know white mice wore dresses." His breath smelled foul with something that wasn't cider. "And Schobe, aren't you a sight? A blinding sight. Whoever told you orange is your color…mate, they were lying."

"Back off Quatas," Schobe said, standing closer to Trinity.

"No need to be mean. I'm only making observations. I'm jealous, is all. The two of you here together. You're lucky to have found one another. Even if it is only for a— short time."

"I said back off." Schobe's voice was growing tenser.

"Or you'll what? Hmm? Take a swing at me, is that it? Well, go on, no one's stopping you."

Schobe stepped forward but Trinity placed her hand on his chest. "Don't. Not now. He's drunk. Or can't you smell the liquor on his breath?"

Schobe backed down obediently. Quatas laughed.

"That's it. Good Schobey. Best listen to your little girlfriend. She's stronger than you. Me. Whole bloody kingdom. Tell you, we'll have a lot less broken walls and roads here come Spring."

A deafening silence fell around them, as the party-goers nearby stopped dancing and drinking and took notice of Quatas and his harsh words. Trinity tried her best to ignore his words, despite their sting. "Quatas, go home. This isn't you," she said.

"Oh? And what do you know about me, Princess? Ain't your kind supposed to be stupid or something?"

"Shut up," Trinity said, a crack in her voice.

"How the hell do you Terkians lose an entire kingdom with that strength of yours in a battle? Whole dumb lot probably sat in the same room waiting for the castle to come down on their heads."

"Stop it, Quatas!" Schobe repeated, angrily.

"I heard they didn't use swords in Terkia," he said, sauntering even closer. "They threw rocks. Didn't they know to start from the top of the rock pile? But then they *were* monkey people." He snickered, and spit flew from his mouth. "Probably too stupid to know what to do with their strength. That would be my guess."

A few not so private comments rose from the crowd. People were beginning to form their own theories about the fall of Terkia. Two lords began mumbling to one another about the Terkian king being at fault. Others in the crowd started whispering that the Terkians really weren't a smart bunch. And some people even started to laugh. Trinity felt at a loss. *Why is he saying these things?* Quatas had been acting so strangely since the day she'd seen him at the dungeon tower. It was as if he wanted her to be mad at him. She felt her chest constrict. It was a soft irritation, different to the other times. It was as if she were trapped in her dream again, and this time her heart was suddenly forcing her to make a difficult decision. She stepped back, clasping tightly to the front of her gown.

"Have I made you upset?" Quatas asked, mockingly. "Careful everyone, those tears of hers are likely to shake the whole kingdom."

The laughing grew louder. And the comments became crueler. Some began claiming that Terkian strength was a myth and that the aqueduct had broken due to natural causes. One old lord started rambling to himself how the Terkians had bankrupted themselves and that Gazenga had kindly put them out of their misery. Trinity struggled to respond. She tried to open her mouth but the words lodged themselves in her throat. She sensed her skin growing warm and wondered how red her face had become. And her heart was splitting into two as the pain inside of her grew more vicious. She likely would've gasped out or screamed had her date not stepped forward when he did.

"I told you to back off!" Schobe shouted, hurling his left fist forward and connecting with Quatas' jaw.

The drunken knight spun back in a stupor and his body hit the ground. Schobe stood over him, shaking, looking shocked at what he'd done. The surrounding remarks had turned to gasps. The king and several of his armored knights stepped forward through the crowd. Evita was there with them.

"What is the meaning of this?" Eslon growled. "Why is there fighting at my daughter's celebration?"

"Sir—your grace...I was only—" Schobe said, choking on his words.

"He was only protecting me," Trinity said, as she stood beside her trembling friend. The nipping pain within her was there still, but it was not stronger than her resolve to help Schobe. "Quatas was saying awful things about me. But...he's just a little drunk is all. Schobe defended my honor."

Eslon blinked several times, apparently trying to judge the situation for himself. "Were there others girl? Who would besmirch you?"

There were, she knew. She was familiar with several faces in the crowd of earlier mockers. Now there was only shame in their eyes, replacing the hate from before. "No. Only Quatas," she replied.

"Very well. Take him away," Eslon said, and as he spoke the disoriented Quatas was hauled from the room by two of the knights. A stream of blood was leaking from his nose. "Let him sober his tongue, before we hear what else he would say against my family," Eslon ordered of his men. Turning back to Trinity, he asked, "Are you alright, my dear?"

Trinity nodded, though it wasn't true. Evita came and hugged her once more. She examined her face with a motherly stare and began comparing Trinity's forehead temperature to her own.

"You're looking pale," she said. "Do you need to lie down?"

Trinity shook her head. "No. I'm fine. I'm not ready to leave."

Evita cocked her eyebrows, looking unconvinced. "You've not been dipping into the ale, have you?"

Trinity shot her an unpleasant, side-eyed glance.

Evita placed her hand gently on Trinity's back. "Right. Just checking." She led Trinity and Schobe back to the nearby refreshment table. "At least have some water, won't you?"

Trinity downed a cup of water handed to her, though the pain in her chest remained. "Aunt E, what will happen to him?" Trinity asked. "To Quatas?"

"For harassing royal family members? I should expect much," Evita said.

Trinity turned quickly and saw Eslon and his garrison heading towards the dessert table. "Grandfather!" she shouted out to him. "Your grace, please! I don't think he was himself. Let Quatas live. Please let him live."

Eslon stared towards her, looking taken aback. "Come now child, it's a party. There'll be no killing here. Come! Let us drink and eat. Make merry! Not every day my daughter turns thirty," he said, guffawing. Cheers rose all around him. Everyone seemed to have forgotten that Evita was only turning twenty-nine. Eslon let loose another hearty chuckle that shook his gut, before waddling back through the swaying crowds as his loyal knights followed close behind.

"Don't push yourself," Evita told her. "We should get you home. You're not looking well."

"I'm fine, really." *More lies.* "I wanted to dance...with my hero."

Schobe's eyes grew big. "Hero? No, I—I just helped him be quiet. It wasn't right what he was saying. And don't you believe a word of it."

"You *are* my hero, Schobe." Trinity removed her hand from her heart and took Schobe's arm once more. The pain—whatever it was—would not stop her from having at least one dance with Schobe. *It's our night together. Ours. Not Hayden's, or anyone else's.* "May I have this dance with you?" she asked.

"You—yes of course. I'd be honored."

"Trin," Evita said, looking as if she accepted Trinity's reasons for staying. "I'll be here. Right here. If you need me."

"...Thank you."

"Schobe," Evita added. "Be sure to watch your feet."

They stepped out to the center of the dance floor. All around them, an exciting energy flowed.

Here in the center of the banquet hall people didn't seem to care about anything. How Trinity envied them. She reveled in their crashing bodies and fits of glee as the swell of bursting music enveloped them. She wanted to be happy, the same as them. But even as she rested her head onto Schobe's shoulder and snickered as he struggled to find a place for his hands to rest, she could sense something unhappy dwelling within her. Her heart was still ripping. *Or maybe*, she wondered, *his heart was ripping. Duke.* Maybe he was experiencing his own share of sadness tonight.

She counted herself fortunate again that she had people in her life, at least for now, who could help her through rough times. There was poor Evita, who had come to her own birthday celebration without a date. A little earlier in the evening Trinity had considered asking someone like Quatas—or even Commander Kuza—to go and have a dance with her aunt. What a mistake that would've been. Besides, Evita never seemed interested in any of the men in the kingdom. And she could've had her pick of any of them. Instead, Evita was always left waiting. For what? Trinity didn't know.

She wasn't sure what had gotten into Quatas either. That was no mere jealousy he was showing. There was hate in his eyes, and his words. Did too much ale make him speak his true feelings, the same as Lady Karin? It was difficult not to think about what he'd said of her people. In a way, he was right though. How did the Terkian kingdom fall? Had her father started a war that they simply couldn't win? Was that why her mother had to stay there and die alone?

Schobe didn't share her concerns. He brushed some of her loose crinkled locks behind her ear and Trinity felt her cheeks grow warm. Perhaps the cruelest fate of all was that Schobe had not been born as the Zayloan prince. Even if he had been royalty, Trinity was certain that she would've been smitten with those warm eyes of his, and that gentle smile. He moved side to side in a wide circle, his hands resting clumsily on her waist and upper back. He wasn't lying; he really didn't know how to dance. Watching him try gave her the greatest joy, even if only for a moment.

"Would you like me to lead?" she asked him, looking up into his eyes.

"I sort of thought you already were."

She cracked a grin. "I like this too. The swaying here with you part. Can I ask you a question? Did you know that your chest smells sort of like…cinnamon?"

He laughed. "You have my mom to thank for that. She put a little in my coat pocket. Said it brings good luck."

"Has it?"

"I'm here with you. So, yes."

"Good. I feel lucky too."

Schobe nervously looked down at her hand atop his other shoulder. "Oh. Did you buy that bracelet from Ellacryse?"

"It was a gift."

"I like it. Matches—"

"My eyes."

He slowly locked onto her eyes. He seemed calmer now. "…Yeah. And your hair. It's perfect for you."

Trinity could feel herself blushing. "I think that was very brave of you earlier. To stand up to Quatas for me."

Schobe snickered. "I was just surprised you didn't stop him. You could've laid him out flat."

"I could've. I wanted to. Only, well, it's strange." She scrunched her face, feeling once more a nagging burn within her chest. "I didn't want to see him hurt. I still don't, even though he's said a lot of mean things to me lately."

Schobe's eyes narrowed. "You like him? Don't you?"

She shook her head honestly. "Not like that. I just wonder about him sometimes. Like his eye color, for instance. My mother had blue eyes too."

Schobe sighed, looking relieved. "Oh, is that all? Yeah, I've always been confused by that too. Not a lot of Hydlixians with blue eyes."

"I guess not."

"He has no parents, you know? Just sort of joined up as a squire a few years back. But I tell you, I don't think I would've made it as a knight if it weren't for him. He always had my back, Quatas. That's why it makes me mad to see him talking about you like that. I thought we were all friends."

The fire within her was growing. "So did I," she said, sounding breathless.

"Hey Trinity," Schobe asked excitedly, unaware of the pain she was hiding, "did you—did you mean what you said earlier? About me being your hero?"

Trinity winced as she tried to focus her thoughts. "Oh. Well, yes. You've saved my life plenty," she said. "I wouldn't be here if not for you."

"Funny how I always thought it was the other way around."

"What do you mean?"

He grinned. It was a goofy, enthusiastic grin. One he wore sometimes when he was reading an engaging book or listening to her go on about one of the adventures she hoped to have someday. "Everyone needs a hero, Trin. Everyone—except for you, of course."

Trinity leaned her head closer to his. Schobe looked hesitant, although he was doing the same. *His breath smells like cinnamon too*. "Even strong girls like to be saved sometimes," she said. "Schobe...I—"

And that's when she saw him out of the corner of her eye...the only other person who had been on her mind that evening. *Guren.* Her former teacher stood tall in the crowd of Hydlixians. He was beaming from ear to ear as he laughed and made jokes. Something she had rarely, if ever, seen him do. For someone who claimed to be sick—sick enough to abandon her to train all alone this last year—Guren looked very happy and healthy.

She could see why. The beautiful woman from the boat was there with him, nuzzling her head onto his shoulder. Both of them were laughing and making merry as instructed by their king.

He shouldn't have mattered to her then. She was going to ignore him. *Remember, you're going to ignore him!* Schobe had been so perfect. So why was she focusing on Guren? But nothing else seemed to matter to her now.

"Trin?" Schobe asked. "Is everything alright?"

She didn't answer him. Before she could piece together what she was doing, she stepped away from Schobe—her absolutely perfect date—and charged clumsily in her heels towards the man who had stolen her attention. This was the same man who had instructed her, valued her, and gave her something no one else had before... confidence. All before turning his back on her as if she were worthless. *A worthless Terkian.* She had to know why. She felt as if this second of embittered poise would leave her as quickly as it had come. There was no way she'd let him turn his back on her again. Not without an answer.

"Guren!" she called across the crowded room. "GUREN!"

He turned to her; his smile was now gone. The girl beside him looked startled and annoyed. Guren whispered something into her ear, causing her to flare up. His face remained unchanged though. He wore the same stoic, passive look that he always had. Except now he appeared somewhat offended by the mere fact that Trinity knew his name. The very thought of it caused Trinity's anger to surge. She stepped with more force than she intended, and her heels went right through the blue glass panel she was on. She fell through the glass onto the stone floor beneath. The dancers around her stopped. Some people even came close to falling into the opening beside her. Still, she continued glaring at Guren like a snake ready to strike. It didn't matter anymore that she was making a scene. The obedient silence ended here tonight.

"You—" her voice fell short as the vexing pain in her chest swelled to a breaking point just then. She screamed out and clutched onto the left side of her face. The pain had risen, centering itself around her left eye. *What in MAI's name is happening?* It felt like her eye was being torn clean from her socket. She shrieked so loud that the band stopped playing. She felt all seven hundred sets of eyes fall upon her. Yet for a moment she couldn't see any of them. There was something else there. A person? No. *A dagger.*

A fuzzy image of a white-hilted dagger—which looked like it was carved from bone—appeared before her, much like the blue-haired woman had done the last time. Blood leaked from the tip of the curved blade. Trinity couldn't see who was holding the weapon, but there beneath the trail of blood lay the remnants of someone's eye. *Who's eye?* Her eye? She felt her eye intact, but still the agony overcame her so. Her head—*maybe his head*—tilted down until she was gazing helplessly over the puddle of dripping blood. There, in the reflection upon the ground, she saw him. He was a fuzzy image also—clad in black armor with a bloodstained face—but there was no mistaking him.

And there, on his left side, was a gaping hole where his eye had once been. *Duke's eye? It's Duke's eye!* He was hurt. Somewhere in the Remsphere, Duke had suffered a fatal injury. And his pain, his sight, and his new nightmare was now hers to share. *Together.*

"Trinity? What's wrong, child?" came a familiar, gruff sounding voice, belonging to the man who was now grabbing hold of her arm. "Trinity, speak to me," Guren said to her.

Trinity snapped out of her vision, returning once more to the stillness of the hushed banquet hall. She saw who was holding her then. She wretched away. "Get off me!" she shouted at Guren. "Leave me alone!" She stepped back as best she could, over the broken glass at her feet. She bumped the hot lantern with her toe and cursed. Her hand was still held over her eye as if it had been plucked out also. "Get away from me!" she cried.

"Trinity, you need help. Let me help you," said Guren.

"I need nothing from you. Nothing! I HATE YOU!"

Guren let go of her arm. Trinity used the remaining sight she had in her untouched eye to jump up and steady herself onto one of the glass platforms beside her. She kicked off her heels and started running towards the entryway. The discomfort from before began to ease in her body, but she still ran with her eye covered. She could hear the frightened outbursts and feel the bodies of the people she shoved past as she pushed through the crowd. She heard Evita's dazed voice too, but Trinity didn't see her. She didn't want to see her. There were cracking sounds after every one of her heavy steps. The floor was going to cave in, she knew. But she wouldn't be there to hear the comments. She was done taking the blame for her strength. And most of all, she was done with being anywhere near Guren. He wasn't worthy of being reasoned with anymore. She had meant what she'd yelled.

She pushed past the posted knights at the door and let her bare feet scrape against the cold, cobbled walkways outside. She was running so fast that she wondered if she were merely an orange blur to those who saw her. She rushed through the courtyard snow and then jumped as high as she was able, knowing confidently that she could reach the one place she needed to be in that moment. It was the only place where she could rid herself of him permanently.

*   *   *

On the night of her rebellious ocean venture, Trinity found Guren in the glass chapel, sitting alone on a pew. He turned to face Trinity as she traipsed up the chapel's carpeted aisle. She was drenched from head to foot, shivering fiercely.

"Trinity!" Guren exclaimed, leaping up from his seat. He ran to her, took off his cloak, and wrapped it around her body. "For MAI's sake, what happened child? Why are you all wet?"

"W-went f-for a s-swim," she managed to say through chattering teeth.

They sat there on one of the dry pews long into the night. He never scolded her. Nor did he look at her with anger. Instead, he sat close to her and helped her warm herself again.

"Did you hear?" she asked, resting herself in the crook of his arm. It was her favorite place to be in all the kingdom.

"About the wedding? Yes. Is that why you tossed yourself into the ocean?"

She nodded slowly. "I wanted to train. Do something. To get my mind off—of things."

Guren snorted. "Do me a favor and pick somewhere warmer the next time."

"Yes, sir. I'll try."

"I'm sorry that happened to you. I can't even imagine what you must be feeling."

"...Fifteen," she hesitantly said, through her quavering voice. "Fifteen. That's what I heard the Zayloan king say before I jumped. Grandfather said it too. They said I'm going to have to marry that boy when I turn fourteen. But...they expect me to give them an heir by the time I'm fifteen. I'm expected to be a mother in six years." Saying it aloud made her both furious and miserable, all over again. But she supposed it was confusion that she was feeling most in the moment. *Why me? And why so young?*

"Fifteen is—that's no age to start being a mother," Guren said, sounding angry for once. Just like she hoped he would.

Her eyes were growing heavy. Soon she would be asleep. She hoped Guren would let her sleep on his arm the whole night through. She never wanted to leave his arm.

"I asked Grandfather," she said, through one of her many yawns. "About being a knight. Only he—"

"Told you what any king would tell you. What any grandfather would say."

"Would you still train me Guren?"

He took a settling breath. "...Yes. So long as you will let me."

"I promise I'll be a good student," she whispered, as her eyes finally stayed closed. "I promise I'll make you proud."

"You already do, Trinity. You always have."

"Guren…"

She fell asleep, never quite remembering if she had told him then just how much he had always meant to her.

*   *   *

Trinity landed into a roll on the bridge leading to the royal mailing tower. *They don't want me to climb? Fine. I'll use the door.* She smashed through the tower's locked door with her body. Stepping over the busted wood, she set to work. She started with the straw dummy, ripping him to shreds barehanded. She laid his remains on the wet ground and spat upon them. She undid the hiding spot where her weapons were and tossed the stone into the wall, crumbling it instantly. Next, she snapped her bow as if it were a twig. Then she broke her arrows. Snap. Snap. Snap! Each one brought her closer to removing herself from him. Each snap meant another forgotten memory. SNAP! Her swords splintered into pieces as she crushed both against the cement aqueduct. It was easier to do than she expected. It was almost as if they had never been whole.

She dropped down, fatigue overcoming her. She allowed the cool flowing water to splash the top of her hair as she rested against the aqueduct. Despite the cold, she was sweating. And despite having destroyed everything that had ever connected her with Guren, she felt no better. Tears trickled down her cheeks and she crawled over to the open hole in the ground, snatching the stack of papers from within. Each one had his writing. Each one had been a lie.

She began to tear them one by one. When she had finished with the stack, she began ripping the scraps into smaller pieces. Again, and again she ripped the papers. She wanted every fragment to be gone. A gust of wind blew through the broken entranceway and claimed some of the remains, including one whole piece of paper that she'd missed. *Damn. Now I'll have to go and find that one.*

Only she wouldn't have to after all. Schobe was suddenly there, standing before her. It was as if he had been there all along. Just like she knew he would be. The missing paper was in his hands. He didn't look jumpy anymore, nor did he seem offended that she had left him alone at the dance. Instead, he looked calm. Sympathetic even. He reached forward, handing her the last paper. Trinity's hand quivered as she took it from him. Then, she ripped Guren's final message into pieces.

PART TWO

TRUST

CHAPTER SIXTEEN

THE ARRIVAL

A few weeks later...

Winter had gone. Spring was at last upon the ruby kingdom. Ordinarily, Trinity would've relished the chance to wear long training tunics once more and dive into the ocean without the fear of catching a cold. The chill in her drafty bedroom though gave her some much-needed doubt about the changing of the season. She laid curled up on her bed, running her fingers along the recent scars on her leg. She'd earned these scars on the night of the ball, when she had fallen through the banquet hall's glass floor. Even now, they proved a great mystery to her. How was it that she had managed to be cut? At first, she began to doubt the thickness of her skin, which had otherwise kept her safe numerous times before. She even tested this theory by trying to prick her finger along a sharp rock edge on her pull away window. The result was nothing. Not even a scratch. So why then had the glass managed to cut her shortly after her last vision of Duke?

Evita knocked at her door, although it was open. Trinity stirred from her thoughts, but didn't bother to turn around and greet her aunt. Evita came and sat beside her on the bed.

"Are you going to get dressed?" she asked.

"Isn't that a handmaiden's job? To dress me."

"You've slept in every day this month. It's not like you. What's gotten into you?"

"I expected that to be pretty obvious," Trinity remarked, speaking into the pillow she was clutching onto. "I'm saving my energy. Hayden will be here soon. He'll be expecting a smile."

Evita gave her a grumbly sigh. "Very well. I suppose you'll have another day of moping. I was thinking of inviting Schobe to supper tonight. He—probably wishes to see you off."

Trinity's stomach did a flip. *How dare she mention him?* Trinity turned to her. She didn't try to hide the raging fire in her eyes. "Don't invite him to supper tonight. I'm not—I don't want to say goodbye yet."

Evita rubbed her shoulder. She hunched down and hugged Trinity right where she was laying. Trinity could feel her aunt's rushing heart beating. *Here come the tears again,* Trinity thought, drearily. Sure enough, the top of her head began to feel wet as Evita broke down.

"Fine, I'll get dressed," Trinity said, budging herself away.

"You will?" Evita asked, wiping at her eyes. "Good. Yes, yes good. You should. May I—may I help you?"

"…Might as well."

The Zayloan parade began later that morning around midday. Trinity watched it from the wide windows of the circular throne room tower. There was a grand procession of over a thousand visiting Zayloans entering the kingdom from the eastern bridge. At the head of the parade were flocks of wine-colored geese being herded into the city's gates. Red geese were not the official sacred animal of Zayloa of course, but it was a fact widely known that no one had ever caught a red mustang—or even glimpsed them. They were said to be so rare that many considered them a myth. The geese were a humorous stand-in, Trinity thought. They waddled and dispersed as the procession entered the market square. Several tenders tried to keep them together with long sticks, but were struggling.

Next came the dancers. Both the women and men of the large troupe, wearing vibrant red outfits showing much of their skin, pranced throughout the cobbled square. The women had sewn tail feathers around their waists for skirts, and the men wore frilly horse heads. Each head had a painted vacant stare which gave Trinity the creeps. The dancers shook and sashayed all the way up the stairways leading to the king's tower. They were accompanied by blaring trumpets and seedy pipes. The musicians followed the dancers, swaying their bodies metrically as they blasted their instruments with reddened faces.

At the end of the procession was the grandest, yet most awkward, sight of them all. A twenty-foot mustang made from red roses sat atop a raised blackwood platform. The platform was carried by many men, each holding onto a taut rope that supported the platform's weight. On top of the mustang sat King Saito, wearing a ruby tunic. He almost blended in with the horse. Trinity could barely make him out, even from her raised vantage point. He was wearing his diamond-studded mane crown again. King Saito waved at the gathering crowds of both Hydlixians and Zayloans alike, who had come to watch the parade entering town. Flags from both kingdoms flew and were hoisted by the common folk. Trinity hated to admit it, but the Zayloan people could sure make an exciting entrance.

Her grandfather and aunt were seated upon their thrones, looking as regal as they could manage while they waited for the arriving king. Eslon was wearing his lion-mane crown, and the top buttons on his pearl robe looked ready to snap. Evita wore a crown of her own, only used for special occasions like today. It was a golden tiara with diamond-encrusted roses forged around the band. It had belonged to her mother, as did the throne which she was seated upon.

Trinity was wearing her royal headwear also. Hers was a…*cuter* design, shaped for a younger princesses' head. A silver circlet that had crafted lion's ears, made from real pearl. Perhaps her crown was the reason behind her given nicknames. She *felt* like a little lion cub every time she had to wear it. All that was missing was a tail. And the ears on the band were shaped incorrectly—too small to resemble a real white lion. They were more like a mouse's ears. Maybe this was why Quatas and some of the other knights had annoyingly called her "mouse princess" for so many years. *Or maybe I squeak when I talk.*

"Come girl, get away from that window," Eslon called. "They'll be here any second."

Trinity sighed. "Whatever you say, Grandfather."

She meandered back over to the wood chair set out on the left side of her grandfather and plopped down. She was a little jealous of his and her aunt's cushioned thrones. *We have stekis for banquets, but not enough for three decent chairs.*

"You look very pretty today," Evita told her, leaning forward and eyeing her from head to foot. "I was against the thought of you wearing that orange dress again, but it suits you."

"Sorry I couldn't find the heels. I lost them at the ball."

"That's quite alright. I'm happy the new ones fit."

"The hell it is," grumbled Eslon, twisting in his throne and peering over at Trinity. "Do you have any idea what that tantrum of yours cost me? I had to replace over seventy tiles you shattered. Not to mention comfort my poor guests who fell into the floor and singed their robes and dresses."

Trinity fought back a smirk. "I'm sorry again, Grandfather. If it helps, I'll gladly donate my wood chair to help with the cost of repairs."

Eslon's eyes bulged out of his head. He craned his swollen neck around until he was facing Evita. "She—she's mocking me. Did you hear that? The absolute nerve."

Evita was resisting a case of the giggles also. "Donate her chair. That's a good one."

Eslon massaged the bridge of his nose. "*MAI*, why was I cursed with daughters and daughters of daughters? Would a son have been so difficult? A grandson even?"

Trinity raised her finger to make an additional point but a stern glance from Evita caused her to retract her statement. She slouched down further into her wooden chair. *I had such a good comeback prepared.*

The throne room doors opened and King Saito appeared. He was escorted by a handful of shimmering knights that looked like they'd been dunked in a pool of blood. Trinity supposed red armor wasn't an awful choice. The enemy would never know when you were bleeding. Their plates were thick and their helmets covered their entire face. They carried with them long, skinny swords tied at their waists. *Who could they harm with those pathetic blades?* Any one of them would crack against Hydlixian steel. She wondered then if they didn't value good swords in Zayloa.

Saito strolled along the white carpet as his servant girls followed closely behind. They brought with them giant yellow rings made of twirled twine, which each servant carried with both hands outstretched. The rings were just as stiff as one on a hoop skirt, and they contained liquid within. When they were waved through the air, they cast glowing pink bubbles as long as a horse's body.

When the Zayloan king approached the throne, he bowed a half bow to Eslon first, then he stepped forward and kissed Evita on the hand. He ignored Trinity entirely. She quickly noticed then that Hayden was nowhere to be seen. She straightened up in her chair, peering through the crowd that Saito had brought with him to see if Hayden was hiding amongst them.

"Welcome, King Saito. The ruby kingdom is honored by your presence," Eslon said, proudly.

"Yes," Saito replied, still sounding as if he were sucking in every word that he said like he was slurping them from a bowl of soup. "I am honored. Such marvelous subjects you have here. Eslon, I am truly awed by your kingdom's beauty. No doubt a result of your glorious daughter's presence. I felt as if I were kissing the hand of the moon princess herself."

"Oh you," Evita said, eating up his compliment with a girlish grin. "Moon kingdoms. Such an outlandish concept. But I thank you kindly for your compliment, your Grace."

"No, no, no," Saito began. "Do not write off the moon kingdom, my glorious child. I assure you; it was more than mere tales. The moon really did have a kingdom. As splendid as you could imagine. And a king with hair so long, and so white, you would think you were seeing a shooting star. And oh, such a beautiful pair of princesses he had. Second, only to your beauty, Princess."

Evita laughed. "I must warn you sir, I am susceptible to kingly flattery."

"And I must warn you young lady, I have only begun to flatter." He flashed a sharp grin at her, and then turned his attention to the king. "How fares the ruby kingdom?"

"Oh," Eslon said, looking surprised that he was being spoken to. "Fine, good. No complaints. Save for a few unexpected repairs to my, ahem, banquet hall."

Trinity was still too focused on Saito's description of the moon kingdom to pay her grandfather much mind. Had they really made a kingdom on the moon? The notion seemed outlandish, as her aunt had said, but it still didn't stop her from imagining what life would be like, ruling from up high. What would Hydlix look like from that far away? She doubted Hayden could find her all the way up there. But then, how did one get to the moon exactly? *Wings, perhaps.*

Saito finally looked at Trinity, catching her still in a daze. "Young lady, you have grown more...*precious*," he said, scanning her from head to foot. His grin widened, and his eyes lingered longer than they should've.

Trinity sat back in her chair, and folded her arms nervously. "...Thank you," she said, as politely as she could manage. Though her thoughts were anything but polite.

"My apologies," he added, finally blinking, "for my son's absence."

"Where is he?" Evita asked, sounding concerned.

"*Yes*." Saito reeled back some and spoke quieter. "He is not so young as the last time, when we could travel together. He is at an age now where he can legally rule, should I not be able to. It is our custom for kings and princes his age to ride separately on royal outings. Less danger, should my royal guard fail in their duties. Hayden will be here tomorrow. His own escort will camp on the outskirts of Sabalean this evening."

"Dangerous place, Sabalean," Eslon grunted. "I'd feel much safer sending an escort party of my own out to meet him."

"You are too kind," Saito said. "I can only hope such kindness and manners are shared by your...*Terkian* granddaughter." He used the same wicked pronunciation of her heritage that his son did.

"I have no doubt," Eslon said. "My Evita has raised her well."

"She is a kind and very clever girl," Evita admitted. "She did this *mostly* without my help. If she is treated with equal respect, I am certain she will make a fine addition to the Zayloan lineage."

Saito glanced once more upon Trinity. He bore a prudish, more dangerous look than before. It was...a *desperate* glare. "One hopes," he said, sounding unconvinced.

Later that afternoon, Trinity met Schobe out by the eastern bridge. Schobe and several other knights were posted along the lengthy stone walkway that towered over the ocean by more than a hundred feet atop cement columns. Despite having never shown signs of weakness, the bridge swayed in the wind, gifting an uneasy feeling to any who crossed. Trinity always felt like she was seconds away from toppling into the ocean whenever she'd visit this side of the kingdom. She'd never been to the other side of the bridge before. Not since she could remember anyway.

Schobe was tapping his halberd rhythmically onto the ground, looking restless at his day's posting. Trinity suspected as much. Every knight in the kingdom was working today, ensuring safe security to the arriving Zayloan companies. There'd be no chance of him being relieved for duty early enough to go and have supper with her and Evita.

"They told me you were wearing your orange dress today for the arriving king," he said, commenting on her recent wardrobe change.

Trinity fanned out her hands and modeled her new maroon tunic with a spin. It was a gift from Evita, who told her just because she was going to be a married woman was no reason why she had to give up wearing tunics. Especially tunics that sported her new kingdom's colors. Trinity loved the outfit in spite of the color. She'd outgrown all of her old tunics; the new one felt more like a dress, resting atop the knees of her blue breeches. She was also gifted with a new pair of sleek, brown boots, with laces running all the way up to her calves. She wore them with pride, wondering why her aunt had suddenly started taking her opinion into account on this latest shopping venture. *She chose well.*

"It's tunic weather," Trinity reminded him.

Schobe smiled. "You always did love your tunics."

They stood along the cemented walls of the bridge and gazed down at the ocean for a while, chatting about the little things they always seemed to go on for hours about. She wanted to know more about his family. He wanted to know what she had done to annoy her aunt that day.

The sun was hot on her skin for a change. While they spoke, she couldn't help but wonder if she had the time to go for a quick dive to cool off. Maybe she could retrieve her sword from the depths after she'd lost it at the start of winter.

Schobe must've sensed her wandering interests, because he turned and resumed his sentry duty. "He's down there. Quatas."

"Is he?"

"Just released yesterday. Commander has him—he's digging latrines."

Trinity laughed. "Perhaps we should go and mock him like he did us."

"Love to. But I'm stuck here all evening. Probably won't even get a supper."

"I'll snake a meal from Phes. Steak, or something. I'll bring it to you. Or better yet, I'll ask Grandfather. Maybe I could have you join us." *It wouldn't be to say goodbye*, she thought, *it's just an invite.* "I'd like to have your company at supper."

"No. You shouldn't do any of that. No, tonight, you should...just dine with your family, Trinity." He looked away, studying the grip on his halberd.

Trinity stood right before him like a pest, searching his eyes for some sort of a more satisfying answer. Though she knew already what her friend was struggling to say about dining with royalty, and about lowborn knights like him not belonging anywhere near her now that her new family was here. *But Hayden still isn't here. Schobe is.* She had wanted to kiss him on the night of the ball. Even after, when he'd come to see her in the tower and gave her the last of Guren's papers to rip. Schobe, however, gave her no such affections. He—being the knightly gentlemen—escorted her home and left when he knew Evita was there to console her. She knew he didn't want to say it, or admit it, but *he* had wanted to kiss her too. She remembered how close their faces were to one another, before she saw Guren and ruined everything. And now Schobe was saying with those downcast chocolate eyes and unspoken words that a kiss was never going to happen between them. But who was he to decide for her?

She rolled her eyes and weakly laughed. "Forgetting already Schobey? I don't like being told that I can't do something. I want you at supper tonight. I'll demand it of Grandfather, if I must."

"Trinity," he said, tensely. "I can't. You know I can't. Please don't say anything."

She shot him a dejected look, then stepped past him and hopped up onto the cemented wall of the bridge, planting the toes of her boots near the edge. She could feel the wind swarming her body, and the ocean's mist sprinkling her clothes.

"W-what are you doing?" Schobe asked, dropping his halberd and clasping onto one of her boots instead to help keep her balanced. "Quit playing games. Get off the wall, Trinity."

She wasn't looking at him. She was staring down at the waves and admiring how far away she felt from the unsettled waters. "I could do it; you know? Jump. And I'd probably survive too. Not even a broken bone."

"*Trinity*," he warned. "Get off of there right now. Just because you're strong doesn't mean you should go risking your life to make a point."

"Be honest…if I jumped, would you join me?"

Schobe's eyes were huge with fright. "Can we talk about this on safer ground?"

"Think of it. They'd both think we were dead. But I would keep us alive. Like with the aqueduct. We could go anywhere. Do anything. Just the two of us. We could be free."

"...No," he said, resignedly. He reached his hand up to her. "We couldn't. I've sworn an oath to your Grandfather. And you—you would never hurt your family that way. Letting them think you were dead. No. You care for them too much."

Trinity clenched her fists and ignored his outstretched palm. She jumped back down onto the walkway, and glared at him once more. "Didn't you hear? I've got a new family. And they don't give a lion's tail about me."

"That's not true."

"All I am is an underhanded deal to them. Just some game piece in their *stupid* alliance."

"You're not. Your family would never do that to you."

"What do you know about my family?" she spat. "They've been planning this for years. My grandfather doesn't even have a proper place for me to sit in the throne room. He doesn't want me there."

"You're angry about...a seat?"

"I'm not angry about—you're missing the point Schobe," she said, gritting her teeth. "I'm angry at—I'm mad at—"

"What? Your aunt? The king?"

"Yes. But no. Not just them. They're only doing what they think is best. I know that."

"Then who? Me?"

"No! Not you. I'm just—I'm angry. So angry. At...ugh—"

"Who?" he demanded, in a way only his kindness, loyalty, and sense of duty could allow, like a tired horse requesting its saddle.

It became too much for Trinity to bear. "THE WHOLE DAMN KINGDOM!" she screamed, loud enough for every knight posted on the half-mile bridge to hear.

"Trinity?" He touched her shoulder, lightly at first, and then he let his fingers rest atop her as he tried to comfort her.

"It's not fair," she said. Her words were calmer now, but still she was upset. "None of this is fair. All I am is a weed ready to be plucked."

"Don't believe that. Don't think that. The kingdom loves you. Your family. I—" He removed his hand from her shoulder.

She stared at him for a second, quietly. "*Schobe*…I have to go." She stepped past him once more.

"Trinity, don't leave yet. Please, don't go." He was begging, not asking.

"It's too late," she muttered, unsure if he'd heard her. She picked up her pace, allowing her fast feet to take her away from him. She headed back towards the direction of where her new life was going to begin. It was a place where Schobe could no longer help her anymore. It was a life where he could no longer be her hero.

CHAPTER SEVENTEEN

THE FLOWER GIRL'S SECRET

Quatas was down at the beach, digging trails against the broken sand. Trinity had debated whether or not she would even come to see him after his month-long dungeon sentence. After all, he was the one who'd treated her and Schobe so terribly at the ball, drunkenly harassing them. But then, this was *still* Quatas. She needed answers, whether he was ready to give them or not.

He and Trinity had become friends not long after her ninth birthday; he was one of the few knights who had been impressed with her feats of strength. After she and Schobe became friends again, the three of them would play games together, laughing at whatever they could, which in those days was usually anything that others would take seriously, like stepping in horse dung or taking bets on which knights would win in a scrap. Trinity's favorite activity with Quatas back then had been spitting. Quatas was the best at spitting. She swore that even from a hundred feet high, she could see his wads hit the ocean when they'd practice off of the eastern bridge.

Schobe hadn't been wrong when he said that Quatas helped him become a knight. The truth was that Schobe probably would've never received his knight's medallion so young if it weren't for Quatas' insistence that he was ready to take the tests. Quatas was a good knight, and always a dependable friend. So why had everything changed?

Trinity approached him along the glimmering afternoon shoreline. Her new boots left light imprints on the wet sand. Quatas saw her, and leaned his sweating, bare chest against his shovel. He was wearing a rounded hat made from dried seaweed, which Trinity thought was strange. Ordinarily, Quatas liked showing off his hair. The sweat, she guessed, must've made him want to hide it. Quatas pulled a kerchief from his pants pocket and wiped at his face.

"Come to check my progress, have you?" he asked. Again, it was hard for her to read his tone. She couldn't tell if he was offended or making jokes. "I admit, I can't shovel crap nearly as fast as the two of you."

"Do you need any help?"

"No," he said, holding back a laugh. "I've got this. Besides, you didn't come here to help me make latrines. Be honest."

Trinity cupped her hands together nervously. "You're right. I wanted to talk to you. About the other night."

"If you've come looking for an apology—I'm sorry. I was drunk." He sat and began drinking from his jug of water.

She'd hardly expected an apology, especially one so halfhearted. "Why were you being that way? You've been saying such awful things to me lately. And then there's times where it's almost like you—never mind."

"What?"

"Nothing. I just...I thought we were friends."

"*Friends*," he said, scoffing. "You're a princess. I could no more be your friend than *you* could marry Schobe. People with different titles can't be friends. It's impossible."

"We *are* friends, Quatas. I wouldn't be out here getting my new tunic all wet if we weren't."

"Since when do you care about ruined clothes?"

"I care." She straightened the fabric with her hand. "It'll probably be the last tunic and pants I ever get to wear. After today it's nothing but Zayloan dresses."

"Oh Princess," he said, pounding his chest. "You're breaking my heart."

Every part of her wanted to turn and end their friendship right there on the spot. What was she still doing talking to him anyway? He, like Schobe and tunics and pants, would no longer have any part in her life soon. Yet, she stood her ground. "You don't really think those awful things about me, do you? That the kingdom would be better off if I wasn't destroying it all the time?"

Quatas sighed softly, and then stood up and began shoveling again. "Said I was sorry. Take it or leave it."

She wanted to say more, but Quatas had turned his back to her. Besides, someone was approaching them from behind. Someone who Trinity hadn't seen since the day of the ball.

"Milady," said the approaching Samboolian flower girl, "you've come to visit." She was carrying with her a bouquet of the orange flowers with green, insect-like thistles. Her hair and face were unwrapped today. Her hair was lovely, Trinity thought. It was soft and raven, and wavy, but not curly. Her round face was a creamy brown. Trinity realized then that the wraps this girl had worn before hid much of her true appearance.

"How are you?" Trinity asked.

"Well, Milady," she said, smiling. "I was hoping to see you again. So sorry about the other day."

"It's alright. I understand."

"*Trinity*," Quatas said in a loud whisper, looking up from his work. "Why are you talking to her kind?"

"My kind?" the flower girl asked, looking uneasy.

"Samboolian trash. The whole lot of you."

"Quatas!" Trinity exclaimed. "Leave her be. She's done nothing to you."

Quatas grunted and resumed his digging. "Anything you say, your *Highness*."

Trinity turned back to the flower girl. "Don't mind him. He's just grumpy about his work is all. I never had a chance to properly meet you the other day. I'm Trinity."

The flower girl still seemed put off by Quatas' comment, but turned to face Trinity all the same. "That is a pretty name. I have never met a Trinity before. My name is Sarai."

"Surrey?"

"No, no. Sar-a-ee."

"Sarai," Trinity repeated, slower.

"You learn quick," she said with a wink.

Trinity smiled. "Have you had any luck selling your flowers?"

"None, Trinity. But would you like one? I'll make you a good deal."

Trinity winced, not wanting to further offend her. "Well…let me smell one once more."

She took one of the orange flowers from the bouquet and held it to her face. Again, the sick feeling from before came over her. Her neck felt a biting tingle. Her eyes began to water.

"I'm sorry, Sarai. I don't think these are the flowers for me. Something about them makes me sick."

"Really?" Sarai asked.

"Yes, even now, holding it. I feel like I'm going to throw up." She reached forward to hand the flower back to Sarai, when she felt a prick on her thumb. "Ouch."

"Careful with the thorns," Sarai warned.

Trinity raised her eyebrows as she stared at her thumb. A pinprick of her tri-colored blood leaked from where she'd been stuck. "Oh. I'm bleeding?" She nursed the wound with her lips. Her hand began to feel numb.

"May I see?" Sarai asked.

Trinity held her wet thumb to Sarai, who examined the blood for only a second before her eyes grew wide. "Your blood, Trinity. It's dark and gray."

Quatas must've overhead them, for he stopped digging and came to examine the cut too.   "Will you look at that?" he asked. "I don't think I've ever seen your blood before. I didn't think anything could hurt you. Has it always been that color?"

"Yes," Trinity said. "It's my Terkian blood."

"Terkian?" Sarai asked, looking shocked. "You are a Terkian?"

Trinity nodded slowly, unsure of what the fascination was all about. She shook out her hand and the numbness subsided. She looked down at the blood and it had already turned hard, like a tiny pebble.

"Please, Milady, Trinity—will you come and meet my old mam? She will be very interested in your Terkian blood."

"I—"

"Leave her Samboolian. This is the princess you're addressing," Quatas commanded.

"Princess?" Sarai's mouth looked like it was going to drop down into the sand. "A princess Terkian?"

"Yes. And it's fine," she said, shifting her eyes warily between Quatas and Sarai. "I'll go. To meet your old mam."

"Oh, thank you, Trinity. Princess Trinity, I mean. Thank you."

She took ahold of Trinity's arm and tried to pull her along. Trinity stepped lightly forward, following after her.

"You there, Samboolian!" Quatas called.

Sarai and Trinity turned back to him.

"Sir?" Sarai asked, uneasily.

"What did you say the name of that flower was?"

"We call it *Irensiya* in my language. But in the TCL, it is called The Perfect Mantis."

"Perfect Mantis," he repeated. He resumed his digging, speaking to himself as he did.

Perfect Mantis? What a strange name for a flower, Trinity thought. Even stranger still was what the flower had been able to do to her. It pierced her skin and made her bleed. Once she had thought that nothing besides a sharp blade could harm her. But then again, she had already been cut by the glass and bowstring as well. *Am I getting weaker?* She didn't feel weaker.

What about the recurring pain which she still believed was her connection to Duke. If he really was her brother, and if it really was him that she'd seen wounded in the pool of Terkian blood, then she knew he was capable of hurting also. She hadn't felt any shared emotions with him since the night he lost his eye. If he were really still alive, then she hoped he was alright.

Sarai led her further along the beach to a place that was packed with refugees. Their numbers seemed to have doubled since Trinity last saw them arriving. The two of them stepped through the crowds of people with the same features as Sarai's; her hair, skin color, and even some dressed in similar robes. Trinity realized then that the refugees most likely all hailed from the same place. *Sambool.* Trinity remembered hearing that the bandits who had attacked her kingdom were said to be from Bayonick. And after thinking back to her encounter with the snowy-eyed bandit leader, Trinity was sure of one thing: *These two groups couldn't possibly be the same. So why won't the king trust them and let them into the kingdom?* Trinity, however, knew the answer for herself. King Eslon didn't go around opening his doors to commoners. Only those born in high society, or those who could add to his riches. *If I was queen, I'd let them all in.*

Some of the refugees watched Trinity with great interest. Others bowed their heads or simply ignored her. She couldn't be sure if it was out of respect or shame. Much like with Sarai, there was little chance many of them even knew who she was. There were children playing swords with dried pieces of seaweed and sticks. Men sat in semicircles, telling stories with great vigor. Sweet smells rose from seeping tents where suppers were being prepared. They were exotic flavors that she'd never caught scent of before, but they were appetizing nonetheless. Some men wore armor, though none seemed to be wearing a full set. There were wrinkled, charcoal-colored breastplates, and tan, loose-fitting pants. Trinity had never seen the material of these breastplates before. They looked like skins, but she knew of no animal with this type of pelt.

Many of the men also wore dark-lensed glasses. She wondered how they could see from them. Her curiosity overcame her so much that she broke away slightly from Sarai's path and went to converse with one man reading a book. When he noticed her, he closed his book and tilted his glasses upward on his nose with his middle finger.

"Hello sir," she said.

"…Hu-lo sar," he repeated, firmly.

"Trinity, what are you doing?" Sarai asked.

"I was going to ask him about his armor. Only—"

Sarai shook her head. "Many here don't speak TCL. What would you like to ask him?"

"I-I wanted to know what sort of skin this was." She touched the man's armor, which had a squishier feel than she was expecting. The man stared at her with visible confusion.

Sarai cleared her throat. "Essi—uh, welleka che malaka?"

"Konoma. Sen konoma," he repeated, tapping on his chest.

"Elephant," Sarai explained.

Elephant? She remembered that black elephants were one of MAI's sacred animals. *I thought it was a sin to kill one.* The soldiers here didn't seem to share her aunt's views. She pointed at the man's dark glasses. "Those. What are they for?"

The man grinned. His teeth were small and yellow. "Esaka, sul ki anota. Mado kide."

Sarai began to chuckle. "He says they are to keep the sun out of his eyes. And the sand. We have plenty of both in our homeland."

The man offered her the glasses from his eyes. Trinity put them on. The day felt dark through the lenses, but she could still see clearly. *Amazing.* "How do I look?" she asked them.

Both Sarai and the soldier nodded. "Like a true-born of Sambool, Princess," Sarai said.

The soldier motioned for her to keep them, pulling out another pair from beneath his wrinkled breastplate. Trinity thanked him and tucked the pair of dark glasses onto the neck of her tunic. After saying their farewells, she was eventually led further along the beach to where a large yellow tent was posted. Ivory tusks were hung over the threshold like mounted trophies. Trinity couldn't believe just how big they were. She wanted to touch them, but thought better of it.

Sarai stopped them before entering so she could quickly wrap her hair back up into her robes. Wherever they were going, Sarai must not have wanted her hair showing. Trinity wanted to ask Sarai why she did this, but thought the question might be rude and decided against it. *I hope I wasn't supposed to cover mine also.*

Inside the tent were many other women, wearing brightly colored garments not unlike Sarai's. They too had their hair wrapped in a way that only their round faces could be seen. They stopped their activities immediately upon seeing her.

Sarai stepped in front of Trinity and took her by the hand. She led her to the edge of the tent where a large, old woman sat in front of a full bowl of what looked to be a steaming, cream-colored broth. The old woman's eyes were crossed and gray.

"Is she—" Trinity started to say.

"Blind, yes," Sarai said, now sensing Trinity's apprehension. She grabbed two rounded cushions and placed them before the old woman on the soft furs lining the tent. She motioned for Trinity to join her, and the two of them sat upon their knees. "Mam, I have brought someone to meet you. A girl named Trinity."

"The one who smells of lavender?" asked the old woman, pleasantly. Her accent was strong, but her use of the Taercion Common Language was flawless. "Such a light step you have, child. I almost thought you were a bathed cat."

"No," Trinity said, laughing at her words. "I usually get yelled at for stepping too strongly."

"Of course," the old mam said. "But you are on your guard with us. So, you step as if you are afraid."

"I…"

"Footsteps never lie. But have no fear, child. We do you no harm. We are not of Gazenga's type."

Trinity did not reply. It seemed as if this old blind woman already knew so much about what she was thinking that any words on the matter seemed unimportant. She looked to Sarai for some sort of hint as to why she was here.

"Mam," Sarai began, "essi vasaka ene Terkian rulaton."

Trinity didn't need a translation for that sentence. She knew Sarai had just revealed who she was. *I hope I didn't just put my trust in the wrong person.*

The old mam nodded and took a spoonful of the steaming bowl's broth. She didn't drink it, but instead poured it out onto the palm of her right hand. Despite the broth's visible heat, the old woman did not cringe or show any signs she was hurt.

"She wants to read you," Sarai explained. "Where we come from, my old mam was one of the last few who knew the secrets to reading a person's story."

"Read a person's story? I don't understand. I'm not a book."

"Everyone has a story," the old mam said. "But we forget parts as we grow older. This is where dolphin broth comes in handy. You know of the golden dolphins?"

"One of MAI's sacred animals. Yes." She was starting to think these people had white lion hearts kept in a jar somewhere around here. *Evita would never set foot in a place like this. Not with her convictions.* Trinity, however, decided to hear them out. "Why do you...boil dolphin?"

"As a Terkian, I thought you'd know the importance of what the sacred animals possess. Think of what the gorilla's strength does for your body. Gives you great power. Power to crush mountains. So too, does the dolphin give power. Over the *mind,*" she said, pointing at Trinity's temple with her dripping hand. "Will you let me read your story, child?"

"You...I..." *Why are you hesitating? Discover your own answers!* She blinked. "Sure. I suppose. Am I—do I have to burn my hands?"

The old mam cackled. "Not at all, fair one. But you must have a drink of the broth."

"I don't think—I'm not so sure I can."

"I understand," the old mam said with a rigid face. "You are a girl of Hydlix also. Very religious the Hydlix. They do not share our views on what the sacred animals can provide."

"The sacred animals were put here by MAI. To help us flourish," Trinity said, in an almost perfect recitation of scripture from the holy text she sometimes skimmed before dozing on Evita's shoulder in church.

"Spoken like a true Hydlixian. But I ask you—do your people honor the sacred ones? Or do they keep them barred in cages? On display to show their might, perhaps?"

Trinity wasn't sure if Sarai's old mam was able to read her thoughts already without having drunken any of the broth. But if the old woman knew what she was thinking, she would've seen the image of the white lion trapped in the dungeons. *Snowflake.* Trinity cast her gaze down upon the steaming broth once more.

The old mam began again, "Even your own people, the Terkians, were not kind to their animals." Her face was pained. "There are…so few gorillas which still roam the canyons of your homeland."

Trinity wavered, but finally raised her hand off of her knee and picked up a cup beside the hot pot. She dipped it slightly into the broth and pulled up a swallow's worth.

"Drink slowly. And clear your mind."

"How did you know I was going to drink? I thought you were blind."

The old mam grinned a curvy grin. "Your heart beats strong, Terkian. Especially when you have made up your mind."

Trinity raised the cup to her lips and drank. The taste was sweeter than she was expecting, and made her think of warm cider beside a fire. But it didn't have the poor aftertaste that Hydlixian cider gave. Instead, she felt like she was washing down a delicious fish supper.

The old mam raised her hand and touched a finger to Trinity's brow. Her gray eyes illuminated, turning many different shades before they became a solid white. Trinity felt a light pressure in her head, as if a thousand thoughts were suddenly trying to break through the front of her skull. She clutched onto her tunic, and winced as the pressure grew more intense. Sarai rubbed the top of Trinity's back and this comforted her slightly. Still, it felt like the pressure would never go away. As soon as the old woman lifted her finger though, Trinity's head had an immediate sense of relief.

"That was—so intense," Trinity said, gasping for air as if she'd just been punched in her lung.

"Were you able to read her, Mam?" Sarai asked.

The old mam's face scrunched and she pursed her lips together. She stared off into something her once-more-grayed eyes couldn't capture. She grabbed onto fur carpets beneath her and hunched over.

"Are you alright?" Trinity asked. Sarai rose and hurried to comfort the old woman.

"I am," the old mam told them. "Never before have I received such a...*complicated* vision."

"Complicated?" Trinity asked.

The old mam nodded. "You know such pain, girl. Pain enough for multiple lives. But all you have ever known is luxury. And love."

Trinity couldn't argue this, but she thought under her current circumstances that she couldn't simply agree. "I *do* know pain. My life has been decided for me. There's nothing I can do to change it."

The old mam shook her head. "It's not that type of pain. This is the pain one gets from feeling tremendous loss. In reading your story...I have only seen this happen six times in your life. One most recently."

Trinity knew this last loss without having to say the person's name. *Guren. His loss doesn't pain me. Not anymore.* But what were the others? Evita, Schobe, and everyone she had ever known were still here with her. For another day at least. "What were they? The others?" she asked.

The old mam clicked her teeth. "One is perhaps your oldest memory. Your first one maybe. You lost your mother, didn't you?"

Trinity gasped, clutching at the furs below her. "You could search that far back?"

"Yes." The old mam was cleaning her hands now, and her breathing had grown heavier. "Dolphin blood has a way of knowing the whole mind. I even know of your time before you were born."

Trinity's eyes grew big as she lurched forward onto her folded knees. "Before I was—tell me! Did I have a brother?"

The old mam stared in Trinity's direction as if she were studying her face. She gazed long and hard, before finally giving a slight nod. "Two of them. Yes."

"Two—" her word was more a breath than an utterance. "Two brothers?"

"Yes," she replied deeply, struggling now to catch her breath. "There were…three of you. Terkian triplets."

Trinity shot up like a geyser. "Please!" she begged. "I have to know more."

The old mam waved her away with a weak hand, and leaned back, coughing violently as she did. The other women in the tent quickly surrounded the elder, who closed her eyes and made Trinity wonder if she was dying. Sarai pulled at her arm.

"We have to go," she ordered.

"What?" Trinity shook her head. "No. Is she alright?"

"She will be. But we must leave her for now," Sarai said.

Trinity wanted to protest, but knew she had no other choice than to follow Sarai back out to the beach.

After stepping out, Sarai closed the tent flaps behind them. Trinity put her hands on her knees and tried to calm herself. There were so many thoughts rushing to her mind that she suspected the dolphin broth was still running its course. "Triplets," she huffed out. "I didn't even know that was something that could—" her voice trailed off, as she dropped to her knees and planted her hands on the cool sand.

"Are you alright, Trinity?" Sarai asked her.

No. She wasn't. Her entire life she'd been lied to. She'd been made to believe something which she had figured for herself wasn't true. But having a second brother changed everything. She knew then that she could no longer keep her silence. She had to confront Evita. Even if it hurt her to do so. "I have to go," she said, getting to her feet.

"Wait," Sarai said. "Before you do, I thought I should tell you something. A secret I've been keeping."

"Whatever it is, it can wait."

"It is about Duke."

Trinity looked at her, gaping. Her head felt so light she thought her feet would give out from under her. "Duke? You know about Duke?"

"He is your brother. Am I right?"

"Is he? *Yes.* I believe he is. No...I know he is. Do you know him?"

Sarai bit her lip so hard that Trinity thought she'd draw blood. There was pain in this girl's eyes. A pain Trinity hadn't realized until now. "Every Samboolian knew of the strobanth. The terrible things he did. Many fear to be within his presence. He is a trained killer."

She gulped, feeling short of breath. "Then...he's a bad person?"

Sarai's eyes fell to the clutched fist across her chest. "It's funny. But if you asked any other from Sambool that question, they would all say yes. No hesitation. He is a wicked boy who serves a wicked king. You once asked me if he is Terkian too. Yes, he is. That is why—what my mam says—I believe the two of you are related. He even sort of looks like you."

I'm not crazy then. I'm not! My brother is alive. I knew it. Maybe they both are. Both? She wasn't sure she was ready to accept the news of this latest brother yet.

Sarai came close and whispered in Trinity's ear. "I cannot tell this secret to anyone else," she said, her voice breaking, "but I know Duke's other side. He saved me. Saved us. Your brother. All of us who are here owe him a debt." She had tears forming, but she did not shrink away or stop. Her voice grew stronger. "Because of him, we are free from Gazenga's clutches. But so very few know this. Duke saved us even when he did not have to do such a thing. At great risk to his own life. And that is why I believe he is like you, Trinity." She reached forward and took Trinity's hand, giving it a gentle squeeze. "I believe...he is a good person."

CHAPTER EIGHTEEN

THE PERFECT MANTIS

Dusk had fallen when Trinity left the beachside camp and reentered Hydlix; her path was clear. She had to see Evita. She had to know the truth once and for all. How many babies did her mother have? Why was Duke forced to go to Sambool? And lastly, and maybe most important of all: *Why did Evita not save Duke? Or the other child.*

Along the way, to her surprise, there was nothing but chaos. The red-armored Zayloan knights ran through the streets, scattering like hungry cats. Meanwhile, Hydlixian knights had posted themselves at different homes and balconies laid throughout the kingdom. They flooded corridors and marched on the cobbled roads. None of their blades were drawn, but there was definite animosity between the two armies. Trinity wanted to stop and ask the reason but suspected the knights would just ignore her. Besides, she had something more pressing to discover.

When she arrived home, Evita was already waiting for her, seated upon the cushioned bench in the hall. Upon seeing her, Evita sprang up and ran to embrace Trinity.

"Trinity! Where were you? I was so worried." She latched onto Trinity's shoulders. "Did you hear about Hayden?"

"Hayden?" Trinity asked, surprised.

Evita searched her expression. "You haven't been told? He's gone missing. The prince's garrison rode across the eastern bridge nearly a half-hour ago. It seems the prince has vanished. They've searched from Sabalean to here. King Saito has—he's ordered that every home in Hydlix be searched also."

Trinity narrowed her eyes. "He can't do that."

"I know. Father thinks it's some sort of trick. Another invasion, perhaps. He's ordered our men to stand guard. Keep them from entering our subjects' homes unannounced."

"That doesn't make sense. Why would he be here? Shouldn't they search in Sabalean?"

Evita sighed, folding her arms nervously. "The kings—they're being paranoid. But they have everyone in a panic. I-I've been ordered to stay here. Oh, I was hoping you weren't out there for long. I'm so happy you're safe. I had gone to order your cake. Raspberry frosting, remember? Just like you like it."

"I..." Trinity found it difficult to meet her aunt's almost naïve gaze.

"Yes, Trinity, what is it?"

"I need to talk to you."

"...Sure, of course," Evita said, motioning to the bench. "Please, let's have a seat. Can I get you some milk? I've just poured some." She turned and lifted a sloshing cup from their center table.

The words spilled from Trinity's lips without warning. "Why didn't you save Duke?"

Evita froze. Her milk fell from her hand and splashed onto the floor. "What—what did you say?"

"Duke." Trinity stared up at her aunt, hesitantly. "I know about Duke."

Evita's eyes were fierce looking inside of her head. Her breathing was silent, almost as if it had stopped completely. "H-how?"

"...I went into your room. On the night of the invasion. I saw what was in your locked chest." Though she was scared to say this, there was no regret in the coolness of her words.

Evita grit her teeth. "You stole from me? After you promised that you would never do such a thing again."

"You wouldn't give me answers. Yes, I stole from you. I took the medallion that had *my* name on it. And the imprint with *my* mother carrying me and my brother. Those were both mine. You had no right," Trinity admitted, more harshly than she'd ever spoken to her aunt before.

"Stop right there!" Evita spat, pointing a finger directly in Trinity's face. "You had no right—"

"I'm not here for another lecture. I have gone my ENTIRE LIFE without answers about my past! Don't you think it was your job to tell me? That I had a brother? Two of them!"

"Two?" Evita looked petrified. "What are you going on about?"

"Admit it! I had brothers. But you only saved me. Why?"

Evita struggled for some sort of answer, but whatever she wanted to say appeared lost within her growing mix of rage and heartache. She bit her finger and stepped back, plopping down onto the bench, and then watched helplessly as the spreading milk rushed and covered the bottom of her dress. "No. You weren't supposed to see—to know any of that."

"But I did. Please—I'm *begging* you." Trinity balled her fists; her whole body was trembling. "Give me an answer. For once in my whole life…give me an answer!"

Evita was crying now. Softly at first, but then she started to wail. Spit and water flew from the crevices of her face. "It's my fault, alright? It's mine. All mine." She buried her face in her hands. "I'm to blame."

Trinity's lip was quivering, but she didn't sense any tears of her own. She was angry. Too angry to try and console. She resented this crying woman who shrieked like a child that hadn't gotten her way. Trinity took a heavy step forward but stopped herself from proceeding any further. She was afraid of what she might do to her aunt just then. "What—" She took a calming breath. "What are you talking about?"

Evita tried to compose herself too, but she was having difficulty. She wiped at her face with the sleeves of her dress. "Everything is all my fault. Everything."

"*What* is your fault, Evita?" It felt like a bitter swear to not address her as her aunt, but right now Evita didn't feel like family. Only a liar who had kept far too many secrets.

"…Gazenga. And that boy. The one who works for him…*Duke*," she managed to say, forcing the word from her mouth. "I could've saved him. Taken him like I did you. But I'm not like you Trinity." She stared up at her, looking powerless. "I wasn't brave."

"...You left him?"

Evita's tears continued rolling down her cheeks. "Your mother was dying. The king had already gone. To join a battle that Terkia was already losing. That wretched, heartless man! He left before he saw you...your mother had just delivered you, see? And she held you in her right arm." Evita looked down at her arm imitating the cradling of an invisible baby. "Duke was on her left. One of the fool nurses in the room didn't sense the danger we were all in. Took that—that haunting imprint. Said it was royal tradition." Evita shook her head and tried to soothe herself, rocking back and forth. "So stupid. Like there was time for things like traditions anymore. The nurse handed me the imprint...as if I needed a reminder of the worst day of mine and my sister's life."

A small part of Trinity wanted to console Evita then. But there were still more questions needing answers. "How did we escape?"

Evita took a breath. "The nurses showed me a secret tunnel leading away from the infirmary. I wanted to—to take you both. Zepolia was so upset. She handed you to me. And then..."

"What?"

Evita squeezed her eyes closed. "She handed me Duke also. I was fourteen, Trin. Can you understand that? Fourteen. I didn't think my actions would have such consequences. I...I stepped away. Holding you only. To be honest, I didn't even know if you were the girl or the boy."

Trinity felt her heart sink. So that was it...the answer she'd waited forever to hear. Her entire life had been based on a circumstance. She had been the closer baby. If

Duke had been on the right arm instead of her, she may have ended up as Gazenga's strobanth. Instead, she was the one who knew luxury like the old mam said. She was the one who was being forced to marry. And Duke was the one who had known *true pain*.

Evita continued, "One of the other nurses handed me your medallion. They led me to the tunnel. I thought—I really believed they were going to follow after. At least one of them. Holding your brother. But no one else escaped from out the tunnel. I had believed for the longest time that everyone in that room had died."

"Duke is still alive," Trinity said, sounding surer and calmer than before. She was getting answers. It was enough to take peace in. She came and sat beside Evita on the bench. "I know he is. I've shared his pain. And I have known his hurt. He's hurting."

"Don't you see? It's all my fault," Evita repeated. "If I had only taken him. If I had only kept him from falling into Gazenga's hands...Sambool wouldn't be as big of a threat as they are now."

There was truth in this. But none of it mattered anymore. Not to Trinity.

"What about my other brother?"

"*What* other brother?"

"I had another. I'm part of...*triplets*." Just saying the word again gave her a strange joy.

Evita shook her head, still trying to compose herself. "I'm sorry, I don't know why you think that. Your mother had twins. It was even prophesized."

"Prophe—what?"

"Prophesized. She met a strange woman of the land, just before she had you and your brother. Some wandering minstrel with long, white hair. The woman offered her a blessing and your mother—kind as she was—accepted.

The minstrel told her and your father to be expecting twins."

"...Are you sure?"

Evita nodded, looking confident with her answer.

Trinity didn't know if there was any truth to the second brother, other than what the old mam had told her. But the Samboolian had seemed so sure, as did her aunt. Trinity supposed though that if there was an answer, she'd discover it. She had to. *He might be out there needing someone to save him also.*

"I'm going to find him," Trinity said, standing up again. "Duke. He needs me."

"You—be serious. You're getting married tomorrow."

Trinity scoffed. "They can't even find my husband to be. And even if they did...I'm going to find Duke. Whether the Zayloans like it or not."

Evita grasped her hand. "Think of the alliance. Think of all the people who depend on us forming a bond."

"I am. And if I can help Duke, then together the two of us might be able to stop Gazenga. And then we can forget all about the alliance."

Evita stared gloomily at the floor where the milk had finished spreading across the stonework. "You still sound like the little girl whose biggest dream was to be a knight. But that's all this is, Trinity. A dream. You have to accept your reality."

Trinity glared down at her, and took her hand away from Evita's. "Why? So I can turn out like you? Someone who *waits* for their dreams to just happen. That's... pathetic."

A hurried knock sounded from their door. Trinity stepped away quickly, thankful that someone was here to break the tension. Quatas was standing on the other side of the door when she opened it.

He was sweating fiercely. His face was drenched in the dark, sticky sweat that she'd once seen on him before. He was wearing his armor now, along with his helmet. And he was panting as if he'd just run ten miles in them.

"Trinity—come quickly," he said. "Guren needs you. He knows something. About Hayden."

"Guren?" *What could he possibly know?*

"Quatas?" Evita asked, looking up from where she was sitting.

"Please Princess Evita, I need to borrow her. This is important. Her intended's life may be at stake."

"Come on then," Trinity said, walking out the door with him.

"Trinity!" Evita shouted. "Don't go. We weren't done here."

Trinity hesitated, before poking her head back inside. "I don't have anything else to say to you."

"Please," Evita begged, "take a moment and think. Doesn't this seem strange?" She rose slowly to her feet. "Why is Guren summoning you now? With all the madness happening out there—how can you be sure there isn't something more sinister at play here?" Her eyes glinted with the remnants of her years of pent-up sorrow. Her voice had grown so fragile. "Please Trinity… we must be careful with who we trust."

There was a truth to her words. And, Trinity supposed, even genuine concern behind them. But she was far past listening. And whether it was respect or love for Evita which would've caused her to question her defiance now, both had grown bitter within her. She glared spitefully at her aunt, no longer swayed by the hurt she saw in Evita's eyes then.

"Don't talk to me about trust," she said, before closing the door shut behind her, refusing to give Evita a chance to say another word.

Trinity and Quatas took the shortest path to Guren's room, straight down to the chapel alcoves. She wondered along the way what Guren was going to say. If he knew something about Hayden, why hadn't he told the king first? And besides, hadn't she made her feelings quite clear? She hated him, and that was all there was to it. No matter what Guren had to tell her, nothing changed between them.

When they arrived at Guren's door, there were already two posted Zayloan knights standing just outside of it. *Strange*, she thought. *What are they doing here?* Neither of the pink-haired knights acknowledged her as she made her way to the front of the door. She went to knock, but saw that the door was slightly ajar. *Since when does Guren leave his door open?*

She had just stepped forward when she felt Quatas grab her shoulders with both of his hands, shoving her through the entrance. The door was slammed shut behind her and she could hear the men leaning up against it, trapping her in.

At first, she considered breaking down the door and dealing with the knights herself, although she had no weapons on her. But as she studied the empty, candle-lit room more closely, a sense of dread filled her. Suddenly, a flash of green filled the room and swirled all around her. Her nostrils were ablaze with a rank odor as an emerald smoke clouded her vision. Trinity felt the vapors scratch their way down her throat as she dropped to her knees, an agony she'd never experienced before coursing through her. Her hands and legs went limp. She wanted to push herself up from the ground, but for the first time in her life, she couldn't find the strength to do so.

As the smoke cleared, a gangly, wavy-haired young man stepped forward holding a golden room key. He placed the key in his pocket, revealing his other hand as he did so, and Trinity saw that with it he was holding an orange flower with green thorns. *The Perfect Mantis!*

He circled her, snickering as he walked. There was a whistling in his laugh, like he was missing teeth. Trinity knew then. Her rapid heartbeats and pulsing headache gave little doubt. *It's Hayden.*

"You know, I've always hated the smell of these flowers," Hayden told her. His voice was deeper than the last time she'd heard him speak, very controlled. Trinity could feel shivers running up her spine; they were the same as before when she'd first met him years ago. The boy had now become a dangerous man. Hayden held the orange flower up to his nose and smelled it with mock enthusiasm. "They're not very common in Zayloa, but I have seen them before. Imagine my surprise when my loyal subject—Quatas, I believe, is what he told you his name was—came running up to me on the shore when I arrived and informed me of your little secret." He stepped over her body as she began to rise, and he kicked the toe of his diamond-encrusted boots hard into her ribs, forcing her to yelp out and drop once more.

Quatas was Zayloan? It was all beginning to make sense now in her frazzled mess of thoughts.

"The mantis is good for healing cuts, you see. They help with clotting blood, and have been known to relax those who ingest them medicinally." He grabbed at the back of her hair and dug her face into the stone floor, causing her to choke out a muffled scream. "How very strange, right? I didn't quite see the connection at first, but Quatas assured me that these flowers made you ill. And now I think I understand." He knelt beside her, and fastened the flower to his draped purple cape. "They slow that nasty ape blood of yours. Keep it from passing properly through your veins."

Trinity believed him. The insides of her arms and legs felt like they were ready to burst.

"I was—" He checked his reflection on a nearby breastplate beside Guren's bed, smirking at what he saw, "—quite lucky one of my men had some smoke powder on hand. And I think, and you'll probably agree, that I've done a fine job mixing up an antidote to that little *strength* problem of yours."

Trinity did her best to keep her head turned up towards him, watching carefully his next move. Hayden's icy blue eyes were filled with a crushing joy. He was enjoying this. And what's more, there was something else in his expression. It was a similar look to the one his father had given her earlier that day.

He began to titter delightedly, whistle and all. He clapped his hands together. "How terrible this must all feel," he said, flashing her a toothy smile, though his eyes were burning with rage. "Now then, I think it's about time you and I had a long-overdue talk, my *little wife* to be."

CHAPTER NINETEEN

RESIST

Her nightmare was now reality. She was unable to move. Trapped without a net. Her muscles squeezed and tightened. She wanted to vomit, but couldn't find a way to let her stomach churn. She tried to reach her hand forward, and clutch onto Hayden's diamond-toed boots, but the pressure atop the back of her hand kept her from moving past an inch or two. All she could manage were weakened yelps. The flower was doing its job; every part of her felt ready to explode. *I can't shake this. Why can't I shake this?*

Hayden turned her body over effortlessly with the tip of his boot. He knelt down beside her and reached for her snowflake necklace.

"What is this cheap trash?" he asked, reflecting it amidst the dark glow of the room's candles.

She couldn't stop him. All she could do was watch as he tore Schobe's gift away. He cast the necklace onto the ground carelessly, snickering as he did.

"What's that? You look like you wanted to say something, dear."

She couldn't force a reply. No more than she could retract her fingers. A thousand vile curses stormed her brain, but she hadn't the strength to give voice to any of them.

He moved his hand towards her face. Trinity expected him to strike her, but instead he did something far worse. He caressed her cheek with the back of his fingers. Then, he raised her head with his hand until their eyes locked with one another. *I'll rip your eyes right out of your head*, she screamed in her thoughts.

"What's wrong? Have I made you angry? Come, come. I'll have no frowning the night before our wedding." He tapped her playfully on the nose. "I see no reason the two of us can't get along. After all, we are to be joined together forever. Under the sight of MAI himself. Which reminds me."

He released her chin, and her head fell hard onto the stone floor. Hayden stepped away, but he hadn't gone far. Her fingers felt a wave of relief, but water rushed to her eyes from the pain. A terrifying thought seized her. Even if she could cry, how was she supposed to let her tears flow anyway? Nothing in her was working like it should. Nothing was going to help her get the blood moving again.

Flow?

There had once been a time when she wanted more than anything to forget all memories of her former teacher. Cast him aside. Erase his presence in her life for good. But as she writhed on the floor waiting for Hayden to do his worst, Guren's was the only face that came to her. She didn't know if any of his lessons could've saved or even prepared her for this wicked turn of events she was now facing. But he had once spoken to her of flowing blood. She would always remember that lesson, because it was one of the very first lessons that he had ever taught her.

*   *   *

"How's that?" she asked Guren, tucking her rusted blades into the belt of her tunic like she'd seen so many knights do.

The remnants of her first training dummy laid strewn across the beachside in the early morning. Clumps of straw were washing away in the darkened waters as the pinkening sky was just beginning to show its first signs of day.

"Let us hope your future opponents wear thick armor. Unless they wish to see their entrails washed out to sea."

Trinity laughed. Guren hadn't meant the praise as a joke, she knew. But the image of a man's gushing corpse being dragged underwater was funny to her at this early hour. She had only been practicing with Guren for a few weeks since meeting him, and her body was still feeling sleep-deprived.

As she bent and helped him scoop what was left of her dummy's stuffing, a nasty shock coursed through her left arm. She wanted to yell, but cursed instead as her knees found the wet sand. Guren rushed to her side.

"My arm!" she cried.

"What? What is it?"

"I can't—my arm won't move."

There was pulsing happening along the tip of her forearm. A bubbling feeling of pain mixed with tingles.

This wasn't like the aqueduct experience. She could think plenty clear still. But her arm was contracting so fiercely that she was beginning to suspect it was broken.

Guren tried to take her arm up into his hands, but Trinity forced it back to her lap, whimpering as she did.

"You've a cramp, nothing more. Stop acting like a helpless baby."

"I'm not a baby! It really hurts."

He nodded and pursed his lips. "Yes, I've no doubt. Especially with that Terkian blood of yours. I can only guess how dreadful it is for someone as naturally strong as you. You've never had to use those muscles of yours before. Not like this."

"Make it stop," she begged.

"I cannot. You have to do it."

"H-how?"

"The blood needs to flow again. Unrestricted. Wiggle your fingers."

"I can't."

"*Trinity*. Do as I say," he commanded.

Trinity powered through the pain and tried to move the afflicted arm's hand. She curled her fingers inward and out, making a fist. Then, she tried her wrist. In what felt like an instant, the blockage seemed to correct itself; her arm grew warm and relaxed. She rubbed at where the pain had been, but couldn't sense it anymore. Her eyes widened with relief and wonder. She looked into her teacher's earnest expression.

"Better?" he asked.

"I don't—do you think that's going to happen again, Guren?"

Guren lightly chuckled. "Most likely. But as you train, you will begin to learn how to resist these natural weaknesses."

"Natural? But I'm—"

"Even Terkians are still human. Fortunately," he said, now smiling and holding onto his own arm, "our bodies have ways of saving themselves."

* * *

Trinity had to work quickly. There was no telling what Hayden was capable of. Or what he had been planning for all this time. She began with her pinky, the same as before when she was young. She tried to wiggle her finger. It was slow, but her pinky definitely moved.

"Yes," she whispered. *Can I talk now too?* It was the same as her pinky. Her voice somehow managed to push through the pressure and give sound like some familiar swing with a sword.

"Did you say something, love?" Hayden asked, sounding uninterested. "So silly of me, I almost forgot to take this off." He dropped a chain pendant beside her. It fell directly beside her snowflake necklace. It was a carved mustang head made from ruby. "Won't be needing that little reminder from MAI, will we?"

Keep talking, Hayden. She had to convince him to speak more. Stall him. *Resist the pressure and let the blood flow.* "That time before," she croaked, "with the invasion. Was that you too?"

"Ah," he said, breathing a triumphant breath. "Remember that, do you?"

"Quatas…he tried to take me to the glass chapel. I always…I always wondered why." Speaking was still difficult for her, but she had to keep trying.

Hayden smirked. "Yes, but he failed of course. If he hadn't, you'd already be dead. I had thirty of my own knights, dressed as bandits, waiting for you in that chapel. They were under orders to put an end to you and bring me your head. A fine gift, wouldn't you say?"

She stilled her worried gasps for air. All of her fingers had begun to wiggle, but she was careful not to let him see. Next came the wrist. And with it, another question.

"Why kill me? That…it'll break off the alliance."

"Who needs an alliance? Your sad excuses for knights aren't going to save us from a Samboolian invasion when it comes. Didn't you know? Gazenga's already wiped out two of the great kingdoms in a single night each." Hayden removed each of his gloves one by one and cast them carelessly onto Trinity's fallen body. You know what's better than alliances, dear? Money."

"…Money?"

"Of course. Your kingdom may smell like rotting fish, but there's plenty of stekis to be had here. Especially in that unpolished old headdress your grandfather wears. I could buy a whole new kingdom with that crown."

"You…you hired the Bayonick bandits then? To steal it?"

"I did," he said, snickering. "Big mistake that was. They were a sorry, desperate lot who had taken up camp outside our kingdom. And that wretched, metal-nosed leader of theirs promised me they'd not only bring back the crown, but you alive as well. Obviously, I hadn't expected them to be able to deliver you. I had my own knights for those purposes, remember?" He paused once more, examining his reflection in the mirror again. His eyes seemed to linger on his imperfect smile. "Whether you were killed here or in Zayloa, it made very little difference to me. With you out of the picture, and no other eligible princesses to marry, Father would have no choice but to retain his crown and find some other fool for the position. I'd then be left to my own plans."

"Plans?" she asked weakly, and as she did the warm flow within began trickling down from her wrist like gentle beads of water. "Why wouldn't you want to be king?"

Hayden threw his head back, laughing. He turned towards her again, and quickly bent down and scrunched his face down beside hers. She froze. She could see him clearly now and, what's more, she could see what he had been doing. The wooden toggles on his shirt had been undone. Trinity stifled a gasp. *MAI. Please. Save me, please.*

"Why the hell would I want to be king?" he asked. "It's only a matter of time before Gazenga takes over all of Taercion. You must know that too, or are you really so stupid?"

Her lips were shaking. "What then?" she uttered. "What would you do?"

Hayden rolled his eyes, standing straight once more. "I've already told you. With that crown of your grandfather's, I'd buy my way off of this wretched continent. Go and live until the end of my days with all the women and ale my money could buy me. He turned away. "I would've already done this some time ago, but as expected, that stupid bandit woman I hired was too overconfident. As soon as we regrouped, I had my knights deal with her and that pesky band of worthless cutthroats."

"You killed them?"

"As many as we could. She—well, she got away. But rest assured, dear. I'll kill her one day. I always…get what I want, eventually." His long, purple cape dropped to his heels. The pinned mantis flower rested on one of the folds.

Trinity's stomach lurched. Her arm was still heavy. But it had to move. *It has to move.* "Did she fly away on her owl?" It was a thoughtless question. But she needed more time. *Move you stupid—yes!* Her wrist fully loosened, as all the blood locked away in her hand started to flow.

"Bloody bird," Hayden said, with evident hatred. "Plucked my horse right out from under me. Crushed him with those talons. I paid a hundred gold stekis that day to the knight that shot the bird down. His spotted head now rests in my trophy room. Right near the place where I intended to mount yours."

"That's terrible."

"Terrible? You think those wretches deserved my mercy?" He kicked her once more, his toe catching her under the rib.

Trinity cried out. She turned and coughed, as blood spilled from her lips, staining the stone floor.

"Disgusting," Hayden told her. "You're just like an animal."

Yes. Look at my blood, you waste of life. Ignore my elbow. It's coming for you next.

The warming sensation trickled through her forearm and surrounded her elbow with a rigid clasp. It was the same feeling one might get after a full day's exercise. She knew this sensation well. Relished it. Wanted more of it. *Keep flowing.*

Hayden tossed his shirt down at his feet. *No!* Every part of her wanted to scream. Beg even. But she had to concentrate. Her arm couldn't move just yet.

"Does your father know about all of this? About ending the alliance? Did he raise a false alarm?"

Hayden laughed again, toothless whistle and all. "That idiot doesn't have a clue. I told my men to ride on and make up some story like I'd gone missing. Meanwhile, a few of us had taken a skiff. Rowed to your beach. That was where Quatas had been waiting for us. Just as I had instructed him to do."

"You did?" *Had Quatas planned on getting arrested? Sentenced to labor on the beach?* It must've been his strategy all along.

"Of course. Quatas has always been loyal to me. I left him here, the last time Father and I visited Hydlix. Oh, I convinced him that Quatas would make a fine knight. A real man on the inside. Father loved the idea. And that hulking commander of yours was never the wiser. After all, Quatas *is* half-Hydlixian. His mother was some Hydlixian harlot, no doubt. But as long as the Zayloan part of him was loyal to me, I didn't care where he served me from."

"Quatas." She said his name as if there was a bitter aftertaste on her tongue. *I trusted you.*

"All he had to do was come up with some story about his parents being murdered. Your clueless commander took him right in. I've promised him a fine lordship when we return to Zayloa."

Trinity's one working fist clenched tight. She still couldn't believe Quatas had been against her all this time. Luring her closer and closer to Hayden's trap. *How could I be so foolish?* She imagined then that she was no different than the dragon who had let the turtle ride on them. Quatas had been waiting to stab her in the back when she least suspected.

"So…you're going to kill me?"

"Now, now," Hayden cooed. "Let's not do anything so rash. I'll admit, it was my original intention to put an end to your life. A girl with strength like yours could prove highly dangerous for me. And with you dead, I could've easily captured your kingdom and all its wealth someday. After all, your grandfather has been so welcoming.

Mounting an invasion here could prove quite easy, as you've no doubt come to understand. But...fate it seems chose a different path for you. To think that all it takes is a simple flower to completely bend you to my will."

"You heartless snake!" she muttered as loudly as she could manage.

"Heartless? No, no. You'll find I'm quite full of heart. And with a...somewhat pretty girl like you, one whom I can control, you'll find that I'll *always* have a reason to let you live."

Hayden crouched down. Trinity stared into his lustful eyes as Hayden smiled back at her with glee, looking like a boy who'd just been gifted a new toy. There in the center of his ugly face was the giant gap where his front teeth had once been. Before she had knocked them out for good.

"Even a stupid Terkian like you can still serve *some* purpose. And after all, this is what your family wanted right? To help unify our kingdoms?" He then whispered, "Isn't that right, little wife?"

She laid there, as the warmth of her flowing blood finally seized her shoulder. It wasn't fair. None of this was fair. If she hadn't been who she was, he'd have had his way with her, and she would have never been able to resist. And her family and friends would've gone on to say how this was only a part of marriage. She was just another *babymaker*, after all. Like every princess who had come before her. And like every maiden, who had to give up on their girlhood dreams and accept the life that was thrust upon them.

Except that Trinity Ikena was nobody's maiden.

"Hayden?"

"Yes, love?"

"...I can use my arm again."

"What?"

Trinity grabbed hold of Hayden's soft neck with the same hand she had been privately nursing. With all her returning strength, she pulled back and yanked at his throat. Her fingernails drove into his skin as he screeched a breathless screech, like a snake being squeezed to death. She whipped her shoulder back and launched him with tremendous force straight into the stone wall behind her. He hit with a loud crash, and then she heard his body crumple to the floor. She was certain without seeing him. His fear-stricken face flying overhead had been all the proof she needed. She wouldn't have to worry about marrying Prince Hayden anymore.

CHAPTER TWENTY

BLOODYEW

Guren's door tore open. Trinity could hear the sounds of heavy, shuffling feet clambering into the room. The men at the door had no doubt been expecting their prince to be having fun with his new toy. They didn't suspect that he'd be lying dead beside the broken wall.

"What the hell did you—" Quatas began to say. At least she thought it was Quatas. There was something different about him. He wasn't wearing his helmet anymore. And though it was still difficult to twist her neck and see clearly in the poorly lit room, the top of his head was unmistakably pink. The beads of watery black sweat from before continued falling from his brow.

"Do you...dye your hair?" she asked, still unable to speak very quickly.

"Shut up!" he shouted down to her. "What did you do to our prince?"

"How did she kill him?" asked one of the knights. There was panic in his voice.

"You said that flower would weaken her," grunted the other, in a deeper, scarier tone.

"How was I supposed to know? She's a filthy liar, that's what." Quatas spat.

He was now standing over Trinity, looking terrified, and more desperate than she'd ever seen him before.

Just then there came a gurgling sound from the room's threshold. Trinity had heard this same sound once before. On the day she watched a man's throat get sliced. Sure enough, the familiar hissing sound followed as she heard a clanging thud hit the floor.

"Wait!" screamed the panicky knight. "Let me explain."

It was too late. The next sound Trinity heard was that of a struggle. Followed by a snap. Another metallic crash sent a ringing vibration beneath her body.

"Y—you weren't supposed to be here!" Quatas shouted to the unknown assailant. "I tried to stop them. I tried to protect her. I was go—" he retched, as what looked to be a shiny ruby-hilted dagger stuck itself into his chest.

Quatas dropped to his knees, as the last of his breath wheezed through his open mouth. He fell beside Trinity. She stared into his trembling blue eyes. They searched her, trying to make some sense of what had just happened. Then, they drifted away, staring at nothing in particular. Lifeless as melting ice.

There was silence in the unlit room. The only sound Trinity could hear was the heavy breathing of the one who had come to her rescue, and the sound of the door being scraped against the stone before being latched close again. The assailant stepped forward, bent down, and scooped Trinity up into his arms gently. The first thing she noticed was his smell. *Old tobacco.* His clothes were warm and sticky with blood. He hobbled as he carried her over to the single wooden-slat bed in the room. He laid her down, placing a pillow behind her disheveled hair, then stayed crouched beside her as she tried to remain sitting up.

Slowly, she lifted her one working hand to his dark and sweating face, or so she had thought it was sweat at first. His razor-thin beard was all wet.

"...Guren?"

"You're—damn it, you're ice cold," he said, speaking with heavy breaths. "I might—I could get some more blankets. I could—"

She felt the top of his stubbly cheek with her thumb. There was blood on his face too, but that wasn't what she had felt. "You're crying." It wasn't an accusation. Only the truth. "Why are you crying?"

"I...Trinity, I couldn't get here faster. I...did he—" but he couldn't finish his question.

She tried to shake her head, but couldn't. "No," was all she could offer instead.

Guren looked past her, towards the broken wall. "How did you stop him?"

I remembered your advice was the first thought she could think of. And it was true. Had she never learned how to help make her blood flow when it was constricted, she would have lost in her struggle against the prince. "I killed him...didn't I?" she asked, confident of the answer for herself.

Guren didn't immediately reply. He sniffed the air around her. "The prince used something. To weaken you. An herb, yes?"

"A flower. But I think it's starting to wear off." Her feet had already begun to feel warm. And her other wrist was finally able to wriggle freely.

"These things do. I can make you some tea. It would help speed the process."

"No, I'm fine." She leaned back against the pillow, as a feeling of lethargy started to overcome her. *I can't sleep here,* she reminded herself.

"Trinity...I am sorry for what—what he was going to do to you." His eyes fished for something else to say. "Had I known—"

Trinity could feel her blood working its way through her abdomen and back now. She was certain that she could lift herself up if she so desired, but still she rested. She was unmotivated to do anything upon hearing these words.

"I stopped him myself. You don't have to be sorry. Not for him."

Guren lifted up and sat on the bed beside her. Trinity wouldn't look at him. She stared intently at the wall beside his bed as she brought her hands steadily to her knees.

"...I do. None of this would've happened if I had been there for you," he confessed.

"You were busy. Or maybe sick. That was always your excuse," she muttered. Her stomach was starting to hurt again.

"I was neither. I left my room some time ago to take a walk. Clear my head. That's when I saw you and the knight running to my room. I would've been here sooner, but I had to work my way through several other of his soldiers along the path."

"I handled him fine. I can take care of myself," she said, her voice now shaky.

"I know." He touched her arm.

Trinity recoiled. She glared at him for a moment. Even if he had meant nothing by the touch, she *didn't* want to be touched. But despite her reaction, she saw that he—the man that she had once respected more than anyone else in the kingdom—was smiling through his sadness.

"I've always known," he said. "I am so proud of the person you've become. You never needed me to be a great knight. You were always going to become one...whether the world approved or not."

She said nothing. He didn't get to make her feel better. He hadn't been there. He was never there for her. *I hate you. I hate you so much*, she kept thinking bitterly.

"I don't suppose your aunt told you," he began, oblivious to her thoughts, "about why I had to stop training you."

"I don't care," she answered quickly. Hot tears were begging to be released. And now that her face was working properly once more, it was hard to battle them off. "I don't care why you stopped. You can do whatever you want."

"I was selfish," he admitted. "I was scared that the king would send you to Zayloa sooner rather than later if he knew the extent of our training. I wanted to keep you here for as long as I could, even if it meant I had to stop speaking with you."

She supposed there was always a part of her that knew this answer. Knew why he did what he had to do. But it didn't lessen the sting any. "I hate you," she said.

"Yes...I know." He stared across the bloody floor. "Your hatred of me is warranted. All I can say is...I'm sorry."

"Why?" she asked, her lip quivering. "Why would you do that to me?" She wiped at her tears.

"As I told you—I am a selfish man. I care about you. I always have, since the day I brought you here from Terkia."

"My aunt brought me here," she said, cutting across his words.

He nodded and said nothing more. Instead, he continued staring at the three men he had killed.

She wanted to punch him. Throw him across the room. Hurt him. *Something!* She couldn't pretend that the private torment of her last year never existed. All the lies and secrets: they were all his fault. This terrible, uncaring, loathsome man. *Why won't you even look at me?* Couldn't he see what his silence had done to her?

And then—without intending to—she started studying the side of his face. She remembered the man he was before all of this. The stoic-faced hero. The one who had come to save the woman who was being attacked in the marketplace, keeping her from a similar fate that Trinity had almost just faced. Guren was the same person who had been a shoulder to rest on, to cry on, when the whole damn kingdom it seemed had turned their back on her. He had been a constant, until he wasn't. But even his cold and unfeeling treatment of her had been something she had come to rely upon with him.

She moved her hand; it was the same one she had killed Hayden with. The hand that Guren had taught her how to move again in spite of the pain. She hesitated, but then tapped him on the arm. He turned to her. For the first time in her life, she saw fear in his eyes. Undeniable fear. She reached both hands forward, but it was Guren who took her into his arms and held her, like he'd done years before. And as he wept freely atop her head, she cried again onto his shoulder. Guren had given her so much grief. But now, there was only a familiar warmth.

It stretched the remainder of her body and touched her deep inside of her soul, lifting the effects of the putrid-smelling flower once and for all. Yes, she hated this man. Maybe she always would. More importantly, though, she loved him too. For now, to know that there was someone real in her life whom she didn't have to be afraid of…that was enough for Trinity to hold onto.

Guren eventually put on the pot of tea. There had been no further disruptions since he had entered, but he told her it was best to make sure they were safe. He barred what was left of his wooden door with his table and chairs. The kettle began to whistle before long. Guren came and poured Trinity's tea into a cold tankard. Hints of raspberry filled her nostrils and she had drunk down more than half the tankard before Guren had a chance to sit and drink his own.

She was still sitting on his bed; her body was wrapped with his blanket. The lit fire now illuminated clearly the four bodies lying strewn throughout the room. It was impressive, she thought, that Guren had managed to kill three armored men with only his single, ruby-hilted dagger. The thrown blade through Quatas' chest must've been tossed with such a pinpoint accuracy and strength as to be able to pierce his armor. She still found it hard to believe that Quatas had betrayed her, but even more shocking was that he was now dead. She wouldn't soon forget those searching eyes of his.

She had been right—or so she kept telling herself—about Quatas' hair. Remnants of the black dye he once used had now seeped out. All that remained was matted tufts of pink. It was how he had blended in with the knights without raising many questions of his background. The weeks he'd spent in the dungeons must've softened his dye. It was the same that morning when she'd caught him off guard at the dungeon tower. It was there, she now realized, where the Zayloans and the bandits hid waiting for their strike. *That's why he wouldn't let me enter the tower. Traitorous wretch.* She wanted to spit on him. After all, he was the one who taught her to spit. It would be fitting. But she wasn't prepared to leave her spot on the bed just yet.

It took her quite some time before she dared to look over and see Hayden's body crumpled on the floor. There was a hole in the wall where his face had been. His body lay still, and gathered around his head was a drying pool of blood. She shivered at the sight and pulled the blanket closer. Even though he had deserved to die, she had never thought she was capable of killing anyone.

The reality of her situation was setting in. She had killed a prince. No apology or explanation would change that fact. *What am I going to do?*

"Now then," Guren said, clearing his throat as he came and sat on the bed beside her, resting his filled tankard atop his knee, "we should discuss our plans."

Trinity stared into what was left of her tea. "I guess I'll just have to tell everyone what happened."

"...Yes. You could."

"I don't want to though. Is that—is that strange?"

"Not at all. You've experienced something horrible. No one wants to relive the terrible moments in their life. And for now, you shouldn't have to. Though there will come a day."

She cringed, feeling queasy all over again at the thought of having to put to words what Hayden had tried to do to her. "What do you think I should do, Guren?"

Guren tapped the side of his tankard with all of his fingers in a rhythmic pattern. He stopped suddenly, and turned to her. "You could run."

"Run? Do you mean...leave?"

He leaned closer and spoke softer. "You know the truth, and I know the truth. And for now, that will have to do. I'm afraid the Zayloans will not see this as some act of defense on your part. Not after seeing their future king lying dead."

Trinity scoffed. "I've done them a favor. He wanted to start a war and flee with all our stekis. Steal our crown."

"But the Zayloans won't see it that way. Killing royalty is...a complicated matter."

Silence passed between them. Trinity warmed her throat with the last of her beverage. "Where would I even go?" she asked moments later.

"I know a place," Guren said. "It's not far. About a half day's ride. There's an unused grotto east of here, before venturing into the Bayonick swamps. In my days as a commander, it would often serve as the final outpost before returning home. You could go there, and stay for a few days until everything here settles down."

"I don't understand. How are things going to settle? I've killed him. The Zayloan king—he'll want blood. Maybe war will happen anyways. Oh, Guren. It's dreadful what I've done."

Guren peered at her over the top of his tankard. "You've done nothing wrong. Nothing. And you are very clever," he said, wiping traces of the pink tea from his lips. "But I think...we might be able to prevent war. If you leave, we may be able to prove that Hayden scared you off and died of other causes. I can mend the wall, and I will make a case for you. Gather whatever evidence I can muster. Did you speak to anyone else in the last few hours?"

"Schobe. My aunt." She looked down at the pair of dark shades she still had fastened to her neck. They had held up surprisingly well, despite being dragged along with her when Hayden was pushing her face into the ground. "Some of the refugees down on the beach."

Guren cocked an eyebrow. "Why did you speak to them?"

"They told me things. About my past. Did you know I…I have a twin brother?" She scooted herself up further towards the edge of the bed's wooden slats. "Maybe two of them," she said, still sounding unsure herself.

Guren leaned back, putting his hand to his chin. "Brothers?" He scrunched his face, but his eyes soon grew wide. "The one in Sambool? The Terkian? That's your brother, isn't he?"

Trinity gradually nodded.

"…Ah, that is interesting. Are you certain?"

"I am," she said. "I'm going to find him. I think he needs me. I want to help him."

"Let's start with *one* problem at a time," he said, almost smiling. "Are you going to the grotto?"

"…How will I know when to come home?"

Guren took a deep breath and glanced over at the broken door. "I'll ride for you. Give me three days. Look for my cloak on the horizon."

Trinity considered his words. Guren did make a good case for her leaving, she believed. But she was scared to venture so far from her home with nothing but the clothes on her back. She didn't know what her aunt would say about all this and wasn't about to go and ask for permission. She worried for Schobe's safety too. If the Zayloans attacked, there'd be a call for arms. Schobe might be hurt, or even killed.

Guren must've sensed her apprehension, because he stood to his feet and motioned for her to accompany him. "I have some things for you. Should you choose to make your journey."

"Are you saying I don't have to go? I can stay?"

"Naturally. A journey can only begin when both feet are in agreement. But this will help protect you, should you choose to go to the grotto. Or further."

"Further?"

"Yes," he said, giving her an understanding glance. "Sambool is to the east also."

He moved towards an iron chest located on the opposite end of his overturned table. He unlocked the metal bolts using a silver key from his pocket, and then turned up the lid. Trinity removed Guren's blanket from her shoulders and stood up from his bed, placing the tankard at her feet. She stepped forward slowly, and was careful not to disturb any of the bodies.

Guren lifted from the chest two sheathed swords, bound in leather casings. They were each about as long as the length of his arms, though one was several inches shorter than the other. The pommels were coiled with brass etchings, and each bore a carved lion's face, encrusted with ruby eyes.

"These were a gift when I retired. Made by an old acquaintance of mine who lives in Kendoro." Guren looked pleased as he handed her one of the swords. "A craftier rogue, I've never met. But the man knows his steel. Claimed to have a forge far beneath the ground. Supposed to make his fires hotter, or some damn lie he came up with. Still, you'll find no finer blades in all of Hydlix."

Trinity's eyes lit up. She loved the feeling of the light-weighted sword. There was a perfect balance to this weapon. She unsheathed the blade and stared at her reflection on the shimmering steel.

"Guren...why would you give these to me? They're too precious."

"Nonsense. They've been collecting dust in there for years. You need something to protect yourself out there. Especially if you intend on looking for this brother of yours. Taercion—as you will learn—can be a dangerous place."

"I...thank you. So much." She held the blade close to her. "I promise I'll return them."

"I am certain you will. Now, you'll most likely be doing some hunting. I can give you what you need to get by for a day or two, but if you should stay in the wilderness longer you could use something like this."

He handed her the second blade and then hunched over the chest once more. He was slower this time in lifting whatever it was he was carrying, looking as if he were struggling. At last, Guren pulled out a long bow that was crafted from a peculiar wood. There were traces of red and black lining the thick wood, and cracks of golden yellow. Trinity gasped, and almost dropped the blades she was holding. She realized then what this weapon was made from.

"Bloodyew?"

"Indeed."

She had heard the stories in church of the sacred trees. They were one of the few annual sermons Palthar spoke on which Trinity managed to keep her eyes open for. MAI had made special golden yew trees all throughout the Remsphere. They were created to be used for making strong ships to sail the oceans and fine homes to live in. But when sin was first introduced to the sphere, man used the bark from these sacred trees to craft their weapons of war. MAI grew angry with man and as punishment cursed what was left of these trees. Their fruits became poisonous, and their seeds produced no new saplings. Their bark became dark and red like the colors of blood that had so invoked MAI's anger. The remainder of these trees became known as the bloodyew and were said to have stopped existing over a hundred years ago. Trinity couldn't believe what she was seeing. *How did Guren get a bow of bloodyew?*

"Where did you—"

"From my father," he said. "And his father before him. Bloodyew is rare, but maintains its strength over time."

She stood nervously before the outstretched weapon. "I can't take that. I'll ruin it. I always break my bows on accident."

Guren stepped behind her and placed the bowstring over her head, so that the weapon rested on her back. "This bow will hold," he assured her. "It always has."

"...I'll be careful. I promise. And I'll return it. When I come home."

"If you insist," he said, kindly.

They wasted no further time. Guren filled a satchel for her with honeybread and cheese, and gave her a thin leather quiver filled with ten steel-tipped arrows. Trinity meanwhile borrowed one of the man's belts. She had to cut a hole into the leather to keep it from sagging on her waist, but she soon fastened her two newly acquired blades to the sides of the belt and examined herself in one of Guren's mirrors. *A real warrior,* she thought, admiring the look of the weapons on her. She grabbed the pair of shades from her neck and put them on. She grinned.

"Take those ridiculous things off. It's nightfall already," Guren said.

"I was *just* looking," she said, approving of her appearance for a few seconds longer.

With her quiver fastened and her satchel around her shoulder, Trinity felt like she was wearing armor again.

But unlike Schobe's armor, this set fit her perfectly. *Why is Guren being so generous?* She supposed he might be trying to make up for his time of neglect, but that didn't seem likely. Guren must have had his reasons. Even if his previous reasons had made her question the love that she had for him.

"Guren?" she asked, standing beside his broken door that he had to peel open for her after removing the furniture. "You are going to come for me? In three days... aren't you?"

His eyes bounced around quickly, but he gave her one of those knowing smiles of his again. The same one that he'd shown on the day they first met at the lion hedge. "Look for my gray cloak," he repeated.

She glanced back once more at Hayden. There was something glimmering beside him, even in the darkness. She approached him slowly. There was still a part of her that believed he would jump up and try to force himself upon her again. She gulped, as she looked down at his diamond-studded boots. *Is that it, then?* No. There was something else. She knelt down and saw the two necklaces. She picked up her snowflake one and put it back around her neck—thankful that the clasp wasn't broken. Then, she picked up Hayden's mustang pendant. The red horse's head twirled in her fingers, casting a reflection onto her tunic. There was a slight crack atop the head of the horse, where Hayden had let it fall onto the stone floor. A crack not unlike the one in Hayden's own head. Without a second thought, she put the necklace around her neck and let the pendent rest on the center of her chest, right beside Schobe's snowflake.

"You're going to keep his pendent?" Guren asked, looking surprised as she approached him once more.

"The mustang *is* a sacred animal after all," she explained. "I prayed to MAI. And I think he heard my prayers. Helped me stop him."

"A sensible decision."

"I wasn't trying to be sensible. I just wouldn't feel right having this buried with the likes of him."

"I meant putting your trust in MAI. There are many evils in this world which can steal the hearts of men. I am happy though that in your dark moment, you chose to trust your heart with your creator."

"My heart?" she asked, defiantly. "My heart was supposed to be his, remember?" She motioned her head towards the dead prince behind her. "Are—are all men like him?" she asked, softly.

"Not all men," Guren said. "But evil has a way of swaying even the stoutest among us. So, you must learn to be vigilant. Protect your heart, and trust only those who deserve it."

"And how will I know who those people are?"

He folded his arms and sort of tilted his head, as if he were giving her question some serious thought. "Love, I suppose. Love makes the heart strong. But it can also break us. You must choose wisely."

Love? Seemed to her that love was never an option. Not the way she imagined it anyway. If love had gone the way she'd expected, she and Schobe might have kissed at the dance. Her beautiful aunt would certainly not be kept waiting for her prince. And her father may have never left her mother on the night she needed him most. *What does anyone know about love?* She stared down at Guren's feet, struggling to make eye contact with him. "Guren… who was that woman with you?" The one at the dance?"

He scratched at the back of his ear, but he didn't appear put off by the question. "I'll tell you about her when next we meet. Promise."

She didn't know if she could believe him, but she was thankful that he had said it anyway. Trinity stepped forward and embraced her teacher once more. She could feel his heart beating, and she was pricked by the heat from his tobacco-laden breath. What gave her the simplest joy though was having his giant hands rest upon her shoulders, protectively. *He* was not of Hayden's type. These same hands helped guide her from the bedroom and nudged her on her way. Trinity knew then what she had guessed since the moment Guren had told her to run. She would have to take her first steps into the unknown world beyond her kingdom alone.

But maybe, just maybe, she could bring someone else along. *A dear and trusted friend, perhaps.* The one who lived in the dungeons.

CHAPTER TWENTY-ONE

THE ROAR THAT SHOOK HYDLIX

Several other red-armored knights had now converged in the center of the market square. Trinity watched them from the balcony beside the glass chapel closely, wondering how she was going to get away unseen.

The dungeon tower lay all the way past the market square and down past the lower districts. If she tried to sprint out into the open, she'd be seen for sure. There was no way of knowing how many other Zayloan knights were in on Hayden's failed scheme. *Think, Trinity, think!*

"Princess," whispered a voice from behind. "Quickly, in here."

Trinity turned towards the glass chapel and to her surprise saw Great Father Palthar standing there, calling her as he peeked out from the chapel doors. He waved his arm frantically, begging for her to join him. She didn't have time for detours, but decided to hear him out all the same. She joined him in the chapel and he locked the doors behind her. She gazed all around, making sure that no one was hiding in a corner ready to attack her again.

"Gracious Heavens child, are you alright? I've never seen our knights so agitated. Do you have any idea what all of this mess is about?"

"...No," she lied. "Great Father, I can't stay. I have to leave."

"Leave? Be reasonable girl, they're blocking every entrance into the kingdom. And what of your family?"

"They're going to have to understand." She stared behind him into the open pantry beside the offering parlor. Several of the ale barrels had been knocked over, but there didn't appear to be a mess."

"Dipping into the sacred ale again?" she asked.

"Now see here," he began, sounding agitated, "I don't need a-a-some uninformed *girl* judging me. And as a matter of fact, no. I have not been drinking."

Trinity gave him a look.

"I haven't. I was trying to get into the basement. I had the entrance covered by the barrels."

"The basement?" *The secret tunnel? Of course!* So, it wasn't just a rumor after all. Did it really lead to the dungeons? *Why hadn't I thought of this before?*

"Yes," Palthar confided. "There's a tunneling system below the chapel. Leads right to the dungeons. They use it for aqueduct maintenance. I myself used to take it all the time when I'd go to hear confessions from the prisoners. Make their final moments cheery before meeting the hangman, what have you. I haven't gone in years though. I figured it'd make a good hiding spot, should I need one."

"M-may I see?" she asked, exuberantly.

"Um, sure. Come along," he said, leading her back to the pantry. "I suppose I could use a strong girl like you to help with these filled barrels."

Trinity quickly helped move the filled containers off of an iron-grated door set into the floor. Palthar lifted the grate as best he could, though Trinity had to go and help him with this also. The entrance below was dark and drafty, and she couldn't see a thing, but Palthar had already planned for this and had with him a glass lantern. He lit a small flame within, and then illuminated the entrance further to reveal wooden stairs leading below.

"The tunnel stretches for a couple of miles, anyway. I think we'll be fine if we take shelter just beneath the stairwell."

"Great Father? Do you—is there a second lantern?"

"No. Why would you need one?"

She grimaced. "I see. Then, I'm sorry to do this. But I'm going to have to take yours."

"How silly. We can share this one. There's plenty of light for both of us."

She shook her head. "Not for where I'm going." She reached forward and grabbed onto the lantern's handle. Palthar put both of his hands onto the thin metal and tried to pull. Trinity, however, gave a simple yank and was able to snatch it away from him. Palthar gasped, looking positively offended. He wretched his wide body backwards until he was between her and the basement door.

"Not a single step forward," he ordered, his round face trembling with anger.

"Please. Don't make me move you," she said, still calm.

"You would attack a servant of MAI? In their own chapel?"

"No. But if I need to pick you up and move you—I will."

Palthar was stricken. He reluctantly stepped aside and Trinity made her way quickly down the darkened stairwell.

"I'll just...I'll leave your lantern at the end of the tunnel."

"Such a wild animal you are," he said, calling out to her as she descended. "Your aunt should've listened to me and put you in an orphanage when you were brought here. They'd have beaten those savage tendencies right out of you."

She stopped herself and stared back up at him. Palthar gave a jolt, looking as if he were afraid that she'd run up and clout him. *Not a bad idea,* she thought, smiling.

"Sorry I have to go on alone. Thank you for showing me this entrance. Now, why don't you be a good Great Father and have yourself some ale. I haven't peed in any of those barrels lately."

Palthar shrieked, and pointed a shaking, accusatory finger at her. "I knew it!"

Trinity ran through the slippery tunnels carrying the lantern ahead of her. There was a lot of moisture down here. She wondered how the aqueduct connected. This must've been the place where the duct funneled the ocean water upwards. Below her were the sounds of scuffling little feet. *Please don't touch me, rats, please don't touch me.* There was something about having their furry little bodies running over her feet that made her skin crawl. But she didn't have time to be afraid.

All the knights in the kingdom—both the silver and the red—would find out about her crime against the Zayloan crown any minute. They'd set up search parties, their blades drawn and ready to strike. If it were only her running away, she'd take to the ocean. She'd swim out with the riptide and then paddle back a few miles down the shore. *None of them could catch me in the ocean.* Unfortunately, she didn't think her partner could swim.

True to Palthar's word, the tunnels opened up to a place right inside the dungeons. She'd never seen this hallway in the tower before and wished that she had known about it after all the times she'd risked her neck to come and visit Snowflake. The swaying lantern light stirred every inhabited cell she passed, and it wasn't long before the familiar catcalls began. She liked to believe that what Guren said was true. That not all men had wicked intentions for every girl they saw. But being here, surrounded by their swarm of lust and foul desires, gave her plenty of room for doubt.

"Leave me alone," she whispered, afraid to speak any louder for fear of being discovered by a posted knight. "Stop speaking to me that way." Her words did nothing to quiet them. Their comments had never riled her up so much before. She kept her head down, and her feet moving forward. She was having desires of her own: to knock out more teeth, and to smash in more faces.

She stumbled in the darkness until she found the familiar steps up to the center cage where Snowflake lay. He apparently had been ignoring all the commotion, but once he smelled her, he jumped to his feet and went to greet her by their familiar spot.

Trinity scratched behind both of his ears, and looked to his trusting green eyes for the confidence she was now lacking.

"I'm going to let you out now. Please...don't eat me," she whispered, knowing it was a foolish request to make. Snowflake was looking very hungry this evening.

She hesitated, but eventually gripped onto two of the iron bars of the lion's cage. She pulled back, expecting the bars to snap. What happened instead was that the cage itself started to lift. She continued pulling back. The iron cage was heavy, but not impossible for her to move. She stepped back and allowed the full weight of the cage to rest upon her two upturned arms. The catcalls stopped as every prisoner in the dungeon watched her feat of strength intently. Trinity launched the iron cage beside her, eliciting yelps from some of the prisoners who thought they were about to be crushed by the flying iron. The cage made a rattling bang onto the stone floors and then toppled over, breaking inwards. No one had been harmed, and she was thankful that the cage didn't have a bottom. Otherwise, Snowflake would've gone along for the toss. Still, whatever silence she'd been trying to preserve had just been broken. She feared the knights would be here soon.

The hungry, prowling lion looked all around him, seemingly impressed by the freedom he'd just been given. She still worried that he might swipe out and maul her, but instead Snowflake leapt from his platform and nuzzled his mane against Trinity's shaking body. She breathed a sigh of relief.

"You're free now," she whispered into his big, soft ear. Snowflake didn't look to understand; he continued purring loudly and nuzzling.

They both heard more banging coming from all around. The prisoners had begun to shake the bars on their cells, demanding that Trinity set them free too. Their pleas soon turned to violent, demeaning requests.

"Get us out, love!"

"Come here, girl! Get over here and turn me loose!"

"Tear off my bars too, sweetie. I'll give you a kiss!"

Trinity's lack of confidence was beginning to sink in again, despite her recent show of strength. The prisoners couldn't harm her behind their bars, she knew, but their words felt as if they were wrapping around her, trapping her like the net from her dreams. All she could picture in that moment was Hayden's face...and that horrible look in his eyes.

Snowflake quit purring then and stepped forward. The white lion growled and let loose a loud, ferocious roar that rattled the cells and silenced the prisoners once more.

Trinity gasped. Never before had she been witness to such a show of power. Snowflake's strength was even greater than her own. She clutched onto his mane and buried her face within his stiffening fur.

"Oh, Snowflake. Thank you. I needed you here. With me."

The two of them walked together along the dark—and now quiet—tower until they'd found the front entrance. She was still surprised that no guards had come to stop them after all the noise from before. Slowly, she peered out the doors and saw a slew of knights—from both kingdoms—squaring off in the streets. They still hadn't drawn their weapons, but they were shouting at one another and many men had their hands on their sword hilts.

"How am I going to get you out of here?" she asked, speaking aloud her thoughts.

Snowflake nipped on the arm of her tunic, causing her to turn. The white lion swayed his head towards his body and rubbed his face onto his shoulder blade.

Am I seeing things? "Did you—are you wanting me to get on your back?"

Snowflake looked intently at her. His eyes were difficult to read. There was a familiar hungered expression about them, but he wasn't licking his lips like he usually did before a meal. He nipped at her arm again, purring as he did so.

She narrowed her eyes and raised a finger to his face. "If I ride on you, don't you dare bite off my leg."

She stepped cautiously towards the large lion's neck. She petted him, comforted him, and then leapt up and threw both legs around his neck. The spot was surprisingly comfortable, even without a saddle. She'd been riding with her aunt a few times when she was younger, but didn't care for the lessons. She'd always come back stiff and sore, and smelling of horse. Snowflake, however, was no horse. She clutched onto the lion's mane, unsure of how she was supposed to get him to move forward.

"You wanted me to ride you, now get a move on."

Snowflake yawned, and then stretched himself out onto the stone floor.

Trinity tried to jostle him. "No, no, get up! They'll find us here for sure."

Snowflake had no intention of moving forward now. His purrs had grown heavier, and his eyes were starting to blink slower.

"Don't you dare take a nap! I'm trying to save you."

Snowflake rolled onto his side, pushing Trinity off of his back as he did.

"Stupid lion," she grunted, standing back up. "How do I get you to go?"

The doors of the dungeon suddenly opened. Two Hydlixian knights were standing at the entrance, looking aghast. Trinity stared at them, then clumsily saluted out of instinct. She recognized their faces, but didn't know the men by name. They had taken very little notice of her though.

"The white lion?!" one of them shrieked.

"He's escaped!" shouted the other.

"TO ARMS!" they both yelled.

They drew their swords and started stepping forward, unhurriedly.

"No please, you don't understand," Trinity began.

"Step aside, Princess. There's a dangerous beast behind you."

Trinity looked back as Snowflake continued purring and resting himself. *Some danger.*

"Stop, don't hurt him."

"I said step aside," ordered one of the knights, who clutched onto her wrist.

"Leave me alone," she demanded. "Snowflake!"

She didn't see him rise but she could feel his growl swelling beneath her feet. The lion sprang forward, leaping over the three of them. He turned to the one holding onto Trinity's arm. She felt the wind of Snowflake's hot breath race through her hair as he unleashed another terrifying roar. Her arms were covered in goosebumps, but she wasn't scared. Her lips curled into a smile as the ground shook beneath her. *Such power.* Both knights clambered back. The one holding Trinity released her. Snowflake looked ready to pursue, but Trinity ran to him and directed his big eyes towards her own.

"We have to go," she repeated. Glancing over her back, she saw more knights running towards them. "Please," she cried out.

Snowflake stared for only a second longer, and then dipped down and threw his head under her body, forcing her back up onto his shoulder blades again, backwards this time. She turned herself, grabbed onto his mane, and kicked into his sides—as gently as she could.

"Go!"

The lion didn't hesitate this time; he sprang towards the rushing knights. Trinity gripped on tight. The approaching men shouted commands, and some readied their weapons, yet none seemed brave enough to face the lion head-on. Trinity continued using Snowflake's mane as a set of reigns and tried to steer him towards the direction of the kingdom's higher districts. The lion charged forward, heading to where she veered him.

The wind whipped through Trinity's hair and an exhilarating sensation overcame her. This was better than any aqueduct slide. She felt like she shared in the lion's overwhelming power. His every step felt sudden but harsh. Everyone they passed looked petrified, but there was jealousy in their faces too, or so she liked to think. This was something else. A thrill unfelt before.

She found the temptation too difficult to pass on. Lifting her head, she screamed loudly, her voice carrying through the streets, not from fear, but sheer excitement. Snowflake, after all, had made it look so fun. She screamed again, as loudly as she could until she felt like her lungs would fail her. *Hear me, Hydlix,* she thought as her heart raced excitedly within. *Hear my maiden's roar.*

A KNIGHT'S CHALLENGE

S nowflake plowed through the streets of the lower district at a full sprint as Trinity clung tightly to his mane. They raced past Schobe's home, which looked like a blur of lights and people. She turned to see Dary and Ellacryse running after her shouting. Schobe's mother was there too, gaping. Snowflake turned sharply and bounded up the stairs that led to the market square. There were more knights here. They had already begun the blockades.

"This way," she yelled into the lion's ear. "Hurry!"

She twisted his fur in her hands and she could hear

him growl at her. Still, he obeyed, padding with his swift and mighty steps. He leapt over stands, crashing into the side of a locked merchant's stall. Blocks of cheese rolled out and away from the collapse as a frustrated shopkeeper ran up behind them, swearing loudly.

Trinity ignored his words. She had to keep looking ahead. "That's it, Snowflake! The bridge isn't far now."

A handful of Zayloan knights were running by their side. They were not holding back their attacks like the Hydlixian soldiers, tossing halberds and spears towards Snowflake and Trinity. One spear flew right by her head and she had to duck to avoid being hit. She was beginning to wonder if they already knew about her killing Hayden. She wasn't about to slow down and find out though. She kicked Snowflake's sides a little harder and forced him to move faster.

The entrance to the upper district was completely blocked by the time they sprinted up to the next set of stairs. The red knights here thrust their spears forward in their hands, ready to catch the lion's vulnerable underbelly should he jump. Trinity pulled back on his mane, forcing him to stop. She looked all around. The knights behind her were getting closer. *How are we going to—The aqueduct!* There it stood, hovering over them. She stood directly beneath the same spot that she'd broken through six years before.

"Come on," she insisted. "We have to try for higher ground."

The two of them bolted to the right of the gathering soldiers, climbing up the wide wooden scaffolds built onto the side of the structure to facilitate it's previous repairs. Trinity could hear whooshes near her head, and she recognized the sound of the thin slices through the air. *Arrows!* She lowered herself onto Snowflake's body and tried to steer his shoulders with her arms.

The lion leapt up onto the flowing slope. They were fortunate to be near one of the wider slopes but she did worry about such a large lion being up here when she and Schobe barely fit years ago. Trinity was instantly drenched by the gushing stream, as was the lion carrying her. Her fingers began to slip and she had to wrap herself tighter around Snowflake's body to keep from falling as the lion crept up the slope. The water slapped at her face, blurring her vision, and she glanced over the side of the aqueduct. The arrows had stopped. Instead, a fight had broken out below. The Hydlixians now had their blades drawn and were battling the Zayloan men. *Are they trying to protect me?* No, that surely wasn't it. They had been looking for their excuse to fight and now they had it. She knew the two of them couldn't waste any further time.

"Hold on," she said, though the water muffled her voice.

She reached out until she was able to just barely scrape the sides of the slope that they were on with her fingers. It wasn't much, but she pulled forward—slowly and with some slips at first—but soon they started moving more quickly up the duct. Her added strength and Snowflake's claws had given them the edge they needed.

Once they'd reached one of the few leveled-out spots on the duct, she pulled back on his mane once more and forced him to leap again. The two of them dropped down nearly twenty feet below, but Snowflake landed gently on his paws. He shook himself out as Trinity surveyed the area where they had landed. They weren't far from the bridge now. She could see it right in front of her.

She was just about to move her lion onwards when a familiar shriek rang out overhead. She peered up and saw Evita standing on the overlook beside the mailing tower. The two of them shared the briefest of distant glances. Even from down here, Trinity could see that her aunt looked mortified.

Guilt overcame Trinity then. She felt like an eight-year-old girl once more, afraid that she was somehow going to get into even more trouble than she was already in. Every part of her wanted to reach out to her aunt—who she had just finished fighting with. But then, she remembered why they fought, and she knew that Evita couldn't protect her. Not this time. Reluctantly, Trinity shook her head and forced herself to stare ahead, looking away from the woman who had raised her like her own daughter. She kicked her lion friend in the sides once more and the two of them set off towards the bridge.

As suspected, there were more knights to be found along the bridge. Only this time she knew the faces she saw. There were knights here that she had seen train down in the barracks ever since she was a little girl. They'd called her the Mouse Princess. Now she was staring them down as if they were on opposite sides of a battlefield. And there amongst the familiar faces of boys—now full knights of the realm—was Schobe. He was holding onto the handle of a spear. His face...was uneasy. *He wouldn't use that on me. Would he?* There was only one way to find out.

She tugged at the lion's mane. Snowflake growled and then bolted towards the waiting knights. They readied their weapons, and Trinity braced for impact by clutching onto Snowflake's mane and pulling upwards. She expected to be slashed, but instead the troop of Hydlixian knights posted along the eastern bridge laid down their arms and allowed for the lion to make a clean jump. Their faces were both frightened and amazed as Trinity and Snowflake soared overhead of the troop. *They're not going to attack me?* Maybe they *had* been loyally defending her all along as she escaped. As she and Snowflake flew through the air, she felt like she'd left her stomach back on the bridge. A scream caught in her throat and her eyes stung in the rushing night air. Still, she looked nervously down into Schobe's eyes who was standing just below her. She wondered in that split second what he could be thinking. He didn't seem angry, or scared like Evita had been. His was a look of triumph. As if he were sharing in her victory. He had always been there to share in the danger that she sought.

With welling sadness in her heart, Trinity looked away from Schobe's pride-filled expression as Snowflake dropped down onto the other side of the soldiers. She realized then that escape was closer than ever. There—*just there on the other side of the bridge*—was a land that wasn't Hydlix. It was a place where Trinity would no longer be a princess, or a knight of any realm. The Remsphere was a dangerous place, she had always been told. But so too was Hydlix. Her decision had already been made, though it didn't ease the pain in her heart any to know her path was set for her. This pain—unlike the shared times with her brothers—was a pain entirely her own.

"...Let's go," she said to Snowflake.

The lion obeyed her soft command, and the two of them raced down the remainder of the vacant bridge. The evening mist lining the way wrapped around her body like an icy embrace. She shivered as the stone pavers below them seemed to disappear. She felt as if she were entering into a world of white nothingness.

Until there in front of them, at a place she suspected to be the end of the bridge, came the bright glow of a dangling lantern. She'd have thought next to reach out and take the lantern to better light their way, if it wasn't for the striking lance which suddenly pelted her in the gut and threw her from the back of the lion. In her second joust ever, she'd just lost to an invisible opponent.

She scraped and tumbled along the bridge's wet stones until she skidded to a stop. The air around her felt like it was spinning. The lance must've shattered against her body because the wood scraps had clasped to her skin and clothes from where she'd rolled. She steadied herself, and stood slowly.

Snowflake was nowhere to be seen. *Did he go on without me?* She didn't have time to wonder. The only light visible quickly crashed to the ground and a great flame erupted. The fire spread amidst the mist and the fog began to lift. She looked down on the ground and realized then that the width of the bridge was lined with lamp oil. *It's a trap.* The fire quickly grew into an unpassable wall, blocking her exit. And there in the fire's glow stood her armored opponent, wielding a steel halberd. The dent in his armor shone a reflective light off the fire's radiance; it was the same dent Trinity had put there months ago with her own lance.

"End of the road, Princess," Commander Kuza said, staring her down with his cold, calculating eyes. "It's time to stop playing at knight now. I'm here to take you home."

Trinity quickly checked her belt to make sure that her swords were still attached. She snapped to her senses, having finally regained the wind she'd lost from Kuza's unexpected attack. She smirked at him.

"I'm not going anywhere with you. You'll let me pass, or I'll be forced to hurt you again, Commander."

Kuza didn't look as if he appreciated her threat. His face grew sour. "I suspected it was you when I heard the calls of a wild girl riding our kingdom's lion in the plaza.

This barrier is meant to be used for enemies. I never thought the first person I'd spring this for would be our very own princess."

"Lucky me," she said, flicking at some of the wood chips on her wet arms.

"Why do you run? You want to be like us, right? A true Hydlixian knight would never run from a fight."

She slid both hands onto her hilts. "So that's a challenge then?"

"That isn't quite what I meant. I was speaking of the Zayloans. You may think whatever you will about me. But I have always been loyal to the royal family. And that includes you."

She scoffed. "Is that why you sprang the fire trap then? To keep me safe?"

"The fire was for the lion. To stop him from hurting you."

"Ohhh, and I suppose that's why you nearly impaled me with a lance. To protect me."

He narrowed his eyes. "I was—pretty sure you would survive. Seems I was right. There really is no hurting you Terkians, is there?"

How she wished that were true. The events of her night were still racing through her head again like a bad dream. One which she'd never wake from again.

"I am curious," he continued, "how you managed so effortlessly to break through our fleets. I thought at least the bridge brigade would be enough to stop the lion. I shall have to have a talk with those boys. See what they say. And punish those who...*purposely* failed to stop you."

She bared her teeth. "You're a pitiful excuse for a commander. Why would you lock up knights who were only doing what they thought was right? I'm the one choosing to leave. The knights have defended their posts bravely, while you hang back here on the bridge. Like a coward."

Kuza snickered. "I don't lock up traitors. I hang them."

Trinity's eyes grew wide. *Did he know?* Had he seen Schobe and the others lay down their arms? She searched his face for an answer, but instead he remained unflinchingly stoic and sure. *If he harms Schobe I'll...*

"Last chance, Princess. Come with me peacefully. Let us end this foolish children's game of yours."

She could've run. She could've leaped through the fire and found the lion on the other side to safety. She could've even jumped from the burning bridge and survived the deadly fall. But none of these things she could've done occurred to her until after she drew the two swords Guren had given her less than an hour before.

"I'm not going anywhere with you." She swung the blades deftly in her hands. They swirled the biting air with a precise, tested weight that her old blades could've never matched. These were no rusted training swords. Though she never thought that the first person she'd be testing them out on would be the knight commander. "If you won't issue me a proper knight's challenge, then I'll pose one to you. Fight me. If I win, you spare our soldiers' lives and leave me be. If I lose...I'll return to Hydlix with you." *Damn it, Trinity. You'd better not lose.*

Kuza smiled a crooked smile, and fought off a chuckle. "That is a good knight's challenge, I'll admit. Fair. Bold. Even, admirable. But you forget Princess...you are no knight." He shook his head and then quietly readied his halberd with both hands. He pointed the pike head towards Trinity. "Seems the Mouse Princess is still in need of a lesson. Well, here's one that even old man Guren didn't teach you." He closed the t-slit visor of his helmet. "How to win."

A daring smile creased along her lips. She shot him a determined glare. "Just don't go crying to my grandfather again when I beat you."

Kuza made no reply. He sprinted forward with a speed Trinity had never seen from a man in armor before. He almost caught her off guard, but she was able to defend herself with her swords and block the halberd's pike. Kuza jabbed the air, swinging her blades with his. He threw his boot onto her stomach and tried to kick her away, but Trinity held her footing and struggled away from the halberd's merciless reach. Kuza's blade smashed down on the stone pavers, leaving an unsettling ripple of gravel which nipped at Trinity's heels.

Every time she tried to counter him, he was there with a metal shoulder or knee. He was so much faster than Guren had ever been during their trainings. A swing of his gauntlet caught her on the lip. Despite her strong skin, she could feel the cut form. *He's not holding back.*

She pushed on his breastplate with the hilts from her blade and caused him to lose his footing. She spun down and tried to trip him, but he was quick to recover. He butted the handle of his halberd against her shoulder, pinning one of her sword arms in the process. Again, he attacked with a sharp knee to the side of her head.

Trinity retreated back, scooting away from her fallen sword.

"Bit different than fighting an old man, eh? Or a straw dummy." He kicked away her sword.

"How do you know about any of that?" she spat, recoiling further back as she did.

"He trained me too, girl. I am no stranger to your

technique. But Guren's time has long passed. Now he is just a tired old fisherman, living on pointless memories."

"He's a war hero. He won the battle for Reiwania."

Kuza snickered. "Some battle. They surrendered when our ships arrived. He likes to tell that they put up a good fight. But the Reiwanians had no army."

"…You're lying."

"I've no reason to. Look, I'm not saying you are without skill. But it was foolish of him to train you in the first place. After all, you're only a girl. A maiden waiting to be wed. Someone to make little princes."

Something snapped inside of Trinity then, like broken chains on a drawbridge. Every horrible thought she'd been suppressing in her mind tonight felt like it was flooding out in a gush of rage. There was nothing anymore—no code of honor, no chivalry, no poised sense of self—which would keep her anger in check any longer.

Dropping her remaining sword beside her, she slammed both fists down onto the ground and made two sizable craters on the bridge. The shockwave of her attack was enough to sway Kuza where he stood. In a flash, she rose to her feet and dashed behind him. Kuza steadied himself and tried to ready his weapon for an attack, but Trinity punched him in the back and sent him hurtling towards the ground.

Kuza used the weight of his armor and grip of his gauntlets to keep himself from rolling too far. But as soon as he stopped himself, Trinity was there beside him with a fast, well-aimed kick to his covered torso. Kuza's body smashed into the bridge's wall before crumpling to the ground. He scrambled to scoop up his halberd. Trinity stepped forward confidently like a spider approaching a trapped insect meal.

Kuza hoisted the halberd towards her. Trinity caught

the pike with both hands and snapped the sharp blade off of the steel rod with a single break. She smacked the broken rod away and then scooped Kuza up by his breastplate. He could've weighed no more than a bag of apples at that point, she couldn't be sure. Her strength felt surreal, as if there were no limits to what she could do. Kuza squeezed her arm, trying to break her arm with his metal fingers. It was nothing more than a tickle to Trinity.

She threw him to the ground and raised the snapped piece of steel from his halberd. She stepped upon Kuza and restrained him in place with one of the new boots her aunt had gifted her. Then she raised the fractured piece of weapon over her head, before thrusting the pointed blade towards the commander's neck.

And then, when all her world seemed tiny and red, she suddenly stopped.

Commander Kuza undid his visor. His face had changed from arrogance to a look of pure teary-eyed fear. It was the same expression so many others in Hydlix, including Evita and Schobe, had given her before. The chant unforgivingly began reciting in her head. *I hate my strength. I hate my—*

"Please," he begged. "Don't kill me."

Trinity's face felt trapped in her death glare. Slowly, she forced her expression to soften, and a tightness in her throat that she'd been unaware of began to loosen. She also hadn't realized how fast her heart was beating until then, and how warm her body had become. *Is this my beast blood?* Her strength had felt so unreal. Now, all she could feel was tired. And perhaps, even a little scared of what she had been able to do.

She threw the remnants of the halberd off of the bridge and down to the ocean below. She stepped over Kuza and collected her fallen swords and refastened them back to the borrowed belt. Guren would've been disappointed that she had managed to lose her weapons so quickly in the battle. The bridge fire had begun to die, but she wasn't planning on waiting around any longer. She readied herself to jump to her destination. Just before she could though, Kuza spoke.

"He's dead, you know. Your prince."

She kept her back to him, as Kuza remained laying on the broken bridge. "...I know," she said.

"I hadn't raised the alarm yet, but I saw him...his body...that face, with my own eyes. We will find his killer, Princess. But even then, it might not be enough to stop war with Zayloa."

She wiped at the blood smeared across her lip. "Then go, and ready your men Commander. You'll need every one you have." She turned to him, piercing his almost sympathetic gaze. "Especially the brave ones from the bridge."

"You and I have different ideas of bravery. Like this," he motioned towards the fire. "What do you hope to accomplish by leaving? And freeing that wild beast? If ordered to, we will go and capture you both again."

"...You cage the wrong sorts of beasts," she said, as the pain in her heart pounded once more. She sprinted forward and jumped across the flames, leaving Kuza before he could say anything more.

Snowflake had remained waiting for her on the other side of the fire, by the place where the bridge finally ended. Deep down, Trinity knew that he would. Their connection had been more than just shared meals in a dank prison cell. She sensed that Snowflake needed her strength, as much as she needed his. It was a good feeling to know that someone did not fear her for being too strong. She nuzzled her face into his mane once more, as his gentle purring calmed her troubled mind further.

"We've a full night's ride ahead of us," she told him.

She climbed onto his back and directed him towards the vast, open fields. The lion charged toward the freedom he'd been given. And, for the first time since she could remember, Trinity rode across the land of Taercion—a place she'd only ever seen from the ruby towers of Hydlix.

CHAPTER TWENTY-THREE

THE GRAY CLOAK APPROACHES

There were many dirt roads along their way, which at this hour blended seamlessly into the rolling grassy hills outside the kingdom, but Trinity continued steering her lion friend east, regardless of what was underfoot. At times, she couldn't resist reaching down from Snowflake's back and letting her hand swim through the tall grass, which tickled and danced across her arm as golden bugs leapt away and out of reach. There soon came a place where she could no longer see the southern sea, as if the fields themselves had somehow swallowed up the vast ocean and left blankets of grass in its stead.

The night was chilly and Trinity's drenched clothes weren't helping. The cool wind rushing to her face made her hunker down onto the lion's matted back. To tell the truth, she wasn't sure if they were even headed east at all. She had expected mountains or more bodies of water. Instead, the longer they rode, the more barren the land became. Grass turned into sand and fields became desert. She was having trouble staying awake, but she held firm to Snowflake's mane and let the whipping wind nudge her out of any tired trances.

Soon, there was a reflecting sheen in the distance. *A pool?* They rode over several more sandy ruts until at last Snowflake brought her to the place she was seeing. Here there were skinny trees that sprouted high into the sky. Their leaves branched out like blooming flowers, and there were large, round fruits nestled beneath them. *Is this the grotto?* Had they ridden half a day already? Snowflake was much faster than any horse she'd ever been on.

The lion shook her off of his back but Trinity found her feet. Snowflake approached the large pool beneath the skinny trees and began lapping up water with his long tongue. Trinity stared into the sky. The clouds were showing their first signs of pink. She came over to where the lion was drinking and checked her satchel; she realized then that she hadn't brought a container for water. She wasn't about to start caring about the cleanliness of the water though—or her lack of cups—after the long night's ride. Snowflake certainly wasn't hesitating to quench his thirst. She knelt some ways beside him, cupped some of the cool liquid in her hands, and drank. *Delicious*, she thought happily. She had some more, drinking as if she hadn't drunk anything for weeks.

Her clothes were still damp. Being away from the lion's warm body had made her cold again. She supposed she'd eventually have to build a fire. She'd seen it done before, but usually by servants in the great hall who had the right kind of wood and flint readily available. She once saw Guren rub two pieces of wood together in his home, igniting a spark. The only wood she could see came from the few trees surrounding the grotto. She stood beside one and tried to strip the bark with her nails, but the bark was rough and flaky. If she could shake it hard enough, she might be able to collect the falling strands of bark.

When she tested this theory, her strength caused the whole tree to uproot from the sand. Snowflake looked up at the commotion.

"I—well that works too," she said. She then gathered some of the strips of broken bark from the fallen tree.

When she'd taken enough, she placed the wood in a pile and took the two sturdiest pieces she could find. Even with her strength, she found that starting the fire was problematic. She rubbed the two sticks together as fast as she could but only managed to strip them. There wasn't a spark in sight. She resigned herself to sitting on the fallen log. *It'll be day soon, anyway.*

Snowflake had quit drinking and was gnawing on one of the fallen fruits that had rolled away from the tree's undergrowth. Trinity went to grab one, and her eyes lit up at the sight of it. She knew this fruit. It was a specialty of Reiwania, or so she had believed. She never would've guessed she'd find a coconut out here in the middle of nowhere. She dug her nails into the hairy shell and twisted. She was able to break the coconut in half. Snowflake watched her intently, still gnawing on the fruit clamped in his jaws.

"Here," she said, walking over and giving him the second half. "Not a steak, but it'll do."

The hungry lion sucked on the broken coconut's meat. Trinity did the same, content with her new survival trick for the time being—despite her failure at building a fire. She sat once more onto the sand and leaned against the log. The morning was still cold. With arms folded and legs tucked to her chest, she finally drifted off to sleep.

The sun woke her sometime later. She'd not rested long enough for dreams, which she found odd. There was so much on her mind that she was still trying to work out. Now that she had time to put her thoughts in order, it seemed she could think of nothing but Hayden's crumpled body. She hated imagining what else he would've done if her strength had not returned to her. She could almost feel his hands caressing her once more. A shiver rose through her body. There was no stopping the tears then. She sat upon the sand and cried.

She wondered what Evita would say if she knew what Hayden had tried to do. Probably something about it being a husband's duty, or some other royal nonsense to help ease the pain. The real sick part though was that they weren't even married yet. *No*, Trinity thought, *he just wanted another trophy.* It didn't matter that they were unwed, or how old she was.

Perhaps that was just it. Maybe she was no longer a child to anyone. All she was, all she felt like in that moment, was something a man could take and call his own. No amount of training, no hidden strength, *nothing* would change that feeling.

She sought shade as the sun rose higher overhead. Snowflake was nowhere to be seen. She hadn't seen him wander away but she did notice his sandy footprints leading off somewhere in the distance. She hoped he would return before long. There didn't seem to be many other sources of water out here in the desert. Actually, there wasn't much of anything. She'd always imagined the area just beyond her kingdom to be full of lush vegetation and wildlife. *Hopefully the rest of Taercion is nicer.*

The rest of Taercion? Would she see it? Was she really going further east? Duke was out there somewhere. Somewhere in a kingdom maybe not unlike her own was her twin. A boy who must've known what she was going through, the same as she'd felt whatever pain he had lived through. She wondered again if last night had given him a reaction of some sort. Maybe his body stopped working, the same as hers. Or perhaps he had terrible headaches as well. *Duke.* No matter what happened, she had to find him. *I will find him.*

Snowflake came loping back around midday. There was a fresh kill hanging from his mouth: a thin deer-like animal with long smooth horns. The lion—clamping onto the creature's skinny neck—laid out beside the pool of water and began tearing into the animal's skin.

Though she had no way to cook this fresh hunt of his, Trinity's stomach growled at the sight of the meat.

"You hunted? Thank you, Snowflake." She stepped closer, but stopped when she heard a low growl coming from the lion. "Don't be selfish. I've shared with you plenty of times." She approached him again and Snowflake looked at her. He licked his bloody lips. She stepped back. "On second thought...I think I'll just have some of my bread and cheese."

The day seemed to drag on forever. Guren had said he'd ride to her in three days. The waiting, however, was killing her. After lunch, she decided to train. Though she knew Kuza was one of the best knights around, it was still embarrassing to have him render her weapons useless. Had all her training been in vain? She wouldn't believe that. *I should've shot him with an arrow.*

She put on her dark glasses, pleased with how well they kept the sun from her eyes. There weren't many targets besides the skinny trees to practice upon. She worked on jumping from tree to tree, launching her ten arrows repeatedly into their trunks as she leapt. The borrowed bow felt good in her hands, easily the finest weapon she had ever held. The bow shot straight and had a tighter pull than the bows she had trained with. The swords handled nicely as well. She was so delicate with them that she didn't even want to scuff them on tree bark.

Kuza had been right about one thing. Training against stationary targets was getting her nowhere. She instead practiced her form and stances by swinging the blades in the air at an invisible enemy. She wondered, though briefly, if Guren had ever killed anyone with these weapons. *They'd certainly get the job done.* She also wondered if he was ever going to train her again. Once everything settled down, would they resume as if there had never been a break? Even if he was an old fisherman now, like Kuza had said, he was still twice the knight of any man in Hydlix. One thing was for certain. *I'm never going to stop training again.*

The heat from the day turned once more to the beginnings of another cold evening. She wasn't about to let another night go by without a fire. Taking one of her arrows and swords in her hands, she began sparking the two pieces of metal together over a pile of kindling and she soon produced several sparks. Soon, a fire started to grow. She basked in the warming glow that she'd created. This...this was *her* fire. And it was the warmest she'd felt all day.

She gathered more wood and watched as her created blaze began to grow higher. Even Snowflake couldn't resist the cozy feeling. He laid beside her, still licking his lips after finishing his latest meal. Trinity settled in beside him, draping herself against the creature's dozing body.

"I *guess* you can share with me too. But you better start being nice," she told him, smiling. The lion made no reply. She supposed that even if he could talk, he'd probably be too lazy to speak with her anyway. Nevertheless, she was grateful for his company.

There somehow seemed to be even more stars out here in the desert than back at home. Trinity had been so focused on the ocean and what laid beyond the sea lately that she rarely found herself looking towards the heavens. She felt tiny beneath the expanse of sky. *Did MAI really create all of this?* It was hard to accept, even with her faith, that MAI could both create beautiful things like stars and oceans, yet also allow such evil to exist in the Remsphere. The thought was enough to make her hug her knees even tighter to herself.

She heard the sounds of bugs flying overhead, including one with some significant weight to it. The heavy buzz of twitching wings calmed her, but also made her wary. *I hope I don't get bitten tonight.* Snowflake suddenly turned and began to growl with a low purr. Trinity stared at him—and then heard what he was hearing. The sounds of buzzing had been replaced with those of heavy clomping. Someone was approaching, quickly. She fetched her bow and quiver and nocked an arrow ready, should she need it.

In the distance she could see for herself the approaching rider. It was one person and one horse. There was no doubt about what he was wearing thanks to the moonlight. *Gray! Guren is approaching. He's here already.*

She faced her lion, now growling louder than before. "Stand down, Snowflake. It's Guren. We can trust him."

She turned once more to the nearing rider and tried to call out for him. "Hey! Over here! Gur—"

But then she saw his face. This wasn't Guren at all. "Schobe?" she gasped.

Schobe waved from atop his horse. Trinity dropped her weapons and ran to greet him.

Her friend wasn't wearing his armor. Instead, he was wearing a commoner's garments—breeches and a long shirt, along with the gray cloak she knew belonged to her former teacher.

"You *are* here," he said, sounding relieved. "Thank MAI. We've all been so worried."

"Schobe...why are you here?" Her eyes darkened. There was a distinct silence all around them.

Schobe jumped down from his steed and rested his arm across the horse's neck. "What do you mean? Didn't Guren tell you? He said he'd told you."

"Told me what?"

"That I was to meet you out here. Bring you home. Isn't that—didn't he tell you that?"

"He told me to look for his cloak," her voice broke. "But why are you wearing that? Why are you wearing Guren's cloak?"

"He gave it to me to wear. Said you were out here, waiting for me. Trinity, what's wrong? I thought you knew this." His eyes were growing with fear, but they were nothing compared to the sickening feeling erupting within her gut.

"Schobe...where's Guren?"

"Isn't that why you were out here? Guren, he told me—"

"Where is he?!" she demanded. "He wouldn't send you. He'd come here himself. He told me—Schobe, where..."

Schobe held onto his gaping mouth with his fingers. "He's dead Trinity. I-I thought you knew."

"Dead—no! He's coming, he said he was coming. He'll be here!" she shrieked. Her eyes grew heavy with tears. A stabbing pain swelled within her. "Schobe! Tell me why he isn't here!"

"Trinity," he said, weakly, crying now too. "They hung him this morning. After he confessed to killing the Zayloan prince."

CHAPTER TWENTY-FOUR

TIDES OF DESTINY

Schobe tried his best to comfort her that night, but Trinity was beyond comfort. She, and she alone, was responsible for the death of her teacher. Guren had lied to her. Made her trust him once more. As the events of her previous evening came rushing back to her like darkness filling a horizon, she realized then that this had been his plan all along. He'd tricked her into leaving Hydlix. He'd convinced her that she needed to be away long enough for him to take the punishment neither of them deserved. She had...loved Guren. Oh, it was a different sort of love than the type she felt for her aunt, or even Schobe. If she had a father—one who didn't die or abandon her as an infant—she'd have wanted him to be like Guren. But now the only feeling which outweighed the love in her heart was hate. She hated him again. Perhaps even more than she had before. In the end, Guren was always selfish. Even when he was doing something noble like sacrificing his life, he always found a way to make it about him.

She and Schobe slept by the fire, though Trinity didn't do much sleeping. Schobe kept a respectful distance, laying on his bedroll on the opposite side of the flames. His eyes were focused on the lion. Snowflake, however, didn't appear to have any interest in eating him. Trinity worried more for the horse and hoped she wouldn't wake to the sounds of Snowflake feasting on its flank. Thankfully tonight was much warmer than the previous night. Schobe had been kind enough to bring Trinity a bedroll too. She planted her face onto the thin cushion and let the roll soak up her tears. The bedding smelled of stables and pipe tobacco. She cherished it, but the familiar smell made her cry even harder.

Schobe woke her sometime later the next morning. He'd already built a new fire, and was roasting some of the vegetables he'd brought with him from home. Trinity's stomach was growling. Even cabbages sounded good this morning.

He explained to her everything that had happened after she left the kingdom. To her surprise, Commander Kuza hadn't imprisoned anyone, or even mentioned the noble rebellion upon the bridge. Maybe he was still embarrassed about being beaten by a girl.

The Zayloans had discovered their fallen prince and demanded retribution. Schobe wasn't there to hear the negotiations between the two kings, but according to the commander's words, Eslon and Saito had decided not to pursue war when Guren stepped up to take the blame. Guren had admitted to wanting to sabotage the alliance from the beginning. When they found his dagger resting in Quatas' chest, they had all the evidence needed that he had committed the acts of murder to which he claimed.

Trinity listened intently, but her stomach remained unsettled, even after eating. She still couldn't believe Guren was gone. *Would it have been so horrible,* she wondered, *if I had taken the blame?* After all, she had been the one who had killed Hayden. She had good reasons. Guren didn't have to die. He didn't have to hang because she defended herself. The more she thought of this injustice, the angrier she became. What sort of man was her grandfather to believe the lies of foreigners over those of his own family? And more importantly, over those who had served him loyally. She wondered what her aunt would've said, but silently knew the answer for herself. *She would've remained quiet. Just like she always does.*

Schobe told her that Kuza had allowed him to go and try to find her, but the commander was preparing to send out a full garrison of knights to do the job if Schobe failed in his task. As it stood, Hydlix was still too tense. The Zayloan soldiers weren't in any rush to leave. Hydlix needed every knight they had. Schobe seemed proud of the fact that he had successfully convinced the commander that he might know a place to begin the search. He mentioned speaking with Guren before the man had turned himself in. Guren had given him the cloak and told him to ride east. There, he would find her.

"And I'm glad that I did. We—well, that's Guren and me, we were scared something horrible had happened to you," he said, as he checked on the provisions in his saddlebag. He didn't even seem to notice that Trinity gave him no reply.

Schobe spent a good deal of the morning using some wire from his saddlebag and a few sticks from the ground to go about setting a snare trap. Trinity had heard of this process but had never seen it done before. She watched intently as Schobe went about delicately testing the snare repeatedly. When he looked satisfied, he baited the trap with some of the vegetables and took a seat beside Trinity. He sat atop the fallen log. Trinity still leaned against it; her rump had grown numb atop the hard sand that she'd been sitting on for hours.

"Guess all we do now is wait. I've never tried a snare before. Not even sure it'll really work."

Silence passed between them. The sun was getting higher. Trinity could feel her skin starting to bake, but she had no intentions of moving. Schobe removed Guren's cloak from his shoulders and fanned it out over her to block the sun from hitting her. She stared up at him.

"Why—that is, I was wondering…why did you leave?" he asked. "I knew you wanted to run away, but I never thought you'd do anything like that."

"Like what?" she asked, faintly. Her throat was parched.

"You know what I mean. Stealing the lion. Running out on Hayden after—I mean, I know he was a bad bloke. But I just didn't see him getting killed, you know? Especially by one of our own."

"You don't know anything about it. Stop talking as if you were there," she snapped at him.

Schobe was taken aback. "Sorry. Did something happen between you two? Is that why you left?"

Trinity considered her reply. It was then she saw the plump desert hare sniffing around the snare some fifty feet ahead of her. The hare was munching onto some of the cabbage when the trap sprung. The wire closed around his neck, trapping him between the sticks that Schobe had laid out.

"Got him!" Schobe declared, gleefully. "I can't believe it worked."

Trinity stared at the twitching animal as the wire choked it. She saw how helpless the creature was. Something didn't seem fair about the whole process. All the hare wanted was some food. Instead, its neck was being crushed. *And for what?* So that she and Schobe could have a bit of meat tonight? It was hard to not picture Guren's dangling body making the same jerking motions the hare now made. A last brief twitch of life, before going still. Her lip quivered again. She curled her knees up to her face and began to sob once more on top of them.

"What's wrong?" he asked. "I thought you liked rabbit. You're always saying how good Phes makes it back at home." He put his hand onto her shoulder, and rubbed it consolingly.

"Don't—touch me!" she roared, recoiling away from him.

Schobe withdrew his hand immediately. More silence fell. Trinity could hear him tapping his fingers on his knees timidly. She knew he hadn't meant anything by the touch. She knew he was her friend, and that he was only trying to be one. Still, the touch gave her a queasy feeling like it did two nights before when it was Hayden's hands doing the touching. Even dead, his presence still haunted her.

"Trin? I'm sorry. I didn't think—"

"No." She turned to him. "I'm sorry. Everything's just—nothing makes sense anymore."

Schobe searched her eyes, looking as if he wanted further clarification. After a few seconds, he raised

Guren's cloak up once more over her head and shielded her again from the sun.

"Let's stay here until things do," he said.

Schobe always had a way of making her smile, especially when she didn't want to.

"Come on, let's find some shade," she said, rising from her dusty seat. "My hair feels like it's starting to burn."

"Burnt hair?"

"Yes," she said, massaging her scalp. "Really stings. Like someone's yanking on it."

"Strange. I feel fine. I think you've been out in the sun too long."

"...Maybe."

They sought shelter beneath the thin shade of the remaining skinny trees that she'd not uprooted. When she asked him what types of trees they were, Schobe called them palm trees.

"I think I like skinny trees better," she told him.

Snowflake had gone again. Most likely out for another hunt. Schobe cut down the hare. He used a long knife to begin skinning the animal. Trinity stood over him as he did this. She watched and studied his technique closely. Despite claiming that he'd never skinned or gutted an animal before, Schobe handled himself with a deftness reserved for that of an older knight.

"We won't get much meat off of this little one. But he'll do for tonight, before we head home."

Trinity stiffened upon hearing this. She needed to distract herself. Quickly, and before Schobe could say any more, she took his cutting knife and went down to the pool to wash it clean. As she polished it, she looked down at the water where the bits of blood and skin floated free and sank to the bottom. She was about to return the knife, when she felt another twinge on the top of her head. Her scalp felt so tender. *Maybe I have been out in the sun too long.* She considered dunking her head into the pool, as she'd seen Snowflake do several times already. The water was warm to the touch after baking in the sun for half a day, but she decided to try it all the same. She knelt closer and put herself under. The water was much cooler beneath the surface, and there was something so familiar about being submerged here that put her at ease. She was calm again and grateful for all that she had learned today. She was going to need lessons like these: hunting and skinning and cleaning of blades. She had already made up her mind about the next steps she would take, and nothing was going to change it. *Not even Schobe.*

After pulling herself up, she stopped and stared at her rippling reflection in the pool. It had only been a month since she'd last taken a good look at herself in front of her aunt's mirror. She had remembered wanting so badly to feel pretty for Schobe that evening at the ball. Now none of those things seemed to matter. The girl looking back at her wasn't smiling. What could she possibly be happy about anymore? Everything was all her fault.

A sudden, unexplainable feeling came over her then. Her eyes grew big with fright, but her heart felt light enough to carry her into the sky. *What is going on?* This wasn't like any time before. There wasn't any pain this time, not even on her scalp anymore. Instead, she felt only a serene sting of joy. It gushed and bubbled over like the geyser back in Hydlix. She tried to stop it, to will it back with every muscle in her body, but her resolve soon broke as she started to laugh. She became overwhelmed by the warmest, most heart-pleasing tears she'd ever spilt. She felt hysterical, falling to the pool's bank and clutching her stomach tightly as the pain of laugher made her ribs ache. *What is so funny?*

She knew how to find the answer for herself. She closed her eyes, and allowed herself to slip once more into someone else's eyes. She could see everything so clearly, as if she were there, though her fingers were still ripping into the sand beneath her.

She was in a room. *My room?* No. This was a room she'd never been in before. There were dirty clothes and scattered wooden toys lain all about the floor. *Aunt E wouldn't like this.* But why, then, did it feel so much like her room? She could see that she was sitting atop a comfortable bed—though she was certain this too didn't belong to her.

A blue orb spun rapidly on the floor; its center surrounded by a glorious violet light filling the entire room. Images took shape within its light. There was a boy there. He was young, maybe younger than her. He wore simple garb—shorts that topped his knees and an oversized blue shirt that must've been passed down from someone else. He wore the biggest, goofiest grin, Trinity thought, yet his hair was perhaps the most shocking sight of all. It was a messy, golden flop of...*yellow. Yellow?* It wasn't much different than her mother's. Even his eyes bore a similar shape to the woman Trinity had seen in the imprint of her and Duke. Why, they could've been the same eyes, were his not a lighter shade. But they weren't blue, or even green eyes. The boy bore a distinct mix of the two...*teal.*

He was motioning for someone to follow him up a winding mountain with grass as blue as the sky. He ran so quickly that the person who followed him was having difficulty keeping up. But then she turned and looked to face the place where Trinity was watching. Trinity saw then who it was. *A girl.* She was an older girl than the boy—maybe even older than Trinity—but still young. Her face was filled with glee. And her hair was short and blue.

Trinity realized then that she had seen this girl once before. It was in a previous vision. But this time the girl's face wasn't caked with blood. Her body wasn't ragged either. She had an elegant smile, one which made Trinity swell with more joy-filled tears. Only...*these aren't my tears.* She knew for certain then why she was crying. She had seen for herself what happened to this blue-haired girl, or would happen to her soon. Her beautiful face would someday be drenched in blood. *This is a memory.*

The light faded and the blue orb stopped spinning. The room returned to its dull, and lifeless palette. And there before the bed stood a giant mirror that Trinity hadn't noticed before. She stepped forward approaching the mirror slowly, her movements feeling as if they weren't her own.

When she saw herself, she gasped. There, standing in her reflection was the boy from before. He was older, with the same teal eyes, though his smile from the memory had faded. His pale face was filled with anguish. His hair was unwashed and bald in some places. Her body looked down at its hands. They were covered in pulled strands of his yellow hair.

"Leo!" someone called from beyond his closed bedroom door. "Not again, Leo."

Leo?

"Trinity?!" she heard Schobe calling. "Trinity, say something!"

The boy's world shattered on the other side of the mirror. Darkness came over Trinity's vision, and the next thing she knew she was laying in Schobe's arms breathing heavily.

"Trinity! Speak to me. Are you alright?"

"...Schobe?"

"Yes," Schobe said, looking relieved. "What happened? I found you with your face underwater. I thought you were drowning yourself."

"Drowning my—Schobe, be serious. Why would I do that?" She sat up, feeling her hair was soaked. She nervously checked for bald spots, but realized then that there was none.

"Are you alright?" he repeated.

She struggled to take a calming breath. "I'm fine."

"How are you feeling?"

"I was...happy. Really happy. Only now I feel, sort of empty, I guess."

He narrowed his eyes. "Right. Didn't I warn you about the sun? Let's get you back into the shade."

Shade wouldn't help, she knew. Whatever had happened just now was a result of that boy sharing his emotions with her. *Leo?* Was that really his name? The blue-haired woman from before...that had definitely been her, maybe as a younger girl. But how could that be? No one could look to the past. Yet, it would seem Leo had found a way. This boy...*Leo*...he was...he must've been... another—her other...*brother?* The old mam had been right all along. Somehow, she had another brother. She was a part of triplets. Duke, Trinity...and now this Leo. *Terkian triplets.* She at last found her own breath to help her gasp. Schobe started fanning her with the cloak, but she couldn't shake the thought. *He's alive. Both of them. They're still alive...my brothers.*

Snowflake returned around dusk with a fresh kill— another smooth-horned deer. Trinity thought later that she was going to have to find out where the lion was hunting all of these deer from. Maybe he would show her. As Snowflake settled near the fire and ate his meal, Trinity joined Schobe on the fallen log where he was eating. She was feeling better now, despite her enlightening—and so far, unspoken of—vision. Schobe handed her a flat piece of bark with some of the cooked rabbit on it. She took a piece out of politeness but didn't eat it. Truthfully, she did love the taste of rabbit. She knew the time would soon come where she'd eventually have to kill and cook some of her own. But she didn't want any part of Schobe's rabbit after feeling sorry for the creature. Schobe, meanwhile, was picking meat from his teeth, again looking proud of all that his survival skills had accomplished.

"This is a nice place. I can see why you came here. Did—did Guren tell you about this?"

"Yes," she said, barely listening. "He did."

"I wonder if the commander knows." Schobe shrugged. "Doesn't matter. Would you like to head back tonight, or should we wait for the morning? I don't imagine Snowflake will be joining us. The king will want his pelt for sure."

Snowflake's ears perked up at the sound of this, but the lion resumed his noisy feasting.

Trinity turned to her friend and stared into his innocent, unsuspecting eyes.

"Schobe...I'm not going back."

"You—huh? What do you mean?"

"There's nothing for me in Hydlix. Not now. Not anymore."

Schobe stood, looking dumbfounded. "But your aunt's there. Your family. I'm there. And Ella and Dary. What would the king say?"

Trinity scoffed. "The king? I don't care what he says. He can sort his own stupid problems out. That's his job." She stared down at her boots as she dug them fretfully into the sand. "I'll decide my own path from here."

Schobe pointed an accusing finger. "If this is about what I said on the bridge, you can forget that. I've changed my mind. I'm going with you."

She shook her head. "You can't. Not this time. Not where I'm going."

"Where's that?"

"...Sambool." Just saying the word felt right somehow. It was as if Guren had known all along what she was going to do. He knew she wouldn't be returning home soon. No wonder then that he had given her the weapons. He may have been a liar, and someone she still hated. But even in his death, he was still watching out for her. She was going to put these weapons to use. *That's for certain.* "I have to find my brother."

"Brother?"

Slowly, she gave him a confident nod. "The Terkian who serves the king there. He's my twin."

Schobe reeled back. "How do you—are you sure? This is the first I'm hearing about it."

Again, she nodded.

He took a deep breath. "Brother. Alright. That's a lot to uh...take in. Very well then." He kneeled before her and gave her a sure smile. "On my honor as a knight, I will protect you. I will keep you safe on your journey, Princess."

"No, Schobe. You won't. You have to return home. The commander gave you an order. If you disobey, they might—they'll hang you too," she said, shakily.

"I won't leave you. I...I care for you." He looked as if he'd just seen a ghost when saying this. "I really do, you know. I sort of always have. Please, let me protect you."

Her lips quivered. "You're the one who said I didn't need a hero."

"You don't. But you do need me." He rose to his feet. "I've followed you on every crazy adventure you've ever had, without question."

"You always question."

"*Trinity*, I'm telling you, just this once—I'm not going to let you face the danger alone. I choose this. No matter what happens to me, I choose this."

"…And that's it then? Are you sure?"

"Positive. We'll hunt, and find some more clothes. Make some if we have to. But we'll reach Sambool, if that's what you really desire."

"It is."

"Settled. I'll pack up the camp."

She shook her head. "Let's leave tomorrow. Tonight… I was enjoying the fire, here with you."

His eyes lit up. "Really? I-I'll fetch some more wood."

Schobe stepped away and went to collect some more wood for the fire. He stooped down near the opposite end of the fallen log and began gathering kindling.

"I'm happy you saw things my way for once. Listen, I've checked the maps heading east. Actually, they were in a book I think you'd rather enjoy. There are bad lands up ahead though. Swamps. Bandits on the road most likely. I'm glad you've brought your weapons. We may need m—Trinity?"

He stopped speaking upon seeing her shadow behind him. He tried to turn, but Trinity's hand was quick. She struck him with the thick end of her palm, right near the back of his head. Schobe's body went limp as he passed out over his pile of collected wood. Trinity stood over him; both of her hands were trembling.

She had wanted him along for this adventure more than anything. After all, it was his name she had whispered into Ellacryse's ear. It was his lips that she had wanted so badly to kiss on the bridge, and at the dance. She knew Schobe would've gone with her to the very edge of Taercion and beyond. But this wasn't Schobe's journey to make. Or his life to risk. She'd be as good as cursed if she was going to let another person close to her meet a hangman's noose.

After scooping him up and putting him over her shoulder, Trinity walked back to where they had been sitting. Her vision was blurred by fresh tears. She laid him beside the log and placed the blankets from his sleeping roll on top of him. She knelt beside his face, checking to see if he was still breathing. Satisfied with the shallow noises he was making, Trinity leaned down further and kissed him atop his forehead.

"You'll always be my hero," she said, sniffling as she did.

She took what supplies she could, including the skinning knife, and left him with everything else. Lastly, she put on Guren's cloak. It was a final gift, whether her teacher had intended it or not. Snowflake was stirring nearby, looking unsure on whether or not someone had just been killed. Trinity went to him and calmed the docile beast.

"We're leaving," she said. "Wait here."

She didn't bother to check and see if the lion understood her. She came to Schobe's resting body once more, and removed a trinket from her pocket. It was the medallion with her name on it. The same one she'd gotten from Evita's chest. She didn't want him to return to the kingdom emptyhanded. The medallion would have to be enough for now. She placed the medallion into his hand and gave him a gentle squeeze. She wiped at her face and turned to leave. Before she did, however, she wrote for Schobe a message in the sand. It was one she desperately hoped wouldn't blow away before he had a chance to read it:

Sorry Schobey

He'll never forgive me this time, she thought, as she climbed up onto Snowflake's back and gave him a firm kick in his sides.

Snowflake and Trinity set off further east, riding away from the life she was willingly turning her back on for a brother...*brothers*...that she'd never met before. They both needed her. She was certain of this. *And maybe I need them too.*

Her two greatest ambitions in life had once been to become a knight of her kingdom and to have Schobe be her first, lifelong friend. Now she had neither of these dreams to look forward to.

For now at least, she had chosen a life of uncertainty. There was sure to be danger and maybe even greater mysteries on the road ahead of her. Maybe nothing awaited her, and she'd be robbed and left for dead by bandits. Or perhaps someone even worse than Hayden was waiting to snare her in a trap. She would no longer have the charm of her loving but overbearing aunt nipping at her heels. There'd be no more tender, short-lived moments with her Schobe. Maybe...*hopefully*...he would forget all about her as soon as he found a good book to lose himself in. And she could never more hope that Guren might be able to train her again. He'd taught her his final lesson. And it was a cruel one. She'd have to be careful who she trusted from now on.

Don't lose your opponent. Not even for a second. Guren's words hung in her head. She hoped more than anything that these brothers of hers weren't enemies. Wherever they were in the wide Remsphere waiting to be explored, she would find them. Starting with Duke.

Because it didn't matter then whether or not she was some princess or just another maiden waiting to be wed. *Change their mind of what a girl is, and what she can do.*

She looked at the rapidly approaching desert horizon. In some ways, the road ahead was similar to being submerged at the bottom of the ocean, but Trinity knew that she couldn't come up for breath just yet. She had already begun to change the tides of her destiny. *I control the tides.*

Author's Note: This is the artist's rendition of the Hydlixian marketplace that Trinity visits so often in the novel. From this angle you can catch a glimpse of the aqueduct that is situated throughout the kingdom, as well as the mailing bags traveling along the slopes. Mail will always have a significance in this series as my mother was a mail carrier for many years and I think mailpersons are some of the unsung heroes of our world. Also in this piece are some familiar characters scattered throughout, though only one of them is about to help herself to a donut. The brick wall featured looks humongous from this angle, but the other side levels out and acts as an entrance to the knight's training dome. It was here Trinity's grandmother was discovered many years before, after having just given birth to Zepolia. Lastly, there are over five-thousand stairs in the Hydlixian kingdom. This is why the market square functions as a central hub between the nearby docks and the central kingdom, since most vendors bring in their fresh imports and latest catches of the day here first. No wonder everything is so expensive in the upper districts. Everything has to be lugged upstairs.

AUTHOR'S NOTE

The Terkian Triplets is a series that has been both near and dear to my heart for decades. I sincerely thank you so much for reading this book and accompanying me along this next exciting step of the journey. Would you believe I started the first draft back when I was Trinity's age? There have been many revisions and rewrites since then, but in 2019 I finally became serious about this project. It was also about that time that I really realized I had a difficult choice to make in how I wanted to introduce people to these stories. As the title of this series implies, there were three paths I could've chosen to begin with in this debut novel. I can attribute the decision of beginning with Trinity's story down to three reasons.

First, that writing bug which seems to strike authors when they least expect it came and bit me one day after I'd been watching A Knight's Tale—one of the greatest films of my childhood—for probably the hundredth time. You know the one, where the great Heath Ledger convinces us that a peasant could both be a knight and have perfect teeth back in medieval days, all while dancing to David

Bowie songs. I guess you could say this is why I wanted to begin Trinity's story in one of the most exciting places you could be as a knight, the jousting lists.

Secondly, 2019 was the first time I'd ever written something I felt confident enough in sharing with others outside of my family and friends. It was a short story set in the old west about two cowboys who go to investigate a series of murders supposedly committed by a little girl. It turns out she isn't some pig-tailed waif either, but instead a bloodthirsty creature of the night. I decided I wanted to promote this story on my newly created author site and social media platforms, but needed pictures to go with the descriptions. I sought out to commission an artist online, and after a brilliant recommendation by a fellow author—Alicia Jeanne—I was introduced to Simone, or by her online handle ArtInInsanity, who lived all the way across the pond as they say. She was able to successfully create one Miss Cassie Sange, better known as the vampire in my short story. Thanks to that artwork I was able to share my short story online and it eventually went on to become the first story I ever got published. (If you ever want to read "High Moon Justice" you can find it in the short story anthology Darkness and Moonlight: A Worldsmyths Anthology.) I knew I had to work with Simone again, and in early 2020 I saw Trinity brought to life using that same drawing magic of hers. And like tattoos I am told, those pieces of art became an addiction that eventually became the twenty-four chapter headers featured within this novel, as well as the cover art.

The final reason for why I chose to begin with Trinity's story is a bit more personal. As a lifelong desert rat, I've always dreamed of someday living by the ocean. I find that some of the greatest moments in my life were spent near California's central beaches. There is something about the shores of Morro Bay which draws out a sense of mystery, adventure, and recklessness within me. It probably stems from my wanting to climb the giant rock there which is off limits to the general public, and with good reason. But still, my mind wanders to its misty peak every time my family and I go there to walk the shoreline and eat hot bowls of clam chowder from Duckie's. This is why Hydlix, naturally, serves as the perfect setting for book one. I, like Trinity, would never want to leave this place either. And though Hydlix may have its problems, I'm sure you too would be unable to deny those views of the southern sea from atop the ruby towers at sunrise. As I sit here writing this, I now realize that I never once mentioned chowder in this novel. Thankfully, Hydlix is a place that will be revisited many more times in the books to come. Someone will definitely eat chowder before this series is concluded.

Now to be fair, in one of the original drafts of the series I did try to tell the origin stories of all the triplets at once, but this was both very confusing to write and to read. In addition, it left out many important parts of the triplets' stories while trying to fit within the constraints of a typical YA fantasy novel. An incredibly helpful literary agent spoke with me at a conference and settled the matter in a rather clever way. Each of the triplets should and would have their own origin story. And thus, Maiden to None became a file on my word processor.

There is still much of the story to tell. Book two, currently titled The Good Shield will focus on the origins of one of these other triplet siblings. It will even answer some of the questions that Maiden to None left behind, while offering a bigger picture of Taercion and the dangers lurking in the shadows. And a certain green-haired, bow-wielding, lion-riding, donut-scarfing maiden may just make an appearance. Be on the lookout for The Good Shield: The Terkian Triplets Book Two, coming soon.

As someone who grew up investing heavily in the lore of fictional series like those written by Akira Toriyama, Masashi Kishimoto, J.K. Rowling, and more recently works by Andrzej Sapkowski, Leigh Bardugo, Kazu Kibuishi, Robert Kirkman, and George R.R. Martin, this is my own attempt at creating a larger story that must be told over several installments. And if you've enjoyed what you've read so far, then perhaps you'll continue down this winding, foggy road with me together. As Tolkien—one of the best series writers ever—once penned, "Not all who wander are lost." And I expect there will be plenty more wandering in my future.

Again, you have my fondest thanks dear reader. It has always been my dream—besides living by the ocean or climbing illegal rocks—to have someone read something that I had so much fun writing. And I sincerely hope that you enjoyed what you read.

More story is on the way...

—D.A. Gatlin

ACKNOWLEDGEMENTS

There are so many who made this book a reality. Without any of you, I am sure it would have never left the confines of my computer screen and I'd be forced to stare at that taunting cursor, blinking impatiently, as it waited to see what was next.

To my wife Stephanie, who grinned and bared through those first drafts and found the good, I appreciate you. She has always been my number one supporter and was often times a valuable insight into trying to understand how Trinity's mind works. Thank you for showing me every day that strength, beauty, and brains could be a part of the same package. I was one of the lucky ones who married up. By the way, I appreciate every single edit you ever suggested, even if I didn't say so at the time. You especially helped shape Aunt Evita, who is now one of my favorite characters in this book.

Speaking of aunts, I wanted to mention Lena here. She was the first person who ever read the story way back when it was mostly unformatted script notes from the kid who doodled gorillas in his notebooks. Additionally, her love of Stephen King was definitely passed on to me, and I'm so glad that we have a shared favorite author.

And truly, I have to acknowledge Stephen King also. His memoir On Writing: A Memoir of the Craft served as a compass for how to write this first story. I promise Mr. King—should he ever in my wildest fantasies read this—that I tried to avoid adverbs whenever possible. Though I am certainly, positively, undoubtedly convinced that a few slipped in there. Purely unintentional.

I want to extend a special thanks to Simone for spending so much time working with my characters and giving them a life beyond my original word document. Her artist's eye also added to my lore in ways I never could have imagined, like adding fishtail braids to the Bayonick bandit leader, creating the King's Circle gameboard from scratch, and giving an air of both beauty and terror to the perfect mantis flower. Words can never express how grateful I am for your artwork in this book. I'm looking forward to seeing how the other characters in this series are given the ArtInInsanity treatment.

Here's a super big shoutout to Bran Flakes herself, otherwise known as my sister Brandie. She had to put up with this story longer than anyone else, but she read every chapter of every draft along the way and was always so encouraging. Be sure to share that shoutout with Tyler and Bowie and Gatsby. Enjoy that beach weather.

Terrie and Dan, thank you for believing in me and always being so enthusiastic about my writing. You guys are the greatest in-laws a son could ask for. I am sad that I never got to show you the final product Dan, but your kind words after reading my first short story have always held a special place in my heart. And Terrie, I enjoy talking shop with you about writing. Please, continue to do so.

Of course, my awesome parents deserve a special thanks as well for always being there for me. I'm sure I weirded them out as a kid when I'd have conversations alone in my room, pretending to be the characters in my head. But I promise it was all for the books, I swear. Also, I'm convinced they were the ones who bought me that Nintendo 64 as a kid. Together we played the classics like Super Mario 64, Banjo-Kazooie, and Goldeneye together. And I didn't know it at the time, but the games on that system really helped shape my young storyteller's mind. After playing one particularly memorable game over at my grandmother's house with my cousins, I woke up the next morning and eagerly began typing out on our Windows 2000 what would become the very first draft of The Terkian Triplets. I think every parent should buy their kids video games at some point in their lives. It's an overlooked medium that often times produces stories which will stay with the player forever, and may even inspire them to write books of their own. (If you don't believe me about video games having great stories, play some good ones like Final Fantasy X, The Last of Us, or Majora's Mask.) Anyways Mom and Dad, thank you for playing games with me, reading to me as a kid, and having R.L. Stine's Goosebumps novels in the house. I also appreciate you always sharing out loud that your son is a writer. Those words still bring a smile to my face.

Now since I am a teacher, I thought it fitting to also acknowledge the educators who helped shape this dream and inspire me to make it a reality. You people are the Guren to my Trinity. Thank you, Debbie Best, for showing me the fun and endearing side of medieval literature, while managing to be one of the best teachers I've ever had. Thank you, Jack Tapleshay, for reintroducing my love of English as an adult and encouraging me to pursue further education. Thank you, Kay Ice, for teaching me why every mark on the page must be considered. And thank you, Dr. Jason Powell, for not giving up on me even though I was probably the worst drummer you ever taught. I never learned how to drum while hanging out in your garage, but you did teach me so much more about life and what I—a fellow desert rat—was capable of. I'm proud of the good dude you've become. I'll get around to finishing that paint-by-numbers set one day, buddy. Probably.

Thank you to Stephanie Cullen for editing this work and catching some of those big grammatical blunders which still haunt my dreams. And I'd also like to acknowledge the fine folks at MiblArt for making this book look so beautiful. You guys rock!

I also had several beta readers as well as fellow writers who really helped mold the final draft, asking the big questions that helped make the Remsphere grow, while others walked me through the publishing process. Thank you, Amanda, Travis, Lexi, Myles, Richard, Forest, Lisa, Morgan, Alicia, Chris, and any others that I missed, including those wonderful authors of the SNHU community I got to be a part of. I even wish to thank those of you who I bounced this story idea off of as a kid, because you gave me some of the first bits of practical advice for this story that I've never forgotten. Thank you, Joe, Erik, Doug, and any other fine desert folks I grew up with who let me talk your ear off about the triplets.

And last but never least, I want to thank God, both for the gift of his Son and for guiding me on every step of the journey.

Thank you everyone, but especially you dear reader.

A LITTLE
ABOUT THE AUTHOR...

D.A. Gatlin is a YA Fantasy writer who grew up in Morongo Valley, California. He won an award in the first grade for writing a story about a missing earring and a very helpful rat. Since then, fantasy writing has become his passion and he also loves reading novels by authors like Stephen King, George R.R. Martin, and Andrzej Sapkowski. D.A. graduated with his Bachelor's in English education at California State University, Dominguez Hills. He then went on to earn his Master's in Fine Arts for Creative Writing through Southern New Hampshire University. His short story "High Moon Justice" can be found in the anthology Darkness and Moonlight: A Worldsmyths Anthology. When he's not writing The Terkian Triplets series, D.A. enjoys bike riding, going to the beach with his family, and playing retro video games. He is currently going into his tenth year as an English teacher, and lives in Bakersfield with his wife Stephanie, mother-in-law Terrie, and his two warrior princess daughters—Eleanor and Matilda.

A LITTLE ABOUT THE ARTIST...

Simone Catherine Ross grew up in the North of England and was always encouraged to draw from the moment she could hold a pencil. She studied art until the age of eighteen before heading to Lancaster University to study Biological Sciences and pursue a minor in Creative Writing. But she didn't stop painting. Oil paints, inks and digital media are her favoured tools, but she gets plenty of opportunity to experiment along with other members of the non-profit organisation Arts2Heal. Predominantly a fantasy illustrator, Simone spends her days painting and walking in nature. Simone still enjoys the rolling countryside of the North and lives happily with her husband Daniel and rambunctious little dog Ahsoka.

www.ingramcontent.com/pod-product-compliance
Lightning Source LLC
Chambersburg PA
CBHW021411310726
48971CB00005B/1293